THE TAGGER HERD

BOOK ONE
(the introduction)

The phone was still ringing, so she hit the answer button and raised it to her ear.

"The Stables," she answered.

There was hesitation before the person spoke. When she did, Dru could tell it was an older woman. "Can I speak with the owner please?" She said quietly.

"I am one of the owners, Dru Tagger."

There was more hesitation. "Oh…good. I'm so sorry to bother you."

She hesitated long enough that Dru could add, "No bother at all, how can I help?"

"Well," another hesitation. Even over the phone Dru could tell she was upset.

"I'm not really sure how to start," the woman paused. "My name is Cora Smith and my husband, Wes, passed away a little over three weeks ago."

Well that was a start, Dru frowned. "I'm so sorry."

"Yes, well, thank you. I received a phone call a few minutes ago," she hesitated again, "I'm a bit confused about the call."

"Was it from someone here at The Stables?"

"No, I got your number from a card my husband had in his wallet."

"Do you have horses? Was your husband looking for somewhere to board them?"

"No horses. We sold all our horses a couple years ago."

"OK…" Dru walked away from the arena and the excited chatter from the two teenagers talking about the last day of school.

"That's what's so strange about the phone call I received. The man who called said he would be delivering the hay in the morning."

"Did they call from Tagger Enterprises for the hay?"

"No."

Dru quietly exhaled in rising confusion. "Hay for what?"

"I don't know; we don't have any animals. I canceled the hay order from the man, but now I'm worried," The woman's voice trembled as she continued. "My husband was being very secretive before he died. He even shipped me to Seattle to spend time with my sister for a couple weeks."

Dru still wasn't sure what this had to do with The Stables.

The woman on the phone continued, "We live in Lenore, but I haven't been there since a week before he died."

"Mrs. Smith," Dru leaned against the back of the building. "I'm a bit confused. How can The Stables help?"

The voice let out a frustrated sigh, "I am afraid my husband bought some animals without telling me and they have been at our home in Lenore, unattended, for over three weeks."

Dru slowly stood away from the building, "Horses, sheep, cattle, chickens…a lot of animals can forage for themselves for three weeks."

"Yes," The woman's voice was a little stronger since she had finally voiced her concern. "After my husband died, we had him brought to Seattle and buried here, with family. I haven't been to our home now for over a month. I have no one there to call to go check the property. With your card here… well, I thought maybe he had talked to you about this."

"No, not with me," Dru frowned. "I'll talk to the manager here to see if he spoke with your husband. If not, then we'll take a drive and check." This could be a total waste of time… she HOPED it was a total waste of time. "You have no idea what kind of animals he may have bought?"

"No," she sighed, "I'm just so worried. The man with the hay was so adamant that my husband had bought the hay AND that it was scheduled to be delivered in the morning."

"Did he say how much hay he was delivering?" It was coming on summer when most large animals would be grazing in pastures and not be dependent on hay. The first hay crop was coming off the fields. He could have been stocking up for winter.

"He didn't say."

"OK, I'll go check it out," Her parents and grandparents had taught her to have respect for animals. Something in her gut told her to make the drive. She wouldn't be able to forgive herself if there were animals suffering because she didn't have time to take a drive 30 miles up the river.

THE TAGGER HERD

Collection One

A Series by

Gini Roberge

THE TAGGER HERD

BOOK ONE

The two men below were the first to know the book existed and were the first to read it. Through their encouragement I continued with the series.

Our 'courier' Emily is Ben's wife and now a good friend of mine as well as their daughter Kenzie.

SPECIAL THANKS TO

BEN SMITH, DVM

For Your Input and Editing Expertise

And the courier Emily!

AND

STEVE ROBERGE, BRO

My sounding board, encouraging voice, and special editor

PROLOGUE

Grayson Tagger hurried down the hallway of the Agriculture Building on the University of Idaho campus. He could see the lecture hall door was still open, which was good since he was running late. The professor hated people coming in late. Only a few feet away from the door an arm appeared and reached for the door knob. It was the professor's and his head turned with a frown as Grayson came into view.

The frown quickly turned to a smirk. "Nice of you to join us, Mr. Tagger." He backed away from the door.

Grayson stepped through the doorway and it was closed behind him.

"Going to blame this on your dad and grandfather?" The professor asked with a raised humored brow.

"Not this time," Grayson answered with a grin. "I came in from the ranch last night."

The professor knew both men. The Tagger family worked closely with the University on agricultural research on the 25,000 acre cattle ranch Grayson had called home all of his nineteen years.

As Grayson took his seat, he grinned at the two girls in the front row. He was normally the only one in the front row. He liked to debate with the professor and needed the extra leg room for his 6' 3" frame. The blonde was cute, so he gave her a wink and a smile then turned to the professor; there would be time for the ladies later.

He barely settled into the chair when the door to the left opened and a young assistant came through. She glanced nervously around the room as she walked quickly to the professor to whisper in his ear. The professor's head came up with a jerk and he looked directly at Grayson. Nodding to the girl, he motioned for Grayson to follow him as he walked to the door he'd just entered.

Grayson stood and followed with a frown. He'd never seen anyone pulled out of class before. He stepped through the door and saw a look on the professor's face that told him he wasn't going to like what he was about to hear.

******

Scott Tagger walked through the doors of the school's fitness room. Tomorrow was game day; the annual rivalry football game between the two river cities, Lewiston and Clarkston. Lewiston had the winning record against the rival city and he wanted to make sure, in his senior year, they won again.

He was the first to the gym which was normal. He was always first to the gym, last on the practice field and studied the playbook excessively. As the quarterback, he wanted to make sure he not only knew what he was supposed to do on a play, but what everyone else was supposed to do.

Tommy, his leading receiver, quickly joined him.

"I think we should break one of the school records tomorrow." Tommy grinned.

Scott laughed as he reached for a set of dumb bells, "Which one?"

Tommy shrugged, "Your dad and brother hold the passing records now, who's do you want to break first?"

"Well, Grayson beat Dad's season passing record so it would have to be one of Dad's single game records. Then, we'll concentrate on beating Grayson." There had always been a touch of competitiveness between the Tagger brothers.

"After the last two games, you're on your way to breaking the season record for passing which gives me one for receiving. So, tomorrow has to be for most passes or touchdowns in a game." Tommy concluded with a grin.

Prologue 2

Scott laughed and pulled off the headband he was using to keep the long dark blond hair out of his face. He and Tommy had decided to grow their hair until the last game. It was long enough now to touch his shoulders, but he didn't mind it, and neither did the girls. They liked the long hair and sparkling blue eyes.

He put the headband back on and stood to switch his weights when the door opened and the head football coach walked through with his head down.

"Hey, Coach," Scott greeted him with a smile. "I don't normally see you in here this time of day."

"Scott, can I see you in my office please?" Coach asked, then turned and walked out.

Scott and Tommy glanced at each other, shrugged, and Scott followed the coach.

The look on the older man's face caused a knot in Scott's stomach.

"Coach?" Scott sat across the desk from him. "What's wrong?"

******

Drusilla Tagger sat on the black horse and stared down the arena at the three barrels. She ran the clover leaf pattern in her mind. It was the first thing her mother taught her when running barrels. Picture what you want, how you want it, and then go do it. Her mom had been a National Champion barrel racer and Dru was determined to be one, too.

Jet, her horse, pranced up and down the arena waiting for the command she had felt so many times before. Dru lined her up at the back of the arena then completed three circles preparing herself and the horse for the run. She counted down in her head as she looked to the barrels. One, two, three….she leaned forward and barely had to touch the horse's sides and the horse bolted.

"Balance," she whispered to herself.

Dru leaned into the first barrel as the horse leaned. The barrel brushed her knee but it didn't go down. She leaned back and repositioned her seat to turn the other direction. They made it around the second barrel and she turned her horse at the third.

"Not too fast." Dru whispered, making sure Jet didn't get carried away and run too fast to make the turn correctly or even run pass it. As they drew closer to the barrel, she could feel the energy of the horse running through her own legs. She leaned back to cue the horse to slow down and she did…just enough. They leaned together as a team, and turned perfectly around the barrel. Jet dug into the ground with her back hooves and got her footing well enough for a huge push off for the final race to victory. Dru leaned down the horse's neck and kicked wildly to push the horse even harder.

"Go, go, go, go!" Dru's yell was barely heard over the pounding hooves hitting the hard dirt. Just before they ran into the fence, the horse slowed and turned to the right.

"Yes!" Dru patted the horse on the neck. "Great job!" They continued to trot around the arena to cool down and lower both their heart rates. "Awesome, girl, just awesome!"

She glanced around at the practice arena and saw…no one. No one had witnessed the best run of her life. Even her kids missed it! She laughed; they were too young to appreciate it anyway.

"That was the best ride ever!" She yelled at Jet excitedly, the horse pranced; her energy matched Dru's. Once they finally stopped, Dru slid from the saddle and wrapped her arms around the horse's neck. She took in a deep breath, filling her lungs with the smell of the horse, leather, and sweat. How could such a combination smell like heaven?

She stepped back and looked at the big beautiful mare. Completely black, long mane and tail that flowed beautifully, contrasting with Dru's own long pale blonde hair as they rode. Jet was a beauty and, unfortunately, pregnant. They had just started running well together when her dad decided to have her bred the previous spring. The ride this weekend at the Lewiston Roundup would be their last for the year.

"We're ready for it." She stroked the horse's neck. Jet bounced her head up and down then walked calmly next to her as they made their way out of the ranch arena.

"I wish Mom would have seen that ride, Jet," she smiled. "She would have loved it!"

Dru sighed happily. Her parents and grandparents had loaded into the car that morning and headed to Missoula to look at ranch equipment.

"Well," she told the horse, "She'll be back in time and we'll just show her, won't we Jet?"

She tied the horse to the hitching post and uncinched the saddle. Dru heard the sound of a vehicle coming up the drive behind her but didn't turn around. It was probably just one of the ranch hands coming in for equipment. She pulled the saddle off and reached for the brush. Both she and the horse loved this time together after a good practice. It was Dru's peace, her moment to give the horse the love she deserved.

As Dru started the long sweeping strokes with the brush, footsteps slowly approached her from behind.

She turned and the smile vanished from her face.

A sheriff's officer was standing next to her. He didn't have to say a word. His face was pale and eyes full of anguish. The brush dropped from her hand and the sound of it hitting the ground echoed through her body. She could barely hear her own voice from the scream vibrating through her head, "Who?"

******

The Tagger Trio, as they would come to be known, stood quietly on the front porch of the ranch house. They nodded politely as friends and neighbors said their condolences and the Trio thanked everyone for coming.

"You have no aunts or uncles?" Andy, their closest neighbor asked. Dru shook her head. "How about your mother's parents and family?"

"No, she was an only child and her parents died years ago, one of cancer and the other had a heart attack soon after." Scott answered.

"So the three of you are the only Taggers left?" he asked in concern.

They didn't answer.

"You're pretty young to be taking care of a ranch this size," he told them. Worry creased his brow.

Silence.

"Well," Andy sighed, finally understanding they didn't want to talk. "I am here for you every step of the way. Anything you need, just ask." He touched Dru's elbow and looked at her earnestly. "I'm serious Drusilla. If you decide to keep the ranch, I'll teach you everything I know."

Dru nodded politely.

Once Andy stepped into the house, Dru walked down the front steps of the ranch house and headed to the barn. There was an empty stall in the back corner; she made her way there and leaned her forehead against the wall. In the 30 seconds the semi driver had closed his eyes, he had clipped the back of the car and sent it over the edge of the mountain. No chance of survival.

Dru turned and slid down the wall, bending her knees to her chest and wrapping her arms around them. She leaned her head down letting the long blonde hair that flowed around her become a shield from the world. At only 22, she had become the matriarch of the family.

She didn't look up when she heard the footsteps. Two sets of them. This was their place to get away from the world; it had been their hideout since they were kids.

Dru felt her brothers sit down on each side of her. They sat quietly for a while, until Grayson finally spoke.

"If..." He shook his head. "What kind of stupid word is IF?" He stretched his long legs out in front of him.

"I couldn't imagine life without the ranch." Scott sighed.

Dru lifted her head and stretched her legs straight out in front of her, matching both her brothers positions. She took Grayson's hand with her left hand and Scott's hand with her right one. Then, squeezing tightly, she closed her eyes and let the darkness and the horror of losing both her beloved parents and grandparents sweep through her. She cried until she could barely breathe.

CHAPTER ONE

"Aunt Dru!" Grace jogged up to her. "You're back early."

Dru lowered the tailgate of her truck and smiled at her niece. "A herd of elk went through the fence at the lower pasture. Matt and Nikki went with Jessup to repair it, so I just loaded the grain and left."

"Did any get hurt?"

Dru chuckled with an eyebrow raised, "Seriously Grace?"

"What...?" Grace started to say then stopped.

Dru watched the fourteen-year -old's expression change as she realized what she had said. Laughter erupted from her. "I was thinking horse, not elk." She explained.

Dru shook her head, amused. "I was hoping. Most elk don't stick around to let us doctor them if they get hurt."

"They would have to be roped first…it would be an interesting challenge." Grace grinned.

Dru nodded with a smile. "And, once upon a time, your dad would have taken the challenge."

"What would Grayson do?"

They turned to see the stable manager's son, Reilly Morgan, pushing a wheelbarrow toward them. He was the same age as Grace. After being raised together the last seven years they were best friends.

"Try to rope an elk so he could doctor it." Grace's giggle was low and infectious.

Reilly laughed which made his blue eyes sparkle. "Oh, I can see him trying that! And see if he could do it faster than Scott!"

Dru laughed with them as she handed Grace the first bag of grain. Grace passed it along to Reilly, who placed it in the wheelbarrow.

"With two girls and a wife to take care of, I'm hoping he would turn the challenge down." Dru turned to get the next bag, then paused and grinned back at the pair. "But I wouldn't bet on that."

They finished loading the grain into the wheelbarrow and headed back to the storage shed to unload it. Dru had driven to the ranch the night before and spent the evening with her two kids, Matt and Nikki. At 18, Matt had just graduated high school and Nikki, 20, had finished her second year in college. They planned on spending the first month of summer on the ranch riding fences and pushing cows.

"I can't believe we're actually going to get paid to work here this summer." Reilly said over his shoulder.

"Can I take that as an offer to volunteer instead?" Dru teased.

"I'd do it just to ride the horses." Grace laughed.

"Part of working here is exercising the horses that belong to The Stables," Reilly chuckled. "So you can volunteer and I'll get paid for it."

Dru listened to the two teenagers bantering between each other. She thought back to the day The Stables opened to the public. It was such a great, yet sad, day. For three years she worked the ranch, filed insurance claims, fought legal battles, had one brother in college, and raised two kids. Once he graduated high school, Scott was able to help her at the ranch, but they weren't able to give him the time to go to college, too.

Once the insurance company and attorneys found out the truth behind the accident, the claim was settled quickly. The owners of the semi-truck that had hit the car carrying her parents and grandparents, had bribed the driver to do a second haul without rest. With the large payout, the Trio was able to pay all the ranch bills and then invest in high end animal stock that would give them better profit down the road. Then, they built their mother's dream; a horse riding stable. It was known to their clients and local businesses as The Stables.

Dru smiled at Reilly and Grace. They reminded her of Matt and Nikki when they had worked at The Stables.

Dru had met Matt's dad, Nick, at a rodeo. He was riding bulls and she ran barrels. Three months into the relationship they were married. After just two months working on the ranch, he told her he was headed back out on the road. Nothing would change his mind, not even when she told him she was pregnant. It didn't matter. He said he was sorry and left. The 'why' had haunted her for years…when she admitted it to herself…it still bothered her.

Matt was only a week old when Nick appeared with a 2 year old girl in tow, Nikki. During their whole relationship, Dru didn't even know the girl existed. But Nikki was his and he had full custody from the mother who was only 17 when Nikki was born. Nick's mother had been taking care of her until she heard about his new son. She pushed Nick into allowing the little girl to grow up with her brother even if their father wasn't around.

Dru talked it over with her parents and they agreed the little girl needed a home and a true family. The adoption papers were signed and Nikki's last name was legally changed to Tagger. She may not have Tagger blood, but she was a Tagger through and through. Nikki and Matt looked just like their dad; tall, dark hair, and eyes that changed from brown to green depending on their moods.

In all the years since he had walked away from the three of them, the only contact was a savings account opened with a $100,000 balance when Matt was five. Eighteen years of child support paid in one lump sum.

It became Matt and Nikki's college fund.

In her 21st year, Dru had married, given birth to a son, adopted a daughter, and divorced. It was a tough year and she was thankful her family was there to support her.

Matt was only 9 months old when the accident happened.

"Earth to Dru…" Reilly was standing in front of her waving a hand at her.

Dru chuckled at him. "What?"

He just smiled and shook his head. "Dad wants help working the back arena."

Dru glanced to the back of the buildings. There was a large and small arena at the back of the property. Plus a round pen for training. They sat behind the two large stable buildings which held twenty horses each.

"Tomorrow's the last day of school," Grace reminded her. "He's getting ready for the riding clinic on Saturday."

They made their way through the buildings and to the large arena. Reilly and Grace ran ahead of her and jumped up on the fence.

Dru's phone started singing just as she reached the fence. After a quick little shoulder wiggle to the beat of the music, she pulled it out of her pocket and glanced down at the number. It was an out of state number.

She looked up as Jack, Reilly's dad and the manager of The Stables, pulled the tractor up next to his son and Grace. There was no mistaking that Reilly was his son. They both had black hair, blue eyes and dimples. Jack's wife had died two years before he answered their ad for the manager's position. He needed a new start, and ended up with a surrogate family with six kids for Reilly to grow up with; her two, Matt and Nikki, Grayson's daughters, Grace and Sadie, and Scott's two kids, Nora and Wade.

The phone was still ringing so she hit the answer button and raised it to her ear.

"The Stables," she answered.

There was hesitation before the person spoke. When she did, Dru could tell it was an older woman. "Can I speak with the owner please?" She said quietly.

"I am one of the owners, Dru Tagger."

There was more hesitation. "Oh…good. I'm so sorry to bother you."

She hesitated long enough that Dru could add, "No bother at all, how can I help?"

"Well," another hesitation. Even over the phone Dru could tell she was upset.

"I'm not really sure how to start," the woman paused. "My name is Cora Smith and my husband, Wes, passed away a little over three weeks ago."

Well that was a start, Dru frowned. "I'm so sorry."

"Yes, well, thank you. I received a phone call a few minutes ago," she hesitated again, "I'm a bit confused about the call."

"Was it from someone here at The Stables?"

"No, I got your number from a card my husband had in his wallet."

"Do you have horses? Was your husband looking for somewhere to board them?"

"No horses. We sold all our horses a couple years ago."

"OK…" Dru walked away from the arena and the excited chatter from the two teenagers talking about the last day of school.

"That's what's so strange about the phone call I received. The man who called said he would be delivering the hay in the morning."

"Did they call from Tagger Enterprises for the hay?"

"No."

Dru quietly exhaled in rising confusion. "Hay for what?"

"I don't know; we don't have any animals. I canceled the hay order from the man, but now I'm worried," The woman's voice trembled as she continued. "My husband was being very secretive before he died. He even shipped me to Seattle to spend time with my sister for a couple weeks."

Dru still wasn't sure what this had to do with The Stables.

The woman on the phone continued, "We live in Lenore, but I haven't been there since a week before he died."

"Mrs. Smith," Dru leaned against the back of the building. "I'm a bit confused. How can The Stables help?"

The voice let out a frustrated sigh, "I am afraid my husband bought some animals without telling me and they have been at our home in Lenore, unattended, for over three weeks."

Dru slowly stood away from the building, "Horses, sheep, cattle, chickens…a lot of animals can forage for themselves for three weeks."

"Yes," The woman's voice was a little stronger since she had finally voiced her concern. "After my husband died, we had him brought to Seattle and buried here, with family. I haven't been to our home now for over a month. I have no one there to call to go check the property. With your card here… well, I thought maybe he had talked to you about this."

"No, not with me," Dru frowned. "I'll talk to the manager here to see if he spoke with your husband. If not, then we'll take a drive and check." This could be a total waste of time… she HOPED it was a total waste of time. "You have no idea what kind of animals he may have bought?"

"No," she sighed, "I'm just so worried. The man with the hay was so adamant that my husband had bought the hay AND that it was scheduled to be delivered in the morning."

"Did he say how much hay he was delivering?" It was coming on summer when most large animals would be grazing in pastures and not be dependent on hay. The first hay crop was coming off the fields. He could have been stocking up for winter.

"He didn't say."

"OK, I'll go check it out," Her parents and grandparents had taught her to have respect for animals. Something in her gut told her to make the drive. She wouldn't be able to forgive herself if there were animals suffering because she didn't have time to take a drive 30 miles up the river.

Dru took the address and directions to her property. She assured the woman they would call and let her know what they found. It would take at least a half hour to get there. She walked back to the arena.

"Hey, Jack." She smiled at him and was rewarded with a relaxed smile in return. "Did you talk to a Mr. Smith about boarding a horse?"

"No, we're booked solid, all the stalls are full throughout the summer."

"It would have been about a month ago?" she clarified.

He shook his head. "No Mr. Smith…oddly enough, I probably would have remembered that name." He grinned, showing off his dimples.

Dru sighed; she needed to make the drive. After a two hour drive home from the ranch, she wasn't relishing doing it by herself. "Mind if I take Reilly and Grace to check out their property? I need to check on their animals." It was the closest to the truth as she wanted to admit.

"Sure, no problem, but the other kids should be here any second." He reminded her.

"Want me to take them?" She asked, hoping he said yes, but feeling guilty for taking all his help.

Jack just grinned; he knew she liked hanging with the kids…what the family affectionately called "kid therapy".

"Yeah, take them." He shook his head with a smile and started the tractor.

Dru, Reilly, and Grace waited next to her silver truck for the bus to arrive. Grace lightly ran a finger around the blue T3E ranch brand painted on the door as they watched the bus slowly make its way down the gravel road.

Sadie was the first one off the bus. At nine years old, she was the most adorable blonde hair, blue eyed girl ever. She wore her hair in a long braid down her back and it just reached the top of her jeans. Her eyes shone bright with the excitement of the end of school. On more than one occasion, due to her looks and fiery temper, Sadie was accused of being Dru's daughter, instead of Grayson's.

"Howdy!" Wade yelled as he jumped off the bottom step of the bus. He was nine, only a month older than Sadie, and had black hair and dark brown eyes which reflected the Native American heritage of his mother Jordan, Scott's wife. Wade had a love of old western movies. All he wanted to be when he grew up was a cowboy.

Nora stepped off the bus shaking her head at her brother, her long black hair swaying around her shoulders.

"Wade stop!" She yelled at him in amusement, then turned to her aunt. "He's been 'cowboy talking' all the way from school, drove everyone nuts." She laughed, her dark brown eyes just as happy as her brothers and cousins.

Nora's passion was in showing horses in competitions rather than gaming or rodeo events. She loved the sparkling clothing and doing her long black hair in big flowing curls down her back. At only eleven years old, she was already winning nearly every show she entered.

"I'm hungry, Aunt Dru," Wade ran up to her. "Do you have any vittles?"

Dru chuckled at him, the light in his eyes and the grin on his face warming her heart, "We're headed down river to Lenore. We'll stop in Lewiston and get you some vittles on the way. Go put your backpacks in the office. We'll grab them tonight when we get back."

After the stop for vittles, they crossed the bridge over the Clearwater River and headed up Highway 12 to Lenore. Everyone was happy and well fed.

It was the calm before the storm…within thirty minutes, their lives would change forever.

******

Dru pulled off the highway and onto a gravel road that led to the Smith property. She still wouldn't let herself believe there was an issue. She was sure the hay man was wrong and had called the wrong rancher. Smith was a common name. Dru quickly glanced around at the kids. She hadn't told the kids exactly why they were headed to the ranch, only saying they were checking on a friend's property; something they did all the time.

Reilly was in the front seat by the door, with Grace sitting between them. He was tall for his age hend had blue eyes that always seemed to be searching for something. He was only five when his mother died of heart failure. He and his father were just the right fit for the Tagger Trio; a broken family looking for more broken families. His best friend, Grace, balanced his moodiness with her exuberance. She always knew when to pull him back from "the dark side" as she put it.

Grace was a ball of sunshine. Her smile lit up the room and her easy laugh was extremely infectious. Her thick, shoulder length, dark blond hair was cut in a cute style and was just long enough she could pull it into a pony tail when riding. At 14, she was already 5' 6" and still had a couple years yet to grow. Her mother Leah was 5' 10" and her dad, Grayson, stood 6' 3". She was destined to be a long tall cowgirl.

Dru smiled as she listened to the excited stories of summer plans from the kids. As much as Dru missed Matt and Nikki, she did love spending time with her nieces, nephew, and Reilly.

For two years, the only family she had were her brothers and her two kids. No parents, grandparents, aunts or uncles; just the five of them. Scott and Grayson had become Matt and Nikki's surrogate fathers. They joked that their family tree was actually a log pole.

Dru finally reached the gate to the Smith property and gave the combination for the lock on the gate to Reilly. She checked the ground around the truck for any sign of animal or human tracks. Reilly searched around the gate but the only tracks were from deer and elk. No sign of any domestic animal or any people going in or out.

Although they had the gate closed to keep people out while they were gone, Dru made sure Reilly closed it again; just in case there were any loose animals running around.

"Not much dust," Grace noted as Reilly crawled back into the truck. "Must have rained here the last couple days as much as it did at home."

They slowly pulled up the driveway and stopped in front of the house. A border of trees ran along the right side of the house;

the barn was to the left in an open field. The house sat in the middle of thirty acres of pasture and timber land.

"Why are we here?" Wade asked. He had to strain his head up and around to see over everyone.

Dru turned the engine off. She didn't open her door and neither did the kids. They just looked around in silence. There was no sound coming from the area and there didn't seem to be any birds flying around. Spider webs decorated the bushes and the corners of the windows. It was very eerie.

"I don't like it here," Nora whispered.

Dru agreed with her, there was something about the place that wasn't right. The house was a normal ranch style, white with a wide porch. The barn was the typical red color and set at the base of a small hill. She could see that the heavy rain had caused a mud slide which pushed up against the barn. There were beautiful green rolling hills in front of the house with pine trees surrounding a large open pasture. It should be beautiful and welcoming, but they all sat quietly in the truck looking around at the desolate house.

"How can such a cute house be so uninviting?" Grace muttered.

Dru shrugged. "Well, maybe because no one has been here for at least three weeks."

She finally decided it was time to tell them the whole story. They all sat quietly listening while she told them the short conversation she had with Cora Smith.

"It's haunted!" Wade yelled from the back. It was so loud they all jumped. "That's why it's so creepy!"

"Wade!" Sadie nudged him, but he just laughed at his cousin.

"No sign of any animals around here either." Reilly said looking around and ignored Wade.

"Maybe we should get out and look around." Grace suggested with a low chuckle.

Dru smiled at her as she reached for the door handle and they all crawled out of the truck. Just as all four doors closed at the same time, Dru was sure she heard a noise coming from the barn. She looked around at the kids but none of them acted like they had heard anything.

They spread out and started to walk…all in the direction of the barn. It seemed the logical place to find any animals Mr. Smith may have purchased. They looked up the hillside, out onto the fields, and into the trees. They looked low at the ground for manure piles or animal tracks.

Dru's phone rang, making everyone jump. It was Cora Smith. Dru didn't have any answers for her yet so she rejected the call.

"I'll call her back," Dru mumbled to the kids.

"Do you hear that buzzing noise?" Nora asked. It was a low hum and she was glancing around trying to locate the source. The young girl quickly shortened the distance between herself and Dru; grasping her aunt's hand tightly. The other kids came in closer too; even Reilly who always tried to put on a brave face.

"It stinks here," Wade whispered crinkling his nose.

Dru could feel her stomach tighten and pulse increase when she realized the sound and smell was coming from the barn. As they walked closer they could see hundreds of flies. It could easily mean dead animals. She took a deep breath and let it out slowly; looking around at the kids she finally realized it may not have been a good idea to bring them.

"Aunt Dru…" Sadie whispered in concern, her blue eyes worried.

The kids understood the meaning, too. They had been on a trail ride at the ranch when they had come upon a cougar kill, a half-eaten calf. It had been there for only a day, but the smell was potent and the flies abundant. The thought of the cougar coming back had made them return to the ranch quickly.

The small group slowly advanced towards the gloomy barn. The windows and doors were closed.

"I feel like we're in a bad horror movie." Reilly whispered.

Grace elbowed him with a frown. "I'm spooked enough Reilly."

Dru glanced around at the kids. There may have been thirty acres on the Smith property, but the six of them were so bunched together they barely took up five square feet of it.

When they reached the barn door, they stopped and listened while they continually waved away the flies that began circling them. It could be a vagrant that found a place to live while the owners were away, or it could be a bear or a cougar that had found a quiet place to sleep out of the rain.

Dru heard a noise. So did the kids and they all stepped in a little closer to her. She glanced over at Reilly who was the closest thing she had to another adult.

"Do you want me to go get the rifle?" he asked. There was always one in the truck when they traveled to the ranch.

Just as she was about to answer they heard another noise. This time they knew what it was.

"That's a horse!" Grace gasped. Reilly's voice had caused the horse to nicker.

Dru grabbed at the barn door and pulled, but it was stuck. Looking down, the mudslide she had noticed earlier had blocked the front of the door. They all bent over and started digging the mud away from the door.

"Grace, see if you can find shovels or something to dig with." Dru called out to her niece as she dug away at the mud with her bare hands.

Grace ran around the side of the barn and quickly returned with a shovel and hoe. Reilly grabbed the hoe and dug as fast as he could. Dru grabbed the shovel and dug just as fast, her mind racing with the images they might find on the other side of the door. She was very strongly regretting bringing the kids but she knew they wouldn't leave now.

There was another whinny.

"At least he's alive and strong enough to call out," Wade said worriedly, his fingers barely making a dent in the mud, but he kept trying.

"Hold on," Dru said under her breath to the horse. She hoped he had hay and water in there with him; that someone had known about him beside Wes Smith.

The horse whinnied again. "Hurry!" Nora cried out as her small fingers made small dents in the mud, but she just kept trying too.

They finally cleared enough to try the door. Reilly and Dru both grabbed the handle and pulled as hard as they could. Their hands just slid off the handle from the slick mud. They quickly wiped their hands off on their jeans and tried again. Dru didn't know what to expect when the door finally came open but what she saw…she would never have dreamed in her worst nightmare.

CHAPTER TWO

Mud, manure, and urine mixed together created an overwhelming pungent odor and a sloppy muck. They waved away the flies and stepped inside. The barn was dark, but Dru could see there were three stall doors on each side and a closed back door at the far end. She glanced around and her eyes stopped on the two sets of eyes that greeted them.

"Oh my!" It was a cry in unison from the girls. The horses were in the first two stalls on the left and the tops of their heads could barely be seen over the short stall wall.

Dru turned to Reilly, "Run down to the other end and open the door, we need to get it aired out in here."

Reilly ran ahead of them as the group stepped up to the two horses. Dru's heart sank when she looked into the sunken, sad eyes of the starving horses. By their size, Dru guessed them to be yearlings. A dirty white blaze ran down the face of the first horse. She could barely make out the color of the hair through the mud and manure caked on their hides. Dru guessed it was the red hair of a sorrel. There was no hay or water in either stall. The floor was at least a foot thick in manure and mud, and there wasn't a dry spot in the stall.

Dru opened the door to the first yearling and stepped closer as she held a hand out to him to let him know she was friendly. He let out a quiet snort and lifted his head a few inches. He tried to take a step to her but he slipped on the wet floor and nearly fell over. She caught the horse to steady him and could feel every bone where her hands touched. The hair should have been sleek and soft but it was matted in mud and manure, in some areas missing. Every rib was visible. The pelvic bones that should have been hidden under muscle and face, were sticking out like butterfly wings. He looked like a hair covered skeleton. His mane was attached to his neck from the dried mud. She touched his muzzle gently and quietly reassured him.

"It's OK, we're here now," Dru whispered to him, her heart aching for him. She had been around horses all her life and had never seen anything as terrible as this.

"Can we come in?" Sadie's voice was low and gentle. Dru glanced over and saw the tears running down Grace and Sadie's faces. Wade was standing behind them, trying hard not to cry.

Dru nodded, "Move slowly so you don't scare him."

They came around the sides and stood next to him. The top of Sadie's and Wade's heads were even with the boney spine of the horse. The horse was shoulder high to Grace. Wade knelt down onto the wet ground and started clearing the muck away from the colt's feet. He didn't care if he got dirty. Sadie and Grace quickly joined him.

Nora had opened the stall to the other horse and he was in the same condition. She reached out to him then quickly drew her hand back.

"He won't hurt you," Dru assured her. They were too weak to harm anyone.

Nora slowly turned to Dru, her eyes full of shock and worry. "He is so skinny, there is nothing but skin and bone." A tear made its way down her cheek. Her eyes glistened from the remaining tears. "I'm afraid if I touch him, I'll hurt him." Her voice trembled.

Dru nodded, the same thought had gone through her mind. "Just touch gently. He'll appreciate a warm reassuring hand."

Nora gently touched the nose of the black horse. The horse lifted his head to her hand. Dru could see Nora's shoulders relax as she touched the dirty white star on the forehead of the horse.

"Grace, help Nora with this one." Dru moved quickly and both girls started cleaning around the horse. They needed to get them out as soon as possible.

Reilly still hadn't returned from trying to open the barn door.

"I'm going down to help Reilly." Dru told them.

As she took a step out of the stalls, a movement caught her eye from the other side of the aisle. Her back stiffened. It was another horse. She quickly moved across and opened the door.

"Oh, you poor thing." She could barely contain her tears. His front legs were stuck in the mud up to his knees. He couldn't move and must have been there for days.

"Wade, come help me," Dru called out. "Over here, there's another one." Dru knelt next to his front legs and started to clear the mud away from him. He was so weak he could barely lift his head. His skin, covered in dirty matted red hair, looked like it was sliding off the bones of his emaciated body.

Dru leaned under the horse to dig at the mud to release his legs but had to move slowly to keep from hitting them. She didn't want to hurt them any more than they were. As she worked, the colt rested his muzzle on top of her head. She could feel his breath run down her back. He must have understood she was there to help and save him. Dru couldn't hold back the tears. They freely rolled down her cheeks and landed in the muck she was removing from his legs.

As Wade walked into the stall, Dru used her sleeve to wipe away the traces of the tears. The two glanced sadly at one another then, Wade lowered himself to the back legs, gently running his hand down the length of them to let the horse know he was there. The little red colt turned his head back toward the young boy. Wade slowly reached out to pet the dirty muzzle of the horse, then turned back to remove the mud from the legs.

Dru finally heard the sound of the barn door opening and Reilly walking back to help. He had only taken a few steps when she heard a quick gasp and the 'dang' that followed. She stood and looked down the barn towards him, her heart racing in dread. He was running between the stall doors at the far end of the barn.

"No, no, no…" Dru muttered as she stepped into the aisle; Reilly's eyes met hers. She could see the anguish in his.

"There's more!" He said in despair and started opening the doors.

Dru took a step farther into the barn and peered into the stall next to the one Wade was in. It was the only stall they hadn't looked in…she knew what she was going to see but wasn't quite prepared.

Another yearling lay on his side in the middle. The horse was so weak he couldn't lift his head more than a couple inches from the ground. His eyes followed Dru as she opened the door.

"Sadie!"

The young girl was next to her in moments kneeling at his head. She began talking to him and cleaning the dirt away from his muzzle. She revealed lighter hair under the dirt; maybe a grey. Sadie glanced up at her, tear streaks running down her muddy face, and her eyes pleading for help.

Dru glanced around the stall. The metal feeder was torn from the wall. There was dried blood streaked on the wall under the screws that had held the feeder. She knelt down by the horse and checked the skin for lacerations. There were none visible; he must have injured the side he was laying on.

Sadie stroked the side of the horse's face. "I hope it's not bad," she whispered.

"I'll see if I can find water buckets for them." Dru turned and glanced down the aisle to Reilly. He had opened the doors on both of the end stalls.

"Six horses, one in each stall, they're all alive." His voice was tight from holding back his emotions. He disappeared into the stall next to Nora.

"One for each of us to take care of," Nora said from behind Dru. "It'll be faster that way."

"I'm going to find buckets and get some water in here." Dru turned and walked quickly out the door.

She didn't let herself dwell on the why's and how's of the situation as she busied herself finding buckets. There was nothing on the side of the barn where they had walked, so she went to the other side. In the back hidden from view, was a lean-to with a few bales of straw and grass hay. She thought of taking the hay to the horses but she decided to talk to Dr. Mark, Tagger Enterprise's contracted veterinarian, before feeding the horses.

She found the water spigot just behind the hay and sighed in relief when she saw buckets stacked next to it. Within minutes she was hauling the first three buckets into the horses. Grace and Nora were in the first two stalls to the left and Reilly in the last. Wade and Sadie were in the first two on the right. She needed to hurry so she could get to the back corner stall and check on the yearling there.

Grace's red colt was free from the muck and was lying down. He was the first to receive water. "A little at a time," Dru told her. "We don't want them to get too much and get colicky." Grace looked at her with a confused expression. "It's a tummy ache for a horse." Dru explained.

Nora's colt was also lying down and the young girl was kneeling in the mud and manure, trying to clean him off while she sang quietly to him. He leaned his head against her. Not caring about the mud that covered the colt, Nora leaned down and wrapped her arms gently around the horse's neck. She kissed him and leaned her forehead against the star on the horse's head. The colt's eyes closed at the touch.

Dru could feel the tears welling in her eyes again at the sight of such a tender moment so she moved on. Reilly's colt was standing but leaning against the wall. There was some red and grey hair showing through the area he was stroking. Dru guessed he was a red roan. Reilly was talking quietly to the horse as he looked up at Dru. She handed him a bucket of water, his blue eyes unreadable. She repeated the instructions; he nodded and turned back to the horse.

She hurried out of the barn and brought back three more buckets handing the first two to Wade and Sadie. As she finally made her way to the last stall, she took a deep breath and tried to prepare herself for what she was going to see. "It couldn't be any worse than the others." She exhaled, stepped into the stall and glanced around. The colt was so dark Dru had a hard time seeing him in the corner.

He was in the same condition as the others with his eyes sunken, dark and head hung low. She bent over and slowly walked to him. He lifted his head and his eyes flickered when he saw the bucket. He tried to walk towards her but slipped and began to fall. Dru put the bucket down quickly just before he hit her with his front shoulder across her stomach. They both slid to the ground with her left leg pinned under him. If he would have been full size he could have seriously hurt her.

He lay still, a bit in shock from the fall. The cold moisture from the mud and manure soaked into her jeans, shirt and her hair but Dru ignored it. She didn't try to move her leg yet, she didn't want to startle him and risk further injury.

Stretching out as far as she could without disturbing him, she grabbed the water bucket and pulled it closer. The colt rolled onto his side and off her leg, his muzzle stretching out to get to the water. She knelt next to him, wrapping her arms around him and gently ran a hand down his dirty neck as he took his first drink in weeks.

The horse was completely black and Dru had a special affection for black horses. As she stroked the horse's neck and pulled the matted mane away from his body she thought of her barrel horse, Jet. She couldn't imagine Jet in this condition. The thought was agonizing to the heart. Her horse had lived a pampered twenty-five years. Dru lost part of her heart the day the horse had died, in her arms, just as this horse was in her arms now.

She took a deep, horrendous smelling breath into her lungs and coughed as she tried to rid her mind of the memory. There was no time to dwell on the past right now, she needed to keep moving so this black horse had a chance to survive.

She wondered how much hay and water Wes had given them the morning he had left. There was an empty feeder and a water bucket nailed to the wall across from it. Even full, the amount of food and water wouldn't have lasted them more than a day.

"Aunt Dru?" Sadie called out.

She stroked the colt's neck and whispered to him that she would be back and went to Sadie.

Her colt was still lying down and had barely touched the water.

Sadie's dirty face was tear-streaked as she looked at her. "What do we do?"

Dru glanced around and each of the kids had stepped to the door of the stalls to hear her answer.

"We take them home," she decided. "Our barn also has six stalls and they're bigger so they will fit without a problem. I'll talk with Mrs. Smith. We'll get them back on their feet and healthy."

Everyone nodded. They were covered in mud and manure from head to toe and all had tear streaks down their faces. Dru knew she reflected their condition, especially in the back where she fell and the muck soaked into her clothing and hair.

"I'll call Grayson and have him get the stock trailers out here for the move. It will take him over two hours to get here so we'll start moving them one at a time out into the walkway where it's dry."

"What about Dr. Mark?" Wade asked.

"I think its best he get here as soon as possible and check them out as we load them into the trailers," she answered.

Dru turned to Wade. His brown eyes were worried and tired. "How's your horse?"

He glanced into the stall with sad eyes. "I have his front legs out, just a little more on the back."

"Let's get him out first." Dru walked towards the stall. "Grace, Reilly, come with me."

As they entered the stall, the little horse lifted his head in curiosity. Her biggest fear was the horse trying to move and hurting his front legs before they could get him released from the mud.

"Wade, finish the digging. Reilly and Grace, go to the other side of him," Dru ordered and pointed where she wanted them.

Once the teenagers were facing her on the opposite side of the horse, she turned back to Wade. "Are you close?"

"Yeah, he's loose." Wade nodded and moved to the front of the horse which was facing away from the door.

"Talk to him while we move him. Keep him calm," Dru instructed and Wade started talking to the horse and stroking his nose. The horse pushed into him gently. Wade's eyes flickered with anguish.

Dru leaned down and reached under the horse. "Reach under his belly and grab my arms to create a sling," She told the teenagers and they quickly did as she instructed. If the horse was full weight, there was no way the three of them would be able to lift him.

"On the count of three, we lift together," Dru said and they nodded.

"One, two, three," They lifted the horse.

Wade's words of encouragement grew louder as he spoke to calm the red horse that didn't kick or fight. He just let them carry him backwards out of the stall.

"He's doing awesome!" Sadie cried out.

Once they had him to the middle of the aisle, Dru nodded and they slowly lowered the horse that immediately relaxed his legs and melted to the ground with the support of the three of them.

"It's probably the first time he's laid down in days." Dru's voice shook with emotion.

Her phone rang. She tried to wipe off as much mud off her hand as possible, then reached in to her back pocket to retrieve it.

It was Cora again. She glanced around at the kids, horses, mud, muck and flies still buzzing around, then declined the call. She needed time before she talked to her. It wasn't her fault, nor was it her husband's either. It was just a bizarre set of circumstances that caused this.

"Do any of you have your phones?" she asked the kids. Only Grace and Reilly had them.

"Yeah," They answered in unison.

"Have you sent out any messages about this yet?"

"No," They answered.

"I know this is awful and it's hard to deal with, but this isn't anyone's fault." They started to speak up and she raised a very dirty hand to them. "Mr. Smith fed them and died in an accident. It wasn't his fault he didn't make it back." She glanced around and saw unhappy expressions. "What I am most concerned about is Mrs.

Smith and these horses. She had no idea the horses were here until this morning. She called as soon as she knew." They nodded in sullen agreement. "I don't want this to turn into a spectacle with people and media. The horses are going to need a lot of time to heal and they don't need a bunch of people coming around and causing undo stress."

"I agree," Grace spoke up.

The others agreed with nods and 'Ok's'.

"You can take pictures so we can document their progress but no one, tweets, posts, or messages ANYONE about this."

They all nodded in agreement.

"I'm going out to call your dads and Dr. Mark. You guys start moving the horses into the aisle just like we did with the little red one. If they can walk, just support them. Don't lift them."

"What about outside?" Nora asked. Mud had plastered her long black hair to her shirt.

"We need to check with Dr. Mark first to see what they can eat. I don't want them near grass that may cause colic." She started to head outside then turned back. "You guys be careful. Reilly take the lead until I get back." Reilly nodded, his expression toughened.

Dru stepped out of the barn to call for help.

CHAPTER THREE

Dru called her brothers and informed them on the afternoon's events. They were just as concerned and dropped everything to gather trailers to get to the property as soon as possible.

Matt and Nikki were with Grayson. He would bring them for help. Scott was going to call Jack and fill him in on the details. Jack would need to get the home barn ready for all the horses.

Dr. Mark was extremely upset and was already in his truck and headed to the property before they ended the call. He approved her giving them a small amount of the grass hay she had found, but not too much until he could check over each one and decide on a diet plan.

She had barely pushed the end button when they phone rang again. It was Scott's wife, Jordan. He had called her and she had left her job at the paper mill immediately. She wanted to know how she could help.

"Food and clothing," Dru answered. It was going to be late by the time the trailers arrived and they could get the horses loaded. They would have to drive slowly so it could take up to two hours to get home. There was no doubt they would be staying in the barn with the horses for the night.

After the calls, Dru stepped back into the barn. The kids were doing a great job in moving the horses. Nora's and Grace's horses were in the walkway. They were leading Reilly's horse out.

When they finally reached Sadie's horse, it wouldn't get up.

"Let him be until he gets more water. Stay with him Sadie," Reilly said. He glanced up at Dru for confirmation so she nodded.

Reilly carried a bale of hay into the barn and gave each horse a flake to eat while they waited. Dru leaned down in front of Wade's little red one that had his front legs stuck in the mud to lightly touch his leg. He quickly pulled it back.

"He's hurtin'." Wade looked at her in concern.

Dru hesitated telling him the truth, but decided it was best to prepare them for the good and bad.

"He could have bone or ligament damage," she told the worried group. "It could be very bad."

The kids glanced around at each other, then to the horse.

"We'll just keep good thoughts that he'll be OK," Sadie looked up innocently, mud covering her face and drying in her long braid.

"Good plan," Dru smiled at her. Oh, to be nine again.

The kids went back to tending to the horses.

Dru sighed and looked around the barn. What was Wes thinking? Why had he bought all these horses and not told his wife?

Just inside the barn, next to the tack room door, she saw a clipboard. Retrieving the clipboard from the wall she stepped out into the sunlight to read Wes' notes.

The first page noted when he fed the animals. The last notation was the morning of the day he had died, 24 days earlier.

He also had a list of items he needed to pick up at the feed store. Tagger Stables was listed with a note that simply said, "Cora's Gift". Dru shook her head; she had no idea what that meant.

She flipped the page up and started reading. It was a list of stall names. Each one had a US or LS next to it with a number. US1, LS1, US2, LS2… and so on. "What the heck, Wes…" she mumbled to herself. What was he noting?

Dru lowered the clip board and looked out into the pasture to clear her mind. "If I was writing those codes, what would they be?" The S would stand for stall… what stall the horse was in. She nodded to herself. The number, of course, would be the number of the stall. Such as Stall 1 and Stall 2 to keep track of the horse. But what were the U and L for?

She watched Reilly walk out of the barn and to the water spigot toward the back. He returned with the buckets only half full because it was easier for him to carry. She glanced around at the house, then saw a chicken coop she hadn't noticed before. She took a step towards it and realized that the door was open so no chickens were inside. They would have been able to forage for food.

Dru stared at the coop. She hadn't noticed it! What else hadn't they noticed? She started walking and reran their movements from the time they arrived. They had seen the house immediately. Off to the right of the house was a row of trees that would block it from the evening sun. To the left was the barn. Once they saw it, their focus was fixed. They hadn't looked for any other structure.

"Oh no, oh no, oh no…," she whispered when she realized what the U and L meant and turned back to the barn. She felt her pulse begin to quicken, the tightness in her throat returned.

"Grace! Reilly!" She yelled. Sensing the worry in her voice, all the kids came running out of the barn wide eyed. They had a pretty traumatic day so far. What next?

"There's another barn!" she announced and the kids stared at her in disbelief. "Wes had a notation next to a DOZEN stalls which stated U for Upper and L for Lower barns." Her heart was racing and she was looking around trying to find another structure.

They stood in stunned silence.

"Grace," she grabbed the girls arm to get her to focus on what she was going to say. "Stay here with Wade and Sadie. You're in charge. Nora, Reilly and I are going to search for the other barn but I hope I'm wrong."

"Me too," she whispered. Six horses starving were bad enough but a dozen!

Grace, Wade and Sadie went back into the barn to tend to the horses.

"I'm guessing this is the upper barn because it's at the top of the hillside," She started walking down the hill and to the backside of the house. "If we didn't see it when we came in, I'm sure it's on the other side of the house."

Their pace quickened and they were jogging when they saw the corral. They broke into a full run when they saw the second barn. As Dru was running, she took note of every detail. There was no mudslide into this building and it looked in good condition. This one was wider and had two large double doors on the end they were running toward. They stopped just in front of the doors.

They hesitated, and listened at the doors instead of opening them right away. Nora took Dru's hand and squeezed tightly.

"Should we make some noise in case there is a bear or cougar in there?" Reilly asked.

A low whinny came from in the barn when Reilly spoke. His voice had alerted the horses to their presence just like at the upper barn. They all reached for the doors simultaneously. This barn was far enough from the other one that they wouldn't have heard the horses if they had called out earlier.

As the doors opened, Dru could see the building was laid out similar to the other except there were four stalls down each side. That meant there could be eight horses in here. A shutter of dread ran down her spine.

They took a step in and jumped as the horse in the first stall whinnied at them. Nora went directly to it. More noises came from down the aisle prompting Dru and Reilly to run down the length of the barn.

"There are six in here too," Reilly called out to Nora.

They were all as starved and skinny as the others. There was no mud slide so the muck wasn't as bad but it was still wet from the mixture of manure and urine.

"Nora, head up and tell the other's what we found, but come back down here to help," Dru told the girl and she quickly ran up the hill.

Reilly started hauling water as Dru sent a quick text to Grayson letting him know there were six more and they would need another trailer.

Three of the horses were standing and they carefully led them out of their stalls and into the aisle. She guessed the first horse they had seen was a palomino but it was difficult to tell because of the mud and straw matted to her body and mane. She looked like a horse version of a scarecrow.

The next horse they walked into the aisle was a dark brown colt. His little legs wobbled as they held him up to walk. There was a bay in the next stall and they used the sling technique to move the horse.

The sling technique was used to move the rest of them. Once they were moved, Dru looked them over. There was a buckskin colt, a filly she suspected was a dun but it was so covered with manure and muck that she couldn't tell, and the third was the littlest horse they had found, a brown colt.

Nora knelt down next to the little brown colt and started whispering to him. As she spoke, the horse's ears started twitching back and forth showing he was listening. Nora kept up her pep talk as they worked.

Reilly handed Nora a water bucket to let him drink, but the horse just lowered his head. Nora turned, "What do we do? He has to drink!"

"He will." Dru laid her hand on Nora's shoulder. "Don't give up. Cup water in your hand and drizzle it into his mouth. Maybe the moisture will encourage him to drink. Keep trying." She paused to think if she had ever had this issue before.

Dru had been around horses all her life and the only time a horse wouldn't drink was when it was over heated. Once it had started to cool off from the ride on the hot day, it had begun to eat and drink normally. "We might have to wait for Dr. Mark."

Reilly found a bale of grass hay in one of the empty stalls and gave each horse a flake.

Dru's phone rang. "Please don't be Cora," she said out loud. It wasn't, it was Grace.

Dr. Mark had just pulled in the driveway. Dru glanced over at the colt that wasn't drinking. "Send him down here first."

"But Aunt Dru!" Grace protested.

"We have one here that won't drink and appears to be in the worst shape. He needs to check him over first," She still didn't seem convinced. "Grace, they all need help, but those six are drinking and have eaten a little. We need to get this little one going as soon as possible."

"Ok," She reluctantly agreed, her voice strained from anxiety. "I'm just so worried about all of them."

"I know, Hon…so am I." She assured her niece.

Dru heard Dr. Mark's truck pull up and took a step out the doors, waving to show him where they were.

He quickly jumped out of his truck and retrieved supplies from the back utility boxes. He was a stocky man with dark hair hidden under his cowboy hat. The dark hair was peppered with grey.

His most striking feature was the large mustache that highlighted his face. He had lived in Idaho for over 20 years but still had a slow southern drawl from growing up in Oklahoma.

Dru knew he was about to retire and thanked heaven he hadn't yet. He was the best, most experienced veterinarian around.

"Tagger Enterprises will cover all the cost," Dru informed him. "Do whatever it takes."

He hadn't seen the horses in the other barn so when he stepped in the lower barn he paused and took in the whole sight. Six skeletal horses looked over at him. They were all lying down. Their dull eyes were sunken in their head with no shine that you would see in a healthy hydrated horse. They were filthy from lying in the manure and a few had sores where they had tried to get out of the stalls and hurt themselves. The kids, covered in mud and manure, continually waved the flies away from the wounds and now themselves.

Dr. Mark looked over at Dru, "There are six more?"

She nodded and his usual calm, cheerful manner was replaced by a stern matter-of-fact shield. She had seen this technique used by many professionals to bury their emotions and focus only on the details at hand.

"This one won't drink," Nora told him as she slowly stroked the neck of the horse. The colt's breathing was more natural now; not as labored as when they first found him. Nora's caring and pep talk must have helped.

Dr. Mark got right to work in checking the horse's vitals as Nora watched intently.

While they were working, Dru received a text from Grayson saying they had reached the gate. Leaving the horses in good hands, she ran back up the hill to meet them.

She walked into the upper barn to see the six horses laying down with Grace, Sadie, and Wade watching over them. Sadie had found a towels and was trying to wash the mud and dirt from around the eyes and nostrils of the young horses.

Dru looked around at the mud soaked kids. Sadie's long blonde braid looked brunette from the amount of mud in it. All of their blue jeans and shirts were brown from the dried flaking muck.

As she waited for the trailer to arrive, Dru walked around the barn and noticed there were a few saddle pads in the tack room. She grabbed them to give the horses something to lie on in the trailer. They didn't want to use straw in fear the horses would eat it and cause digestive problems. There wasn't any other bedding around. The pads were the best they could do.

Dru opened the door to a small office and found a small box containing a number of folders. She recognized them as horse's registration papers. She heard the trucks arriving so she grabbed the box and quickly placed it in her truck.

In the first truck, Matt was in the passenger side with Grayson driving. In the truck behind him, Scott was driving and Nikki was on the passenger side. Dru motioned the directions for Grayson to back the trailer to the barn and for Scott to park where he was. They needed to focus on one set of horses at a time.

Grayson backed up the trailer to the barn while Matt, Nikki and Scott walked towards her. As they approached, Dru could see the looks of disbelief when they saw her. Like the kids, she too was covered in mud and manure from head to toe.

"That bad?" Scott asked.

"Brace yourself," she answered with a disheartened sigh. "It's absolutely awful."

CHAPTER FOUR

After a quick walk through, they decided on a plan. The saddle pads were placed on the floor of the trailer for the horses that had sores on their sides. Six healthy horses could fit into the stock trailer but these young horses needed to be lying down as they traveled, so it would be a tight fit. They would load the horses from the upper barn in one trailer and the lower barn in the other. Once the upper barn was emptied they would take the other trailer to the lower barn.

"Mom?" Nikki asked. "What can I do to help?"

"Head down and help Dr. Mark," she answered. "He's probably overwhelmed and your experience with him should help."

Nikki turned and jogged down to the barn.

Scott walked up to the first little horse and bent to help him up.

"Wait!" Grace cried. Scott, her uncle, stopped and glanced up at her in surprise.

"He has a bad left hind quarter, so you can't pick him up that way. You have to have someone help on the other side and create a sling." She showed him what she meant. "That way you don't hurt him as much."

Scott glanced up at Dru and she nodded. "They've been taking care of them for the last couple hours," She smiled proudly at Grace. "The kids can tell you what to watch on each horse."

With that, Grace, Sadie and Wade took over the instructions for the loading of their horses. The men listened respectively and took their time with each one.

The horse's weak legs wouldn't be able to hold them up for the whole trip in a rocking and bouncing trailer. Dru sighed in relief when she saw the horses begin lying in the trailer.

The last to be loaded was Sadie's little grey colt. The nine-year-old informed the men that the colt had not been up at all, so they would need to find another way to carry and load him. She showed them the dried blood on the wall under the feeder screws.

Grayson knelt down and stroked the small colt's muzzle. "Well, little one. We need to see if you have injuries on that side." The colt's eye focused on the man talking to him. His ears flicked forward in interest and he lifted his head.

Grayson motioned for Matt to help him lift the colt. Matt took the hindquarters and Grayson the front. Sadie watched them intently and spoke encouraging words to the horse. He seemed to understand what they wanted and tried to get up. His weak body flayed around on the ground and he kicked out. His hoof connected with Sadie's hip sending her flying back against the stall wall then down to the ground.

"Sadie!" Grayson called out to his daughter; she was already trying to get up before she hit the ground.

"I'm OK, he didn't mean it," Sadie cried out and ran to the horse to defend it. The colt had stopped trying to get up and lay quietly on the ground, groaning from the effort. Sadie was on her knees in front of the colt, before her dad could grab her. "He didn't mean it, Dad!"

"I know, Honey," Grayson knelt by his youngest daughter and the horse she was protecting. "I didn't mean to yell." He touched the side of her dirty face and her blue eyes began to well with tears again. "It's OK, Honey. He was just trying to help us." She turned her face into her dad's shoulder as the tears began to fall.

Dru watched her brother quietly comfort his daughter. She sighed heavily. It was a hard thing for a parent to see their child hurting physically and emotionally as Sadie was now.

When Sadie leaned back she left a mud stain on her dad's shirt; "Oh, Dad! I'm sorry."

He smiled at his daughter, "I think a little mud is the least of our problems right now." He leaned down to kiss the top of her head, the only spot that wasn't dirty. "Now, go get in the trailer so he can see you in there as we carry him."

Sadie slowly stood, ran a soothing hand down the horse's jaw and headed for the trailer.

Grayson looked over at Matt. "OK, let's try this again."

The colt didn't try to help this time and let the men pick him up. They held him securely to see if the horse could put its weight on his own legs. The colt wobbled but took the weight. As the horse stood, Dru inspected his side for injuries.

"He OK, Mom?" Matt asked with concern in his voice.

She couldn't distinguish between the mud and blood but there was a wide gash from the top of his shoulder to the top of his leg. There were other smaller wounds that were matted with mud. "Pretty ugly cuts," Dru answered.

"The mud probably kept the flies out of it." Grayson looked around and assessed the situation. "We can't lift him from his sides; it would hurt him too much."

"There is a canvas in the back of the truck. We can try and get him down on his good side and carry him." Dru suggested.

Grayson nodded and she retrieved the canvas. They heard Dr. Mark drive up from the lower barn as the canvas was placed under the colt. With great relief to the group, he lay down on top of it. The colt's large eyes moved from one person to another, his ears flicked back and forth trying to anticipate the next move.

Dr. Mark, Scott, Matt, and Grayson each took a corner of the canvas tarp and lifted slowly. The colt bounced his head a few times then relaxed. Dru walked next to him and stroked his neck while talking to him softly.

Grace and Wade were in the trailer keeping the other five horses calm. The horses didn't have enough energy to do more than just lie there. All the excitement of the last couple hours had worn them out, more than they already had been.

The stress worried Dru. She knew it could be deadly to the starving horses.

Sadie paced back and forth in front of the trailer. She began bouncing nervously when she saw the men carrying the horse out. "Oh, oh, oh…" she cried out. "Is he OK?"

Dru nodded. "This was the best way to carry him without hurting him."

Sadie stepped up into the trailer. "I'm riding back here with him."

Dru hadn't thought of that. Would the horses be safe in the back of the trailer by themselves? "I don't believe that's legal Sadie…or safe."

Matt and Grayson stepped up into the trailer and the men placed the colt onto the pads. Once the colt was down, it rolled up onto its side and moaned. Sadie knelt next to him and encouraged him. She glanced up at her dad pleading with her eyes to let her ride in the back.

He didn't answer. "Keep these doors open, and the trailer here while we load the others." It was going to be a close squeeze for all six horses to lie down in the trailer.

"I'll look over these six while you load the others." Dr. Mark said and stepped into the trailer.

Grayson, Matt, and Dru walked down to the lower barn as Scott drove the truck. All of the horses were lying down with the kids and Nikki talking quietly to them.

Dru placed her hand on her daughter's shoulder. "You OK?"

Nikki nodded with tears in her eyes. "This seems like a dream…a really bad one."

They repeated the process of loading each of the horses.

Reilly and Nora oversaw how each was loaded. Again, the men listened carefully and followed the instructions from the kids.

Once the last horse was loaded, Reilly turned to Dru, "I want to ride in the back with the horses."

"Me, too," Nora stood defiantly.

She looked up at the men and Nikki for opinions.

Grayson spoke first. "You can ride in the back, up to the other barn." Nora and Reilly jumped in the trailer. "Stay in the corner and be careful if they start moving." He turned to Matt and Nikki. "Ride on the outsides and watch them carefully." They nodded and jumped on the wheel wells and held onto the open bars on the side of the stock trailer.

Scott slowly pulled away from the barn as Grayson and Dru walked behind the stock trailer while watching Matt and Nikki.

"What do you think?" Grayson asked.

"I understand how the kids feel and I feel the same way myself. I want to watch over the horses and not leave their sides," Scott was driving very slow and careful up the hill. "I would feel better if Matt and Nikki rode in the trailers for a while to make sure the horses ride ok. They are bigger and older and can handle an emergency faster."

Grayson nodded. "I agree, but the kids are gonna be pissed."

"Well then," Dru glanced up at her brother with a grin. "I'll let you be the bad person and tell them."

He chuckled but didn't say anything.

Matt and Nikki jumped off the trailer when it stopped.

"No problems," Nikki reported.

"How do you two feel about riding with the horses out to the highway to see how they do?" Grayson asked.

"I'll do it." They answered in unison.

"The kids aren't going to be very happy they aren't allowed to." Nikki warned.

Grayson nodded and opened the trailer door slowly so as not to spook the horses. He motioned for the kids to come out. They did so reluctantly and were visibly upset when Grayson told them they weren't riding with the horses. They looked to Dru for help.

"Sorry kids," She shook her head. "Matt and Nikki will ride with the horses to the highway to make sure they travel OK." This news didn't help their moods. "We'll stop every fifteen minutes and check on them."

Nora and Reilly rode with Scott so they could check on the lower barn horses.

Grace, Sadie, and Wade rode with Grayson so they could check on the upper barn horses.

Dr. Mark drove ahead of the group. He was headed to his clinic to retrieve the supplies he needed and then meet them at their barn. The Tagger barn was bigger and stress free giving the horses a better chance to recover than taking them to the busy clinic.

The trip from the house to the road was long and arduous. The men drove slowly to keep the trailers from bumping and swaying too much. Half way down, they stopped and the kids bailed out of each truck to check on the horses. They looked through the openings on the side instead of opening the doors. Dru was following the group and they all gave her a "thumbs up" as they climbed back in the trucks.

She dug her phone out of her back pocket and was surprised that it had lasted the day. She had landed on it and soaked it in mud and manure more than a couple times.

Everyone had washed their hands and faces before getting into the three vehicles, but the odor was a bit strong inside her truck so she lowered the windows. "Man, I stink," she whispered to herself as she glanced at the messages and incoming calls.

Jack had texted asking for an update and letting her know the barn and dinner were ready. She responded with the E.T.A. It was going to be a long trip.

Once they got to the highway, Matt and Nikki were let out of the trailers. The horses were resting quietly and not trying to stand. They jumped in the truck with Dru. As she reviewed the first part of the day's events with her son and daughter, they followed the trailers down the highway which ran parallel with the Clearwater River. They stopped at each large pullout to check the horses.

There were two options to get home and to the barn from the highway. They could go through town and deal with a long uphill grade and many stop lights or they could go the back way, which was a flatter road but had one short steep grade at the end. The horses would lean to the back of the trailer as they made the climb and they couldn't stop half way up. Their house was within minutes once they got to the top.

They decided on the flatter road with the steep grade that ended close to their property. Their home was affectionately called The Homestead. It was a large two story house built to fit three families.

Once turning off the main road, there was a long driveway to The Homestead. The moonlight lit the white vinyl fencing that lined each side of the driveway. It looked like it was glowing. A circular driveway would allow the men to pull the trucks around and backup the horse trailers right into the barn.

Currently, there were only two horses at the house. Libby was big, black and had a long flowing mane like her mother, Jet. Nikki, riding Libby, had won many horse shows and Nora had started showing with her a couple years before. Kit, a dark red bay with black mane and tail was Libby's daughter. She belonged to Nikki and was also the barrel horse that Sadie and Grace were riding at the local arenas.

The pair of horses saw the trailers and began whinnying and running with the trucks. They ran excitedly, bucking and kicking up their heels at the anticipation of new horses. Dru could hear the little horses whinny from inside the trailers.

Grayson and Scott came to a stop and the kids slid out of both trucks and jumped on the trailer running boards. Nikki and Matt joined them. They would work on keeping the colts and fillies calm as the group drove down the long driveway.

Dru watched all six of the Tagger kids and Reilly talk with the horses from the sides of the horse trailer. All of them were more concerned with the horses than they were with their own safety. The mud and muck had dried in everyone's hair, skin, and clothes.

Dru looked at her phone to check the time; they had driven away from The Stables at 3:30 and now, at 11:30, the moonlight lit the surrounding pasture and house. The afternoon had been long and stressful. The next few hours wouldn't be any easier.

CHAPTER FIVE

On a normal day, two red Australian cow dogs, Bart and Mavis, would welcome all incoming vehicles. Tongues hanging out, tails wagging, they would run circles around each other to be the first to greet the visitor to their home. Tonight, there was no sign of the dogs. Someone had kenneled them so they wouldn't disturb the horses.

Jack, along with Grayson's wife Leah and Scott's wife Jordan waited at the large barn doors, lights on and ready. Leah stood 5' 10" with dark blonde hair and blue eyes; Jordan just barely hit 5' and had the black hair and dark eyes of her Native American ancestry. While Grayson and Leah complemented each other's coloring and height, Scott stood a full fourteen inches taller than his wife.

Dr. Mark's truck was off to the side with all the side doors open and the contents removed. Dru parked next to his truck and glanced into the barn. He had set up a table and his supplies were organized across it. He had prepared for triage.

Nikki and Matt joined Dr. Mark to assist. Nikki had spent a summer working at the veterinary clinic before her first years in college. Matt had worked in the clinic the summer before. Matt enjoyed the time working with the large animals but decided to attend the University of Idaho for Forest Management so he would spend his working years outside in the mountains. Nikki was attending the University of Idaho too but, thinking of the growth of Tagger

Enterprises, she was working towards a degree in Resort Management.

"How did they travel?" Dru asked as the kids walked up to the barn.

The mud was starting to flake off their faces causing a reptile scales look to their skin.

"They seemed pretty comfortable," Matt answered. "A couple tried to get up when they heard Libby and Kit but gave up."

Jack was directing Scott as he backed the trailer into the barn. He looked over at the kids and then to Dru. His eyes opened wide and he shook his head in disbelief. "You guys look like you've been through a mud and manure war...and lost."

Leah looked at all the kids. "I don't think I have ever seen you kids so dirty." She looked around at each. "While the men unload the horses, you all go and get in the showers."

The kids looked at her in horror and instantly started talking over each other about how they needed to be there with the horses.

Grace finally turned to Dru. "Help!" She mouthed in desperation.

Living together in the same house as the kids grew, the adults were very respectful of each other's parenting skills and rights. They worked hard to not step on each other's rules and orders but this time Dru couldn't help but say something.

"Leah," she finally said. Leah looked at her with an arched brow showing surprise that Dru would go against what she said. "They need to work with the men unloading the horses."

"The men are quite capable of unloading the horses." Leah said tartly.

Dru kept her voice calm so she didn't upset her sister-in-law. "The kids need to help unload these horses and help them to the stalls." Leah's shoulders went up in defense.

The kids remained quiet.

Choosing her words carefully, Dru continued, "Each one of them took care of a couple horses and they know where each horse is hurt. Once you see the horses, you'll understand."

Grayson stepped up to the group and looked at the kids. He hadn't heard the exchange. "What are you waiting for? Scott parked, go help." The kids took off without looking at Leah.

Grayson looked between his sister and his wife. He could tell there was tension. "What?" he asked innocently.

"Nothing," Leah replied and followed the kids.

Dru shook her head at him, silently letting him know to leave it alone.

She stepped up on the side of the trailer and took a look at the horses inside. They were all lying up on their sides, heads hung low, and barely a movement from them. They were exhausted. Dru was worried they didn't have enough energy or strength in their bodies to handle such commotion. It had been a stressful day for them and she was concerned that the stress was beginning to takes its toll.

"Let's take them out one at a time, do a complete exam and get them to their stalls," Dr. Mark told the group. "There would be too much commotion if we tried to do too many at a time." Everyone nodded.

Jack stepped up to the back of the horse trailer and started to open it.

"Be prepared," Scott warned him, Leah, and Jordan.

Jack slowly pulled the door open and wide to the right. A long low "Dang" was all he said. Leah and Jordan audibly gasped and glanced up at Scott in shock.

"The kids are in charge of the unloading," Dru stated. "Reilly, Nikki, Nora, get over here and prepare your horses." The kids climbed into the trailer to talk to the horses and keep them calm.

Reilly reminded the men what to watch for on the first horse; the little buckskin. Grayson and Matt removed him carefully using the sling technique to lower him to the ground. They walked slowly to Dr. Mark's triage area.

Every rib was protruding. The horse's backbone stood at least three inches above the top of his sides. Skin drooped from the bones, and there were patches of hair missing. Matt stepped away to make room for the doctor and Grayson cradled the horse's head and neck in his arms. The colt leaned his head into the man and tucked his nose under his arm. Grayson gently stroked the horses face and neck and whispered soothingly to him.

All four legs of the horse shook as he was examined. Eyes, teeth, hooves, ears; every inch of the horse was poked and prodded and noted in Dr. Mark's book. All sores cleaned and antiseptic applied.

Leah stepped beside Dru and quietly took her hand. "I understand," she whispered as they watched the kids take charge and work with the men. "I've never seen the kids like this…so in control," They watched quietly for a moment. "…and the men are listening and following their lead."

Dru nodded. "They worked as a team to get this far. It's the only chance these little guys have."

The kids had done a good job of cleaning the horse's faces but their bodies were still covered with dried mud and manure. They would wait until they started to regain their strength before bathing them.

There were six stalls in the barn; four to the right and two to the left. A small office, tack room, and horse washroom were also on the left. They would have to double up the horses. The stalls were covered in a deep layer of soft cedar shavings. The shavings were warm, absorbent, and they didn't worry about the horses eating it like they would with straw. Fresh water and a flake of hay had been placed low and easily accessible to the horses while lying down. Outside of each stall was a white board to write notes about each horse inside. Nikki was writing instructions on them as Dr. Mark dictated to her.

As the horses were being examined, the men set up a table in the washroom for Jordan and Leah to place the food and beverages. It didn't take long for the food to disappear.

The first trailer was emptied and Scott moved it out of the way. Grayson backed up the second trailer as Matt hopped on the side to check the horses.

"Little grey is leaning up on the door," he yelled out. "Little black horse looks like he tried to get up and fell across the roan…he's lying on top of him…roan looks like he's hurting."

Reilly jumped on the side of the trailer and started talking to the roan horse. He put his arm through as far as it would go but couldn't quite reach.

There was no other way in the stock trailer than the back door so Jack opened it slowly and Grayson slid in grabbing the canvas they had carried the grey horse on. He braced the grey horse with the canvas until Matt could slide in next to him and grab a corner. The little grey tried to use the canvas as a brace and stand up. He slipped on the floor mat and started to roll onto one of the red horses. Grayson jumped in the trailer and caught the horse before he fell over. Matt followed him in and helped brace the weak horse.

"He's a little fighter." Grayson looked up at Matt who nodded in return. They both had a smile of respect for the grey horse.

"He's hurt on his left side," Sadie reminded them anxiously with her hands in nervous fists just under her chin.

Matt had his arms around the back end of the horse and Grayson around the chest. They were working hard to avoid the sores on his sides.

"Now what?" Matt asked. They glanced back at the roan that was under the little black one. They needed to move quickly.

"We have to get him moved," Grayson glanced over at Jack and Scott. "We're going to hand him off to you and get the black one out."

"Here we go," Grayson counted to three then he and Matt lifted the horse, who groaned deeply making Sadie cry out. They were quickly handing the horse to the other men when he began to slip and Dru jumped in to balance him. They took three steps back and quickly laid him on the barn floor.

Sadie remained at his side and held a hoof as if holding a friends hand. She sat quietly and watched as the very tired Dr. Mark cleaned the wounds. His strained face registered concern as he listened to the lungs and internal organs.

Sadie stared intently at the doctor. "Is he going to be OK?" She finally whispered with a voice shaking in worry.

Dr. Mark sighed and looked at her anxious face. "Let's get him settled in his stall and we'll have a group talk about all of them, OK?" She nodded and moved out of the way so the men could place him in his new home.

Grayson and Matt moved the black horse off the red roan and were relieved that neither horse was further injured. Reilly crawled in the back of the trailer to talk to the roan while Dr. Mark looked over the black horse.

Once the trailers were emptied and moved, the kids took turns taking showers. Leah and Jordan found cots, lawn chairs, sleeping bags, anything that would make a good bed for the kids. Both mothers had realized how hard the kids had worked and supported them sleeping in the barn with the little herd.

As each kid reentered the barn, they chose a stall to be responsible for. Sadie insisted on the little brown horse and grey horse that were connected to IV's. "They need my love the most," she rationalized.

Each of the five younger kids took charge of a stall which held two horses. Matt and Nikki took the sixth stall and would take care of one each and assist as needed with the younger kids.

Nikki and Matt helped clean the medical supplies and repack Dr. Mark's truck. The kids brought their chairs and cots into a circle so they could all see the vet as he talked to them. They were very quiet. Nora, Sadie, and Wade sat next to each other and held hands. Grace and Reilly were right behind them. Grace had her arms wrapped around one of Reilly's as he stared at the stall where the red roan and little black where resting. They were his chosen horses.

They all looked like they were having a simple weekend sleep-over.

The adults stood behind the kids and waited. Everyone in the room was entranced on Dr. Mark's every move. He finally sat on a bale of straw and addressed his worried audience.

"I'm going to be very honest with you." Looking at each of the kids and adults; he made eye contact with each of his captive audience. "There is a very good chance that not all of these little ones will survive the next couple days." He paused, letting the news sink in.

Dru sighed, it was a fact she already knew but didn't want to be told so blatantly.

The doctor continued, "These horses have been without food and water for over 3 weeks. Every horse here has gone through a very thorough examination, as you saw." He leaned his elbows on his knees so he could be more at eye level with the younger kids. "We took blood samples for tests which will let us know if the liver, heart, and kidneys are functioning properly."

"We listened to their bellies to make sure they had gurgling sounds in them. This lets us know that their digestive system is working; that they will be able to process and pass the food and water they've been given. Now, we also wormed each one of them to get rid of any parasites that might have gotten in them. This is going to be very rough on their digestive systems. Some of the horses won't make it because of this process."

He paused and looked around the group. "It is very important that they do not get ANY grain or extra supplement besides grass hay for the next month. Their stomach and intestines must get used to having food again and the grain and supplements are too potent," He glanced at Wade and Sadie. "Do you know what potent means?"

They nodded, "Too strong" Sadie whispered.

"Good." He smiled. The kids were listening intently. "The main issue we have to watch out for is what some people call the re-feeding syndrome that can occur when we start introducing food to them. I won't get into the scientific details, but if given the wrong food or too much food it could cause their heart, kidneys or liver to fail." He paused. "That's when we lose them. If they can get to the tenth day, they have a good chance of pulling through."

"We've only given them grass hay so far," Reilly pointed out. "Is that OK?"

"Yes, it's OK." Dr. Mark then went over the feeding schedule for the next couple days. They would be on a four hour schedule. "They need water at all times and we'll be putting a white salt block in their stalls. Remember, they shouldn't be without either salt or water." The doctor repeated and everyone nodded.

"How long before they get better?" Grace asked.

"They will get worse in the next couple days because of the introduction of the food and their systems getting used to it. Passing the parasites will also be rough on them. You may see more hair loss too." He let this sink in before answering Grace's question. "After the first couple days they should start gaining two or three pounds a day. They need to gain at least 200 to 300 pounds of muscle and fat before we start to call them healthy." He paused and took a deep breath then continued. "We have a couple that draw extra concern. The little red one with white back legs…the one that had his front legs stuck in the manure and mud…he has some ligament issues that we need to watch. We don't want him active so he'll need to be contained in the stall. He needs to rest those ligaments. I've bandaged them to keep them supported." He paused, no one spoke. "The next is the small grey on the canvas. He had some serious gashes we've cleaned but it's too late to stitch, so we've bandaged them for now. This means he's going to have a couple good size scars.

"Watch for flies or anything else that might get in his wounds. They'll need cleaned daily. He is on an IV for the night to help rehydrate him and keep antibiotics in him. Same as the little brown colt from the lower barn; he is on IV for at least the night."

He paused to emphasize the next point. "Stress will be their worst enemy. Keep them calm and resting," The doctor looked around the group. "You've done a tremendous job in getting them here and helping them. Now we just take as much care as possible and wait for their weakened bodies to recover. I'll be back in the morning before I head to the clinic." He stood up which signaled the end of his review.

As the adults walked out with Dr. Mark, Dru called Grace, Reilly, Sadie, Nora, and Wade over to the side. They were all showered and dressed in t-shirt and sweat pants to sleep in the barn for the night.

"I just want to tell you kids…" She hugged Wade and Sadie into her sides. "…how proud I am of all of you. When I realized what we had gotten ourselves into at the barn, I questioned my logic in bringing you with me." She could feel the tears stinging the back of her eyes and her throat constrict from the emotions that were building. "There isn't another group of people, adults or kids, that could have worked any harder then you five did. You put the horse's needs in front of your own and that really says a lot about who you kids are," They all smiled. "Every horse that survives will do so because of the effort and love you guys are giving them."

She hugged each of them. "I am so proud of you." They had their five minutes of mushiness then moved on to check on the horses.

CHAPTER SIX

It was 2 o'clock in the morning when the kids finally laid down and fell asleep. Dru walked quietly through the barn and stopped at every stall and watched for the horse's chest to rise and fall as they slept. The kids weren't allowed to sleep in the horse's stalls. With two horses in each stall it was too dangerous but Sadie had moved her blankets to the floor and stretched her arm in as far as she could, her small arm lay limp over the brown colt's front legs. Dru smiled, she would have done the same thing at her age.

Even at 39, Dru wanted to cuddle each of the horses and promise them they would do everything they could to help them through this terrible ordeal and make sure they had a good productive life. She had a strong feeling the horses knew that now as they slept. It was probably the best sleep the horses had in weeks. After such a hard physical and emotional day it was also a solid sleep for each of the kids.

Dru turned off the main barn light and retrieved the box of files out of her truck that she had collected at the Smith property. She piled the files on the desk in the small barn office, tiredly sat in the chair, and slowly reached for a file. The top file contained Wes' calendar. He had taken detailed notes on when he was to pick up each horse or when someone was dropping them off at the ranch.

The week before his death had been a busy one. According to her calculations, the horses had been without food or water since the morning of his death. Twenty four days. It was a miracle they had all lasted so long.

She frowned at the last notation in his calendar. "Tagger Stables" was written and circled in red next to where he had written Colfax. Tagger Stables had no business currently in Colfax which was a small town about 60 miles north of Lewiston. Dru searched the internet on the laptop in the barn office and looked for the information on Wes' accident. He was only 15 miles outside of Colfax when the accident happened. The autopsy revealed that he had a heart attack which was believed to be the cause of him swerving and rolling off the side of the road. Dru wondered if the farmer with the hay, who called Cora, had been from Colfax.

She looked again at her phone to see if she had missed any calls. Cora hadn't called again. The last time was right after they found the horses.

It was at that moment Dru saw lights flash the house and barn. She looked out the window to see a vehicle had turned off the road in front of The Homestead and was headed up their driveway. Since the whole family and Jack were here at The Homestead, she had no idea who it was.

Dru stepped outside and listened. It sounded like a car. The motion detector light turned on as she rounded the side of the barn and looked down the driveway. The car had started to slow down but must have seen her and continued to drive towards her. The lights blinded Dru so she couldn't see who was driving and she didn't recognize the car.

The car stopped and the door opened. Just as she began to wonder if the driver was going to get out, a head appeared above the top of the car. It was an older woman with short brown hair. Dru guessed her to be in her late sixties. She walked stiffly from the car and shut the door. As she came around the front, Dru noticed the slender woman was dressed casually in jeans, tennis shoes, and a T-shirt.

"Cora?" Dru guessed. The woman nodded and leaned against the car.

Cora took a moment and stretched her arms up then out. "When you didn't answer my calls, I knew something was wrong. I found your address on the internet, programmed into my GPS and here I am." She stopped stretching. "That's a long drive."

"You drove here from Seattle all by yourself?"

"I did," She paused, looked at Dru then up to the stars. Dru knew she wanted to know what they had found but was afraid to ask. "Do I need to sit down for this?" Cora finally asked.

Dru sighed. There was no way to make the situation better.

"Yes." Dru motioned for the older woman to follow onto the back deck of the house. It was a warm night and Dru wanted to be able to hear any commotion from the barn. As they started to sit, Jack, Scott and Grayson stepped out the back door. They had heard the car come up the drive. There were looks of surprise on their faces when they saw the older woman.

"Cora, these are my brothers Grayson and Scott, co-owners of Tagger Enterprises and Jack Morgan, our stable manager." They each shook her hand and took seats. "Guys, this is Cora Smith." They knew the name. "She drove from Seattle today to find out what we found at her ranch."

There was silence. Dru knew the men were waiting for her to tell Cora the story.

"Tell it straight." Cora said and looked Dru in the eye, preparing for the worst.

By the time Dru finished telling her about the fillies and colts, tears were streaming down Cora's face and she was shaking. Scott retrieved a glass of water and a wet towel from the house so she could cool her burning eyes.

"I just don't know what to say," Cora whispered in despair.

The group sat in silence. Kit let out a light whinny and a soft whinny came from inside the barn. Scott stood. "I'll go check on them."

Cora began to rise to go with him, but he politely motioned her to sit back down. "Now is not the right time," he said softly. "Other than the twelve horses, the three of us have two kids and all six of them, plus Jack's son Reilly are bedded down out there to be close to them."

A small sob came from Cora as she sat down. "Bless them, just bless them." She mumbled as she dabbed at her eyes with the towel.

The three sat quietly in the warm night air while Scott checked on the barn. Dru could feel her whole body screaming for sleep.

"Cora, it's been a long day and will be daylight soon. We have a guest bedroom you can use while you're here." Dru stood hoping the woman would understand.

Cora nodded, retrieved a bag from the car and followed Dru into the house. When Dru came back out, Scott had returned and he, Jack, and Grayson were still out on the deck. They were discussing the upcoming cattle drive; moving the cows from spring to summer pasture which was supposed to happen that Sunday.

"We're not going to get the kids away from here for a of couple days," Scott stated.

"I won't be leaving either," Dru added. "With the horses on 24 hour watch for the next week, it's going to be a long one."

"We have two choices," Scott continued. "We can use a smaller crew and move a few at a time or we postpone until next week when the little herd gets an all clear."

"How's the pasture look where they are now?" Dru asked.

"Pretty good, with all this rain we can make it another week or two if the temperature doesn't spike and start drying out the top pastures." Grayson answered.

June weather in the valley was always unpredictable. Rain could pour most days or there could also be drought. It could be 90 degrees on Monday and 50 degrees on Wednesday.

"We don't have to do it on a weekend," Grayson pointed out. "Let's postpone the decision for 48 hours and see where we're at."

They all agreed.

"We have the riding clinic at The Stables on Saturday," Jack reminded the Trio.

Dru nodded. "We'll work it out and make sure you have help." She stood. "but, for now, I need sleep."

The men nodded and stepped into the house to go back to bed. Jack was sleeping in Matt's bed instead of going home.

Dru went out to the barn, walked by the office and briefly glanced at Wes' files. She shook her head, switched off the light and kept walking to check each of the stalls.

Matt and Nikki were in front of the first stall on her right, sleeping in lounge chairs from the patio. They had a brown colt and bay filly in their stall.

Nora was in the next stall with the palomino and the black horse with the star on his forehead. He was the second colt they had found.

Next was Sadie. She was still stretched into the stall where her horses were and had a grip on the hoof of the little brown one.

Dru took a light blanket and covered her. No sense moving her back to her cot; she wouldn't have stayed in it anyway.

Reilly was in the last stall on the right. He was sleeping at the stall with the red roan and black colt.

Across the aisle from him were the two lighter horses. Grace was tucked down deep inside a sleeping bag outside their stall. All Dru could see was a mass of blonde hair.

The red colt, who was the first to be found, and the little one stuck in the mud were in the next stall with Wade sleeping on a cot at the door.

All horses and people were breathing and sleeping soundly.

Dru lay down on her cot and closed her eyes; it was time to end this very long day.

****

She heard boots walking next to her head and barely opened an eye to see Matt going into Sadie's stall.

Dru closed her eyes again, "Is everyone up?" she whispered. Her body just wasn't ready to move yet.

"Not really. Sadie went to get the hay. I'm checking the IV bags"

"Everyone still breathing?"

"Yep."

"Well, that's a good start. Let's see if we can keep it that way today." Dru finally opened her eyes and looked around.

Everyone was in different stages of waking up. Wade was lying in his cot with his two red horses up and leaning over the top of him. The little one with the bandaged legs was resting his nose in Wade's neck making him giggle as he stroked their faces and chests.

Grace and Nora were quietly watching their horses eat and Sadie was coming into the barn with a wheel barrow filled with hay. It was daylight behind her but it couldn't have been for very long.

"Who's that?" Matt was looking behind Sadie.

Dru rose from the cot and looked. Cora was already up and walking towards the barn.

"Cora Smith," she answered and stood to greet her.

Cora paused just before the barn doors and didn't look in. Her presence made all the kids sit up and stare openly which they normally didn't do. Those that were still lying down quickly stood and started moving their bedding into the tack room.

Dru stepped out to greet her.

"Give me a minute." Cora whispered. "I thought I was ready for this but…"

"Take your time." Dru nodded in understanding and turned to the kids.

"Let me introduce you to our herd of kids and they can introduce you to the herd of horses." Dru pointed to each and said their names. They all politely said good morning or hello except Wade. He walked over to Cora and put his small, nine-year-old hand on her arm.

"I'm Wade," he started. "I just want to thank you for calling Aunt Dru about the horses," Cora stared at him in surprise. No doubt she was expecting admonishment of guilt. Her hand was shaking as she covered Wade's hand as he continued. "If you hadn't called so fast, we might not have got there in time."

He turned to walk next to her as she made her way to the first stall door. "We each took responsibility for two, except Matt and Nikki, they only have one each," he told her proudly.

Cora hesitantly looked into the first stall. "Oh, my heaven." She whispered and leaned against the stall to steady herself. Wade stood quietly holding her arm.

He silently waited for her to compose herself. When she nodded to him, he took her around and introduced her to the rest of the horses.

Jack, Scott, Jordan, Grayson, and Leah walked into the barn with both Jordan and Leah already dressed for work. Scott and Jordan smiled with pride as their son walked Cora around the barn.

Matt moved all remaining cots and blankets into the tack room for the day. Chairs and bales of straw were set about for everyone to sit on.

After her tour, Cora sat in the first chair she came to. "I can't believe this is happening," She looked at each of the kids who were quietly standing by the stalls. Her eyes were moist from the tears and her face tense from shock.

"I don't know what Wes was thinking when he bought all these horses." She paused, looking around at each of the group. "I appreciate everything you have done to save these precious animals."

There was silence as they waited for her to continue. She sighed heavily, feeling the weight of the animal's condition on her shoulders.

Nikki was the first to speak. "With your permission Mrs. Smith, I've decided to call my filly *Harvey*." There was a round of giggles. Nikki had succeeded in breaking the tension. She later admitted she had a much better name picked out, but the reaction to Harvey was fun so she decided to keep it.

"It's a filly, silly girl." Wade laughed at his cousin.

"And what great name have you chosen then?" Nikki asked him.

"*Dollar and Rooster*," Wade announced proudly. He was greeted with knowing smiles.

"Well," Cora nodded, "It seems as though we have a John Wayne fan in our midst." He looked at her with surprise and awe that she would know that. "Dollar must be the sorrel with the four white socks and big blaze down his nose?" Wade nodded so the older woman continued. "…and Rooster Cogburn from *True Grit?*"

"Yes!" Wade grinned. "…and *Rooster Cogburn and the Lady.*"

The round of name announcements continued.

Matt's brown colt was named *Trooper.*

Nora announced hers as *Scarecrow* and *Arcturus;* Scarecrow from the straw stuck to the horse when she was first found made her look like one and Arcturus because he was black as the night with a white star on his forehead. She had searched the internet on Grace's phone and Arcturus was one of the brightest stars in the sky.

Reilly named his black horse *Cooper* after Gary Cooper but hadn't named the red roan yet.

Grace's little buckskin was *Eli* and the little dun was *Buttercup;* Eli after her grandpa's old horse and Buttercup for Grace's favorite spring flower.

Everyone turned to Sadie expecting very creative names from the family scholar. She named the little brown horse *Angel.*

"But it's a colt!" Wade laughed at her.

She raised her eyebrows at him with a little attitude thrown at him. "If Nikki can have a filly named Harvey, then I can have a colt named Angel," she smiled, "Angels can be boys too, you know." She walked over to her stall door. Both horses were lying down. Everyone watched as she knelt down by the little grey colt that had been carried on the canvas. "And you," she lightly touched his muzzle, "…shall be *Little Ghost.*"

"You have an Angel and a Ghost…" Cora tried to smile. "How ethereal of you."

They heard a vehicle pulling down the driveway. "That's got to be Dr. Mark…get ready everyone," Dru told the kids and they returned to their stalls.

The adults turned and greeted Dr. Mark as he came in to the barn.

Cora stood, "What can I do?"

Dru looked around. Everything was taken care of except the empty makeshift dining table. Cora followed her gaze. "I'll take care of it." She stepped past Dru and walked to the house and the back door that led to the kitchen.

CHAPTER SEVEN

Cora's breakfast was more of a feast. Dru couldn't believe it when they started bringing food into the barn; a parade of blueberry pancakes, biscuits and gravy, sausage, eggs, muffins, and mini quiches with bacon. Within minutes the food disappeared into the bellies of some satisfied kids and adults.

The phone calls started a little after eight. It was the junior high calling about Grace and Reilly. Everyone had forgotten about the last day of school. Jack and Grayson handled those calls and the grade schools were called about the other kids. Jordan and Leah had gone to work and Jack was back working at The Stables. He was within 20 minutes away if he was needed.

Grayson and Scott shared the job of working with the horse's hooves. As the two brothers were raised on the ranch, they had learned farrier work from their dad and grandfather. Wade's little colt Rooster was the biggest concern. The hooves themselves had been stuck in mud and manure and the constant moisture had done damage to the hoof wall. They were considering having a specialist come in to give a second opinion.

Nikki and Matt changed the bandaging on the animals with the younger kids watching them closely.

The wind picked up and blew in ugly dark clouds that brought rain soon after breakfast. The doors and windows were closed to cut down on the draft and keep the rain out of the barn.

Dr. Mark's prediction that the first day would be very hard on the horses was coming true. Most of them had developed diarrhea and Matt's colt, Trooper, had stopped eating. If he didn't begin to eat soon, he would have to be tubed to get food in him. Matt and Nikki replaced the IV's on Sadie's horses throughout the day. Dr. Mark had hoped to remove them first thing in the morning but they were also stricken with diarrhea. As a precaution, the IV's remained.

Their water, food, and salt intake were monitored closely. They received a flake of hay every 4 hours. All food and water amounts were written on the white boards so Dr. Mark could easily see how they were doing. He planned to return at the end of the day to check the horses unless he was needed sooner.

Around ten, Wade's colt Rooster, with the bandaged legs, tried standing and slipped in the soiled bedding. He went over backwards banging his legs against the wall. He let out a moan, a groan, and a bit of a whinny that scared everyone in the barn. Dru had just started looking at Wes' files again when she heard the commotion. Since they were in tight quarters, they couldn't afford any more crashes so every time the bedding was soiled it was removed immediately and sawdust used to soak up any moisture.

Dru made sure everyone was settled again and went back to the office desk.

She nearly cried when she opened the first file. A gorgeous well rounded quarter horse was pictured on the registration papers. It took her a minute to realize that it was Grace's Buttercup. Her coat was shiny and creamy and highlighted with the dark main and tail. About six inches of white hair created boots between the darkness of her legs and hooves. Her eyes were bright and alert as she was looking at something just out of camera range.

Dru looked over the papers and the lineage and was amazed at the names. There was Two-Eyed Jack, Jessie James, Peppy,

Wimpy, Doc O'Lena, Zippo Pine Par and Poco Bueno lines. They were top of the line quarter horses.

The biggest shock was when she reviewed the foaling date. Buttercup wasn't a yearling; she was a two-year-old! Because of her loss of muscle and stature, Dru had assumed they were only a year old and hadn't confirmed her belief with Dr. Mark. She quickly reviewed each of the other files and saw their foaling dates were all within four months of each other; they were all two-year-olds.

Dru flipped through each of the files and identified each of the horses. No one could have guessed the horses out in the stalls were these magnificent animals in the files.

She glanced up as Cora walked into the office. With the tip of her boot, Dru pushed a chair from the desk towards the woman and handed her the horse's files for her to review. Dru looked over the financials. He had spent anywhere between $2,000 to $10,000 on each horse.

She let out a low whistle. "I think he spent your retirement."

"We had talked about selling the ranch," Cora exhaled loudly. "I guess this was going to be his way of saying *no* to that idea…or he was going senile." She had a slight smile on her face.

"These are quality horses. Did you raise quarter horses before?"

She nodded. "Not this many, but he always bought top genetic horses. He said the extra money was worth it. He was a logger, but we raised the horses as a hobby."

"What about fencing?" Dru asked. "Why did he keep them inside when he left?"

Cora sighed, "I'm not sure how the fencing situation is at the property. I was supposed to be headed home the day after he died. But when he died, I just stayed in Seattle. I couldn't face going home without him there," She smiled sadly. "It sounds odd, but some of our best days were out working on the property including building fence. So maybe he was waiting for me."

"Did you have any kids?" Dru asked, as she leaned back in the chair. This was the first time she had to really talk with Cora.

Cora shook her head. "No, Wes couldn't. We thought about adopting, but we just never got around to it." She turned as Grace walked by the door.

"When I was introduced to the kids, I was a bit rattled," Cora admitted. "The two brunettes…the sweet Wade and Nora are your brother Scott's? And his wife is Jordan, the tiny brunette?"

Dru nodded.

"The tall young man with the blue eyes, Reilly? He has to be Jack's."

"Yes, his mother died when he was five and Jack moved them here from Texas when Reilly was only seven." Dru smiled. "He's pretty much a brother to our group."

"Then the little blonde, Sadie, with the long braid, she's yours?"

Dru chuckled and shook her head, her own long pony tail swinging down her back. "She's Grayson's youngest, Grace is his oldest, and Leah is his wife. Mine are the two older ones, Matt and Nikki."

"So you each had two kids?" Cora nodded in understanding. "So, you're not married?"

Dru shook her head. "No, not since Matt was born. I adopted Nikki, she and Matt have the same father…"

"Aunt Dru!" Nora's panicked shout echoed through the barn.

The chair fell back and landed with a bang as Dru ran out of the room. Nora's face registered terror as she came around the corner. "There's blood coming out of Arcturus."

Matt was already on the phone to Dr. Mark.

Arcturus was laying down flat on his side. His stomach seemed even more sunk in than it had before. His breathing was labored. Dru knelt down at his back side and found a pool of blood mixed in with his diarrhea.

"Get me some towels." Dru instructed.

She took a picture and texted it to Dr. Mark so he could judge how bad the situation was. Then she cleaned up the mess.

Matt was sitting with Nora at the horse's head, the young girl lightly touching the star on the horse's forehead. Everyone else was peering quietly over the stall with Scarecrow lying quietly in the opposite corner.

They waited.

Dr. Mark arrived shortly thereafter with Erik, one of his vet assistants. Though Dru was concerned, she didn't say anything about his decision to add another person to the rescue of the horses. Arcturus's health was more important.

Dru took Nora's hand and led her out so the men could doctor the horse. She pulled the kids away from the stall. They sat on a bale of straw and Dru wrapped her arms around her niece. Tears were running down Nora's cheeks.

"He just has to be OK," Nora whispered and leaned into Dru's embrace.

The emotional attachment to these horses had come quickly. The kids had been taught compassion for animals and people that were in need. They learned at an early age to appreciate the horse and how the animal helps them work the ranch. The horses the kids ride aren't just animals, they are friends and family.

Twenty minutes later, the men came out of the stall.

Dr. Mark knelt down and patted Nora's leg. "Everything sounds good internally. Like I said yesterday, it's hard on their internal organs to get back to processing food after being without for so long. They will have sores inside their stomachs." Just like everyone else, he was beginning to show signs of how exhausting the last 24 hours had been. "We have to wait and watch now. If he's still with us in the morning, then he should pull through."

"Thank you." Nora whispered and wiped away her tears.

Dru was watching Erik, concerned with the look of disgust on his face.

He was moving from stall to stall looking at the young horses. "I can't believe someone would do something like this," he muttered.

Dru could feel Cora stiffen. She put a hand on Cora's to give her reassurance.

"It wasn't done on purpose." Reilly spoke up defensively.

Eric shook his head and pulled out his phone to take a picture. Reilly and Matt both stood and reached for the phone but Dr. Mark had already taken it from the assistant's hands. "No pictures," he said sternly.

Eric reached for his phone back. "This needs to be reported," he argued, then glanced over at Dru, as if she had purposely starved the horses.

"You know better than that." Dru stood and faced him.

"This doesn't happen to a dozen horses on accident," Erik said sternly.

Matt placed himself between his mother and Erik. "There's more to this story than what you're accusing us of. You've been working with us for over a year Erik, you know we wouldn't do this on purpose. We *rescued* them."

"Erik, go out to the truck," Dr. Mark ordered. Erik looked between Dr. Mark and the group of nine. "I'll tell you the story on the way back to the clinic."

"Give me my phone," Was the only thing Erik said.

"Not until we're in the truck," Dr. Mark responded.

Erik's body tensed and his face began to turn red. Dru wasn't sure if it was anger, embarrassment, or a little of both but he turned and left the barn.

Dr. Mark turned to apologize to the group. "I had no choice but to bring him along. We were on another remote checkup when I got the call." He took the time to check on the other horses. "Keep the feeding schedule the same," He said as he walked to the door. "Keep me posted on how Arcturus is doing."

After the kids settled in with the horses, Dru wandered back to the office and had just started working on her cattle books when a blonde and brunette head peered around the corner of the door. Even though there was only a month between them in age, Sadie was already three inches taller than her cousin.

Dru smiled at them. "Yes?"

"When Erik said that this doesn't happen to horses on accident, does he mean people do this on purpose to horses?" Wade asked.

Dru sat back and looked at the two 9-year-olds, asking her this simple question that had such a horrible answer. She let out an audible sigh and sat up to the computer. The best answer was in front of her on the internet.

"There are times that people can't feed themselves let alone their animals," she started as she began typing on the computer. "There are times that horses are just abandoned by their owners; they think the horses can forage on their own."

For the next half hour, they looked at all the horrible stories on the internet of horses that had gone through starvation for one reason or another. There were stories of how people found and saved the horses, although none were the same situation as theirs with so many horses starved unintentionally.

The rest of the kids and Cora had come in to see what they were doing. They went through every story they could find, which included all the places that help rescue horses and other animals.

"Can we donate to the rescue places?" Grace asked.

"Of course," Dru told her. "Anyone can donate and all donations are helpful. We donate yearly to the Retired Equine and Care Habitat in Deary, with our extra hay and some monetary funds. We did research to make sure the business' were credible and not scams. We wanted to make sure the money was going for the rehabilitation of the animals, so they could return to a purposeful life," she paused, "Of course, now I have a greater appreciation for what these rescue places do and what they have to go through."

Dru wanted to make sure the kids had all their questions answered, so she continued from one site to another until there were no more questions. They came upon a site for a farm in Georgia called the Dancing Cloud Farm Horse Rescue. The site showed many horses that were just as starved as their little herd. They had documented the horses they saved over the years; showing before and after pictures. The kids perked up when they saw the condition of the horses a year after being rescued.

"They look beautiful," Nora said excitedly. "It doesn't look like they were ever starved."

Dru nodded. "Well, our goal is to rehabilitate the little herd so they can have happy, productive lives, too. Once they've healed completely, then they'll be like all the other horses we have."

"What about Rooster?" Wade asked her. They were all worried about his front legs. Dr. Mark informed them he may have to wear the bandages for quite some time. Surgery was also a possibility.

Dru sighed, "Well, he's going to have to be a wait and see." Wade's shoulders drooped and his eyes looked back into the barn.

"We'll do everything we can to make sure his legs heal." She assured him.

"Any of you know who Doris Day is?" Dru asked the kids.

"I do!" Wade and Sadie said in unison.

"She played in the western 'Calamity Jane'." Wade nodded, excited he knew the answer.

"I'm impressed," Cora smiled at him, which made Wade's smile even wider.

"He's our western movie fan." Dru chuckled.

"Why did you ask about her?" Reilly asked.

"Well," Dru typed into the computer. "She has an animal foundation that also helps horses and all other animals."

They spent the next ten minutes reviewing the foundations website.

When they were done, the kids went back to the horse stalls, excited about the possibility of the horses having full recoveries and happy lives.

"Dru?" Cora said as they were left alone again.

"Yes?"

"You and your brothers own Tagger Enterprises?"

"Yes, equally."

"How does that work?"

"Scott handles the farming, Grayson works the ranch with Jessup, our foreman, plus Grayson is our horse trainer. I work The Stables with Jack as the manager. Plus I handle Tagger Enterprises as a whole." She explained. "I make sure all three portions of the company are working harmoniously and keeping us moving forward. If there is a major decision to be made, the three of us vote on it," Dru grinned. "It keeps us from strangling each other."

"You three must work well together," Cora seemed impressed. "What about your parents?"

Dru hated that question. It always made her think of the accident and the days following the funerals.

After a brief hesitation and a deep breath, she told Cora about the accident.

The older woman listened quietly, while shaking her head in disbelief.

******

Cora headed back to the house to fix lunch for everyone and Dru walked the barn for a stall check. Grace, Wade, and Reilly had fallen asleep. Nora had positioned herself between her two horses and was singing softly to them.

Sadie had placed a chair in the stall with the little brown and grey colts. She was reading out loud to the horses from the computer tablet while they ate their hay.

Dru leaned her arms across the top of the stall door and listened to her niece read about a horse in battle. "What are you reading them?"

"The stories about Sergeant Reckless," Sadie answered proudly.

"The hero horse from the Korean War?" Dru shook her head in amazement. Sadie was the scholar of the group. She loved school, loved learning, and seemed to be able to remember it all.

Sadie nodded, "I thought it would help them be strong if they heard about other strong horses like Sergeant Reckless."

"You couldn't have picked a better example."

Sadie nodded as the grey, Little Ghost, placed his nose on her shoulder. Her eyes shone when she looked up at him and ran a hand down his nose.

"You get back to eating," Sadie told the horse. "I'll get back to reading."

Sadie started reading and the horse turned back to his hay.

Dru smiled at the two; that was going to be a special friendship.

She wandered back to the barn office and found Matt and Nikki sitting at the desk reviewing the horse files.

Dru looked out the window at the falling rain. The mood had darkened. The websites were depressing and she was worried about Erik's reaction to the horses and what he may say to others. She wasn't sure what to do.

They had decided to keep the rescue quiet to save Cora the horrendous accusations that would be thrown her way about her and her husband. But now, if Erik announced it, and made it sound like Tagger Enterprises was in a cover-up of a dozen starving horses, it could ruin the family business. She needed to talk to Scott and Grayson.

"I'm going in the house, call me if something happens. I'll be right back." She said to her kids.

They nodded while reviewing the horse registrations.

Dru made a run for the house through the rain. Her brothers were in the library huddled around the computer looking at the weather forecast.

"It looks like we'll be missing riding in the rain for the cattle drive. It's supposed to rain for the next couple days." Grayson told her as she entered the room.

"We have a bigger problem." She told them of the incident in the barn. They were just as concerned.

"We'll have to believe that Dr. Mark is going to control this situation." Scott said. "He's been there from the start so he knows the truth."

"Should we go ahead and get this out to the public our way? Before it gets ugly?" Dru asked.

They debated for a while until the phone rang. It was Dr. Mark assuring them he had explained everything to Erik and he was sure that the assistant would keep the rescue quiet.

"Well?" Dru asked her brothers as she ended the call.

"I say we hold off saying anything because we may not have to." Grayson suggested.

Scott nodded. "Let's get Benny, the brand inspector, here as soon as possible and Walter, the head of the animal shelter."

Grayson nodded in agreement and Dru left the house with an uneasy feeling.

The rest of the day was filled with cleaning up after the horses. Each time they had diarrhea, they had to clean up the bedding and wash the horse's skin. No one shirked the duties of the cleanup. Even when Reilly offered to do it for the girls, they politely declined. They would handle it which made Dru smile...tough young ladies.

She finished reading Wes' files and reviewed the horses with the kids. They all looked in amazement at the pictures of the horses when they were healthy.

Cora prepared dinner for everyone that night. She was becoming quite popular with the kids and parents. The cots and sleeping equipment were pulled from the tack room and set back up by each of the stalls. The temperature had dropped at least 20 degrees since the night before so Leah and Jordan brought in more bedding from the house.

The evening progressed with no new emergencies, and the group of kids took turns feeding the horses every four hours.

Dru woke to Reilly walking by her with an arm full of hay. He walked into each stall and whispered softly to the horses as he fed them. He stopped and stroked each of the horses, making sure they were comforted and eating. The last stall he went into held the red roan and Cooper. She waited for him to come out but he didn't. Leaning on an elbow, she listened but didn't hear him.

Quietly, she rolled off of the cot and made her way to the stall to find him sitting on the floor with his back to the wall. The little red roan was lying next to him and the horses head in Reilly's lap; he was stroking the muzzle very slowly.

He glanced up in surprise as she stepped into the stall, "I'm sorry if I woke you." he whispered.

"You didn't," She sat down next to him. Cooper made his way over to her and not so gracefully plunked himself on the floor. She reached over and began caressing his neck.

"I can't believe how dark he is. I have a special affection for black horses," she whispered. "He reminds me of Jet."

"Your barrel horse? Libby's mom?"

"Yes, and Jet's mom, Nan, was also black."

Reilly nodded and looked up at her; his blue eyes questioning without him saying a word.

"What is it Reilly?" She asked with a soft and encouraging voice. "Just spit it out."

"I don't really know..." His voice trembled slightly as he looked between the two horses. "I just can't believe how I feel about these two so quickly."

Dru didn't speak; she didn't want to say something that would make him stop talking. The barn was quiet with just the sound of horses and people breathing. She waited for him to continue.

He leaned his head back against the wall, then twisted so he could look at her; eyes full of anguish, voice tight as he fought back tears. "Sometimes, I just feel lost and I don't know why."

Dru felt her throat constrict from the raw emotion in his voice. She couldn't speak so she nodded.

"Dad is always there for me," he continued. "Sometimes too much." He smiled sadly, "…and you Taggers…all of you… I couldn't ask for more. You guys have been everything to us."

She smiled, but remained quiet.

"Grace is my rock." A tear escaped and he quickly wiped it away. "There are times that I get so lost that I feel like I'm drowning," he confessed and looked at her with pleading eyes, "Does that make sense?"

After her parents and grandparents died, Dru had felt herself drowning in the sorrow and loss. "Oh, yes," She whispered.

"Grace is my life preserver," He touched his hand to his chest. "She brightens my heart."

Dru had felt herself letting his sadness overwhelm her but when she thought of Grace's smile and 'life is good' laugh, she could feel the happiness pushing out the sadness.

"I understand," She took his hand and squeezed.

"When I went into that barn and saw all these little guys suffering…" He closed his eyes which pushed another tear down his face. Again, he brushed it away quickly and looked down at the red roan, "When I was with this guy and you brought me that first bucket of water something changed inside of me. I didn't know what it was then, but I think I'm beginning to understand."

"What was it?" She asked softly.

He looked back up at her with a sweet smile she hadn't seen before. "The more I'm with Cooper and this guy, the more I don't feel lost." His voice was barely over a whisper and cracking with emotion. "They give me purpose. So many people have asked me what I'm going to be when I grow up and I never knew. I feel like

I've never really had any reason for being here." He fiddled with the horse's mane.

"Here, as in…"

"Life," he admitted. "But, not in the bad way… just as in who and what am I? Since Mom died, I've been such a focus for Dad that I didn't really have anything for me to focus on. With these guys, I do…they are my purpose in life."

Dru looked at the two guys he was talking about. They were sound asleep.

"I'm healthy, and between the ranch and The Stables, and you Taggers, I couldn't ask for more," He paused and smiled mischievously. "Don't tell him I said so, but I've got a great dad."

Dru grinned, "Yes, you do."

They listened to the stillness of the barn and caressed the animals that were giving Reilly what he needed for his soul.

"Are you ever going to give that little guy a name?" she asked.

"I have," he grinned, all the tears were gone now. There was a different aura around him; his soul seemed to have lightened.

"Really?"

"Yeah, but I didn't think anyone would understand, so I've just been whispering it to him," He looked over at her. "Rufio."

She grinned with a knowing look; "He was one of the lost boys on Peter Pan."

He nodded, "Now, when I feel lost, I can say his name and know I'm not lost anymore and neither is he."

She put her arm around him and hugged him tightly, "I understand."

The horses heal us, as we heal them.

CHAPTER EIGHT

Dru woke at five the next morning and walked through the barn checking on the horses and kids. She stopped and watched Reilly sleeping on the cot that spanned across the stall opening.

"A lost boy…no longer lost," she smiled.

Rufio and Cooper were standing and eating on the flake of hay in the feeder.

She stepped out of the barn and glanced up at the gloomy sky. It seemed even darker and the rain had slowed to a light drizzle. Every muscle was sore and she had a light headache from the stress, lack of sleep, and dreary weather.

She released Mavis and Bart from the kennel and stepped up to the front porch to get out of the rain. On a normal day, she loved to stand on the porch and listen to the rain fall but today…they just needed the sunshine.

The rain didn't bother the dogs; they were just excited to be out of the kennel. Her eyes caught the movement of Libby and Kit grazing. There were two large pastures that separated The Homestead from the road. The driveway split them. The house, horse barn, hay barn and a shed lay behind the pastures.

There were few trees on their property to give the pastures shade so they had designed a large island in the middle of each pasture. Each fenced island had two large oak trees that provided the shade with benches and flowers creating a nice sitting area at their base. The two large trees in the south pasture were planted in honor of their parents and the north pasture trees were in honor of their grandparents.

Even though they grew up at the ranch, their family had a small house in town so they could attend school in Lewiston. Every weekend, summer, or day off from school was spent at the ranch. Their parents and the Trio had graduated from Lewiston High so now it was a family tradition.

The Tagger Trio had decided to build The Stables near Lewiston and Clarkston, the largest cities within a two hour drive from the ranch. They wanted the kids to be able to work and practice at The Stables and go to school in Lewiston.

After reviewing the housing options, they decided it didn't make sense to have three houses, so they built one large house for all three families. It worked well since they split their time between the ranch and The Homestead. The kids may be cousins, but they were as close as brothers and sisters.

Dru had just turned to head into the house when she saw the first news van drive by the main gate. If she stretched out over the railing far enough, she could see if the vehicle had turned left to go to Highway 95 or right to head towards The Stables. She held her breath then, with a sinking feeling in her gut, she saw the van had taken a right. They were headed to The Stables. The secret was out, she was sure of it.

She quickly put on her raincoat and a Tagger Enterprises T3E logoed hat and walked down the driveway to the road. It was a long walk down the driveway in the sunshine, but it seemed like forever in the rain. She was almost to the main road when the second news van went by. She stopped so she didn't attract any attention. Once cleared, she made her way to the gate and closed it so no one could come up the driveway…legally. She turned and made the long trek back up to the house. The dogs had followed her and weren't very happy when she put them back in the kennel.

Once in the house, she started the coffee and turned on the computer, immediately going to the Facebook pages of the local newspaper and television station. Her heart sank as she melted into the library chair and read the reports about a dozen horses having been starved. There was no mention of the Tagger name or of Cora and her husband. They were obviously going to verify the story before attaching a name.

Dru reached for the phone and called Jack because his house overlooked The Stables property. He needed to know that the media had headed to The Stables to see if they could find the horses or gather any information. After answering on the first ring, he told her there were three news vehicles in front of The Stables. He would try to handle it from there.

Scott, Grayson and their wives had entered the library and listened to Dru's conversation with Jack.

They all gathered around the small kitchen table, coffee in hand.

"We don't have a choice," Scott started. "We have to put it out there and get ahead of it before it gets ugly."

"I don't want a bunch of people hanging around the barns." Grayson leaned forward. "Dr. Mark said to keep the stress on these horses low. We're not losing one because of reporters and nosey people."

They all agreed.

Leah stood to get the coffee pot and glanced through the large living room and out the front window. She stopped, turned and walked to the front room. "Who is that?"

They all stood and joined her at the window. Dru worried that someone had come through the gate she had locked but it was someone walking down the driveway to a number of waiting news vans. The media had moved from The Stables to The Homestead and were waiting, cameras ready, on the other side of the gate.

"I can't imagine one of the kids would go down there." Jordan said.

"Too big for the kids," Scott shook his head. "Unless it's Grace or Reilly."

"Where's Cora?" Leah asked. None of them had seen her.

Dru hurried to the big open closet by the backdoor where she had just hung up her coat. "My raincoat's not here," She yelled back to them.

"What the heck is she doing?" Scott exhaled.

"Doing what we just talked about," Grayson said. "She's getting ahead of the story. She must have been the one to call them."

"What do we do?" Dru asked. "We can't go running down to stop her. That would look really conspicuous on camera."

Scott shrugged as he walked by her and grabbed his rain coat, "We don't stop her, we go and support her."

Grayson reached for his coat and Dru grabbed Grace's coat. Leah and Jordan stayed at the house to watch for the kids.

The Trio jumped in one of the silver trucks with the T3E ranch logo on the side and made their way down the driveway and arrived when Cora was about twenty feet from the gate. Cora turned and looked at them with a concerned expression but waited for the Trio to join her.

"I didn't want you to stop me," She whispered and took Dru's outstretched hand, "I'm so sorry, I heard you talking last night about Erik. It needed to get out there the right way."

"It's OK," Dru smiled in encouragement. "We'll be right here to support you." Cora looked up at Grayson and Scott; relief had taken over the concern. She took a deep breath and turned to walk the rest of the distance to the gate and face the reporters.

The local Lewiston station was there as well as a couple from Spokane, which was two hours north of Lewiston. She must have called them early.

Cora stepped up to the gate and introduced herself. The Tagger Trio stood right behind her to show their support. The reporters were very respectful of her and listened intently while filming her. She explained about her husband and the phone call that made her call Tagger Stables. Once she mentioned the Tagger name, the cameras lifted to take in all four of the group.

She explained how the kids were taking care of the horses and they were getting all the love and attention that they would need to survive.

"Can we see the horses?" The local reporter asked.

Dru could feel the tension in Scott and Grayson increase.

"I can't answer that," Cora responded. "This is not my property and they are no longer my horses." She glanced back at the Trio then turned back. "Due to the amount of the veterinarian bills, the feed, and time it will take to rehabilitate the little herd, I have signed over the horses to Tagger Enterprises."

Dru hoped her internal stunned reaction didn't show on the outside. Neither brother made a move or changed expressions. As far as Dru knew, there had been no discussion about this. She had told Cora that they would take care of the bills, not that they wanted the horses in exchange.

The reporters glanced up at the Trio and moved their microphones closer. "Can we see the horses?" Was repeated but directed at them this time.

They all three shook their heads. Grayson stepped forward and spoke. He explained the need to keep the barn as stress free as possible for the horses to have every chance of survival. As he spoke, Dru noticed how charming he was. He was precise, but there was compassion and honesty in his words and the way he delivered them. All of the reporters and camera people seemed to hang on his every word.

"We need to go do our morning chores and vet check of the horses," Grayson said. "But, we, at Tagger Enterprises and the entire Tagger family, want everyone to know that we are doing everything we can for these horses. It is very unfortunate what happened to them, but because of Mrs. Smith's quick reaction, when she first learned they might exist, they at least have a chance now," He paused and looked around the group. "Please have respect for Mrs. Smith and the loss of her husband of over forty years."

He paused again to make sure they understood what she was going through. "We will work out some way to keep you all abreast on the condition of the horses."

"Can we get pictures?" The Spokane reporter asked.

Grayson turned to Scott and Dru. His expression said he had no idea what to say.

She had never spoken to reporters before, so Dru took a deep breath and exhaled quickly. Before she lost her nerve she spoke, "We understand your interest and the public interest in the horses. We would be just as curious," She paused, not really wanting to give pictures out of the terrible condition the horses were in. "We will work on sending you photos as soon as we can, but right now we need to get Cora out of the rain and do our morning chores."

With that, they all turned and loaded into the truck.

"That went better than I thought," Cora said as Scott helped her into the back seat with Dru.

"We'll see how they edit it and respond to the reaction from the public," Scott answered her.

"We've never said you had to sign the horses over to us," Dru told her. "I said I would handle the bills."

Cora didn't answer right away. "If you don't want them, I understand."

Dru shook her head, "Seriously, Cora. That isn't the point. They are very expensive horses."

"I have no means of rehabilitating them without you or taking care of them afterwards," She sat up straighter in the seat. "I want the horses to stay with the kids," she said firmly.

"I understand," Dru responded. "I feel the same way, but we're also not going to take them from you."

"You're not. I've already downloaded the transfer papers and signed them. I'm giving them in exchange for their care."

"Cora…" Dru started.

"Really, Dru," Cora chuckled. "It's done; I've given them to your company and the kids so it's doing you no good to argue with me." For the first time since they had met, Cora's eyes had a slight flicker of humor in them.

"You'll learn Dru likes to argue until she gets her own way," Scott grinned.

"I do not," Dru said, but nodded guiltily with a smirk to Cora who laughed in return.

Scott stopped the truck behind the barn. "I called Benny last night; he'll be here around nine. Same with the head of the human society. They're going to want to track the animal's progress and double check the story. We need someone outside of the family that will verify and track it all."

"Dr. Mark will verify," Cora reminded him.

"Yes, but he's been Tagger Enterprises contracted vet for years," Scott explained. "Some people wouldn't consider him outside the company. You calling the news first is probably the one thing that will help show that we aren't trying to hide anything illegal."

"We have to tell the kids about the reporters," Dru added while they were getting out of the truck and walking into the barn.

It was only 6:30, but all the kids were up and had made a circle of straw bales for chairs. All seven were there waiting for the adults to arrive.

"Did Erik tell everyone?" Nora asked, her dark eyes showing the worry and concern for the horses.

They all took a seat in the circle. Leah and Jordan joined the group bringing out cinnamon rolls and juice for the kids and more coffee for the adults.

They heard a truck come up the drive and Scott quickly walked to the door to make sure it wasn't a trespasser.

It was Jack. He had waited until the reporters left and came through the gate, locking it behind him.

They all took seats on the straw bales with the kids.

"Well," Dru said to get everyone's attention. "Since we're all here, let's have a Tagger family meeting."

Cora started to stand but Wade on one side and Grayson on the other, pulled her back down without saying anything. Her jaw dropped in surprise, but then her expression quickly turned to a pleased smile.

Dru explained to the group what had happened with the reporters.

"So how do we handle it now?" Jack asked. "If the reporters were mixed up between The Stables and here, you know that any curious public will be too."

Options were discussed about handling the public and the newspapers. Who would answer phone calls, how would they update the public, and then Dru finally approached the subject of the pictures. No one in the room wanted the photographs they had taken at the Smith property out into the public.

"We've taken photos here while Dr. Mark was working on them," Scott reminded them. "Let's put those pictures out. They have a positive feel to them, showing how they are being taken care of."

Dru and Grayson agreed. There was general agreement with everyone else.

Dru turned to Cora, "You were on the internet and working a GPS to find this house, which means you're comfortable with computers?" Cora nodded. "We keep very thorough medical, training, and horse shoeing records on our horses. Would you be comfortable taking that over for our dirty dozen here?"

Cora looked pleased, "Oh yes!"

"But she's still going to cook…right?" Leah asked with a grin and glance to Jordan.

"Of course!" Cora smiled.

Grayson's phone rang. It was Benny and he needed in the gate. Reilly volunteered to go and ran down the driveway.

Scott's phone rang again then Grayson's, Grace's, Dru's. It continued until everyone that had a phone was answering phone calls. The news reports had hit the air and internet. The local news station declared the horses 'The Tagger Herd'.

They received phone calls from major television networks wanting interviews, smaller market news organizations, and reality shows that wanted to feature them on their shows. All requests were declined. They were told that all information would be posted on an internet page that would be up and running as soon as possible. That way, the Taggers kept control of the information that was shared with the public and there was no undo stress on the horses.

About an hour into the phone barrage Grace and Reilly turned off their phones so they didn't have to answer any more curious friend's phone calls.

Grayson and Cora met with Benny in the barn office. Benny had checked on each of the horses, reviewed the pictures taken at the Smith property and reviewed Dr. Mark's notes. The head of the humane society also arrived and reviewed the information and horses. There were no issues. They agreed that no one was at fault and that the horses were being taken care in the best possible way. They would make sure their reports were made public.

Dru pushed the end button on her phone as she watched Matt remove the IV's from the grey and brown colts. She had been answering phone calls for three hours. It rang again and she went to hit the ignore button when she saw it was Andy, their neighbor at the ranch who had helped her for years in running the ranch and now Tagger Enterprises. She pushed the accept button. "Andy."

"Come open the gate." Was all he said.

"What?

"I need you to come open the gate so I can come up the driveway. It's locked and there are cars showing up like crazy out here."

She walked to the end of the barn and looked down the driveway. She motioned for Grayson and Scott who were sitting on the deck answering phone calls.

The Tagger Trio looked down the drive at their ranch neighbor who was pulling a large trailer load of hay. Scott jumped on the four-wheeler and headed down to unlock the gate. Grayson and Dru stood quietly watching as they made their way back.

Andy stopped his truck next to them. "Where do you want it?"

"What?" Dru asked confused.

"The hay," Andy waved his hand toward the trailer. "I spoke with Dr. Mark this morning to make sure your horses could eat it. It's certified weed free grass hay and from my best haul last season. It's for the Tagger Herd…at least that's what the press is calling them."

The Trio stood stunned listening to him.

"So," Andy repeated. "Where do you want it?"

They spent the rest of the morning accepting and declining donations of hay, grain, vet supplies, and food for the kids. The outpouring was tremendous. Dr. Mark's assistant, Marie, called and said that enough money had been donated from around the country and internationally, for all current and future vet bills for The Tagger Herd. Nikki was put in charge of handling the donated money.

Dru was climbing into her truck to drive over to The Stables to help Jack with the riding clinic when Cora stopped her.

"Everything is going much better than expected," Cora smiled. "Leah is showing me the computer program to track the horses and Jordan is writing out a list of all the food likes and dislikes of the family. They are going to the ranch for the evening to handle the donations that are being taken to the ranch so don't worry about anything here. I'll be watching over everyone." She turned and waved.

"She's fitting right in," Dru said to herself as she started down the driveway.

******

It was late when Dru arrived back at The Homestead, but she had called throughout the day to make sure everything was alright. Leah and Jordan were at the ranch. Grayson and Scott were still at

The Stables unloading the donations of hay and grain into The Stables storage barn that wouldn't fit at The Homestead.

The lights were out in the barn, which meant everyone was asleep, so she went directly to the house.

Slowly she climbed the stairs to the back deck of the house. Her body was finally starting wear down. Thank goodness for Jack. She had a hard time focusing at the clinic and he did the majority of the work.

Hoping for something quick to eat for dinner, she opened the door of the refrigerator. A bowl full of Cora's spaghetti greeted her.

"Oh, fantastic," Dru grinned and pulled the bowl out and set it on the counter. A movement out the kitchen window by the barn caught her attention.

It was Cora, flashlight in hand, running towards the house.

Dru instantly forgot about the food and headed for the door and met her in the driveway.

The older woman was breathing hard, her face was ashen, and her voice shaking when she spoke.

"One of the babies," She finally managed to say, then turned and headed back for the barn.

Dru's heart was sinking, Dr. Mark had warned them, but she didn't want it to happen. Facing death wasn't one of her strong points but she had no choice but to follow Cora into the barn.

They didn't turn on the light, Dru wanted to see the horse before they woke the kids. As Cora started walking down the aisle, Dru held her breath at which stall she was going to stop. She went to the right. Grace and Wade's horses; Rooster, Dollar, Eli and Buttercup were on the left. They were safe. Cora passed the first stall on the right which meant Trooper and Harvey were good. She kept moving. She passed Nora's stall…Scarecrow and Arcturus were safe. Only Little Ghost, Angel, Cooper, and Rufio were left; either Sadie or Reilly's horses. Cora started to slow down.

Dru's heart sunk when Cora stopped next to Sadie who was sleeping peacefully on a cot. The older woman waited until Dru was next to her then aimed the flashlight over the top of the sleeping girl and towards the little colts inside; then turned it on. Dru peered into the stall.

Little Ghost was lying down on the far side; his head lifted at the light. It wasn't him, it was Angel. Dru could feel her throat constrict and the tears burn the back of her eyes when she saw the horse. Angel was laying out flat, his little muzzle stretched out as far as it could go. He was struggling for every breath.

She stepped around Cora and carefully over Sadie to kneel next to the horse and run a hand down his little neck and to his side. She sighed heavily. He was too far gone. Dr. Mark was too far away to get there and she didn't believe it would matter. She looked up at Cora who was standing at the stall door trying not to wake Sadie.

"Turn on the light," Dru told her reluctantly. Cora's shaking hand went to her chest. They both knew what that meant.

Cora turned and Dru prepared herself for what was next. When the light shown through the barn, she heard instant movement. Matt's head was the first to pop up. He glanced at his mom and then down at Angel. His shoulders slumped in defeat. She waved him over. Sadie hadn't moved yet so he stepped lightly around her. They heard Reilly swear and Matt waved him quiet. Nikki poked her head over the stall door and had to cover her mouth to keep from calling out. Her eyes were wide in shock and tears instantly sprung into them.

"We need to move Little Ghost out," Dru whispered.

Matt looked around to assess the situation. It was still raining, so he couldn't take him out the back stall door. The only choice was out the front next to Sadie. Since she was still asleep, they wanted to wait until Little Ghost was moved before they had to wake her. Nikki and Matt both took an end of Sadie's cot and lifted slowly. They worked their way to the other side of the aisle. Sadie whimpered once but was so tired she didn't wake.

"Call her parents," Dru said to Nikki.

Matt stepped into the stall with the two horses as Dru stepped out and pointed to the end of The Stables to the washroom. Reilly and Grace, who was silently crying, went to the room to prepare it for the grey horse. Matt helped the colt to his feet and led him across the walkway.

Angel hadn't moved and his breathing was getting shallower. Dru had been through this before with animals and knew the horse didn't have long. All the kids were awake except Sadie.

Taking a deep breath and letting it out slowly, Dru knelt down next to the young girl. Sadie's hair had been worn in the braid for so long that it was starting to unravel. Dru brushed away a couple loose strands that were across the nine-year-old's face. She looked so young and innocent. This was going to be one of the worst things Dru ever had to do.

She leaned down close to her sleeping niece, took a deep breath, and said her name, "Sadie." She stirred and turned on her side facing Dru. Her eyes flickered open, then closed.

"Sadie", Dru repeated and caressed her cheek gently.

Sadie's eyes flew open and she sat straight up. Her eyes were still a little glazed and she looked around but wasn't really seeing anything. When her eyes finally focused, they were looking right into Dru's eyes. She frowned in confusion herd swung her legs over the edge of the cot. Sadie looked down at her cot then over to the stall door.

"Why am I over here?" She asked softly. Dru cupped her hand under Sadie's chin and turned her so she was looking at her again.

"It's Angel," Dru whispered sadly.

Sadie's eyes grew wide and instantly glistened with tears. She slid off the cot and ran into the stall. "No!" she cried out. The crack in her voice made the tears well in Dru's eyes as she followed her niece into the stall. Sadie had fallen onto her knees, feet spread out to the side.

Dru sat next to Sadie who turned her desperate blue eyes up at her, "Can he be helped?"

Dru slowly shook her head causing Sadie's shoulders to slump and little sobs escape. Reilly appeared and sat next to Sadie with Grace sitting on the floor on the other side of him. Slowly Nora and Wade came in next to Dru.

The young colt's eyes were closed. He took another laborious breath and let it out. They were getting farther apart. Sadie reached out and laid her hand over his hoof. Wade and Nora did the same with the back hooves while Grace lightly stroked the horse's nose. Quietly they waited for each breath.

Slowly, Sadie leaned over onto Reilly's shoulder. His face muscles stiffened. He took her hand that wasn't holding onto Angel, and squeezed tightly giving his silent support.

Another breath...

Dru found herself holding her breath between each of Angels.

No one spoke; the barn was eerily quiet.

Another breath...

Matt and Nikki stood by the stall door with Matt's arm around his sister's shoulders.

Another breath...

Dru looked at the five kids who had fought so hard and long to save these horses and here they were, supporting each other…waiting to say goodbye.

Another breath…

Sadie's fingers slowly started caressing the little hoof; tears streaming unchecked down her cheeks.

Another breath...

Dru and all five kids had a hand on Angel to comfort him; to let him know he was loved in his short time with them.

Another breath…

Silence…

There were no more breathes, Sadie's little Angel was gone.

No one spoke.

The sound of a truck racing down the driveway echoed in the quiet barn. The gravel gave way as the truck slid to a stop then a door slammed and running footsteps made their way into the barn.

"Sadie!" Grayson's voice rang out.

Sadie's head tilted back, her eyes closed. A long gut wrenching little girl cry came from her, "Daaaaddddyy!"

Reilly and Dru quickly moved as Grayson slid behind his little girl. He wrapped his arms around her as she turned and buried her face in her daddy's neck. Her whole body shook.

Dru turned to Nora and Wade and wrapped them in her arms. Sobs had taken over, crying just wasn't enough.

Grace and Reilly stood and walked out of the stall and were quickly embraced by Matt and Nikki.

Cora had been standing at the stall door but had disappeared.

Grayson rocked Sadie in his arms until she leaned back and looked up at her dad; her eyes pleading. She tried to say something but the words wouldn't come out.

"It's OK, Honey," He cupped her sad face in his hands. "We did everything we could, it just wasn't meant to be. But always remember, you gave this horse something that every horse should have."

"What?" She whispered between the tears.

"The love of a little girl."

She cried out and buried her face in his neck again. They sat rocking while Dru, Wade, and Nora made their way out of the stall.

Wade glanced around. "Where's Cora?" He asked through the tears he was trying to wipe away.

Dru shook her head. "I didn't see her leave."

He peered into each stall looking for the distraught woman and found her in the office sitting in the chair; her head in her hands as she leaned on the desk. She was silently crying. He put his arms around her and leaned his head on her shoulder but didn't say anything.

"I don't understand," Cora cried. "I don't understand why he bought these animals."

In just days, they would all know, but right now, even that knowledge wouldn't have eased the pain of losing Sadie's little Angel.

CHAPTER NINE

The next morning, they buried Angel on the hill behind the hay barn. The wind began to blow and the sky was an ominous dark grey as it threatened to start another rainstorm at any moment. The entire Tagger family, all eleven of them, and their extended family, Jack, Reilly and now Cora were there holding hands to complete a circle around the grave.

Matt was Wade and Sadie's age when Dru's barrel horse, Jet, passed away. He had known the horse all his life and had a hard time dealing with her loss. To help, he wrote a poem for Jet and it had been recited after every horse they'd lost.

Matt's voice was low as he began, but grew stronger as the rest of the family recited it with him.

Thundering hoofs
Flying manes
A tail that trails
The love that remains

You leave us now
To fly in the sky
Green pastures to run
Under a warm sun to lie

Carry my heart
In your enchanted spell
Of unconditional love
As we say farewell

Your love we share
Without End
As we saddle up
Fly high my friend

As they recited the poem, Dru looked down at the family homestead. The large white multi-family house with the wide wrap-around deck, the horse and hay barns painted red with the traditional white trim. They were nestled in the rolling hills of the neighboring farmer's fields. It was a beautiful final resting spot for Angel.

After a moment of silence, the kids returned to the barn. Leah and Jordan returned to the computers to announce to the media and public that one of the Tagger Herd was gone. An outpouring of condolences came through on several different social media sites. There were comments as far away as London and Australia.

Dr. Mark and Erik came by to check on the remaining horses and give their condolences to Sadie and the kids.

"Why did he die?" Sadie asked sadly; tears threatening to fall again.

Dr. Mark sat on a bale of straw to talk to her. He held her closely trying to console her.

"There was just too much damage to the stomach and other internal organs. It was just too much for the little guy." With tears in his eyes, Sadie closed her eyes at a failed attempt to stop the tears.

******

Dru stood on the back deck of the house and stared at the barn. She heard the back door open and close. Scott and Grayson appeared at her side.

"Jessup just called." Grayson leaned against the railing with his back to the barn. "There's been a number of volunteers call wanting to help us move the cows to the summer pasture. That way the kids can stay here."

Dru nodded sadly. She had never missed a cattle drive, so with a heavy heart she turned to her brother, "I need to be here, just in case." Grayson nodded and reached over to cover her hand on the deck railing. Scott joined them and covered her other hand. She felt her insides tremble at the memories.

They stood quietly for a while until Dru finally spoke, "It reminds me of the weeks after the accident." She didn't look at her brothers; they knew she was talking about the accident that took the lives of their parents and grandparents.

"So many people came out to help with the ranch for the first couple weeks," She sighed at the memory. "It seemed like months before we were left alone."

"That's probably why we survived it." Scott squeezed her hand tightly then turned and walked down the steps and out toward the barn. Grayson soon followed.

After checking on the kids and horses, the men and their wives headed to the ranch to move the cows. They weren't expected to return until late the next day. Jack was at The Stables, so it was up to Cora and Dru to handle anything that might happen.

Dru remained on the porch long after they were gone. Finally deciding she couldn't stand there all day, but not wanting to go to the barn, she checked the outside stock tank. Kit and Libby wandered over to her so she brushed them and combed their manes. Every once in a while they would whinny out to the barn and wait for an answer back. It was their way of checking on the little herd.

While Dru was with the older horses, Cora left the house and headed to the barn. She was picking up the files that Dr. Mark had left so she could enter them into the computer. Five minutes later, she appeared from the barn, walking calmly to the house.

"No disaster this time." Dru said to Kit and Libby.

She finished filling the water tank, moved hay from the hay barn to the lean-to at the side of the horse barn and took inventory of the hay and sacks of feed that remained on the property. There were significant amounts of donations so she wanted to make sure everything was accounted for.

Dru slowly made her way back up the steps of the porch and stood leaning on the railing again and watched the barn.

"How long are you going to avoid going in?" Cora said from behind her.

Dru didn't turn. "I don't know," she answered honestly.

"Want to talk?"

"Not really."

"Kids are doing fine and horses are all eating and drinking."

Dru nodded, took a deep breath and turned. "I've seen too much…I don't handle death well." Dru said as she walked by Cora who nodded in understanding.

It started to rain again as she made her way to the barn.

When she stepped into the barn, Dru glanced over the first stall door and saw Nikki and Matt in with Harvey and Trooper. They were sitting against the closed doors that led to the outside stall run. It reminded her of the nights she and her brothers would hide out in the barn at the ranch and have their life discussions.

"What are you two doing?" She smiled at her kids. The eighteen and twenty-year-olds were not just brother and sister, but for years they were the only kids on the ranch growing up and were also best friends.

They returned her smile. "Just talking about all the horses we've known in our life-time," Matt answered. They both scooted in opposite directions, inviting her to sit between them. She happily joined them.

Dru had a quick flash of the night of the funeral when she and her brothers huddled in the back of the stall at the ranch barn. She pushed it aside and looked proudly at her kids. She loved these quiet moments with them.

"So, which one do you remember first?" she asked them, although she already knew the answer.

"Jet." They answered in unison.

Dru chuckled. "First horse I remember was Jet's mom, Nan," She smiled at the memories. "Black as ink, just like Jet and Libby."

"How old were you when Jet was born?" Matt asked.

"Six," she answered. "I was there when Nan was bred, babied her all year long, and was there when she gave birth to Jet, out in the lower barn pasture at the ranch. Jet and I grew up together. Libby was born when you were just a year old."

Dru smiled as Nora, Wade, Sadie, Grace, and Reilly entered the stall and sat comfortably around the walls. With Trooper and Harvey in the stall too, it was a tight fit.

"I was nine when your grandpa started training Jet. She was so trusting that she didn't give him any problems, she knew he wouldn't hurt her. Took the first bit with no problem, saddle pad with no problem, and saddle without any issues. He trusted her so much by that time, that he let me be the first one on her back." She glanced up at the other kids. "That didn't happen very often."

"I was so worried when I put the boot in the stirrup that first time but Grandpa told me to trust him and Jet. So, I did, and with a quick grab of the saddle I pushed myself up into the seat. Jet just turned her head around and looked up at me. That was it, so Dad led me around the arena for a while until we got into a good rhythm together."

"When did you start racing on her?" Grace asked.

"A year later; I just did some smaller shows for a long time with her as we learned. I used Snowball, your grandma's barrel horse, most of the time growing up. Jet and I started serious barrel racing when I was in high school."

"You didn't race after the accident?" Sadie asked.

Dru sighed, remembering the last perfect ride. "No, I was too busy after that."

"Did you miss doing the rodeos?" Nora asked this time.

"Not as much as I would have missed the ranch if we would have lost it." She glanced up at the kids on the far side. "Sometimes, even when you want something with all your heart, you have to understand the consequences of having or doing it. If all is good, then do it, but if it's going to hurt someone or something else, then you have to weigh your decision on whether it's worth it to continue."

"Did you always love horses?" Wade asked.

She smiled at his change of subject. "I always *liked* horses, but when Jet was born it was a whole new love. There's just something about finding the right horse."

"What do you mean?" Reilly asked.

"Horses have personalities just like people do. There will be people you like and some you tolerate and others you just don't like at all. Same with horses," she explained. "Monty, Scott's horse, was one I just didn't get along with, but he and Scott are just perfect for each other; stubborn and pig-headed." She grinned at Wade and Nora, who were nodding. "Grandpa found his match with the original Eli and Mom with Snowball. Sometimes you could look most of your life for the perfect match."

"Dad doesn't ride just one horse." Grace pointed out. "Did he ever find the perfect horse?"

Dru thought back to all the years riding on the ranch; Grayson and Scott didn't ride much at The Stables, just when they had large events. "I don't think he ever did, even when he was team roping. He always rides the younger horse and works them with the cows. He trains them for everyone else."

"But Jet was yours." Nikki smiled.

"Yea, she was," Dru nodded. "When she was a foal, I would go out to the pasture and walk up to her and Nan. When Jet would see me, she'd try to walk up to me so I would move around to the opposite side of Nan and away from her. I'd play peek-a-boo with Jet around Nan until Nan got tired of us and would walk away." The girls giggled.

"Tell them about when you were sick." Matt said, having heard it at least a dozen times.

"How sick were you?" Sadie asked.

"Pretty sick… It was the summer I was eleven and had the flu or something like it. I woke up in the middle of the night, wrapped a blanket around me and snuck out to the pasture. The evening breeze felt really good on my hot skin. I laid down under the fence." She grinned at the memory. "Your grandparents would have killed me if I would have gone in with the horses. They were going to be mad enough that I was outside. Jet came up, sniffed me, and then stood next to the fence as I fell asleep."

"You were out there all night?" Wade asked his eyes wide in surprise.

All the kids were entranced by her story.

"I was, and the whole next day. When Mom and Dad found me the next morning, Jet was still standing over me, protecting me. I was sound asleep, the best sleep I'd had in days. They kept bringing me water and something to eat but just let me lie there in the sun, protected by Jet."

"She stayed with you all day?" Nora asked.

"She did," Dru's heart warmed, she could still see black horse standing over her. "Mom and Dad finally brought her some water to drink too and a flake of hay."

"That is so cool." Wade smiled.

"Yes, it was." Dru agreed; the memory seemed to ease the pain inside her.

"Do you have more stories?" Reilly asked.

All the kids agreed they wanted more, so she told stories throughout the day. What she didn't tell them, was how she would stand at Jet's shoulder for days crying after the accident. The horse seemed to know that she needed solace and would let her wrap her arms around her neck and just let the tears flow.

******

Dru's eyes flickered open; it was just starting to get light outside and she could see enough in the barn to make out all the sleeping kids in their lounge chairs and cots. No emergencies during the night, so it was her best night of sleep since the little herd had come into her life.

She quietly slid off the cot and stretched her tired back muscles then she folded the cot and moved it into the tack room. Stall check time to make sure everyone was OK.

Trooper and Harvey were standing and eating their hay. Matt and Nikki were sleeping soundly in the chairs just outside the door. Dru smiled down at her kids, she loved them with all her heart and soul and had to fight the urge to lean down and hug them both.

Nora lay on a cot in front of her stall; Arcturus was leaning out the stall door and over the top of her. Dru stroked the neck of the horse then leaned down and pulled the blankets over Nora's shoulder. With her eyes still closed, the girl reached up and touched the nose of the little black horse with the star, then turned to lie on her stomach. The palomino, Scarecrow, was lying in the back of the stall.

Next were Sadie and Little Ghost. Dru glanced in the stall and sighed, it was sad not seeing the brown little colt in with the grey. Sadie had opened the door of the stall and put her cot across the front. Little Ghost was lying right next to the cot and Sadie's arm lay over the back of the horse as they slept.

Dru took out her phone and took a picture of the two. Sadie would cherish that picture.

In the corner stall were Reilly, Rufio and Cooper. Reilly wasn't on his cot as she approached; Dru frowned knowing exactly where he was. She stepped to the door and saw him sleeping in the corner of the stall, Rufio standing over the top of him and Cooper eating at the feeder. They were all calm and peaceful so she let him be for now, she'd talk to him later.

Sleeping bag and blond hair was all Dru saw on Grace's cot. She giggled softly and glanced over the door to see Buttercup, the cream colored dun, and the buckskin, Eli, eating at their feeder. Both glanced at her but didn't move away from the food.

Wade's two little red horses were standing at the back of the stall, heads hung low as they slept. Wade was half off his cot, sound asleep. Dru shook her head at him and gently pulled his upper body back onto the cot and covered him up with his blankets. A slight smile crossed his sleeping face.

Dru walked to the small side door of the barn and turned back. All day yesterday there was a doom and gloom filling the building. The horse stories helped, especially for Dru. Remembering the good times always helped ease the pain of loss.

She stepped out the door and was surprised to see a beautiful blue sky with just a few puffy white clouds dotting the horizon. The sun was up and starting to warm up the brisk morning. It was a spectacular refreshing morning.

Libby and Kit's head popped up from the pasture and they whinnied excitedly at her as they trotted toward the fence. Dru smiled, it was always heartwarming to be greeted so happily.

She missed Mavis and Bart who were with her brothers.

"The cattle drive should go well today." Dru said to Libby while stroking the horse's long sleek neck. She retrieved a brush and started brushing her black and bay horses. They did their usual dance of trying to get to the brush in front of the other one.

Dru found herself relaxing and smiling at the pair. It was an invigorating and refreshing morning; just what they all needed. She turned and looked at the barn and grinned. "Why not?" She said to Libby and retrieved their halters and lead ropes from the tack room.

Kit was tied to the hitching post just outside the barn. She was young and would be too ambitious with the weakened horses. Dru made her way to the barn with Libby prancing excitedly by her side.

"This could be a mistake," She turned to the excited horse and stroked her long nose. "Just play nice."

Dru opened both of the large doors on the barn and blocked them open to let the sunshine in. She hesitated a moment and glanced up at Libby. The tall black horse's ears were perked up showing excitement. This was her first meeting with the little whinnies she'd been communicating with all week.

Dru took a step into the barn and Libby let out a loud whinny that echoed throughout the barn.

The kids jumped up immediately and looked at Dru as if she was crazy. With a chuckle at their expressions, she just ignored them and continued into the barn. Matt and Nikki scrambled out of the way as Libby met Harvey and Trooper first. She was calm and sniffed at the excited little horses. She wasn't aggressive, just nurturing as she sniffed them each again and pushed to move to the next stall.

"Mom, what are you doing? They aren't supposed to have stress." Matt asked worriedly.

Dru answered but remained focused on the large mare and the young horses.

"They need energy," Dru explained. "It's been dark, dismal, and depressing in here." She glanced over at the surprised kids. Kit let out a few whinnies from outside the barn, letting them know she wanted in too.

"Open all the doors to the outside. Get some fresh air in here for the horses. It's beautiful out. Shut the inside stall doors so they can't get out and Libby can't go in." She continued her introduction of the mare to all the excited colts and fillies, each nickering excitedly.

As the doors were opened and the light breeze made its way through the barn, the energy from horses and kids grew. Wade giggled in delight when his red horses tried to push one another away to get to the mare. Rooster was getting good at walking with his bandaged legs. All of the horses were up and leaning their heads out the stall doors.

"This is the first time they've all been energetic and at their stall doors." Grace said excitedly. She started grabbing the bedding and moved it into the tack room. The straw bales were moved to the sides so Dru unhooked the lead rope so Libby could move freely between the stalls.

She and the kids gathered at the end of the barn and watched as Libby mothered the horses. Matt and Nikki walked up to their mom and wrapped an arm around her.

"Look at Rooster's eyes!" Wade exclaimed. "They look all excited."

"It's not just Rooster!" Nora cried out happily. "All the horses are excited."

They spent the next 45 minutes standing and smiling as the little horses began to move around with energy. Cora entered the barn to inform them that breakfast was ready but everyone was enjoying the morning horse visit and refused to leave.

Dru walked in and took Libby's rope to lead her out of the barn but the mare didn't move. They were her babies now and she didn't want to leave them.

Understanding the horse's need to nurture the horses, Dru ran her hand down the nose of the mare and down her neck. "I know, sweetheart, but they need their rest now."

She pulled again and the horse reluctantly moved, but she let out a loud whinny and danced excitedly as she left the barn and joined Kit. The older horses were returned to the pasture but remained by the gate ready to go back.

They repeated the routine every couple of hours. The life and energy in the barn increased with every visit.

As Dru walked Libby toward the barn for the last visit of the day, she heard George Straight's voice floating out of the barn. He was joined by a chorus of voice's singing about a *Clear Blue Sky*. She giggled softly to herself as she stood at the barn doors and watched the kids singing to each other and the horses. There was a definite change in moral from the day before.

The riders returned from the cattle drive during Libby's last visit and they couldn't believe the change in horses and kids since they had left the night before.

The cattle drive had gone without incident and they had over twenty volunteers that had helped with the move. It was twice as many people that were needed and all the volunteers were thankful for the chance to help out in any way they could. They sent their best wishes to the kids and the Tagger Herd.

******

The next morning Dru was standing at the end of the barn as Matt and Nikki walked Libby and Kit to the barn. Libby was nurturing like a mother to them as she was let loose and wandered around the barn. Much to her distress, Kit was left outside again.

Scott and Grayson were in the library working while Leah and Jordan had gone to their jobs.

Dru's phone started to sing. "Good morning." She smiled as she answered Jack's call.

"Dru," His voice was full of excitement, "I just got a phone call from a guy confirming as to whether Wes Smith had made arrangements for a horse that he was to deliver today."

"What?" Dru exclaimed and turned to Cora who was standing next to her watching Libby greet the horses.

"The guy said that Wes had told him it was a gift for his wife."

Dru remembered Wes' note; "Cora's Gift".

"What did you tell him?"

"I explained to him that Wes had passed away but Cora was at The Homestead with you so he going to take the horse there," he hesitated. "He didn't seem to know about the other horses so I didn't say anything to him."

"What's his E.T.A.?"

"About an hour and a half, he's coming from this side of Colfax."

"OK," Dru answered and wandered to the side of the barn so Cora couldn't over hear her. "I'll get the kids ready and let Cora know. He's the last man that talked to her husband. Hopefully, he has some answers for her…us."

"I'll set things up here then be over in an hour." Jack stated and ended the call.

Dru turned to Cora. How to tell her…

"Alright everyone, head in to get breakfast." Dru took Cora's hand to keep her from going in. The older woman looked at her in surprise. "Cora and I will watch the horses."

She sent a quick text to her brothers to come out to the barn; they walked by the kids as they joined her.

Dru motioned for Cora to sit. She took a deep breath and repeated what Jack had told her. Cora's eyes widened as she spoke.

"My gift?" She whispered. "Do you think he knows what Wes was up to?"

"I don't know," Dru took her hand. "But I do know that he's the last chance we have of knowing."

They heard a truck making its way up the driveway. The gate was locked so it had to be Jack. Dru took Libby's lead rope and had to pull the mare away from the horses. When she walked out of the barn, Cora was grilling Jack for information about the phone call. He repeated everything to her, Scott and Grayson again.

Dru made her way into the house to tell the kids before the driver got there.

When Dru finished, Nora was the only one to speak. "Another horse? Are we going to keep it?"

"It's Cora's horse," Dru answered, looking around at the group. "Be respectful and remember, it's Cora's decision and she's going to be very emotional about this. It's only been a month since her husband died."

"I keep forgetting," Sadie sighed. "She had a whole life before she came here."

Dru smiled in understanding. They had known Cora for less than a week, yet it seemed like years.

She looked out the window at Cora who was still talking to Jack. His phone rang, he answered it, walked forward and looked down the driveway, then walked down to open the gate.

"Here we go kids." Dru said as they all made their way down the steps of the back porch of the house and to Cora's side.

CHAPTER TEN

Dru stood nervously next to Cora. The information the man had was more important than the horse itself. She saw Wade reach over and take hold of Cora's hand. She squeezed it tightly as they watched the horse trailer make its way down the drive. Libby and Kit had left their place by the barn gate and were running alongside the trailer. Whinnies were echoing throughout The Homestead; from inside the trailer, the pasture, and in the barn.

Jack had gotten in the truck with the driver for the return ride. The truck pulled next to the waiting group so the end of the horse trailer was even with them when it stopped. A tall slender man walked around the end of the trailer. A large straw hat nearly covered his grey hair. Dru guessed he was in his sixties.

"Wow," He glanced around the group waiting for him, "You have quite a herd here," he smiled. "I'm Ray James."

Grayson took a step forward and stretched out his hand. He shook it firmly and turned to introduce the group. The kids stood looking at the horse trailer wondering about the horse inside. When he introduced Cora, Ray took a step to her and smiled warmly.

"I am so sorry for your loss," he paused, "I only met Wes that morning and really enjoyed talking with him."

She was still holding Wade's hand tightly but she stretched out her free hand to his outstretched hand. "I have so many questions…" Her voice quivered when she spoke. Wade took a protective step in closer to her.

"Jack tried to explain everything as fast as he could as we came up the drive," he looked towards the barn. "All twelve were at the property?"

There was a sharp intake of breath from Sadie. Ray glanced down at her then back up at Grayson.

"We lost one," Grayson confirmed with a sigh and a nod.

"I am so sorry." Ray said glancing down at Sadie. Grace was standing next to her and she leaned into her big sister for support.

Ray took a step backwards. "He's been in the trailer for a bit now; I'd like to get him out before we talk."

"How old is he?" Dru asked as he lifted the gate release on the trailer.

"A two-year-old." Ray answered.

Same as the others.

He pushed the gate back and Scott held it open for him. Dru inhaled deeply as Ray stepped inside the trailer. Her stomach tightened from the anticipation.

"I want to see, but I don't want to see." Reilly whispered.

"Same here." Was chorused from the group. They all knew, under better circumstances, their herd should be in the physical condition as this horse. It was a reminder of the terrible ordeal the Tagger Herd had been through.

They could hear the horse start walking out of the trailer, the hoof beats echoing. Libby and Kit were leaning over the fence trying to see in the trailer.

Dru held her breath as the horse stepped out of the trailer and exhaled sharply when she saw him. He was magnificent! His coat was shiny dark red with black mane and tail, a slender white blaze ran from his forehead to the tip of his nose and his eyes were bright, alert, and curious. The white on his legs came up to his knees to make 4 perfect stockings on the long legs. He was now dancing across the driveway but even as excited as the horse was, he was well mannered and didn't pull against the rope that Ray was holding.

There were gasps from the group. Ray was smiling, pleased the horse had received such a reaction.

"Cora!" Wade cried out.

Dru turned as Matt and Scott caught her before she hit the ground. They helped her to the porch steps that were just behind her.

"Are you OK?" Scott asked. The whole group's attention had shifted from the beautiful colt to the woman that had quickly become their friend.

Cora nodded. Tears began to fall down her cheeks. Nikki ran in the house for tissues and glass of water.

Dru knelt in front of her. "What can we do?"

The older woman just shook her head. "Give me a minute."

The only sound came from the colt's hoofs hitting the ground and the horses nickering between each other.

Cora finally lifted her gaze and looked at the horse. She dabbed the tears from her eyes and smiled down at Wade. She patted his hand. "They are happy tears," she assured him and told him the story as if they were the only two there. "The day Wes and I were married, he gave me a horse for a wedding gift. He was the son of Zippo Pine Bar. I raised the colt, training him myself. Other than Wes, he was my best friend. I called him Zipper. The colt helped keep me sane when Wes was away in the service." Her eyes glazed as she remembered the horse. She sighed, "He passed away just days away from our 29th wedding anniversary."

Cora looked at Ray and nodded towards the horse. "He is Zippo Pine Bar lineage?" All eyes turned to Ray.

"Yes, ma'am," he confirmed. "His grand-dam is full blood sister to your Zipper."

Cora sat staring at the colt as he looked around his new home. She finally stood and slowly made her way to the horse. He nosed her hands looking for a treat but finally gave up and leaned his head against her shoulder as she whispered to him and stroked his neck. "He is identical to Zipper; same blaze and four white stockings."

"Did he tell you that?" Cora asked Ray.

"Yes, ma'am. Wes said that a little part of you died the day Zipper did." he answered

The group remained silent as they watched Cora stroke the horse's neck. She finally turned back to Ray, "Did he tell you why he bought these horses?"

Ray nodded, "He told me the whole story. We had a nice chat before he left." He hesitated, "He died about 20 minutes from my farm. I didn't know about it until this morning. I was busy getting the hay baled and then picked up. Then I went down to Boise to visit my grandkids while it was raining, made it back late last night."

Scott stepped up to Cora and took the lead rope from Ray. "I'll put him in the corral. Then we can talk on the porch."

Dru watched the horse walk down the driveway, excitedly prancing at the whinnies coming from the barn. He had a large round quarter horse rump, no ribs were showing, and he had energy and life resonating from him. Her eyes went past him to the barn where the skeletal horses were recovering. She glanced at the kids, then over to Cora. She wanted the kids to hear about Ray's conversation with Wes but knew it was Cora's decision.

Grayson helped Cora up the stairs and to the patio furniture. The kids looked at each other, then to Dru; they didn't know if they should go to the barn or remain. Dru looked to Cora.

"Cora?" She started up the steps. When the older woman turned, Dru glanced down at the kids.

"They deserve to know," she said and motioned for everyone to join them.

Scott put the colt in the holding corral between the barn and pasture. It would give the colt, Libby, and Kit time to get to know each other before he was pastured with them.

Ray sat in the chair next to Cora and waited for everyone to sit. There were two long tables and more than a dozen chairs on the porch. It was a normal family gathering area and evening dining table in the summer. No one spoke, they were waiting for Ray.

"I'll start at the beginning," Ray told Cora. "My daughter, in Boise, had purchased the horse last year in California before she found out she was pregnant. We moved him up here for the winter so I could take care of him with mine. But once my granddaughter was born, she realized there wasn't going to be time to train and ride him like she had planned so she asked me to sell him." He paused looking around the table at the curious faces.

"He wasn't even in the paper yet when I got a call from your husband," Ray chuckled. "I'd taken the horse to the veterinarian in Pullman for a health check to prepare for selling him, and that vet had been in contact with Wes. Wes had asked him to call if he happened to see a Zippo Pine Bar horse come through. He did, and Wes called me immediately. I was barely pulling back in my driveway when I got the call."

Everyone remained quiet.

"Wes came up the next morning, cash in hand...didn't even dicker on the price." Ray chuckled again.

"Did he tell you about the other horses?" Cora asked anxiously.

Ray nodded, "He said he had purchased other horses and was done buying the dozen he wanted when he heard this colt come up for sale." He smiled at Cora. "Wes said he was buying you a dozen horses instead of a dozen roses for your anniversary."

"Anniversary?" Dru asked while others just gasped at the news. She looked at Cora. The older woman's eyes were misting over. "When is your anniversary?"

Cora's voice was a low whisper from emotion. "Forty eight years today," More gasps from around the group. She shook her head and raised a calming hand, "I didn't want anyone to know, I *needed* this one to myself," She paused then sighed, "I needed today to say goodbye to him." Dru took her hand and squeezed. Wade had ahold of the other one.

There was silence from everyone as they respected Cora's grieving. She looked up at Ray and nodded for him to continue.

"The dozen horses were for the two of you, but he kept calling this colt 'Cora's Gift'." Ray smiled.

"I'm 68 years old," Cora told him. "Why would he buy a dozen horses for us?"

Ray leaned forward, "Wes said when he married you and gave you that Zippo colt, it was to start your life together and to live your life. He said recently you had sold all the animals and were talking about selling the ranch." He shook his head.

"He felt like you and he were just setting yourself up for dying instead of living your life." He paused when she gasped in surprise. "He figured you had many more years to live by enjoying raising young horses, training them, and selling them. *He was buying you a dozen reasons to live every day, instead of just waiting around to die.*" Ray said flatly.

Cora let out a long sigh. "Since we didn't have children of our own, Wes always called our horses our kids." She reached out and touched Ray's hand. "And your colt was a baker's dozen."

Ray chuckled, "Yes ma'am."

"Well, with Angel gone, we have that dozen he wanted." Sadie whispered to Cora.

"The colt that died was called Angel?" Ray asked in surprise.

Sadie nodded, looking over at Wade, "I figured there were boy angels, too," Sadie said defensively.

Ray held up a hand, "No, it's a wonderful name," he assured her and stood. "I'll be right back." He left the table and went to the front cab of his truck waving a file folder when he returned. He fumbled through the papers a moment then pulled out one and handed it to Cora.

She took the paper and began reading. "It's the colt's registration papers," She announced to the group and continued to read until she gasped and put her hand over her mouth. Her surprised eyes looked up at Ray. He nodded with a knowing smile.

"What?" Sadie asked.

Cora motioned for Sadie who quickly stood and made her way down the table. Cora handed her the paper.

Sadie's jaw dropped and her eyes welled up in tears. "His name is Pine Bar Angel." She looked up in amazement.

Sadie turned to Cora, "Happy Anniversary, Cora." She whispered and kissed the woman on the cheek. "I wish he was here to be with you."

"Honey," She looked into Sadie's big blue eyes. "I believe he is here." She looked around at all the people, smiled, but was too emotional to speak.

"Can I go look at him?" Sadie asked.

"Absolutely," Cora answered and all the kids, except Nikki and Matt, quickly scattered from the table to crawl up and hang on the fence and look at the new colt. He quickly trotted over to them, happy to take in all the attention and love they wanted to give him.

They told Ray about the condition of the other horses. He was heartbroken and knew Wes would be too.

"I would be willing to take a couple off your hands to help out," Ray told them. "I'll work with the animal hospital at WSU to make sure they get whatever is needed."

There was silence when he stopped speaking. Matt's jaw had dropped and Nikki had gasped. Scott, Grayson, Dru and Cora were completely silent, not letting their shock show.

Ray looked around at everyone.

Dru looked over at Grayson and Scott. With Cora having signed over the horses to Tagger Enterprises it was their decision to make. They turned and looked at her. They didn't know what to say either. None of them had thought of separating the herd, yet they couldn't say yes or no without taking a vote between the three of them.

"Can you excuse us a minute?" Dru asked Ray and she and her brothers stood.

"Mom, you can't be seriously considering this?" Matt asked in amazement.

She didn't look at him; she just followed her brothers into the house.

CHAPTER ELEVEN

"No." Dru's vote.

"No." Scott's vote.

"No." Grayson's vote.

Dru shook her head. "I couldn't imagine telling those kids that we were taking those horses away."

Scott nodded. "How would you even choose which ones to give him?"

"I think Matt, Nikki, and Cora just about had strokes when we came in to vote," Grayson chuckled as he glanced out at the barn. "Those horses have only been here a week but…they are already part of the family."

"Just like Cora," Scott added.

Dru smiled up at her brothers. "We need another vote." When she told them what she had in mind they smiled and agreed without hesitation.

Dru glanced out the window. Cora was politely talking to Ray but nervously looking at the back door. Matt and Nikki were both staring quietly at the table, their faces expressionless. "Should we put them out of their misery?" She smiled wickedly.

As they walked out the door, Matt and Nikki's heads sprung up searching their faces for the answer. The Tagger Trio took their seats and Dru spoke.

"Ray, we don't make big decisions that affect Tagger Enterprises without voting between the three of us," She explained and he nodded in understanding. "We would like to thank you for the offer, but the horses are not and won't be for sale…ever."

"I knew it." Matt whispered with a grin.

Ray nodded and said he understood. He left soon after the vote. The kids had moved from looking at the new horse and disappeared into the barn.

After seeing Ray off, the adults returned to the back porch.

"Wes loved you very much." Dru smiled at Cora.

She nodded, "He wanted to continue living and not just wait around to die." The emotion shook in her voice.

"That's a dang good reason to buy a dozen horses." Scott told her with a warm smile.

"It doesn't help with the loss of Angel and what those poor animals have gone through, but at least now I understand," Cora agreed. She looked up at the Trio. "I just couldn't imagine going through this last week without all of you." She looked out at the barn. "I couldn't imagine what would have happened to all of them."

"In an odd way, it seems like it was meant to be." Scott said. They all agreed.

"Now what, Cora?" Grayson asked. She looked up in surprise. Dru didn't think she had thought about what's next. "The horses are on the mend and you now have all your answers."

"I guess," she hesitated, "I can't take care of the property myself, so I'll sell it," she sighed. "We had it paid off a long time ago in preparation for retirement. It should be a good retirement fund and my sister has invited me to stay in Seattle with her permanently."

"No way," Nikki gasped.

Dru glanced over at her. Her kids really needed to work on their poker faces.

"The vote on the horses was not the only vote we took in the kitchen." Dru told her.

Cora's eyebrows went up in surprise.

"We would like to offer you a permanent position with Tagger Enterprises." Grayson smiled as Cora's eyes widened and her smile grew. Matt and Nikki sat up straight in their chairs, anticipating her answer.

Scott continued, "Jordan and Leah will be thrilled to have you stay on as cook."

"Oh! Of course!" Cora beamed.

"We would also like you to continue with the computer work on the horses but we want to add in The Stable and ranch horses." Scott finished.

"Yes, yes!" Cora clapped her hands excitedly. "Does that mean I get to see the ranch I've heard so much about?"

They all laughed then headed out to the barn.

They stood at the barn doors and watched the kids and horses. They were reaching the end of Dr. Mark's cautionary period of 10 days for the horses to survive and didn't want to lose any just because their focus was slipping.

They waited until Jordan and Leah returned from work and Jack arrived from The Stables before they called a family meeting. They stressed how important it was to continue to watch the horses. Everyone understood.

The news of Cora's employment with Tagger Enterprises went over as well as they thought it would. Dru noticed Jordan and Leah were all smiles but had glanced hesitantly between each other. She also noticed, in the last week, that Wade had attached himself to Cora. But now with the news that she would be staying, he was standing in the back of the group looking out the barn door; his face unreadable. Dru touched Cora's arm to get her attention and nodded towards Wade.

Cora walked to Wade and stood next to him. His large brown eyes turned to her.

"I'm very happy to stay here with your family and the horses." Cora told him.

"I'm very happy, too."

"Then what are you worried about?"

"I'm not worried."

"Then why do you look worried?"

"I was just wondering if your husband would be happy you have a new family."

Cora was overwhelmed, and pulled him into a hug and held tightly.

******

Over the next couple of weeks the kids and adults shared their time between taking care of the horses and running the summer events at The Stables. As Libby continued to mother the horses, the new Tagger Herd continued to put on weight. Kit and Cora's colt had become fast pasture buddies and wouldn't leave each other's side.

On a quiet Saturday morning, the Tagger Trio walked towards the barn where the kids were waiting for a surprise. Jordan, Leah, Jack, and Cora were guarding the barn door making sure no one peeked.

The Trio smiled at each other. This was a good day at the Tagger Homestead.

As they stepped into the barn they spread out their arms showing the kids the dozen halters and lead ropes for their horses. Their eyes widened.

"Dr. Mark approved taking the horses for walks in the pasture for an hour a day." Grayson announced.

The barn filled with excitement with the kids running to grab the color of halter they wanted for their horses.

As the halters were placed on the horses, Leah, Cora, and Dru haltered Libby, Kit, and the Zippo colt.

Dru walked Libby to the gate that led to the north pasture. The two watched their herds make their way into the green pasture.

The first to walk by them were Leah and Kit who excitedly turned to welcome the little herd to her pasture. The parade continued;

Matt and Trooper
Nikki and Harvey
Wade and Dollar
Jordan and Rooster
Nora and Arcturus
Scott and Scarecrow
Reilly and Rufio
Jack and Cooper
Sadie and Little Ghost
Grace and Buttercup
Grayson and Eli
Cora and her Zippo Colt

The horse's bodies were beginning to show signs of healing. Their hindquarters and backs were starting to fill in with muscle and the missing hair was growing back. Eyes were shining with excitement and ears were twisting non-stop taking in all the new sights in front of them. They bit at each strand of grass like it was the first time they had seen one.

While Libby grazed, Dru leaned against the fence and watched the herd enjoy their first visit to the pasture and her family and friends enjoying the moment. There was laughter, excitement and most of all…*love*.
Whether four-legged or two-legged, their lives had changed forever and their stories had just begun. ..

THE TAGGER HERD

BOOK TWO

WADE TAGGER

CHAPTER ONE

"I have the most boring dad in the world."

Sitting in the front seat of the truck, his arm wrapped in a bright blue cast from fingers to shoulder, Wade watched his dad talking to the man at the hardware store. His arm was resting comfortably on a pillow on the middle console. As hard as he tried to keep his eyelids up, they fell back down and he was in darkness again.

When they opened, his boring dad was talking on the phone in front of the Kubota tractor store. The collar on his denim jacket was lifted up and the black cowboy hat was pulled down low to protect him from the chilly October day. He ended the call when a man came out of the store and handed him a box, "Here you go, Scott."

"Thanks Greg…I appreciate this. I didn't want to leave him out here alone," He handed the man a credit card in return and the man went back in the store. His boring dad stood quietly staring down the road until the man returned with his receipt. They shook hands and his dad returned to the truck. Everything went dark again.

When the light returned, they were driving down the road towards the white plumes of smoke coming from the paper mill where his mother worked. Wade loved coming this way because there were trains all over the place. His mom told him they used the trains to move product the mill manufactured.

The train track ran between the road and the security building that led into her work. A train was moving slowly down the track keeping pace with their truck. Its path blocked the entrance to the security gate, so they stopped and waited behind a large semi-truck.

As the train cars passed, Wade could see his mother's car in the gap between them. She must have driven from the far side of the manufacturing plant to meet them at the gate.

His head was so heavy it felt like someone had filled it with a bunch of rocks, but he finally managed to turn his head enough to see his dad. He was watching her car, too. Everything went dark again.

Wade could hear his mother's voice but couldn't get his eyes to open to see her. She asked how he was and his dad said he was sleeping a lot then there was silence.

"Jordan," His dad called out. "We need to talk."

Wade managed to get his eyes open long enough to see his mother walking away carrying papers in her hand and ignoring his dad. See, she thought he was boring too.

Wade looked up at his dad who was sitting quietly watching her walk away. Her straight shoulder length black hair was swinging as she walked. She climbed in her car without looking back at them, then turned to drive back to her office building.

Wade sighed…so boring….and his eyes closed.

When they opened again, they were driving through town, the radio on, his dad humming to the tune…it went dark.

Bells were ringing…the ones that signaled the end of school… his eyes flew open. They were sitting in front of the school and he lifted his tired eyes up to his dad.

"Those pain killers are kicking your butt today," He smiled warmly then reached over to brush Wade's hair away from his eyes. "Are you still hurting?"

"I don't know," It came out as a dry whisper.

His dad chuckled as he reached down on the floor in front of Wade. "I stopped and got you some Gatorade," A bottle appeared and his dad opened it and lifted it to Wade's mouth. The cool liquid felt good on his lips and down his throat. A few drops ran down his chin. Wade tried to lift his unhurt arm but it was filled with rocks too.

"I'll get it, Buddy," His dad wiped the drops from his chin.

Wade tried to smile, but he wasn't sure it actually happened. He loved his dad calling him Buddy.

"Want another drink?" He was leaning across the truck console so he was close. He smelled good...Wade's eyes closed again.

Somewhere, in the fog in his head, he could hear Sadie talking about Wade's tenth birthday party and Nora was talking about not going to school on Thursday and Friday because of the teacher's conferences.

Wade's eyes opened again and he could see the rodeo grounds...they were headed home. The Homestead was only 5 minutes away from the big arena. Everything went dark again.

The truck slowed down and made the turn into The Homestead driveway. Wade's eyes opened to see his dad only drove half way up the drive and stopped. He was pointing his phone at the little herd that were walking and trotting to them; the same they did every time they saw a truck.

"Can we get out Uncle Scott?" Sadie asked. The door opened before he answered. She was headed for Little Ghost, it's where she went every night after school. Her parents had to drag her out of the cold barn every night.

"Don't get your school clothes too dirty," He called out to them.

Wade tried to see what his dad was doing with the phone but he had a hard time focusing. When his eyes finally cleared, he could see his dad recording the herd as they neared the fence. Wade tried to lift his head to see, "Dad?" He whispered.

"What's up, Buddy?" He asked and laid the phone on the seat.

"Can I get out?" His throat was dry making his voice gravelly.

"I don't think that's a good idea right now."

Wade leaned back against the seat. He could feel the tears fill his eyes and tried to make them stop by squeezing his eyelids tight.

He felt a hand on his forehead.

"I'm sorry, Buddy," Wade could hear the concern in his voice and his eyes opened to see sad eyes looking back at him. "I know you want to see Rooster and Dollar but you're a bit warm right now." He gently wiped the tear away that had escaped. "I promise we'll come out tonight and see them, but now, you need to get some solid sleep."

"OK…" Wade sighed. His dad would keep the promise, he always did.

The truck started moving and Wade tried to watch the horses as long as he could but everything went dark again. The truck stopped and he heard a door open and close; then the door next to him opened. Wade could feel his dad lean in the truck and pain shot up his arm and shoulder when the casted arm was lifted from the console. Wade groaned loudly and cried out.

"Sorry Buddy, I tried to move it as careful as possible." He was lifted and another groan escaped as the ache began to increase.

"It hurts, Dad." Wade moaned as he leaned onto his shoulder.

"I know, Buddy. I'll get you upstairs and get you another pain killer."

"Where's Mavis and Bart?" The cow dogs usually greeted them.

"Up at the ranch with Jessup."

He was carried up to the back deck of the house and he heard the back door open.

"Scott, is he alright?" Wade opened his eyes in time to see Cora's concerned expression.

"Hi Cora," Wade tried to smile at her. She always made him smile and he always felt warm and protected when she was around. He wondered if that's how grandparents made you feel. His eyes started to close again.

"Hi back, young man," She smiled softly and stepped back as he was carried through the door.

"Need pain killers," His dad told her and carried him down the hall then up the stairs to the bedrooms. "They're in the truck."

He felt Matt's big bed engulf him as he was lowered onto it. Matt was at college and the bigger bed was safer for him and the cast. The pillow was adjusted under the casted arm and the pain started to subside. "That's good," Wade whispered.

He opened his eyes enough to look up at a very worried expression, "I love you, Dad." He whispered and saw the smile spread across his dad's face.

"Stay awake, just a couple minutes longer, Buddy."

His shoes were removed and since he was wearing sweatpants the blanket was laid over the top of him and tucked in around the sides.

Wade stretched his eyebrows up to keep his eyes open. Cora came in and handed his dad the medicine. After swallowing it, Wade nodded…or tried to…and closed his eyes. A hand touched his forehead again and then nothing.

******

Wade was riding Rooster across the north pasture at the ranch. Dollar, Eli, Scarecrow, Harvey and Arcturus were running next to them. "I wonder where the other horses are," He shouted to Rooster. They galloped across the top of the mountain with trees to the left and pasture to the right. The wind stung at his eyes, but he didn't care, he just reached up and pulled his cowboy hat down lower and tighter. The energy from the horse passed into his legs and up his body so he leaned forward and encouraged Rooster to run faster. Both their hearts were racing.

Wind in his face and the other horses running and jumping over fallen trees and rocks; he was in heaven!

Wade saw his dad's big grey horse, Monty, run out of the trees next to them. He suddenly felt cold and his heart began beating wildly; this time out of fear instead of excitement. The fear was rising up into his throat, he needed to scream but it wouldn't come out. The large horse's hooves were hitting the ground so hard it made the ground shake and Wade could feel the vibration move through Rooster and into his own stomach.

Monty turned from running with them, to running at them. His eyes seemed to glow red. With each stride Rooster took, Monty took two. He was catching up to them! Steam started coming out of Monty's nose as he ran at them. Wade kicked Rooster harder to make him go faster. He was breathing so hard his lungs hurt and the fear was so intense he thought his heart was going to explode.

Monty was right next to them, he was going to run right into them! Wade needed to keep the grey horse from Rooster. Trying to distract Monty and protect Rooster, Wade screamed and jumped off his red horse.

As he was hurtling through the air, he could hear voices; it sounded like his mom and Matt. Wade looked down and saw the ground getting closer. His whole body tensed to prepare for the imminent impact as he screamed.

"Wade!" It was Matt's voice.

Wade's eyes flew open. There was no pasture or mountains, no Monty, no Rooster, but his heart was racing and he could feel the pain from his arm. It felt like someone was stabbing it.

His mom's scared eyes were looking down at him. Matt was looking just as scared.

Wade didn't say anything, but just lay quietly trying to slow down his breathing. A trickle of sweat ran down the side of his face; his mom placed a cool towel on his skin and wiped it away. Her soft touch and gentle smile helped calm his heart.

"That was one heck of a nightmare," She said nervously. Her dark brown, almost black eyes glistened with unshed tears. "Take deep breaths," She demonstrated a deep breath for him. He copied her and they breathed together a couple times until Wade could feel himself gaining control. His lungs didn't hurt anymore.

"I'm OK," He whispered.

"You had us scared there," Matt knelt next to the bed. His cousin's eyes were more green than brown today as Wade smiled up at him. Matt was his hero, but he had been gone the last couple weeks at college.

"You're home." Wade told him.

"I came to check on you."

"Are you staying for my birthday?" Wade hoped. His voice was barely a whisper.

Matt grinned, "I wouldn't miss your big double digit birthday, you goof ball." Matt brushed away the hair from Wade's eyes, just like his dad always did. "I have to head back in the morning but it's only an hour away, so I'll be back in time."

"The party's not until Saturday." Wade reminded him.

"I'll be here Friday." Matt promised.

Behind Matt, his dad appeared at the door with a panicked look; his chest heaved from breathing fast. He must have run up the stairs.

"Hi, Dad," Wade smiled. "Matt's gonna be here for my birthday."

His dad's shoulders relaxed, "Jordan…?"

"He was having a bad nightmare and we couldn't get him to wake up," She told him. Her voice sounded angry, but his dad just nodded then turned back to Wade with a smile.

"Want to talk about it?" He asked softly.

Wade frowned, he felt the heaviness in his heart returning. He looked down at the cast and didn't say anything…he was too afraid. The tears started building and he had to take deep breaths to make them stop. His chest starting heaving uncontrollably. His lungs hurt from breathing too deep, then the breaths started coming too fast and his head was getting foggy which scared him.

"Wade, it's OK," He could hear his mom…the tears were running down her cheeks. He was scaring her again, too. The guilt made Wade feel even worse and made his tears start flowing and he couldn't stop them. The sob coming up in his throat tasted bad. Before he realized what was happening, he was throwing up then gasping for air.

Matt reached behind and lifted his shoulders so the vomit wouldn't choke him. His dad raced to the other side of the bed to support his cast.

"Relax, Wade," Matt whispered to him.

"It's OK, Buddy," His dad spoke softly.

Wade looked into his dad's concerned eyes. His face was just inches away from his own.

"It's OK," His dad tried to reassure him with his eyes.

Wade took a deep breath to try to stop all the little rapid breaths. It made his lungs hurt even more and he started to panic thinking it would never stop. Another breath and his lungs seemed full…he couldn't get any more air in his lungs! He looked up at his parents with terror in his eyes.

His dad grabbed the blankets and threw them off the bed. "Matt, you have a better angle. Pick him up and follow me."

Matt did as he was told and lifted Wade from the bed with his dad helping position the cast over Wade's body. "You got him?"

"Yeah," Matt answered.

Wade looked to his dad then at Matt. He didn't want to go back to the hospital. The panic rose again as they made their way down the hall making Wade gasp again and the air filled his lungs but he started breathing even faster from the fear. His whole body was tingling.

Wade felt the sob coming up again. "I'm going to throw up!" He gasped out between breaths.

"Don't be doing that, kid." Matt started moving faster down the long hallway. "You throw up on me and I'll throw up on you and we'll have a real mess."

Wade looked down through the fog and saw everyone at the base of the steps looking at them. All their faces showed concern. Sadie and Nora were crying. It made him feel worse and the air started coming out of him in large gasps and he dug his face into Matt's neck.

"Backup!" His dad ordered everyone.

"Scott, where are you going?" Wade could hear the panic in his mom's voice.

He peeked out from under Matt's chin. His dad didn't answer because he was already out the back door with Matt walking quickly to keep up with him. Wade couldn't stop the panicked breathing…his whole body started to shake.

"No…hospital…" Wade cried. He couldn't tell if it was out loud or not.

His dad ran past the trucks and headed to the barn. Matt was running behind them, Wade bouncing in his arms.

Wade's eyes started to roll back into his head and a blackness was taking over.

The movement stopped.

"Wade!" His dad shouted.

Wade tried hard to open his eyes but couldn't. Someone started lifting his eyelids up for him, so he could see his dad through the haze and then Dollar and Rooster behind him. Their heads were up and ears alert.

The stall door had been opened and a bale of straw placed in front of it. His dad sat down on the end of the bale, straddling it and then he reached for Wade. Matt lowered him into his arms and they stretched his legs out over the rest of the bale.

Both horses' noses immediately lowered and nuzzled his face. He could feel their breath go down his neck.

"Concentrate on their breathing," His dad whispered in his ear.

Their breath on his skin tickled and he wanted to laugh but his lungs wouldn't let him. He listened to their breathing and tried to match his breaths with theirs. His lungs start to relax and the breathing started to slow down. The fog slowly cleared out of his head.

"There you go. Just look at the horses," His dad's voice made it through the haze.

Wade reached up with his good arm and touched Dollar's face. He loved the smell of horses and the feel of their soft hair. It was thicker now that winter was coming so they seemed fuzzier. He felt something hitting his cast and looked down to see Rooster trying to bite it.

"I think he's trying to free you," Matt said. Wade looked up and smiled. Breathing was easier now; the breaths not as rapid. He had stopped shaking and could see clearly.

"No," Wade whispered to Rooster and gently moved the horse's mouth from the cast. Rooster went for his hand instead to see if there was a treat in it. Wade giggled and leaned back against his dad. He could feel his dad's racing heartbeat against his back; his arms were wrapped tightly around Wade's waist.

"It's OK, Dad, they stopped coming," Wade whispered about the shallow breaths. The arms relaxed.

Rooster turned his attention to Matt and tried nibbling on his hair making Wade grin. Matt turned up his face and blew air up at the horse. Rooster bounced his head up and down then checked Matt's hands for treats.

The strength and warmth from his dad's arms made Wade's body relax. He felt loved and protected; like nothing could hurt him. He looked down at his cast and wiggled the fingers coming out the end. A twinge of fear rose to his heart. If his dad ever found out how he broke his arm, he would lose his dad's love forever.

CHAPTER TWO

It was quiet and comfortable in the barn. Matt had pulled up another bale of straw for a seat and the two men were talking about college classes he liked and didn't like. Matt had thrown hay into the stall to keep the two horses close to the door and Wade. They were grazing quietly. He had fed the other horses too and although Wade couldn't see them, he could hear them eating and moving around. Other than on a tractor with his dad, this was his favorite place on earth.

Uncle Grayson walked into the barn looking even taller than normal from Wade's view on the straw bale. His stomach grumbled when he saw the tray of food his uncle was carrying. He also had a shirt over his shoulder. Wade forgot that he had puked and looked down. There was vomit down the front of his shirt.

"Gross," He whispered.

Matt laughed. "Just be glad you didn't vomit on me going down the hall or we would both be covered in a whole lot more than that."

Uncle Grayson handed Matt the food, then walked into the office. He returned carrying scissors.

Wade chuckled as his uncle cut his shirt off.

"One less shirt in the laundry pile," Uncle Grayson winked.

They carefully maneuvered the clean shirt over his cast and head. He snuggled back into his dad when they were done. "What's for dinner?" Wade asked.

He drank the cup of soup slowly and enjoyed sitting with the men. They were talking about trucks, tractors, and cows; all the good stuff.

Wade glanced over at Rooster who was eating next to Dollar.

It had only been four months since they found the horses in Cora's barn. Rooster's front legs had been stuck in the mud and he hadn't been able to move for days. The horse had worn leg wraps for weeks trying to support the ligaments and tendons as they healed but he still walked awkwardly.

When Rooster shifted close enough, Matt reached over and patted him on the shoulder then rubbed down his legs to his knees. The red horse stood quietly and took in the attention.

"I took video of him walking today and sent it to Dr. Mark," His dad said. Wade's eyebrows went up; that's what his dad was doing!

"He answer back?" Uncle Grayson asked.

Wade felt his dad move but couldn't tell what the answer was.

"It may be time to take him up to WSU," Uncle Grayson turned to Matt. "Press harder and see if he reacts."

Matt slid his hand down again until he reached the knee. He squeezed lightly then slowly worked his way around the knee. Rooster didn't react so he lifted the hoof and bent the knee as if putting shoes on the horse. Rooster jumped backwards away from him.

"He didn't like that," Wade said. He looked over at his uncle who had leaned over and was resting his elbows on his knees watching the red horse walk back to Matt who stretched out a hand and petted him, apologizing for hurting him.

"All the horses look a lot better," Wade said. "Rooster's back bone is almost all gone." Nikki and Dr. Mark had worked together on a nutrition plan and the horses were gaining weight.

"They do look better, Buddy." His dad squeezed him tighter. Wade smiled down into his soup. Even after he scared them tonight and made them worried, his dad still called him Buddy.

"They've all put on a lot of weight," His uncle agreed with him. "Arcturus hasn't gained as much, actually looks like he might be losing. We should talk to Nikki about changing his feed."

Rooster's nose appeared above his soup cup, and he sniffed. Wade giggled and tried to get the horse to drink some. His dad stuck his finger in the soup and put it into Rooster's mouth. The horse stuck out his tongue a few times then lifted his head in the air; his upper lip curled up towards the ceiling, showing the pink underneath. He stretched and stretched trying to get rid of the soup.

They all laughed and the sound echoed throughout the barn. Wade turned and could see all the horses come to the stall doors to see what was happening. He loved being in here with all of them. Over the summer, he and the rest of the kids had spent a lot of time with them. They spent more nights sleeping in the barn than they did sleeping in the house.

Rooster finally gave up trying to remove the soup and went back to eating his hay so Wade looked down at the horse's knees. He thought about what his uncle had said about WSU, the hospital for animals in Pullman.

"Dad?" Wade said.

"Yeah?"

"Do you think Rooster will have to have surgery like I did?"

He saw his uncle and Matt look at his dad. Their expressions were unreadable.

He felt his dad sigh before he answered, "Yeah, he probably does, son."

Wade turned and looked at the horse, "Will he be OK?"

"I honestly don't know, but before we do any more worrying about him, I'll call tomorrow to see if we can get him up there as soon as possible."

"Can I go, too?"

He could see the look of concern on Matt's and his uncle's faces.

"I promise I'll be a grownup. Rooster will be scared going by himself without his friends. He'll need me…like I needed him tonight."

His dad's arms squeezed Wade again and his chin rested on top of his head. "Well, who could argue with that? If it isn't during school hours. I think you'll be missing enough school time with your broken arm."

"I don't think we have school this Thursday and Friday." Wade snuggled into his dad. The soup had warmed him and made him tired.

"We'll see in the morning. I don't know that they will be able to do it that quickly."

"We're headed to Cora's property tomorrow," Uncle Grayson reminded them. "We need to winterize the house."

"She hasn't been there since before her husband died," Matt nodded. "That's going to be tough on her."

Only Aunt Dru had been to the property since they had found the horses. She had driven into the property to check on the place but never stepped out of her truck. Wade could barely remember what it looked like, besides the barn, which he remembered as dark and haunting.

He watched Dollar lay down with a plop. The horse groaned; he always did when he laid down. The horse's pelvic bones used to stick out but now there was barely a bone showing. Rooster and Dollar looked so much better…he sighed as his eyes slowly closed.

******

Wade felt the pain in his arm and opened his eyes to see what was wrong…his mind was fuzzy. It took him a minute to realize he was back in Matt's bed. The sky out the window was just starting to lighten. He tried to move but his legs seemed to be stuck. He looked down and saw Nora sleeping at the end of the bed. Wade smiled; it seemed like forever since he'd talked to her.

He tried to move, but the arm pain shot through him again. He pushed his foot against his sister to wake her up.

"What?" She gasped frantically as she rolled off the end of the bed, jumped up and looked at him nervously. Her long black hair was loose and looked wild around her head. She was wearing her white pajamas.

He giggled, "You look like a crazy ghost."

She grinned back and lifted her hands over her head and waved them around. They both laughed softly and she climbed back up on the bed.

"Will it hurt if I come up there?"

"It already hurts, so it doesn't matter."

There was just enough room between the cast and the edge of the bed for her to crawl up and lay her head on the other pillow. He and Matt had shared a room. When Matt left for college he told Wade to sleep in his bed when he was away. It was a lot bigger than Wade's bed. He looked over at his bed, but Matt wasn't there.

"Where's Matt?"

"He's sleeping downstairs. He didn't want his snoring to wake you up."

They lay quietly for a few minutes before she spoke again.

"You really scared us tonight," she whispered.

"I scared myself."

"What happened?"

"I don't know." He didn't think he could explain it.

"Mom yelled at Dad again."

"For what?" Wade frowned. "It wasn't his fault."

"She said it was because he asked you if you wanted to explain your nightmare."

"We do that all the time…we always talk about our bad dreams to them so the nightmares will go away. It wasn't Dad's fault."

Nora sighed, "I just think she needed to yell at him, because he got you to calm down and she just made you cry more."

"That's not fair."

"Nope," She turned on her back and then twisted her head so she was facing him. They looked into each other's eyes. "Mom, Aunt Dru, Aunt Leah, and Cora stood outside the barn doors all night holding hands until Dad carried you back in the house. Mom was afraid to go in…she thought it might upset you again."

Wade felt the sadness in his heart again. He hated making them all feel bad. "Do you think I'm the reason they're fighting all the time?"

Nora shook her head with a frown. "No…they were arguing way before your accident. I think it just added to what they argue about."

"Are we supposed to take sides?" He hoped not.

"I don't think so."

"We just wait until they get better?"

"I guess so," She turned back on her side to face him and tucked her hands under her cheek. "Will you tell me how you broke your arm? I promise I won't tell anyone…pinky swear."

Wade turned his head and looked up at the ceiling. He didn't feel the short breathing coming back or the tears. Maybe he should tell her…he needed to tell someone. Then he remembered that the last time he told her a secret she told Sadie. Nora never kept secrets.

He didn't answer, but tried to adjust his arm and the pain shot into his shoulder making him grimace.

"Do you want me to get your medicine?" She asked and sat up.

"I don't think they would be happy if you gave me one."

"Do you want me to get Mom or Dad?"

He sighed, "Aunt Dru," He didn't want to make his parents fight again.

***

The next time Wade woke was when Nora climbed out of the bed. Aunt Dru had given him the pain killer and let Nora stay in the room with him. He moved his casted arm a few inches to see if it still hurt. There was a dull ache but not the sharp pain. He used his good arm to adjust it in front of him and tried to sit up. He couldn't get up.

"I feel like a turtle on his back," Wade chuckled.

He was looking around trying to figure out how to get up when his mom appeared at his door. She was smiling warmly.

"Hi, Mom," He smiled back, his voice barely a whisper.

"Feeling better?" She walked into the room, sat next to him, and touched his forehead.

"Lots better."

"Well, it looks like your fever broke," She softly ran her finger down his cheek like she had done since he was a baby. He smiled at the touch and her warmth.

"Have the kids left?"

"They're eating breakfast."

"Can I go down, too?"

"Of course."

She helped him sit up and slide to the side of the bed then carefully put the sling for the cast over his head and adjusted it tightly around his arm.

"Careful," She put an arm behind his back and one under his cast to help brace him. "You might get a bit dizzy."

Wade stood motionless next to the bed until the dizziness went away. He nodded, "OK."

They walked slowly out the bedroom and down the long hall to the top of the steps and stopped. Looking down the long stairwell then to each other, they smiled. "I don't think I can do the steps, Mom."

"Grayson?" She called down the steps.

Wade's head jerked up and he looked at her in shock. Why didn't she call for his dad? Was he gone? Did he scare him away last night? Did he find out what happened and stopped loving him and left? The tightness in his lungs returned and reached his good hand to his chest. He looked down the steps and saw his uncle AND his dad at the bottom. He took a deep breath and the tightness went away.

His dad ran up the stairs while his uncle stayed at the bottom. When he reached the top, he glared at his wife before smiling at Wade. "Good morning, Buddy."

"Hi, Dad." Wade grinned. He called him Buddy, so everything was OK.

He was carried down the stairs and into the kitchen where all the kids greeted him excitedly. Matt had already left to go back to college.

Cora gave him a smile and a careful hug then scrunched her face. "You stink, young man."

"He threw up!" Sadie laughed.

"Well, you're going to need a bath before I ride in a truck with you." She ruffled his hair and turned to get his breakfast. Wade's eyebrows shot up in surprise.

"Blueberry pancakes…my favorite!" He looked up at Cora with an appreciative grin. "Thank you."

She smiled back. It was the smile that made him feel warm inside. "I was hoping you would have an appetite this morning. Just eat slowly so you don't get sick again."

He nodded and started eating. All the parents and kids came in, greeted him, and slowly left until it was just him, Cora, and his dad sitting at the table.

He took one last bite of pancake and leaned back in the chair. Stomach full, he looked down; he had only eaten half of his normal breakfast but there was no way he could eat more.

He looked up at his dad, "Have you called about Rooster yet?"

His dad laughed, "It's not even 8:00 yet, son."

CHAPTER THREE

Wade sat in the back seat of the truck with his dad on his left side and Cora on the right. His casted arm was resting comfortably on his dad's leg. Uncle Grayson was driving and Aunt Dru was in the shotgun seat in the front. He rested his head back and watched the blue river pass by. The leaves on the trees along the river had turned yellow and he liked how the blue and yellow looked together.

His mind went to Rooster and the video they had sent up to the school. The professors and doctors had been reading about the herd's progress on Facebook and the different magazine articles that had been written. Dr. Mark had sent them information about the herd and they were very interested in seeing Rooster. The clinic had just had an appointment cancellation for the next day and wanted Rooster brought to them by 10:00 in the morning.

Wade still wasn't going to school so his dad agreed he could go with them to the appointment, if he promised to be an adult. He leaned his head against his dad's shoulder. Wade had been so eager to go with them earlier, but now, as the time got closer, he felt the nerves in his stomach. He loved Rooster and the thought of him going into surgery just hurt his heart.

"Are you OK?" His dad asked.

Wade looked down and realized he had touched his chest again. He wanted to tell his dad that it was his heart hurting, not his lungs. Instead he leaned his head up and looked at him. He had his brown cowboy hat on and he looked like a cowboy from the movies, "I'm scared for Rooster."

"So am I, son," he sighed. "But if he's in pain, we have to think of what's best for Rooster."

"He doesn't act like he's hurting unless you bend his knee," Wade reminded him.

"We don't really know that. Sometimes you just get used to being in pain," He touched Wade's cast. "Do you still hurt from your arm?"

"Not as much as I did before."

"Is it because it doesn't hurt or because you've gotten used to the pain?"

Wade lifted his arm and realized it did still hurt. "It still aches, but since it doesn't hurt as bad as it was, I don't notice it as much." He admitted.

His dad nodded, "That could be what happened to Rooster. I'm also worried because he doesn't run in the pasture when the other horses start running"

Wade sighed and looked down at his cast, "Will Rooster get worse?"

"It could…as he grows and puts on more weight, it will put a lot of stress on his joints. If he's just putting up with the pain now, then it might become very painful later."

"Do you think there's a chance they can fix him?" He asked hopefully.

"I hope so, Buddy. I really do." He grasped the fingers that were sticking out of the end of the cast. It was the closest he could come to holding his hand.

Everyone had become quiet; listening to their conversation. The truck started to slow down.

Wade looked up and recognized the turn up the dirt road to Cora's house, then turned and looked at her. She was staring down the road, tears rimmed her eyes, and she seemed really pale. He reached over and took her hand and squeezed tightly which made her turn and look at him. She smiled sadly.

"Are you OK?" He asked. She nodded but didn't say anything. "You look kind of sickly." He told her honestly.

She chuckled quietly, "I'm just thinking of the past and all that is back there." She smiled, squeezed his hand and her eyes returned to the road.

Wade looked at his dad. He was looking at her too and his face showed his concern.

They stopped at the gate and Aunt Dru got out and opened it. Wade smiled. It was nice to ride shotgun until you realized you're the one responsible for opening all the gates. This time it wasn't bad, but their ranch had four gates to go through before you got to the house.

Aunt Dru left the gate open. They weren't worried about anything getting out or anyone getting in while they were there.

The house was even scarier this time, Wade thought. The sun was hidden behind the clouds so the house looked dark and gloomy. He wondered what it looked like when Cora had lived there. What did the inside of the house look like?

They stopped in front of the house and, like last time, they all hesitated before leaving the truck.

Aunt Dru turned in her seat to look at Cora. Her eyes widened in concern, "Are you OK?"

Cora's hand was shaking in his which made him look up at her. She seemed even whiter than she was a few minutes before.

Cora nodded, "I didn't realize it was going to be so hard. It looks so forlorn...and haunted." Wade quietly agreed. Haunted was the word he used the first time they were there.

"Take your time," Uncle Grayson said from the front seat. "We're not in any hurry."

Cora sat quietly in the seat and stared at the house. They all waited for her to reach for the door handle before they did.

As Cora walked to the front door, Wade's dad helped him out of the truck then turned to retrieve the empty boxes out of the back for the items she wanted to take with her.

Wade stood outside and watched the adults disappear into the house. He sighed heavily. As curious as he was to see the inside of her house, he also wanted to go out to the barns. He had to move fast before the adults stopped him. Walking quickly, he passed the house and headed to the upper barn that had held Dollar and Rooster. He turned once to see if he was being watched…no one had seen him yet.

The doors to the barn were closed. He looked down to see if there was any mud blocking the doorway like it was the day they found the horses. No mud but the shovel and hoe were still resting where they left them.

Wade gripped the door with his good arm and pulled hard. He struggled to push it open all the way, having to lean against it and push with his back.

It was just as dark on the inside as he remembered. With one final glance at the house, he stepped into the barn. His mind went back to the first time he had been there. Dollar was the first horse they had seen; in the stall to his left. The horse's big eyes looked at them desperately. Wade walked to the stall and glanced in; the floor was still covered in mud but it was dried and hard. The next stall had been Arcturus' then it was Rufio's.

He was at the back of the barn and looked towards the main doors. It was really gloomy and spooky in there, he couldn't imagine what the horses felt when they spent weeks alone and starving in such a dark cave.

Across the aisle was Cooper's original stall. Wade looked in…it was the darkest stall of all, which had made it hard to see the black horse when they rescued them. A bucket still lay in the middle of the stall. It looked desolate.

He moved to Little Ghost's stall. The feeder was still lying on the ground and the dark marks of dried blood were on the wall where the horse had cut himself. The wounds were healed but the scars would be pronounced. Sadie didn't care, she loved him anyway. After Angel died, she and Little Ghost had become almost inseparable. Only when she was forced to, did she leave the horse's side. As much as she loved school, she loved the horse more so the beginning of school had been hard on her.

Wade walked to the next stall; Rooster's. He hesitantly walked in and looked at the ground. The holes were still visible where he and Aunt Dru had dug the starving red horse out of the mud. He knelt down, and with his good hand put his fingers in the holes. He closed his eyes and remembered the sad look he and Aunt Dru had shared when they had begun digging at the mud.

"Wade?" Aunt Dru's voice echoed in the barn but he didn't open his eyes. He realized that he was crying again…the sadness of the memory taking over his heart.

His aunt's arm slowly slid around his shoulders and she pulled him into a hug; he leaned his head on her shoulder. They sat quietly for a few minutes remembering those terrible hours.

He opened his eyes and looked up at his aunt. Her eyes were sad but she was smiling, trying to comfort him.

"I want to go into Angel's stall," He whispered. She nodded and helped him stand.

She moved around to his good arm and took his hand as they left the barn and headed down to the lower barn.

"I never did go down to this barn," Wade reminded her. As they came around the corner he stopped and looked at the barn. "It's pretty." He said. It was red with white trim; kind of like the one at home.

He started walking again and she opened the doors. Walking past her, he wandered down the aisle looking into the stalls. They weren't muddy like the other ones.

"This one," Aunt Dru walked into the second stall to the right.

He looked up at his aunt. Her long blond hair was pulled back in a ponytail which was sticking out the back of her ball cap that had the Tagger Enterprise's T3E logo on it. The brown ball cap matched the brown denim jacket she was wearing. "This is a nice barn."

"Yes it is," She agreed.

"I don't know why, but I always thought of them as terrible places." He looked around again. "I don't think Cora would have had a terrible place; she would have nice things."

"You're right. She has nice things."

The comment made him think of the house. "What does the house look like?"

"Let's go up and you can check it out yourself."

"OK."

They walked quietly out the barn and shut the doors behind them. As they walked up to the house, he forgot about the barns; they weren't haunted after all.

Cora's house wasn't very big compared to The Homestead. Wade stood in the large living room and knew Cora was to the left in a bedroom. To the right was another bedroom. In front of him, down a little hallway he could see the bathroom and a kitchen. Just beyond those was a utility room. That was it. He figured they didn't need much more for only two people.

The pictures on a table against the wall caught his attention. One of Cora and her husband caught his eye. It was the first time he had seen Wes. He wasn't much taller than Cora and was wearing a grey cowboy hat. Wade looked closer. Their arms were around each other and they looked really happy.

"We were at my sister's 50th birthday party in that picture," Cora's voice came from behind him.

"You look happy."

"We always were," she smiled.

She took the picture he was looking at and put it in the box she was packing. He helped her gather the rest of the pictures and put them in the box.

Wade continued to look around. He didn't see anyone else, "Where is everyone?"

"They turned all the water off and prepared the house for winter, so I sent them out to the tack room to get everything. No sense it being stolen or ruined up here. We can put it to use at The Homestead or the ranch."

She continued to pack so he wandered down the hallway to the kitchen. There was a single plate, fork, and coffee mug in the sink that were covered in a heavy layer of dust. Wade frowned at them. They were from Wes' last meal… a sadness came over him which made him look down the hall to Cora. If he felt that sad…how bad was it for her?

Wade looked around the kitchen…everything was covered with dust but it was orderly and there were pretty plates decorated with birds on the wall. They were nice and he was sure that she wanted them so he carefully took them from the wall and placed them on the table.

Another glance at the fork, plate, and mug in the sink …he didn't want her to see such a sad sight, so with a little difficulty he washed and dried and put them away.

He heard his dad talking to Cora in the living room. Wade turned and went to the bedrooms. They were nice too.

"Cora?" He called as he walked down the hallway to find a box for the bird plates. He turned the corner and saw her leaning against the wall, holding her stomach. "Cora! Are you OK?" He hurried to her, took her arm, and walked her to the chair.

"I'm fine, Hon." She smiled up at him.

"No, you're not." He started to walk past her to find his dad.

"No you don't." She grabbed his arm. She might be sick but she still had a pretty strong grip.

"I need to go get Dad, you're sick," he argued.

"Just a little emotional," She assured him. Wade frowned because he knew it was more than that.

"I have something for you," She changed the subject.

"I don't want anything but Dad to help you."

She chuckled. "Wade, I'm fine," She leaned back around the chair. "It's an early birthday gift." She pulled out a lariat.

Wade gasped. It was a big one, like his dad and uncle's.

"This was my husbands," She said as she handed it to him.

He slowly raised his good arm and took the rope.

"I gave this to him a few years ago for his birthday."

Wade didn't know what to say. He just looked at the lariat in amazement. It was coiled perfectly. He rubbed his thumb over the ridges of the rope and bounced it in his hand to feel the weight.

"On the ride back to the house, I'll tell you about some of Wes' best roping moments."

"I wish I could have met him," Wade smiled at her.

"He would have liked you. He had a lot of respect for kids that were hard workers like you, your sister, and cousins."

"How come you didn't have kids?"

"Wes couldn't have them and we never really decided to adopt…then it just got too late in life. My sister had five kids and they had kids…she has twelve grandchildren. We go visit them during the summer and at Christmas. I like Christmas with kids around."

"Does it bother you to talk about him?"

"It did at first, but now I like to talk about him."

"Will you tell me stories about him? I'd like to know."

She smiled gently. It was the smile that made him feel warm inside.

"I'd love to," She looked around the room. "We have a couple photo albums around here somewhere."

"Over here," Wade said and walked to the bookshelf. He lifted the books and put them in one of the boxes.

"Thanks, can you put the other books in there too?"

Wade nodded and placed all the books in the box. "There's some bird plates in the kitchen…I just need a box."

"Oh, good…I love those plates. Wes gave one to me each year on Valentine's Day."

She went to stand up and fell back in the chair.

Wade didn't wait for her to stop him this time…he ran out the door yelling for his dad.

When he turned the corner of the house towards the barn where they were loading the tack into the truck he saw his dad had started running up to the house. His aunt and uncle right behind him.

They began to slow down when they saw Wade, so he waved at them to move faster. "It's Cora!" He yelled. His dad and uncle ran past him; his aunt turned around and ran to the truck.

Wade barely made it to the door when he heard the truck start and the engine grow louder as Aunt Dru was racing to the house.

Both men were kneeling next to Cora when Wade made it back into the house. She was reassuring them that she was fine, but had just lost her balance when she tried to get up. Wade had run out the door before she could stop him. The men looked at each other; by the looks on their faces, they didn't believe her either.

The lariat was lying in the middle of the floor…he didn't realize he had dropped it. He quickly picked it up and sat in the corner chair to stay out of the way as they loaded the boxes Cora had packed. He told Aunt Dru about the bird plates and she carefully packed them.

Wade watched Cora who had leaned back and closed her eyes since they weren't letting her get out of the chair. Her hair had grown a lot since they first met her; it was now down to her shoulders. She looked younger than the 68 she said she was. Before today she always seemed healthy; she did her yoga exercises every morning.

He stood as they started turning off lights. Uncle Grayson helped Cora out of the chair but she insisted on walking without help.

As they rode back to The Homestead, Wade ran his fingertips over the ridges of the rope following the coiled length of it. He was worried about Cora who was now asleep next to him.

She was still sleeping when they parked in front of the doctor's office. Aunt Dru had quietly called them and made an appointment for Cora.

When his dad opened the door, her eye's flickered open and her body stiffened. She was instantly upset.

"I'm not going in there!" She glared.

"You don't have a choice about that," He reached out to her. "Your only choice is if I'm carrying you in or are you walking in?"

CHAPTER FOUR

Wade held the back door open while his dad helped Cora walk into the kitchen of The Homestead. She smiled and thanked him politely.

Behind Cora, Aunt Dru walked up the steps of the patio.

"She'll be fine," Aunt Dru assured him. "The doctor gave her some medicine that will help her out."

Wade nodded then turned and saw his uncle start to unload the tack from the truck into the barn.

"Can I go help Uncle Grayson?" He asked.

"Sure."

The screen door slammed behind him and he carefully stepped down the patio steps. He started running across the driveway to the truck; his new lariat bouncing on his shoulder.

Uncle Grayson came out of the barn, "Stop running." He ordered. "The last thing we need is for you to fall and re-break that arm."

Wade slowed down to a walk, "Would it break again with the cast on?"

His uncle grinned, "You want to find out?"

Wade grinned back, "No."

He handed Wade a saddle pad to take into the barn. The barn was too quiet. All the horses were out in the pasture and Mavis and Bart were at the ranch. Thinking of the dogs up at the ranch was depressing. It was because the family left so fast the night he broke his arm, that the dogs were left at the ranch and not down here with all the kids.

Wade helped unload the truck the best he could. With each trip in the barn he felt his energy waning and he began to drag his feet. When they were done with the tack going in the barn, the truck was backed up to the deck so they could unload Cora's boxes.

Wade held the door open as his uncle carried the boxes into the house and back to Cora's room. He leaned his head back on the door frame as he waited for him to return. The lariat was in his hand; the end resting on the floor. Wade meant to close his eyes for just a second, but it must have been longer. His head jerked down and to keep from falling, he threw it backwards and banged it into the door. "Dang," He mumbled and then heard the laughing. He opened his eyes to see his dad, aunt, and uncle standing in the kitchen watching him. He gave them a tired smile.

"Come on," His dad reached out to take his hand. "You may be 'almost ten' but I think you need a nap."

Wade took a couple steps and realized just how tired he really was, "Dad?"

He stopped and looked down at him.

"I've gotten used to you carrying me," he smiled. "And I'm really, really tired."

The adults laughed at him again as his dad leaned down and picked him up.

"Can I just sleep on the couch and not in bed?" Wade leaned his head on his dad's shoulder.

"Sounds like a good idea, Buddy." He leaned his chin on top of Wade's head so he missed the smile that spread across his son's face when he called him Buddy.

******

Wade woke and heard the adults talking at the small table in the kitchen. He leaned forward to see if Cora was with them. She wasn't. He leaned back and looked at the clock. It was only one o'clock, which meant the kids wouldn't be home for over an hour. He sat up so the sleepiness would leave his head. The lariat was on the floor so he picked it up and set it in his lap and with the tip of his finger traced the coiled rope.

Cora must still be napping. She really didn't look good when she came out of the doctor's office. Although she wasn't in there very long, she seemed worse, not better. He leaned his head on the back of the couch. What if the same happened to Rooster? What if he went into the clinic and came out worse? What if he didn't come out? What if Cora didn't get better?

He shook his head really hard to get the bad thoughts out.

All the bedrooms were upstairs, except for Cora's, and the guest bedroom which Nikki used when she came home from college. He looked down the hall to see if Cora's bedroom door was closed but couldn't see that far down the long hallway. He wanted to talk to her but he was nervous. What if she got worse while he was sleeping?

He felt the depression in his heart. How could he lose both Cora and Rooster?

The dust covered dishes from Wes' last meal flashed in his mind…how sad was that image?

Wade listened to The Trio for a few minutes. He couldn't hear what they were saying, just that they were talking.

How did they make it through the accident that killed their parents and grandparents? The sadness was heavy just THINKING about losing Rooster and Cora. Wade couldn't imagine losing his parents. How did they do it?

He stood up slowly in case the dizziness returned. It didn't, so, lifting his rope over the shoulder with the cast, Wade walked slowly towards the kitchen. With his boots off, he didn't make a sound and their talking continued. They were at the table with their cattle books scattered in front of them. Aunt Dru was writing something in one of the books.

He leaned on the door-jam and watched them for a minute before he blurted out. "How did you do it?"

They looked at him in surprise. "Do what?" His dad asked.

"How did you handle the sadness of the accident?" He didn't have to say what accident; they knew.

They didn't answer; they froze in place. Wade thought they looked like they were playing a game of statue. His aunt stared at him in shock, pencil frozen in place, tears sprung to her eyes. His uncle had been lifting his glass to take a drink and it was frozen in mid-air. His dad had been reaching for one of the work books and his hand froze in place over it. They just stared at him.

"Never mind," Wade sighed and turned away from them and headed down the hallway. He stopped half way and leaned against the wall; depression making it too hard to walk. If they weren't handling the loss, eighteen years later, then how would he be able to handle losing Rooster and Cora?

"Well, we handled that well." He heard Aunt Dru say. They must have thought he had left.

"I don't think that's called handling it at all." His dad answered.

"Where do you think that came from?" Uncle Grayson asked.

"Rooster," His dad answered.

"Probably Cora this morning too," Aunt Dru added.

They were quiet so long he almost left.

"I lost count on how many times people told me I was handling 'it' well or asked me how I was handling 'it', after the accident," His uncle said and sighed heavily.

"How can anyone handle 'it'?" Aunt Dru asked. "One foot in front of the other, one breath after the other, one day goes by, then the next."

"I think it was Matt and Nikki," His uncle said.

"Yeah," She agreed. "Focusing on those two kept me sane."

Wade heard a chair move and footsteps. He waited for them to come into the hall. Instead he heard someone moving away from him then walking back to the table. The chair moved again as they must have sat back down.

"Are you going to talk to Wade?" Aunt Dru asked.

"I honestly don't know what to say," His dad admitted. "Until you go through something like that, you don't know how to handle it." There was a pause. "Well…" Wade heard his dad say. "Next time…you two need to handle questions like that better."

Wade could tell he was joking.

"Us?" His aunt and uncle asked in unison.

"Yeah," His dad chuckled. "I'm the baby brother. I shouldn't have to answer the tough questions."

"It was your son that asked!" Aunt Dru laughed.

"It was your nephew," His dad responded with a chuckle.

A chair moved across the floor making Wade hurry down the hall towards Cora's room. Her door was open, so he peeked around the corner to see if she was awake.

Cora's bedroom wasn't as big as the adult rooms upstairs, they were like mini apartments, but it was big enough to have her bed and a small sitting area next to the big window. There was also a large private bathroom. She was sitting in one of the chairs staring out the window. She saw him and waved him in.

"Are you feeling better?" He asked and walked to the chair across from her. He glanced out the window and saw the herd of horses.

"I am," She smiled. "I was just sitting here watching those beautiful horses," She sighed. "It's so relaxing just watching them wander the pasture grazing."

He pulled his legs up into the chair and settled his lariat on top of them.

"Thank you for the lariat."

"You're welcome. I'm impressed you call it a lariat and not a rope."

"Dad taught me."

"You have a good dad."

Wade nodded, "Are you going to be OK?"

"I am," She shifted in her chair so she faced him. "The doctor gave me some medicine to help. I had a bad reaction to the new vitamins I started taking, so it's not contagious."

"You scared me," He said honestly.

"And you've scared me the last few days," She countered.

"You looked sad when I came in. I'm feeling really sad about you and Rooster."

"I'll be fine…going back to the house…the memories are tough sometimes…and I'm concerned about Rooster, too."

"How do you handle the sadness?"

"Patience," She said softly. "Knowing that it will start to ease and something good will come along and make you forget the sadness for a while. Each time that happens, it eases the loss a little more." She glanced out the window. "Watching the horses...they remind me of how much Wes loved me, and that helps to ease the pain," She looked back at him. "Wes' gift ultimately led me to a whole new family and I adore each and every one of the Tagger herds; horse and human. Being around you and the rest of the kids just fills me with energy."

"I like having you here," Just talking to her made him feel better.

"I like the ranch, too," she commented.

Wade sighed and leaned back against the chair and glanced around. He didn't want to talk about the ranch, so he looked for something to change the subject. He saw her TV and DVD movies lying next to it. "You were watching a movie?"

"Just finished one of my favorites," She smiled at him. "A John Wayne movie, of course."

He sat back up, "Which one?"

"*The Quiet Man.*"

"That's a good one…Mom's favorite," He nodded. "Have you seen *The Cowboys?* It's my favorite. I'd love to be one of the boys."

She chuckled, "I have the DVD over there in that box if you'd like to watch it. It was one of Wes's favorites too."

Wade glanced down at his cast and wiggled his fingers at the end of it. "Nah, what other ones do you have?"

"You don't want to watch *The Cowboys?*" She asked in surprise.

"Does that one have that bad word in it?"

"No, we bought the edited one. Neither Wes nor I liked that word."

"Me either."

"Do you want to watch it?"

He just shook his head.

"Alright," She said but gave him a concerned smile. "Go ahead and pick one out. Wes had all kinds of westerns. I love them all."

Wade stood and went to the box next to the TV. He picked up the DVD box that held *The Cowboys* and looked at the cover…John Wayne…each of the kids…he set it aside. He was going through the rest of the movies when his dad came to the door.

He talked to Cora for a few minutes before turning his attention to Wade. "Did you want to talk?"

Wade didn't want to talk about sadness anymore so he just shook his head, "No, it's OK Dad. Cora and I are just gonna watch a movie and rest."

His dad nodded and reached to pick up *The Cowboys* DVD. "Watching this again?" He smiled, but the smile left when Wade shook his head.

"Nah," He looked back into the box so he didn't have to see his dad's reaction and ignored the uneasy feeling in his stomach. "I'm looking for something different."

It was quiet for a few minutes; Wade kept going through the movies. He wasn't really seeing them; he was just trying not to turn around to his dad.

"So what other choices do you have?" He finally asked. Wade picked up the next one in line and without looking at it handed it to him.

"No, I don't think so." He chuckled. Wade looked at the DVD and saw it was a movie with Clint Eastwood, *The Unforgiven*. It was R rated. He quickly looked in the box and saw another favorite movie and handed it to his dad.

"*Silverado*," He nodded. "That's more like it."

"It's a fun one, so it will lift our spirits," Cora smiled.

His dad put his hand on top of Wade's head and when he didn't look up, he moved his hand down and put a finger under Wade's chin and lifted it up. Wade looked up at him and tried to smile. He didn't think it worked too well because his dad's expression was concerned.

"We're going out back to go through Cora's tack," Dropping his hand from Wade's chin he continued. "You let me know if either of you need anything."

"We will." Cora assured him.

Wade didn't say anything…he was afraid his voice would show his nervousness. He nodded and concentrated on putting the movie in the player.

Wade could see Cora in the mirror nodding at his dad. Her expression showed her concern, too.

He crawled back in the chair next to Cora after his dad left. Part way through the movie, Sadie, Grace, and Nora arrived home and jumped on the bed to quietly watch it with them.

Wade must have fallen asleep, because he could feel himself being lifted. Then there was the motion of climbing the steps, then the feeling of the pillows on Matt's bed surrounding him.

"I tried to get him to talk about the ranch, but he just changed the subject," He heard Cora say.

"Did he say why he didn't want to watch *The Cowboys?*" His dad was talking. Wade kept his eyes closed so he didn't have to answer their questions.

"No," Cora answered. "He just picked it up, looked at it for a minute then set it down again."

"That doesn't make any sense," His dad said. "He loves that movie…there's been times he would watch it two or three times in a row…on the same day."

Their voices began to drift as they walked down the hall.

Wade opened his eyes and stared at the ceiling wondering if he was ever going to be able to watch that movie again.

CHAPTER FIVE

Wade woke early and wiggled himself down into the blankets, they were warm and soft and he didn't want to get up yet. He opened an eye and glanced at the other bed; it was empty. Reilly was at home and Matt was in college. He always wondered what it would be like to have his own room and now that he had it, he wasn't sure he really liked it.

He heard footsteps in the hallway and harsh whispers. It had to be Sadie and Nora, they argued all the time. He wasn't sure how Grace could stand to share a room with them. The three girls shared one large room with big rugs on the floor to designate which part of the room belonged to which girl. There were fancy room separators blocking the girls sections from each other.

Wade and Matt didn't need a separator; they got along really well for their eight year age difference. Wade's side of the room was covered in tractors; toys, replicas, and posters. There were pictures lined on a long shelf of Wade at various ages riding with his dad in the Tagger Enterprises tractors. Some of his best days, in his whole ten years, were spent farming with his dad.

Matt liked them too, but his side was more 'mature' with family snapshots, pictures taken at the ranch, and a few baseball trophies he had won with the teams he played with in school and over the summer. There was one large picture of deer at the ranch. So both boys liked each other's side of the room and got along well.

The girl's whispers faded as they made their way down the hall and staircase.

Wade debated whether to stay in bed or go referee the two again. He closed his eyes and tested whether he was going to be able to go back to sleep…his mind went to Rooster and the impending trip to WSU. Lifting the covers off him with his good arm he decided to get up; he wouldn't be able to go back to sleep anyway. He needed his mind busy until they were ready to go. Might as well let the two arguing girls do that for him.

He positioned the cast over his stomach and rolled onto his good side. Using his legs to move himself to the side of the bed, he pushed with his good arm to sit up. The dizziness just lasted a few seconds then he put the sling over his head and cradled his arm in it. He headed out the door and to the barn where he knew the girls would be.

They were still arguing when he walked in…they were just louder.

"I just asked a dang question, Sadie." Nora grumbled.

"I don't know why you did," Sadie answered tersely.

"What are you two arguing about this time?" Wade asked as he held out his coat for one of them to help him put it on.

They both moved forward and helped. Neither one answered his question.

"Is it that stupid that neither of you want to tell me?" Wade smirked.

Nora shrugged and moved into the stall with Arcturus and Scarecrow. Sadie stood on the outside and glared in at Nora.

The girls looked as different to each other as the two horses did. Sadie was tall for her age, her mom at 5' 10" and her dad stood 6' 3". She also took after their light complexion with blonde hair and blue eyes. Nora was shorter even though she would be turning 12 in November; a week after Sadie turned 10. Nora and Wade both took after their mother's Native American coloring along with dark brown eyes and black hair. Since their mom was barely 5 foot tall, Nora didn't have a chance to catch Sadie in height. He desperately hoped he would.

The only thing the two girls had in common was their long hair. Sadie's hair was to her waist, Nora's only half way down her back. Both girls had their hair loose this morning with just a headband holding it back.

Scarecrow was a golden palomino with white mane and tail. Arcturus was totally black except the star on his forehead. After putting the weight back on, Scarecrow was turning out stockier than Arcturus' more long and elegant conformation.

Little Ghost, Sadie's grey horse, was in the next stall. Sadie stopped glaring at Nora and entered his stall.

Dollar and Rooster were on the opposite side of the aisle from Little Ghost so Wade turned to them as Nora walked her two horses out of the barn and headed for the pasture. She would go directly to the house to get ready for school instead of coming back to the barn after letting them go.

Jack had dropped Reilly off to catch the bus with Grace, and the two teenagers had already put their horses in the pasture, along with Trooper and Harvey.

"Want me to halter Dollar for you?" Sadie asked.

"Nah, he can stay in here and keep Rooster company until we leave."

"I'll get some hay for them," Sadie headed to the bale at the barn door.

Wade opened the door to the stall when she returned. Both horses made it difficult for her to get to the feeder but Sadie just laughed at them.

"What were you arguing about this time?" Wade asked as she walked out of the stall and headed back to Little Ghost.

A shoulder shrugged as she reached for the horse's halter that hung on a hook just outside the stall. "She asked me if she should thin down Scarecrow's mane to keep it shorter or just let it grow."

"What did you say?"

"That she needed to make up her own mind…it wouldn't matter what I said…she would just do the opposite."

Wade nodded, that part was probably true. "Why didn't you tell her the opposite?"

Sadie shrugged as they walked along with the grey horse and out of the barn.

"Scarecrow is hers…"

"So?"

"I wouldn't let anyone else make that decision about Little Ghost."

"And she wouldn't for Arcturus," Wade opened the gate to the pasture for her to walk through. "So why would she about Scarecrow?"

"I don't know," Sadie turned back to the barn.

Aunt Leah was standing on the back deck of the house, "Sadie hurry up, you need to eat and leave in the next 5 minutes."

"Ok, Mom." Sadie answered.

"Why do we go through this every morning?" Aunt Leah asked but, not expecting an answer, walked back into the house.

Wade and Sadie grinned at each other and walked toward the back of the house.

He glanced at his cousin and wondered if he should talk to her about his arm. She always kept secrets and they had a lot between the two of them.

"Sadie?"

"What?"

Wade wiggled his fingers at the end of the cast, "How come you never asked me how I broke my arm?"

Sadie stopped at the bottom of the steps and looked at him; her brows wrinkled together showing her seriousness. "We share everything."

He nodded.

"Well, I figured, if you wanted to tell me, you already would have."

Wade looked into her blue eyes and sighed, "It's just that…"

"It's OK, Wade," Her eyes softened. "You have your reasons."

Wade looked down at his cast and wiggled his fingers again. He nodded.

"Then, when you're ready, I'll be here for you to talk to," She smiled at him to let him know she wasn't upset.

Her mother opened the door, "Get in here."

Sadie grinned again and headed up the stairs.

Wade sat on the bottom step and rested the cast on his lap. He stared out at the barn, thinking of Sadie and Nora…wondering why they couldn't go a day without arguing. The back door opened and closed.

His mother sat down next to him and took his right hand and squeezed.

"I wish I was going with you today."

"It's OK, Mom," Wade smiled to reassure her.

"Work is just…there's a deadline…" She exhaled. "I don't know…"

Wade squeezed her hand tightly, "Dr. Mark said it was just like a checkup today, he'll be home tonight."

"But I should be there with you."

Wade turned and looked into her tear filled eyes, "I love you, Mom and I know you love Rooster, too."

She nodded and exhaled loudly.

"It's Ok," He told her again.

"If he has to have surgery, I don't care what's going on at work…I'll be there for you."

The back door opened. Nora, Sadie, and Aunt Leah walked out.

"Jordan, they missed the bus again," Aunt Leah told them.

"I'll drop them off on the way to work again," His mom said. She squeezed his hand then leaned over and kissed the top of his head. "I'll be thinking of you and Rooster."

As Sadie passed by him, she looked down and had a guilty twinkle in her eye. Wade grinned and watched them leave. It was their secret. When they didn't feel like riding the bus, they spent too much time in the barn in the morning so a parent would take them in.

He looked down at his cast and wiggled his fingers… secrets…so many secrets…but his was the biggest of all. He wasn't going to tell Sadie, he didn't want to burden her with having to keep it. The consequences of the truth were too great.

CHAPTER SIX

Wade stood behind the trailer and watched his dad and Uncle Grayson try to load Rooster into it. They were headed to WSU for Rooster's appointment, but Rooster was not going into the horse trailer. No matter what they tried, the horse wouldn't go in.

"Wade!" His dad called out.

"Yeah?"

"Let's see if he'll go in if you're in there."

"OK," He said and his uncle braced him as Wade stepped into the trailer.

It wasn't the stock trailer that was more open and airy. It was the one that had closed windows to protect the horses. He walked inside and looked around.

"Wade?" He heard his dad's voice. "What are you doing?"

Wade walked back to the narrow opening which was only half the width of the trailer due to the tack room on the other side.

"Checking it out to see why Rooster doesn't like it." Wade answered.

His dad looked up at him, hands on hips. "And what did you find out?"

He smiled at his dad, who wasn't wearing a hat yet but still looked like a western movie star. He was smiling up at his son.

"Come in and I'll show you," Wade said and walked back in. He figured it would be easier to show them. Only his dad stepped in.

"You too, Uncle Grayson!" Wade called out and his Uncle stepped into the trailer.

Wade looked out and saw his aunt walking towards them.

"What are you guys doing?" She asked. "It's supposed to be the horse in the trailer, not you guys."

Wade chuckled, "Can you come in?"

She stepped into the trailer so he had all of the Tagger Trio standing next to him. He looked up at all three of them. "Do you see it?" He asked his aunt.

She looked around and finally nodded.

"What?" His dad and Uncle Grayson asked in unison.

"It looks dark and scary like the stalls at Cora's property." Wade told them. It reminded Wade of the day before when he revisited the barn and looked from the back of the barn to the front…if he was Rooster, he wouldn't want to go in either.

They both looked around and slowly nodded.

"Smart young man," His uncle said and walked out of the trailer, followed by his dad and Aunt Dru. She turned and helped Wade step out of the trailer.

His uncle was already climbing in the truck to move the trailer and unhook it. He hooked up the stock trailer to the truck instead. Once done, Rooster went into the open airy stock trailer without a problem.

During the drive, the adults worked hard on keeping the conversations going as they tried to keep Wade from thinking about the appointment. Wade just sighed…at least they were trying.

They made it to the top of the Lewiston hill grade and pulled over to check on Rooster. The highway out of the valley was a long gradual climb, but you had to do it to get to Pullman and the University. His dad opened the back of the horse trailer and braced Wade as he climbed in to check on his horse. Wade used his good arm and patted the horse's nose and made sure he was alright.

"He's OK, Dad."

They made it the rest of the way to the University without having to stop.

When Uncle Grayson pulled up next to a large brick building, Aunt Dru slid out of the truck and walked through large glass doors. They waited quietly until she finally came out and told them the directions to take Rooster. They drove around to the back of a large building with a lot of white framed entrances in it. Wade could see a horse arena that looked like a race track. On the outside; the place looked nice.

Wade stood at the foot of the horse trailer waiting for his dad to walk Rooster out.

The horse groaned when he stepped down off the back of the trailer. Wade cringed inside, wondering how painful it was for him.

He reached out for the lead rope but his dad shook his head.

"Sorry Buddy, this is a strange area for him and lots of things that could spook him. I don't want him accidently hitting your cast."

Wade nodded with a dejected sigh and followed behind the group of adults as they walked into the building; his new lariat swinging over his shoulder.

There was a really wide hallway they walked down and toward other horses that were already there. They looked like they were in cages not stalls which made Wade start to get nervous. In different rooms he saw big machines. He heard the doctors say they were used for testing. That made his heart really race.

There were so many long words being tossed around that they all started to sound like a foreign language. He pushed his lariat up high on the shoulder that had the cast and looked around for the first hand that belonged to a family member. He reached out and grabbed ahold and squeezed. His uncle looked down supportively and squeezed back.

They walked by a room that had large pipe stalls like Dr. Mark had at his clinic.

Then they walked by a hole in the ground that looked like a miniature swimming pool. The lady in a white jacket said it was for horses. His eye's widened. She smiled and said it was for the horses to rehabilitate from injuries.

"Will Rooster go in there?"

She nodded, "More than likely; but it will depend on the type of surgery he has and how he needs to exercise to recover."

The lady followed them around and explained different scary thing to him. By the time she was done, he wasn't as nervous anymore; but he kept ahold of his uncle's hand…just in case.

A man in a white jacket took Rooster away. Wade didn't even get a chance to say goodbye to him. He took a deep breath and let it out slowly to keep himself calm.

"He'll be OK," Uncle Grayson said. "It's just like when you went in for your arm. They just poke and prod and then tell you what's wrong."

"Will they put his legs in a machine for an x-ray like they did my arm?" He asked and his uncle nodded.

"Can I watch?"

"They have to put Rooster to sleep before they do that. It might be a bit scary." His uncle said honestly.

"OK," Wade shook his head emphatically. "I'd rather not."

They walked into a big room and waited for the doctors to finish examining his red horse. When done, there were two veterinarians that sat in the chairs next to them to explain what they needed to do.

Wade couldn't listen. The words were really long and made his head hurt. He looked out the window and watched a lady exercising a horse in the big arena they past when they arrived.

He heard the word euthanized…he knew that word; Sadie had told him what it meant. It was the one word they didn't want to hear. His heart trembled and his stomach turned. Wade slowly turned his attention back to the adults. All of them were frowning.

"You're not going to kill him are you?" Wade asked calmly, trying to sound like an adult. They all turned and looked at him. His uncle squeezed his hand tightly.

"Wade," His dad answered with soft, concerned eyes. "You wanted us to be honest with you?"

Wade nodded.

His dad continued, "If there isn't a way to get Rooster out of pain, it may have to happen. It would be best for Rooster."

Wade just stared at him for a minute then turned his eyes back to the lady exercising the horse in the arena. Why did he keep asking them to be honest with him? They should lie to him and tell him everything is fine. He felt like he was in a bad dream. A different kind of nightmare than the one he had about Monty.

The horse in the arena with the lady changed from a walk to a trot as he went in circles. Then he moved to a gallop. He looked like he was in good shape. Wade wondered if that would be Rooster someday. Maybe he would come up here and watch the lady exercising Rooster, not euthanizing him.

He concentrated on the horse moving and the feel of his Uncle's hand holding his own. It always surprised him when just holding hands made him feel better. It made him feel like he wasn't alone. Wade glanced up at his uncle and wondered if it felt the same way to him.

Uncle Grayson noticed him looking up at him and smiled down, his blue eyes looking concerned. "You OK?" He whispered.

Wade shrugged his shoulders, "I don't know." He looked at the other adults who were still discussing Rooster's legs.

"Do you understand what they're saying?"

Wade shook his head. "Just the part about putting him to sleep if he's in pain," He sighed. "I guess that's the important part." He felt like crying, but told himself to be strong for Rooster. "When can we take Rooster home?"

His uncle leaned down a little more so he didn't disturb the other adults.

"He should be awake enough in about a half hour so we can take him home. Then we'll decide on a surgery date for him to come back."

Wade nodded. His dad turned to him and glanced between him and Uncle Grayson who nodded to let him know everything was OK.

The other adults stood so Wade and his uncle did too.

It was a very quiet ride home. The Trio didn't want to talk about Rooster with Wade there, but he wanted all the kids to know what happened today.

He was in the back seat with his dad so he looked up and asked; "Can we have a family meeting?"

"About?"

"I think it would be better to tell everyone about Rooster at the same time. So it doesn't have to be said over and over again."

His dad nodded, "I think that's a great idea."

They arrived in Lewiston in time to swing by the junior high school and give Grace and Reilly a ride home. They were both excited about not having to ride the bus but bummed they wouldn't be told about Rooster until the family meeting.

Rooster groaned and Wade cringed again as the horse stepped out of the trailer. Wade led him to the south pasture to join the rest of the herd with Dollar and Buttercup trotting to the fence to greet them. Grace had followed Wade to open the gate.

"Thanks," He told his cousin as they turned from the gate. Wade made his way to the front steps and sat to watch the herd graze…or try to since the grass had gone dormant. They put the horses in the pasture for exercise.

Grace sat on the step next to him.

"I like just sitting here watching them." Grace said softly.

"Me too."

"You OK?" She asked without looking at him.

"I don't know."

"Want to talk about it?"

"What?"

"Whatever…I'm always here for you to talk to."

"I know."

"Well?"

Wade sighed, "I'm worried about Mom and Dad…Rooster…and Cora…and then there's all that homework Sadie is going to be bringing me from school today."

"Who ever said that being ten was easy?" Grace grinned at him which helped raise his mood. She had the best smile and her laugh could brighten the darkest of days.

"I'm still nine for a couple days," Wade reminded her. "Hopefully ten will be easier than nine."

Grace nodded, "Then there is the arm…"

"Yep," Wade wiggled his fingers at the end of the cast. "Then there's that…"

He trusted her…but he wouldn't tell her either…for the same reason he wouldn't say anything to Sadie.

They sat quietly and watched the horses until Sadie and Nora arrived…then their mom's and Jack arrived from work and the family meeting was called.

Everyone gathered at the table and chairs on the back deck. The temperature had warmed for the day, so they took advantage of one of the last times to gather there before winter weather started.

Wade looked around at all the kids and adults gathered to hear about Rooster. His dad was sitting to his left and Reilly was to his right. His eyes went to the lariat in his lap when his dad started talking. He was listening intently this time because he knew his dad wouldn't use all the long words.

Rooster didn't just have knee problems. His hocks, the ankle for a horse, were also damaged and causing the issues.

There was the possibility that surgery could be attempted that would ease the pain and possibly repair it all together so he could have a normal life. The other kids were excited and hopeful until he raised his hand to quiet them down. That was never good.

The doctors believed that if they did surgery, they would find that he was either too injured to save and would be in pain the rest of his life, or they could ease the pain but not eliminate it. Either way, he wouldn't be able to have a normal life.

Everyone was quiet.

His dad spoke directly to the kids. "The most important thing to do is what is best for Rooster. It would be cruel of us to make him live in pain." All the kids sadly nodded. Nora and Sadie were crying. Wade continued to stare at his rope…his fingers running over the ridges.

"He could go into surgery and they find the damage is too extensive and put him to sleep there, or, they can fix him as best they can and hope it eliminates the pain. Even with the surgery, he may still need to be put down."

"Did you vote? Is he going to have surgery?" Grace asked nervously.

Wade looked up at his dad, his eyes wide and hopeful.

"There wasn't much to vote on," Aunt Dru spoke. "We would never put him down without at least trying everything possible." She looked at Grace. "Yes, he will have surgery."

"When?" Grace asked excitedly.

"Well, that's up to Wade," Aunt Dru said.

Wade's eyebrows went up in surprise. "Me?" He sat up in his chair.

"They have an opening this Friday or the Thursday after." His dad told him.

"Friday is my birthday." Wade reminded him.

His dad nodded. "That's why it's up to you. You now know the possibility that Rooster may not make out it out of surgery," He paused until Wade nodded. "Do you want to take the chance that Rooster is gone on your birthday?"

Wade thought about it very carefully, remembering the groan as Rooster stepped out of the horse trailer. Was he tolerating the pain like his dad had said? "I think we should do the best thing for Rooster and get him out of pain right away." Wade paused and took a deep breath. "One way or the other."

His dad nodded.

Reilly leaned over to Wade, "That's the right thing to do."

Wade smiled up at him and sighed. He was glad Reilly agreed with him. He looked around to see if everyone else did. The only person that didn't look happy was his mom.

"Can we go with him?" Sadie asked.

His dad shook his head, "That would be too many people."

Wade sat up in his chair and looked at his dad who had turned to him. "Me, Dad?" His voice cracked. He looked at Uncle Grayson who could confirm that he was good then back to his dad. "I was really good today and tried to be an adult. I will be good, I promise. Please Dad?" Wade took a deep breath. "Rooster will need me… you said I could in the barn when Rooster helped me…I promise I will be an adult again…"

Wade stopped talking when his dad raised a hand to stop the nervous fast talk.

"Yes, Wade. You did great today and we think you will help keep Rooster's stress level down." Wade smiled nervously. He saw his mom put her head in her hands…she really didn't look happy.

CHAPTER SEVEN

"Stupid girls," Wade walked through the front door of the house and made his way to the kitchen. He looked out the back window and saw all the adults sitting around the tables on the deck. Out the side window, the girls were braiding all the horse's hair…even Rooster's and Dollar's. He'd told them not to, but they laughed and did it anyway. "Stupid girls." He repeated.

Wade was tired of the cast on his arm and tired of all the girls. Why did Reilly have to go home with his dad? Why did Matt have to go back to college? He was the only boy left at The Homestead. He turned in circles in the hallway, the lariat swinging around him. He didn't know what to do and felt grumpy and didn't want to talk to anyone. He stopped and looked around. The door to the no-media room was open. It was the one place no one could watch TV or use their electronic games so hardly anyone ever went in there…unless one of the kids got in trouble.

Deciding it was a good place to get away from everyone, he walked down the hall. The girls wouldn't find him in there.

Wade walked in the room and passed the gaming table to the left. There was a chair to the right of the door; hidden in the corner. It was big and fluffy with lots of pillows. He could sink into it and hide from the world; no one would find him there. Kicking off his boots he crawled up into the chair. The cast fit perfect up on the arm of the chair and he sunk back into the pillows with the lariat across his lap. He traced the coil with his fingers, the ridges of the rope were rough on his skin but he liked the feel…it was mesmerizing…a deep breath…let it out and try to release the bad mood…he watched his finger…concentrated on the feel…another breath and he felt his body relax.

Wade lifted his eyes from the rope and looked around the big room. It had 3 couches and 4 chairs; lots of sitting room for the family. A large rock fireplace was on the wall that connected to the outside wall that had all the windows. Over the fireplace was barb-wire that was looped and bent in the shape of the ranch T3E brand. Around it, were four large coils of wire, one for each generation of Taggers' that owned the property. His dad had told him the barb wire was from the original ranch fencing constructed by Wade's great-great grandfather.

On the wall, to each side of the fireplace, were large canvas prints of Mavis during a branding. The one on the left was Mavis walking next to his dad's legs; they were headed to work the herd and she looked like she was glaring at the cows. The canvas on the right was Mavis lying down looking up at his dad who was leaning down petting her head. They were awesome and Mavis looked great in them. They always made him think of her working the cows at the ranch.

Wade could see the adults outside sitting at the table talking about Rooster and sighed. He didn't want Rooster to be in pain but he didn't want the horse gone either. Tears threatened to fall when he thought of the night Angel died. Sadie was heartbroken and cried herself to sleep in Uncle Grayson's arms. He took another breath and tried to blow away the tears. He was tired of crying.

A movement out the window caught Wade's attention. His mom had stood up quickly and turned to the house. Her chair had fallen back on the deck. As his mom walked to the house, Aunt Leah picked up the chair and followed. His dad's head was back and he was looking up at the sky. Both Aunt Dru and Uncle Grayson were leaning on the table and talking to each other. They didn't look happy either.

Wade heard the back door open and footsteps quickly coming down the hall. Holding his breath, he hoped the footsteps would go past the door; they didn't. His mom walked in the room and he was about to say something when Aunt Leah walked in.

"What was that all about?" Aunt Leah asked his mom.

Wade debated whether to get up fast and leave or wait. Wanting to know if they talked about Rooster, he shrunk back in the chair and tried to disappear into the pillows.

His mom turned and glared at Aunt Leah. "You know exactly what it's about! They made the decision that Wade would go to WSU without discussing it with me. They made the decision about the horse without any input from us. The horse is Wade's and yet I have no say in what happens to it."

"Rooster is Wade's responsibility but he belongs to Tagger Enterprises," Aunt Leah corrected. "So the decision is between the three of them."

"Everything is between the three of them." His mom was almost yelling.

"Jordan, calm down."

"Why? I've been calming down for years and I'm tired of it." She turned her back to Wade, so he couldn't see how mad she was.

"Well, that's bull," His aunt walked farther into the room. "It's been a great life, Jordan. There is no better life out there. I don't know what's up with you."

"I'm tired of being the outsider."

"The outsider?"

"In this whole family! Don't you feel it?" She turned back to his aunt. "There's those three and all their kids, then there's us."

Aunt Leah shook her head, eyebrows raised in surprise, "I have NEVER felt that way, so don't lump me into that. I love my husband, my kids, and the entire family. I am not a fifth wheel to anyone or anything."

"Then I guess I'm on the outside all by myself."

"You're putting yourself outside, Jordan."

"It didn't upset you when they hired Cora?"

It was Wade's eyebrows raised in surprise this time. What did this have to do with Cora?

"Since it had to do with part of what we do here, yes it did. But I support the decision completely. I love Cora and am thankful I don't have to work all day, then come home and have to feed this herd of a family."

"I love Cora, too. But they should have asked us first."

Out the window, Wade saw Aunt Dru stand and step toward the house.

"As I understand it, Dru brought it up to them and they both agreed, so what's the problem?"

His mom sighed, "Of all people, I figured you would understand."

"Well, if she doesn't, then maybe you can explain it to me," Aunt Dru walked into the room; her voice tense. "Attacking Scott like that was uncalled for, Jordan. HE made the decision about Wade going up for the surgery, not the three of us. He was fulfilling the promise he made to Wade in the barn the other night."

The room was quiet. Wade looked at his mom while silently wishing he had left the room. No 'almost ten years old' should have to witness this.

His mom glared at Aunt Dru.

"Jordan, this has been going on too long. You have to talk this out so we can get past this." Aunt Dru pleaded.

His mom turned and faced her. She took a deep breath, "This is not what I wanted when I got married."

"What did you want?" His dad walked in the room behind Aunt Dru.

Wade hadn't seen him get up. He glanced out the window and saw Uncle Grayson still sitting at the table and staring towards the pasture where the girls were playing with the horses.

Without saying anything, Aunt Leah walked out of the room. Wade could hear her footsteps echoing down the hallway. He should leave too, but he couldn't get his legs to move.

"What did you want?" His dad repeated.

Wade could feel his heart pounding and hoped they couldn't hear it. He really didn't want to be there.

"I wanted a husband and family."

"What part of that didn't you get?" His dad asked.

"I got a husband and his family. Not our family."

"You knew that they were part of who I am and part of the marriage. So what changed?" His voice was angry and confused.

"I became the afterthought." She said.

"Since when?" He asked in disbelief.

"Since the beginning," she answered.

He shook his head. "We were fine until last spring when the horses came into the family. Are they the issue?"

Wade held his breath. How could the horses be the problem?

"The horses are not the issue," She said gruffly.

"Is it Cora?" Aunt Dru asked.

His mom glared at her again but didn't answer.

His dad looked between the two women. "What about Cora?"

"When we announced that we hired her, I saw you and Leah exchange a look." Aunt Dru said to her.

"I thought you liked Cora doing the cooking." Wade's dad seemed as confused as he was.

"I do," she answered.

"I don't understand, Jordan." His dad sighed.

His mom walked over to the window and looked out; she saw Uncle Grayson and quickly turned around.

"It's now or never, Jordan," His dad stepped towards her. "You have to tell me what's wrong so I can fix it."

"You can't fix it," She responded angrily.

His dad rolled his eyes and shook his head. "Then what do you suggest?"

She glared at him, "I'm going to pack up the kids and move into town for a while."

Wade's eyes opened wide and his heart raced. Before he knew what happened, he stood up and yelled, "No!"

All three of them jumped and turned surprised faces towards him.

"Wade!" His mom gasped and walked over to him. "What are you doing here?"

"I was in here by myself when you and Aunt Leah came in," He took a step towards her, his heart pounding. "I don't want to go anywhere!"

"Wade…" She began.

"No!" He said again. "I don't want to leave. I don't want to leave those bratty girls, or the horses. I don't want to leave Dad just because you do!" Wade was nearly yelling at her. His heart was racing with a mixture of fear of leaving and anger at his mom for wanting to leave.

"Calm down, it'll be OK," His dad whispered in concern and took a step forward.

Wade's mom knelt down next to him, "Please calm down." She pleaded.

He realized they were worried of another panic attack, "I'm OK." His breathing was fine; it was his heart that was scared.

"I don't want to go anywhere," Wade repeated looking between his parents.

"You're not going anywhere," His dad said firmly.

His mom stood and faced his dad and aunt.

"Aren't you going to vote on that?" She glared at him.

"What does that mean?" His dad asked angrily.

"You vote on everything else! So aren't you going to vote on whether you take my kids away from me?"

"Are you listening to yourself, Jordan?" His dad yelled, then stopped and took a deep breath. "I am not taking the kids away from you. You were threatening to take them away from me and the family."

"The family…" She said sarcastically.

It sounded like she was cursing.

"Jordan," His dad waited until she looked at him. "What is the problem?"

She didn't answer.

"What is the problem?" He repeated.

"Just spit it out, Jordan," Aunt Dru pleaded.

His mom looked out at Uncle Grayson, who was now talking with Aunt Leah, then turned and looked at Aunt Dru then his dad.

"I can't compete," She said bluntly.

His dad didn't say anything but his head tilted to the side like the dogs do when they are confused.

"I don't understand," Aunt Dru said.

"I feel like an outsider when it comes to this family," Her voice was shaking.

Aunt Dru looked over at his dad who was still just staring at his mom. Wade looked up at his mom because he was confused, too.

"Since when?" Aunt Dru asked.

"Leah and I should have been consulted before hiring Cora," She said flatly.

"So it wasn't the horses, it was Cora?" His dad asked.

"I love Cora." His mom added quickly.

"But you didn't want us to hire her?" Aunt Dru looked frustrated, her neck was turning red…that only happened when she was getting mad.

"Hiring her was fine, but Leah and I should have been consulted," she said curtly.

"She was hired on by Tagger Enterprises," Dru argued. "So it was put up for a vote between the three of us, like everything else is that involves the company."

"It involved the responsibility of me and Leah, so we should have been included in the conversation," His mom replied.

"It wouldn't have changed the outcome," Aunt Dru reminded her impatiently.

No one spoke for a few minutes. Wade shifted his weight from one foot to another. It seemed like they forgot he was there.

"What did you mean you can't compete?" His dad finally spoke. Wade thought his voice was very soft compared to the tension in the air. He looked up at his mom. She was looking at his dad with angry eyes.

"I can't compete with the three of you," She answered tersely.

"You feel like you are competing with us?" His aunt asked, her voice raised an octave in confusion.

"I feel like everything I do, or want to do as a family, I am competing with the relationship between the three of you," His mom paused. "I wanted to marry Scott, not all three of you."

"You knew they were part of the deal when I asked you to marry me," his dad said.

"Yes, I did," She admitted. "But I didn't think it would become a competition between our relationship and the relationship between you three."

"We've been married for over 13 years, Jordan," His dad pointed out. "Why is this an issue now?"

"I guess it's been building," She answered, her voice still angry. "But when you hired Cora, without talking to us, it just showed how it was going to be forever."

"You want us to fire her?" Aunt Dru asked in angry disbelief. Wade just about yelled again but his mom answered before he could.

"Of course not," she said.

"Then what do you want?" His dad asked.

"I wanted that job," His mom finally replied.

"What job? Cora's?" His dad asked in disbelief.

"Yes," she answered.

"Why didn't you say something?" He asked; looking confused and frustrated.

"Because I didn't think it was an option," She crossed her arms in front of her.

"Jordan," His dad took a step towards her. "Why didn't you say you didn't want to work at the paper mill?"

"I didn't say that," She turned away from him and looked towards the fireplace.

There was silence in the room again. Wade looked at his dad and aunt to see if they understood what his mother was saying, because he sure didn't. They looked just as confused as he felt.

"I am so confused right now," His dad finally said. "You wanted the position we gave to Cora but you don't want to quit your job?"

His mom still didn't look at them, "Yes."

"You couldn't do both," Aunt Dru pointed out.

"I know," She agreed.

"You know Tagger Enterprises is self-sufficient," His dad said and his mom nodded. "You don't have to work; you've known that all along. Your job has always been your choice."

"I know," She glanced back at him.

"Then what do you want Jordan? I am not going to tell you that you have to quit your job, or keep it. It's your choice." He said again.

"I love the people I work with. My job and the company are great," She started. "But I want to be more to this family and not feel like I'm competing against the three of you."

"I don't understand the competing part," Aunt Dru said. "There is no competition."

"Yes there is," His mom was frustrated again and Wade was confused. This adult stuff was hard.

"What do you see as competition?" His dad asked.

"I want to have what you three have," She yelled. "I want that bond, I don't want to compete against it."

"You do not want the bond that my brothers and I have," Aunt Dru said stiffly.

"Yes, I do Dru," Wade's mom glared at his aunt. "How can you stand there and tell me that I don't want what the three of you have? I want that bond; that strong of a relationship."

"There is no comparing our relationship to your relationship," Aunt Dru told her, taking a step forward. "There is no competing because it's not the same." His mom started to say something but his aunt continued, "You don't want the bond we have, no one does. Your relationship is between the two of you, built on love." Dru waved her hand to point at his parents. "It grew from love and is shared with the family; born of that love," Aunt Dru glanced at his dad and out the window at his uncle. "We were born as brothers and sister…but you have no idea what we went through to become the friends and partners we are now." The redness moved from her neck to her cheeks and her eyes were glaring, "You have no idea what it is like to be riding your horse on the best ride of your life one moment, and five minutes later have your whole world torn from you. In a blink of an eye you're part of a happy family, then BAM, you're an orphan." Her voice quivered. "You have no idea what it feels like to cry in agony until you can't see or breathe. You feel like you're falling in a hole of despair with no way out. You have no idea what it's like to hold onto each other so hard that you begin to bond in a way that no one should ever have to," She paused to take in a deep breath. "I was drowning in agony in the barn the night of the funeral, and the only things that pulled me out, were the hands and love of my two brothers. It took all three of us, *together*, to have the strength to pull ourselves out of that hole and emerge from that barn. We knew when we dried our tears and walked out, that we only had each other, hearts and souls. There would be no one, besides the three of us, who would know the agony that we were feeling. " She paused, her voice had been shaking. "Your relationship is built on love," She looked over at her brother. "Ours was built on family but bonded with the need to survive."

When she stopped, the room was eerily silent.

While Aunt Dru was talking, his dad had walked up beside her and taken her hand. She had tears sliding unchecked down her face and his dad was fighting hard not to let his tears fall. It's not right that Wade should be seeing his dad like this. Wade looked up at his mom and saw she was crying too. Then to his surprise, Wade's hand was reaching to wipe away the tears rolling down his own cheeks.

Aunt Dru wiped her face with her sleeve.

"I love you with my heart and soul Jordan," His dad said, the emotion made his voice crack and his eyes were anguished. "I don't give that love lightly because I know what it is like to have it ripped away," He looked at his sister. "No one can change or expect the relationship I have with Dru and Grayson to change. We have a bond that runs thicker than the blood we share in our veins," He paused and looked back at his wife. "I would not have survived without them."

His eyes dropped to look at Wade then back up at his wife. "I don't want that type of bond with you. I want to be man and wife; the same way I felt the moment I met you. If that isn't enough anymore…then I can't give you more. You have to decide if that bond is enough for you. It's your choice."

His dad left the room. Wade nodded at Aunt Dru when she looked down at him then followed her brother. He stood there not knowing what to do or say, so he just took his mom's hand and squeezed it. She had quit crying but didn't move or say anything either, she just squeezed back.

CHAPTER EIGHT

Wade sat at his bedroom window and looked at the lights of the city. His mom had left right after the argument. She had hugged him tightly and apologized to him that he had to witness the fight then after saying she loved him…she left.

"Why can't she just stay?" He mumbled to himself.

The moon was bright enough he could see the horses grazing in the pasture. For some reason, no one had put them back in the barn for the night. Nora, in her pajamas, walked in and sat down next to him.

"They look like ghosts out there," Nora leaned her forehead against the glass. She twisted her head to look at him, "Are you sad?"

"I wanted Mom to stay." Wade mumbled and his shoulders slumped in defeat.

Nora sighed, "I don't know why she had to leave."

He didn't tell her about the conversation he witnessed. It wasn't his story to tell…he wasn't really sure whose it was…his Mom's…Dad's? There would be no good reason to tell Nora what happened anyway…it would make her just as sad and worried as he was.

"No matter what happens," Nora punched his shoulder trying to make him smile, "We'll always have each other."

His frown deepened; she made him think of Aunt Dru's story about the night of his grandparent's funeral. Wade's eyes started to tear up again.

"I'm not that bad!" Nora punched him harder. He lowered his eyes; willing the tears to go away.

"OK," She stood and headed for the door. "Let's go play with the horses."

"In the dark?" Wade hesitated, but when she disappeared down the hallway, he ran to catch up even though he knew they would get in trouble if someone found out.

Nora lifted her fingers to her lips to shush him. He walked on tip toes behind her. When they got to the top of the stairs and looked down, no one was there and they couldn't hear anyone either. Slowly they made their way down and looked out the back. The Trio and Aunt Leah were sitting on the back porch so they went to the side door. There wasn't a motion detector light out that way that would announce their late night adventure.

Once out the side door, they ran quickly to the fence and sat quietly. When they were sure no one saw them, Nora helped him crawl through the fence towards the horses that they were in the pasture between the front of the house and the road. Nora and Wade talked quietly to the horses so they didn't spook them.

"I'm surprised you like it out here in the dark," Nora whispered to him.

Wade looked around and up at the moon. "It's not that dark," He answered and glanced at his cast.

Wade looked over at Nora who was smiling and petting the horses while walking through them. In her white pajamas she looked like a ghost again. He walked carefully through the horses so he didn't accidently hit them with his cast.

He walked slowly between each one. They were so relaxed and calm as they grazed, that he began to feel the same way. All the trouble and stress of the last couple days was starting to flow out of his arms and legs…he felt like he was floating. This was the best idea

Nora had ever had. He walked through making sure he touched each of them. Little Ghost seemed to glow in the light, living up to his name. Scarecrow's blonde hair stood out in the moon, too. Arcturus' star shown like the bright star he was named after. The moonlight shone off the horse's black hair.

Wade and Nora were giggling softly when they heard a truck start. They froze and went silent. He stepped around Buttercup to see which truck had started. Nora came up behind him.

"It's Dad's truck," Nora said without seeing it.

"How do you know?"

"I recognize the sound of it. Sometimes, I lay in bed at night waiting for their trucks to come home, so I know they're OK."

The lights shone down the driveway…they waited. Soon the front of the truck passed the side of the house which caused the motion detector light to turn on. The light confirmed Nora's statement; it was their dad's truck.

"Where do you think he's going?" Wade whispered as he stared at the truck slowly making its way to the road.

"Well, it's been a bad day for him," She said and Wade silently agreed. Nora really didn't have any idea just how bad.

Nora continued, "If he turns left, he's going to the ranch and if he turns right, he's going to town, probably to Mom."

As the truck slowly moved down the driveway, Nora took Wade's hand. "Please go right, please go right…" She started whispering. Wade felt all the stress and anxiety make its way back through his body. How could one left or right decision make so much difference in their life?

The truck was half way to the road when it stopped.

"What is he doing?" Wade whispered.

"I don't know," She knelt down between Buttercup and Harvey and pulled Wade down with her. They were still holding hands while staring at the truck.

A little light glowed in the cab, "It's his phone." Wade whispered. He felt like a spy.

The light went out and the truck started moving.

"Nora," Wade looked at his sister's face, which was lit by the moon, "I don't want them to get a divorce, I don't want it to change."

"I know…me neither," She put her arms around him and they stared intently at the truck; quietly willing it to turn right.

Wade knew it wasn't the same, but he understood Aunt Dru's talk about the brother and sister bond now. He knew that in this moment, as they watched their dad, that no matter if the truck turned left or right, he and Nora would be closer than ever.

Wade leaned into his sister, understanding that she would always be there for him. He promised himself to always be there for her, too. They watched as the truck stopped. There was no indication if he was going right or left, the light came back on.

"This is killing me!" Nora squeezed tighter.

The light went out.

The sound of footsteps came from behind them. They hunched down even further, wishing one of the horses would lay down so they could hide behind it. Their eyes never left the truck even when the noise of the gate opening reached them. Wade realized he was holding his breath and slowly let it out. Every muscle was tense as he listened to someone walking towards them, while watching their dad sit in the truck at the end of the driveway.

The truck started moving again; it turned right.

Wade's eyes widened as he realized his dad could be going to his mom. He looked at Nora and she was grinning back at him. Then, slowly, the smile faded as her eyes slowly moved above him. He turned and saw jean covered legs. His eyes moved up to see Uncle Grayson staring down at them with an amused look on his face. Instantly Wade knew that their dad had seen someone in the pasture with the horses and had texted their uncle; busted!

"Care to explain?" Uncle Grayson asked.

They stood quickly and reached out to pet the nearest horse.

"We couldn't sleep, so we came out to check on the horses," Nora smiled, her eyes darted to the lights of her dad's truck making its way up the road.

Uncle Grayson turned and watched the truck lights turn the corner into town. "I understand," He said softly. The three of them watched the tail lights disappear into the mass of lights from Lewiston.

Rufio came up behind Uncle Grayson and rubbed his head against his arm, indicating the horse wanted some attention so he turned and stroked his neck. He moved to the next horse and did the same. He didn't say anything, so Nora and Wade went back to petting the horses. The three of them quietly wandered between the herd, Wade and Nora would giggle softly when a horse nudged them.

Under the moonlight, the three of them played with the animals until the horses started to ignore them again. Cooper had lain down next to the fence. He was so dark it was hard to find the horse but Nora knelt at his head and stroked his neck.

Wade watched his uncle walk between the horses. He didn't have his hat on, so his dark blond hair was shining in the moonlight as he stroked Scarecrow's long neck. Then he turned to the next horse. He seemed really relaxed as he was talking to Harvey. A wide grin spread across Uncle Grayson's face when Eli put his head over the man's shoulder and lowered its long neck and head to pull Grayson to the horse's chest. The girls called it a special horse hug.

Wade decided it was just as relaxing for his uncle as it is for him. He turned to Nora. She was watching Uncle Grayson with a relaxed happy smile.

Wade walked to Rooster and ran his hand down the horse's neck to his shoulder, down his sides and up and over the horse's rump. Almost all of the bones were now covered with muscle and fat. He walked a complete circle around him and stopped at his head. Rooster leaned his nose onto his side so Wade leaned into him trying to forget that he might be gone forever in two days. Taking a deep breath, Wade filled his lungs with Rooster's essence.

Uncle Grayson came up behind him and put a hand on his shoulder causing Wade to look up to see understanding eyes looking down. His uncle understood the turmoil he was going through which caused tears to sting the back of his eyes again. The emotions of the week raced through Wade as he wrapped his good arm around his uncle's waist and leaned into his side. His uncle's arm draped around Wade's shoulders and he squeezed tightly giving him his silent support and love. It was a moment that Wade would never forget.

"Let's head in," His uncle motioned for Nora.

The three of them quietly walked to the gate. The horses continued their nightly grazing as if having their people out in the dark with them happened every night.

"No more coming out in here in the dark," Uncle Grayson told them as they walked through the gate, "Unless you invite me."

******

The next morning at the breakfast table, neither Nora nor his uncle mentioned their midnight visit to the horses, so Wade didn't either. It would be their secret.

Cora still didn't feel well and was sleeping, so Aunt Dru and the girls were making breakfast. It was Thursday, so the kids didn't have school that day or the next. Wade was happy that Jack had dropped Reilly off at the house to spend the day with the kids and horses.

There was no sign of his parents.

"Are we going to take Rooster up to the hospital tonight or in the morning?" Wade asked. Reilly and Wade were sitting at the table with Uncle Grayson.

"We'll take him in the morning," Uncle Grayson answered and picked up the lariat that Cora had given Wade. "This is a real nice gift."

Wade nodded and watched Uncle Grayson playing with the rope. His uncle was the best roper he'd ever seen. He never missed a cow.

"Why did you quit competing in the rodeo?" Wade asked.

A memory filled smile spread across his uncle's face, "To go to college…then to take care of the ranch," He ran a finger around the coil and over the ridges, just like Wade did when Cora gave it to him. Wrapping his hand around the rope he swung it back and forth getting the feel for the rope. "Scott and I had a lot of fun team roping and traveling from rodeo to rodeo. Aunt Dru was there too, running barrels."

"How come you never talk about it?" Grace sat at the table next to her dad; Sadie quickly joined them. They liked to hear stories from their parents past…it didn't take long for Nora to join them too. Helping Aunt Dru with breakfast was abandoned. They all sat quietly waiting for his uncle to tell stories.

"It just seems like a lifetime ago," He answered Grace. "It was done and over years before you came along."

"Did you win a lot?" Reilly asked.

Uncle Grayson nodded with a big smile that made his eyes shine, "We did, but that wasn't the most important part."

"What was?" Grace asked.

He smiled at her, "Just riding, chasing the steer, throwing the rope, and having fun." He grinned at Nora and Wade. "Your dad was the best partner ever. If one of us missed we'd shrug it off and figure we'd get the next one. That's probably why we won so much…because we put the fun first. You guys have seen on TV… team roping is really fast," He looked around at the kids. "World record time is 3.5 seconds," All the kid's eyes opened wide. "A good header only throws after two turns and a healer will be there in five or six."

"Did you and Dad do it that fast?" Nora asked.

Uncle Grayson shook his head. "No, we usually averaged around 6 seconds."

"That's still really fast," Wade said. His uncle smiled and nodded. "What about calf roping?"

"The record is just over 6 seconds and the best ropers are consistently around 7 seconds." He answered. "You definitely want a fast and experienced horse." Uncle Grayson paused, "Every rodeo weekend started the same way," He told his entranced audience. "Your grandma would visit the horses as we loaded them into the horse trailer."

"Why?" Reilly asked.

Uncle Grayson smiled, "She would tell the horses to take care of her kids."

"Telling them to win?" Grace asked.

Uncle Grayson shook his head, "No, telling them to make sure we didn't get hurt."

"In team roping?" Nora looked surprised.

He nodded at her, "Oh yeah. Many horses tripped coming out of the box or, the steer would dart in front of them and the horse would trip over it, sending the rider flying or rolling on top of him," He leaned back in his chair. "We watched one girl start out of the chute and the rope barrier snapped and wrapped around the back legs of her horse. She and the horse went rolling. She stood up and just walked off. They came back later and had a great run."

"Sounds scary!" Nora shook her head.

"Did Grandma and Grandpa go to all your rodeos?" Sadie asked.

"Not all of them, but they made it to some," He continued to bounce and swing the rope. "They had the ranch to take care of."

"What horses did you use?" Nora asked. Wade glanced over at her. She was always thinking of the horses and not the rodeo.

Uncle Grayson grinned at her. "Scott had a horse called Abraham, a little buckskin like Eli. He could stop and turn on a dime, so he and Scott were the header."

"Who did you ride, Dad?" Grace asked, enthralled with her dad's story.

"I rode a couple different horses," He handed the rope back to Wade. "I always seemed to be training a new horse."

"Did you or dad ever crash?" Wade asked. Watching buck-offs and crashes on TV was always the best part.

"Couple times, but nothing bad," He leaned forward in his seat. "Worse I saw was a steer dart in front of the horse and try to stop. The horse went right over the steer, tripped then rolled, sending the heeler up in the air and down on both legs…bent them backwards."

The girls groaned and the boys smiled.

"Dang!" Wade cried out and touched his cast. "That must have hurt!"

"Carried him off on a stretcher," His uncle chuckled. Men have such a weird sense of humor. "He was back competing two months later in Walla Walla and won."

"Did you or Dad break anything?" Nora asked.

"Not in the rodeo, but at the ranch," He nodded at Wade's casted arm. "We both broke our arms when we decided to ride a couple steer in the back pasture."

Wade looked down at his cast and frowned. Was his uncle going to ask him how he broke his arm? He glanced up at his uncle and was surprised to see him looking at Grace instead.

"At the same time?" Grace asked.

"Yeah, and both the left arm," His uncle's eyes shone with mischievous memories. "We challenged each other to see who could stay on the longest. So, at the same time, we slid off our horses and onto the steer," He laughed. "We didn't even get bucked off."

"Then how did you break them?" Sadie asked.

"Some really pissed off mama cows!" He laughed and all the kids joined him. "Both of them chased their wild babies down a hill and we jumped off to get away from the mad cows. We both hit rocks and broke our arms."

"What did Grandma and Grandpa say?" Grace laughed.

He leaned back in his chair, "Well, they sure weren't as mad as we thought they would be." Wade waited for his uncle to turn to him accusingly, but he didn't. He just continued looking at Grace and telling the story. "Grandma just loaded us in the truck and took us into the doctor."

"And Grandpa?" Sadie asked.

His uncle chuckled and glanced up at Aunt Dru. "He just called us idiots and said, 'Well, I guess you won't do that again.'"

Everyone laughed but Wade. He looked down at his cast then up at his uncle. It wasn't the same. His dad wouldn't laugh or just call him an idiot; he would hate him and not love him anymore.

"Dad?" Grace said and everyone turned to her.

"Yeah?" He leaned forward with his elbows on the table.

She glanced over at Reilly who nodded at her. "Reilly and I would like to team rope with Buttercup and Rufio," Her dad raised his eyebrows in surprise. "Would you help us train them?"

"Mine, too?" Sadie added. "Little Ghost and I can do breakaway roping. Please, please, please!"

Wade sat up straight thinking about Dollar and Rooster.

"I haven't trained a horse for rodeo in a long time kids." He answered.

"It couldn't have changed much," Reilly said. "Team roping hasn't changed much…besides getting faster."

Wade watched his uncle look around the table at all the kids. They all eagerly waited for his answer.

"I'm older now," Reilly added quickly. "And will help with the ranch more so you can have time for training. I'll ask Dad and Scott if they will train me with shoeing so I can help with that, too."

"I'll help with the ranch, too," Grace added. "Anything you need."

Aunt Dru leaned against the kitchen counter with her arms crossed in front of her, she watched the group closely. Uncle Grayson sat back in his chair and glanced over at her. She grinned at him; obviously amused by the conversation.

"Uncle Grayson?" Wade said quietly and his uncle looked over at him. "I believe these horses came into our life for a reason." He looked down at the lariat that started the conversation then back up at his uncle. "Maybe getting back to rodeo is what the reason is for you."

Uncle Grayson smiled at him and nodded, "Maybe you're right, Wade."

"So you'll do it?" Reilly asked hopefully.

His uncle looked around at all the kids. "It's a lot of work," He warned them.

Before he had a chance to answer, Wade's mom walked through the kitchen door with his dad right behind her and they were both smiling.

Nora and Wade quickly glanced at each other then at their parents. Their mom went to Aunt Dru and hugged her. Wade felt the relief inside, he smiled up at his parents.

"So what's going on here?" His dad asked and came up behind Nora and Wade; he kissed them both on the top of the head.

"Your brother is about to agree to train our little herd of kids and horses to rope in the rodeo." Aunt Dru grinned.

His dad laughed. It was a really happy laugh that Wade hadn't heard in a long time.

"Well kids," He looked around at them. "You couldn't ask for a better trainer. He sure trained some great ones for us," He started to sit on one of the empty chairs. "Let me tell you about Abraham..."

CHAPTER NINE

Wade lifted the rope and twirled it the best he could. He couldn't hold the rope in his casted hand so he watched Reilly throw the rope again. The loop sailed high, and just as it looked like it would land over the top of its target, it just kept going and missed.

"Lots of work and lots of practice," Reilly grinned at him. Wade nodded.

They had put the plastic calf head in the end of a straw bale to practice roping. The calf head had been in the barn for years and they had occasionally pulled it out and played with it. Now they had a mission.

"Dad said he was going to buy us mechanical training calves. They even have one to pull behind the 4-wheeler." Wade told Reilly. "That way we can practice roping without wearing out the cows."

"I've seen them," Reilly swung the rope in circles over his head again then threw it towards their make-shift calf. It went high again. He grinned at Wade, "…and I need one."

Wade laughed, "You, me, Grace and Sadie all roping, we're gonna need more than one." He glanced over his shoulder and saw the girls walking towards them with lariats in hand. "Like right now."

Reilly looked over and saw them too. He looked back at Wade. "It's guy time."

Wade happily agreed and coiled his lariat and tucked it under his arm. They took off running behind the house to get away from the girls. They started laughing when they heard the girls yelling at them and ran faster around the side of the house and all the way to the front yard only stopping when they saw the horses in the pasture.

Wade looked at Reilly and nodded. He used his good arm and hooked it over the top rail of the fence. Reilly balanced him and gave him an extra push to get all the way over. Once Wade was over, Reilly crawled up and over and they ran for the island in the middle of the pasture.

Reilly opened the gate for Wade and they each sat on one of the benches that faced each other.

"Sometimes, I really get tired of hanging out with just girls." Wade grinned at Reilly.

"Just need some guy time," Reilly grinned back. He stretched out on the bench with his arms behind his head. Wade copied him the best he could.

"Reilly?"

"Yeah?"

"I turn 10 tomorrow."

"I know that."

"How long have you and your dad been with Tagger Enterprises?

"About seven years."

"So I was three."

"That's the math," Reilly laughed.

"I don't really remember life when you weren't in my life."

"Are you getting mushy Wade?"

"Sort of," He chuckled. He was staring up through the limbs of the large oak tree...most the leaves had already fallen.

"OK, I'll sit through this," Reilly teased. "Consider it your birthday present."

Wade laughed, "I like Rufio and Cooper."

"Me, too. They're going to be great roping horses." Reilly said. Then he turned towards him. "I'm really sorry about Rooster. I'll be thinking about him all day tomorrow. So you better call as soon as you know anything."

Wade nodded, "We all spent a lot of time with the horses. He's mine…but ours too…"

They turned and looked back up into the trees.

"I miss Matt," Wade said.

"Where'd that come from?" Reilly laughed. "We were talking about horses."

"Yeah," Wade sighed. "My brain has just been jumping all over lately."

"So what's the mushy stuff you wanted to say?"

"I just wanted you to know that, no matter what happens, you'll always be my brother."

Reilly didn't answer him so he turned to look at him.

After a few minutes Reilly spoke; "I remember when I first got here, you used to follow me around like a puppy dog."

"So…that hasn't changed." Wade giggled.

Reilly laughed, "But I remember thinking back how I needed to protect you like you were my brother. Our parents didn't even have to ask me to help you if something happened or they were busy; I'd just be there helping you."

Wade smiled up at the tree, "You and Matt have always been there for me…us guys sticking together."

Reilly's legs flew up in the air and he twisted and sat up, slamming his feet on the ground with a bang. Wade laughed and awkwardly repeated Reilly's move the best he could with the cast on his arm. They were facing each other.

When he looked over at Reilly his smile faded. Reilly was looking at him with a serious expression.

"What?" Wade asked.

"You're about to get your first big brother advice," Reilly warned him.

"What?"

"How did you break your arm?"

Wade felt the tightness in his lungs again. His hand quickly went to his chest. He grimaced from the ache when he looked at Reilly.

"You OK?" Reilly asked in concern and moved to the bench next to Wade.

Wade slowly took a couple breathes. He didn't breathe too deep because he didn't want to have another panic attack. He looked over at Dollar who was grazing quietly in the pasture in front of them. He watched the horse's lips open and close and his teeth pull at the grass. Wade looked to Dollar's big soft brown eyes. Then he glanced to the back of the horse and watched the tail flick back and forth. His lungs quit hurting.

"You don't have to tell me HOW," Reilly started, "But can you tell me WHY you're scared to tell anyone how it happened?"

Wade looked at the ground and considered the question, "Promise you won't tell anyone?"

"If that's the way you want it," Reilly nodded, "A brother's promise." He stuck out his hand. Wade hesitated then finally reached out and shook it.

Wade looked up at Reilly then down to the ground. He knew Reilly would keep his secret. "Dad will hate me if he found out how I broke it and I don't want to lose my dad." His stomach felt ill for just saying that much. He felt like throwing up.

Reilly nodded and admitted, "I've felt that before, but not to the extreme you're feeling it. You're making yourself sick over it."

Wade remained quiet. He was willing himself not to throw up.

"Wade," Reilly waited until he looked at him before he continued, "The other night, when you had your breathing attack, I saw how scared and worried your mom and dad were."

The guilt hit Wade as if Reilly had physically punched him. His eyes closed and he groaned… his heart began to hurt again.

"No," Reilly said loudly. "Look at me." Wade opened his eyes and met Reilly's worried blue eyes. "I didn't say that to make you feel bad. I said it so you could know how much you mean to Scott and Jordan."

Wade nodded but didn't say anything.

"You should tell your parents what happened." Reilly said.

Wade shook his head. "I can't."

Reilly sighed. "Do you think that there is anything that I could do to make my dad hate me?"

Wade frowned. "No."

"Does my dad love me more than Scott loves you?"

Wade didn't answer.

Reilly moved back over to the other bench so they could face each other again.

"Remember what Grayson said this morning about him and Scott breaking their arms?" Reilly asked. Wade nodded. "He said that his parents weren't as mad as what they thought they were going to be."

"I know," Wade whispered.

Reilly's phone announced he had a new message. He read it and sighed, "Dad's on his way."

They sat quietly a few minutes.

Reilly stood up and started jumping up and down.

Wade looked at him like he was crazy, "What are you doing?"

"Getting rid of the bad mojo," He answered with a grin, "You can't be serious if you're jumping up and down."

Wade laughed and stood up to join him. They were still jumping when they saw Jack's truck stop at the end of the driveway.

Reilly went through the gate then turned around, "Wade, there is nothing you can do that would make Scott hate you," He started to turn then hesitated. "Except maybe murdering someone," He had a mischievous grin on his face. "You didn't murder anyone did you?"

Wade chuckled, "No."

"Well then, tell your dad what happened." He turned and yelled. "And that's your first advice from your big brother!"

He watched Reilly, rope in hand, run across the pasture and meet his dad at the lower gate, then watched as the truck made its way down the road and round the turn to town. He lay back down on the bench with his good arm behind his head. All he could hear was the horses walking around and eating. Every once in a while a car would drive by.

He heard his mother calling out to him so he sat up, grabbed his rope that had fallen to the ground, and slowly moved over to the gate. As he started to push the gate open he looked up and saw Monty standing on the other side staring at him. He froze, fear gripping his heart. Why was his dad's horse here? He'd never seen him off the ranch. Wade felt his heartbeat getting faster…it was pounding in his ears. With shaking hands he slowly closed the gate, keeping the fence between them, but trapping Wade in the pasture island.

He didn't move anything but his eyes as he looked for the other horses. He could only see Eli, Buttercup, Cooper, Arcturus, and Trooper, so he slowly turned his head. Monty took a step towards him, he froze again. Wade's pulse was racing and his breathing started to increase. He took a deep breath and slowly let it out trying to stop a panic attack; no one was around to help him.

Wade took a step back away from the gate and Monty came running at him. Terror took over and he began walking backwards as fast as he could; he tripped on one of the plants and landed on his back. The big grey horse hit the fence chest first; his eyes staring right at Wade. With lungs on the verge of bursting Wade sat very still hoping Monty would leave.

The horse took a few steps backward then rammed the fence again. Wade stood up and ran to the far end of the island. Monty followed him snorting wildly, throwing his head in the air causing his mane to fly wildly; his eyes glowing.

"Stop!" Wade yelled at the horse as his panic heightened. He looked over at the house, someone was on the front porch. It was his mom.

"Mom!" He screamed. She turned away and walked in the front door.

Monty began ramming the fence next to him which made Wade's lungs start to hurt again. His hand grasped at his shirt trying to pull it away to make more room to breathe. He ran down to the other side of the island. "Go away!" He screamed again and started gasping for breath in big gulps. He looked around desperately trying to find something for protection. Monty rammed the fence again and Wade could see the top rail crack. The fear began bubbling out of his stomach and up his throat. The next push caused the rail to break in half and fall slowly to the ground. The horse stopped and stared at him. Wade knew that Monty could get to him now. He'd seen the horse jump brush and fallen trees that high.

He tried to yell but vomited instead, making him gag and fall to his knees. Monty took a step backwards and the horse's head swung to the left. Wade looked in the same direction, Monty was looking at Rooster who was grazing peacefully unaware of the monster of a horse aiming for him.

"No!" He tried to scream. Wade forced himself to stand up and leaned his head back and took a slow deep breath. He would have to calm down to save Rooster. Lowering his head, Wade looked for Monty.

The horse was prancing around wildly until he suddenly stopped and reared up on his back legs. He looked huge…a monster of a horse. Monty lunged forward, flying in the air directly at Rooster. Wade screamed and ran for the fence slamming into it then falling backwards on the ground. Everything went black.

Wade sat up. He was breathing so fast his whole body was tingling, his head back in the fog. He looked up in time to see his dad jumping over the fence Monty had just rammed and his mom running behind him. Nora was running behind her. Wade looked around trying to find Monty and Rooster.

Rooster and the other horses were standing at the fence watching him.

He had fallen asleep on the bench and was having a nightmare. He lifted his arms as his dad grabbed him. His dad's whole body was shaking. His mother opened the gate and ran to their side, wrapping her arms around them; tears streaming. Nora quickly joined them and was pulled into their family hug.

No one spoke; they just held each other tightly.

Wade realized they were all too scared to speak. He must have screamed when Monty attacked. He turned his head and saw Rooster. Monty wasn't attacking Rooster…Rooster was OK. He tried to get his breathing to slow down by watching the horse.

His arms were wrapped around his dad's neck, cast and all so he could feel his dad's heart racing. Wade took a few deep breaths to relax, then concentrated on his dad's heartbeats; they both started slowing down.

Then he thought of Reilly's brotherly advice.

"I didn't murder anyone, Dad." Wade whispered.

"What?" His dad's arms relaxed but didn't let him go.

"Reilly said you would love me no matter what, unless I murdered someone." He explained.

"Reilly started this?" His mom asked.

"No," Wade leaned back to look at them. Their faces were still tense and now a little confused. "Well, sort of."

"Wade?" His dad said softly.

Wade looked up at him. "Yeah?"

"Reilly is right."

CHAPTER TEN

Holding onto the corner of the cattle ramp, Wade stood on the wood fence; stretching as high up on tippy toes as he could. He tilted the cowboy hat so it shielded his eyes from the sun. The cows had started coming up over the hill a few minutes ago so at any second now he should see the riders. Wade looked to his right and saw his mom and Jessup.

Jessup was one of his favorite people ever. He had started working at the ranch before Wade was born. After The Stables were built, Aunt Dru started working more at new business than at the ranch, so they needed a new foreman at the ranch. Jessup had broken his hip at the ranch where he worked before Tagger Enterprises, and that ranch wouldn't hire him back when he healed. The Tagger Trio had hired him as fast as they could. They didn't want someone else to get him.

Wade didn't know how old Jessup was, but he knew he was younger than Cora…they told him that much. Jessup walked with a limp, which Wade thought was cool…it made the older man look like he came out of a John Wayne movie. If he couldn't ride with his dad, Wade always wanted to ride with Jessup.

Wade looked behind them and saw Aunt Dru and Aunt Leah. Reilly and Grace were next to the horse trailers talking. He couldn't see Sadie and Nora. All of the cows that their groups had gathered were already standing and mooing in the large corral and out in the pasture.

The people at the corrals were all waiting for the men to bring in the rest of the herd. They had ridden deep into the canyon where it was too dangerous for little kids to ride.

Mavis had helped with his group and Bart ran with Aunt Dru and Aunt Leah. The dogs did the hard work of chasing the cows out from under brush and down from steep hill sides.

Wade turned his attention back to the incoming herd of cows. He stretched higher, wanting to get that first glimpse of his dad. The calves were running around trying to find their mothers. The moms were mooing… trying to call their babies. It was so loud Wade could barely hear himself think!

He looked down at the fence he was standing on. It was 2 inches wide and he knew he could walk on it to the other side…maybe then the riders could be seen. Slowly putting one foot in front of the other and balancing with his arms he walked across; the last few steps he finished quickly. Hearing his mom yelling, he glanced over, waved and turned back to the cows. She was going to tell him to stop walking on the fence so he pretended he couldn't hear over the mooing.

There they were! His dad, Jack, Matt, and Uncle Grayson were riding behind the cows. Wade bounced on the fence in excitement. "Look at them," He whispered. They were wearing their cowboy hats and their chaps. It wasn't too cold, but they had long shirts on and his dad and uncle wore their black vests…they looked like they were in a movie.

He watched their every move, "I want to be there." Wade said out loud.

"Where?" Sadie said from behind him on the ground.

"Out there with Dad and the men," He answered without moving his eyes from the riders.

"You will someday," She encouraged.

Suddenly, a cow bolted from the back of the herd and ran up the hillside. His dad and Monty took off at a gallop after it. They ran up above the cow then down in front of it to push it back into the herd. *It was magnificent!*

As his dad made his way back down to the riders, Matt, Jack, and Uncle Grayson turned in their saddles to face him and started clapping; giving him a round of applause for his performance.

Wade laughed. He couldn't hear them over the loud cows but he knew they were joking and laughing and he just wished he was there.

He heard someone ride up next to him, "I'm going in to help Cora with dinner," It was his mom. Wade kept his eyes on the riders but nodded. "Do you want to ride with me?"

"Nah, I'm OK, Mom."

"Are you sure?"

"It's OK," He assured her without looking.

He didn't hear her go; just watched the cowboys pushing the cows. The corral was nearly bursting with all the cows that were in it already. It was a lake of red and black backs.

Wade quickly looked around and saw that only Reilly and Aunt Dru were still there; off their horses and ready to shut the gates. Everyone else had ridden up to the house for dinner. He couldn't believe they didn't want to see the riders come in, it was one of the best parts of the day.

 Before his dad could see him, Wade quickly fence walked back over to the ramp.

"Wade, knock it off!" He heard his dad over the mooing of the cows. Busted!

Wade turned and grinned at his dad like nothing was wrong. His dad rode up beside him, wrapped his arm around Wade's knees and pulled him over his shoulder. Still on horseback! Wade screamed with laughter.

"Dad!" Wade had to brace his hands on Monty's rump, his feet high in the air over his dad's head.

"You said you wanted to ride Monty today," His dad laughed and walked the horse back to where Matt, Jack, and his uncle were.

"Yeah, but not upside down and backwards." Wade laughed.

"That's the way you ride all the time," Matt teased.

Wade just laughed as his dad walked Monty closer to Matt, who helped him get turned around and sitting behind his dad. Wade wrapped his arms around his waist tightly and looked around. Aunt Dru and Reilly had shut the gates to the pasture and were looking over the cows. Reilly was standing next to Jack who was still mounted on his horse.

Uncle Grayson sat quietly looking at the cows.

"Wade," His dad had turned in the saddle trying to see him.

"Yeah, Dad?"

"Promise me you will stop walking on the fence tops."

"OK, Dad." Wade looked over at Matt who had lifted his cowboy hat off his head and was wiping the sweat from his forehead. He smiled at Wade, "Want me to lead your horse back?"

Wade nodded, he may be "almost ten" but he still liked riding with his dad on Monty.

"I'm hungry, I hope dinner's ready." Matt hollered over the noise of the cows as he untied Wade's ranch pony and led him in the direction of the house; Uncle Grayson and Jack falling in line behind him. Aunt Dru and Reilly quickly mounted their horses and followed.

That left just Wade and his dad coming up the back.

"Can I ride him today?" Wade asked once they got away from the loud cows.

"Not today, Son. He's a bit riled up after chasing cows. You need to grow a little more. He needs a strong rider."

"OK," Wade sat quietly behind his dad as they made their way up the road that led to the house. Monty was relaxed and walking with ease. His dad barely moved his hand to turn him left or right so Wade was convinced he could ride him.

Wade turned and looked back at the corral full of cows, "Are we going to work all of them tomorrow?" It was time for pregnancy test, shots, and separating out the cows that weren't bred.

"We'll get them all done, but it will be late when we finish and head home."

"Headed home on Saturday?" Wade was surprised. "I thought we weren't going home until Sunday."

"Seems, someone has a birthday coming up and presents have to be bought and party arrangements need to be made."

"Well…that's a pretty good reason if you ask me!" Wade said happily. He glanced over and saw a new trail cut through the trees. "Where's that trail go?"

His dad glanced over. "Jessup must be working on something." He turned Monty to head up the trail instead of the road.

"Oh cool!" Wade grinned. He was off on an adventure with Dad.

He sat quietly enjoying the motion of the horse. Every once in a while he bent sideways around his dad to see where the trail was leading.

"Can you tell where it's going?" Wade asked.

"It looks like it's going to meet up with the other road. Probably a shortcut so you don't have to go all the way up to the house and around the big corner to move between the barn and the corrals."

"That's a great idea."

The trail came to an end between the barn and the house. They turned and saw Matt and the other riders just coming into the driveway.

"That's quite a shortcut." Using his dad's arm he swung off the horse.

His dad agreed as the other riders approached and wanted to know how they got there so quickly. Wade walked proudly next to his dad as they made their way into the house for dinner.

******

After a full day of school, the drive to the ranch with Cora, and riding all afternoon, the kids were tired; except for Wade. Even the parents were tired. By nine o'clock the whole house was asleep except Wade and Jessup. Jessup had driven to their ranch neighbor Andy's house to pick up supplies for the next day.

Wade lay in bed looking around the bunkhouse. It was just one large room with eight sets of bunk beds placed along the walls, four on each side. The lower bunk was larger than the upper bunk, so the adults slept in the lower beds and the kids in the upper beds. Dressers were placed against the wall in between the bunks. Matt was on the bottom portion of the bunk bed that Wade was in. There was a small kitchen area at one end of the building and a bathroom at the other end by the door. It was always fun to sleep in the same room as everyone else. Jessup and Cora were the only ones that slept in two of the three bedrooms in the ranch house.

Wade sat up in bed and looked around. Light snoring echoed throughout the room. Bart was curled up on the foot of Matt's bed and Mavis was curled up on Nikki's bed. Looking outside the window, the moon was almost full. He could see the outline of the barn on one side of the bunkhouse and on the other side he could see the roof of the house.

There was a window next to the bunk bed Wade was in so he quietly slid out of bed to stand at the window and look at the sky. The moon lit up the house and the little white fence that created a yard around it. Trucks were lined up in front of the house.

"I bet you can see the stars real good from the back of the truck." He crawled back up on the bed and lay quietly. His legs started getting restless and he had to keep moving them so they didn't itch.

Finally, giving up and climbing back down the bunk ladder, he walked carefully down the row of beds to the door. It was still warm out, so the brown hoody he was wearing was warm enough. All their boots where lined up along each side of the door. It took him a minute of searching to find his own boots then tucked them under his arm before he slowly turned the handle of the door. There was no sound as it opened. One last look in the bunkhouse; there was no movement from anyone except Bart. The dog jumped off the bed and trotted to him then out the door. Wade glanced around the room one more time and then slowly slid out the door and closed it carefully.

He took a few steps away from the door and slid on the boots then walked around the corner of the house to see where Bart went. The dog had lifted his leg on the nearest tree.

Wade walked over to the trucks intending to crawl into the back of one of them and watch the stars from the top of the tool box. Bart followed right behind him, but when Wade stopped the dog kept going.

"Bart!" Wade whispered as loudly as he could. The dog just kept trotting down the road toward the corrals where the cows were penned in the large enclosure and the horses in a small corral next to them. He took off running behind the dog.

"Matt and Dad are gonna be mad if you get hurt, Bart." He mumbled after the dog.

The dog didn't care, so Wade continued to run after him until he got to the big corner that led to the corrals. It was so dark he couldn't see the corrals in the distance so he turned to look at the bunkhouse.

Wade was too far away and couldn't see it anymore, so he continued down to the corral…he needed to get the dog back.

When he arrived at the corrals he stopped, but Bart was nowhere to be seen so he walked over to the horse corral and climbed on the gate. He sat quietly and stared up at the twinkling stars. The large bright moon lit the area around the corrals. He looked back up the road to the corner that led to the house. There were no lights; it looked like a black oasis. The outline of the trees could be seen because the sky was so light. If it hadn't been for running after Bart, he wouldn't have been brave enough to walk through the dark night to the corrals.

Wade felt a nudge on his back. He jumped and turned quickly only to see the horse that Jack was riding standing next to him. The horse was curious about Wade so he reached out and petted it between the ears. The horse shook his head, not liking his ears played with. Wade chuckled then looked around the group of horses. They were so tired there was still hay in the feeders and the horses were either lying on the ground or standing along the fence sleeping.

Wade looked for Monty and found the grey horse standing on the opposite side of the corral, head down, and eyes closed. Wade climbed higher on the fence. The cattle ramp was to his right and the posts were high enough for him to use as a brace as he stood on the fence. Out of habit, he turned to look to see if anyone was watching him, then laughed at himself.

He climbed the fence and stood high above the horses feeling like the king of the cowboys. He wanted to get over to Monty so he looked around the corral and planned his path; without touching the ground of course…what kind of an adventure would that be?

He needed to jump from one side of the cattle ramp to the other, then swing his leg back to the fence and pull himself up. From there he could stand and fence walk over to the corner of the corral to

Monty. There was a large four post brace in the corner and he could stand comfortably to see the horse.

Wade leaned back, holding the side of the cattle ramp, and jumped to the other side. Both hands wrapped around the top of the ramp holding him up. His legs dangled free. Swinging his legs over to the fence and catching his boot on the rail, he walked his hands across the top of the ramp to get his body all the way over. When he got there, it took all his strength to pull himself all the way on top of the fence. He stood. "Yes!" Wade grinned; proud of his accomplishment.

Now for the fence walk…he braced himself with the tall ramp post and took a first tentative step. He began to fall to the right and grabbed the post to keep from falling. The horses were in the corral to his left and there were cows to his right. A few cows were black with white faces; all the others were either solid black or solid red. He couldn't see the cows well, but every once in a while he would see a flash of white from their face.

"Don't fall," He said to himself and took another step; all was good so he took another, then another. Now, he was too far away from either side to grab anything for balance, so he began to walk faster. He started to fall to the right, and balanced himself by leaning hard to the left and walking faster to make it to the four post brace. "Yes!" He shouted and stood proudly on the corner post.

Bart barked, Wade turned quickly to see if he could see the dog…too quickly. He felt himself going backwards and turned to try to catch the fence. He was falling into the cattle corral! He lunged to catch the fence and missed. There was no way he could protect himself and looked to see where he was going to land; the metal cattle squeeze chute was under him. It had bars over the top and side and was used to catch and hold the cows while they were doctoring them.

Wade put his left arm out to try to catch himself on the chute, he grabbed for a bar but missed and continued to fall until his arm caught between two of the bars as his body hurtled to the ground. A scream escaped when he felt the arm catch then break; shearing pain ran from his upper arm into his shoulder. He hit the ground, landing on his back. The force freed his arm from the chute but caused it to slam into the ground painfully. He lay stunned. The pain was so bad he couldn't even cry.

Then he heard them…the scream had scared the cows. They were beginning to mill around faster and faster; closer and closer. The ground under him started to vibrate. Fear shot through his stomach as a large calf appeared with its mother right behind it. She stopped and stared at him. Streams of snot were running out of her nose and her eyes looked frightened. More cows came up behind her.

Wade's mind went to Charlie in his favorite movie *The Cowboys*. When Charlie went down into the cows to get his friends glasses, he spooked the cows and they trampled him to death. Wade could see them wrapping Charlie in a blanket and lowering him into the grave.

Terror screamed out of Wade, causing the cows to start moving around each other. The cow that had stopped and stared must have thought he was going to hurt her calf. It charged him. Despite the horrid pain shooting through his arm, Wade turned onto his stomach and tried to crawl away from the cow. The ground shook under him…he closed his eyes and prepared to be trampled. A loud crash sound echoed through the night…it was louder than the cow's hoof beats…then silence. All he could hear was animals breathing.

When the cow didn't hit him, Wade slowly turned his head to see where she went. The scared cow was so close, the snot was dripping only inches away from his face. Her breath pushed its way down the top of Wade's head and down his back. He lay frozen; not knowing what to do.

Another loud crash rang out. The cow shook her head and turned to leave. Then another crash! The cow swung around to run away; she bucked with a twist and a kick- out with her back legs. A back hoof landed on the lower portion of his already injured arm, breaking it too. He screamed again as another loud crash echoed and the cows moved away.

Wade began to cry from the fear and the pain. He knew his arm was broken; twice. When the tears finally stopped, he remembered the loud crashing that scared the cow away. What had caused it? Flipping his head around in the direction of the noise; his eyes widened in horror. Monty was standing at the fence…his chest bloody from where the horse had slammed against the fence. The top rail was broken and the second rail was cracked. He'd hurt Monty. His dad was going to kill him! Dragging his broken arm along the ground, Wade crawled to the fence.

Monty was leaning over the broken rails. When Wade got to him, the horse's breath ran down his back as the horse nudged his ear.

"Monty, I'm sorry," Wade cried. He looked at the horse's wounds and saw two deep gashes running across the whole chest; blood dripping. "I'm so sorry."

Wade lay quietly with Monty standing over him. He didn't know what to do. It wasn't very late and no one would be getting up for six or seven more hours. He couldn't lay there that long. He looked down at his arm but couldn't really see anything, but there was a sensation of something running down the inside of his sleeve. Wade guessed it was blood…now he and Monty were both bleeding.

There were bears and mountain lions on the ranch and he knew they were attracted to blood…they could smell it from long distances. He remembered seeing the half eaten calf from a cougar kill. It made him sick to his stomach to think of Monty that way. Wade needed to get help for Monty.

CHAPTER ELEVEN

With his right arm, Wade pushed himself into a sitting position; streaks of pain ran up the left arm and into the shoulder. He cried out making Monty bounce his head up and down.

"Thank you, boy." Monty had saved him from being trampled to death like Charlie, so now he had to save the horse.

Wade took a deep breath and let it out slowly. His mind had to be clear to be able to get help for the horse. Reaching up with his good hand he petted Monty on the nose.

The broken arm began to throb. He needed to get back to the house before the pain took over and he couldn't move.

There was no way he could go over the fence. He would have to crawl under the bottom rail. One more pat on Monty's nose and he rolled over on his knees to crawl under the fence to get out. His left arm dragged helplessly along the ground as he crawled to the fence. When he reached it, he lowered his body and dipped his head under the rail and used his right arm to pull his body under the bottom rail. Once through, he laid on his stomach to catch his breath. Sweat was running down his face and he could still feel the blood trickling inside the arm of the sweatshirt.

Wade looked up the road toward the house, seeing nothing but black…but he knew how to get there. He just needed to move. Should he crawl or try to get up and walk? He decided walking would be faster and pushed up with his good arm, which caused the broken arm to move forward. Shooting pains ran up the arm and across his back and he nearly passed out. Wade remained on his hands and knees until the searing pain subsided. He leaned up with his good arm grabbing the fence…again the searing pain when the arm fell to his side. Pulling up with his good arm he finally stood and leaned against the fence.

"Don't pass out." Wade told himself and held tightly to the fence rail. He felt dizzy and needed to vomit. Taking a deep breath…letting it out slowly then doing it again…the dizziness started to clear.

He looked up the road into the darkness that led to the house…fear and doubt racing through him. "I can't do it."

Tears pushed behind his eyes and his shoulders slumped. One of the horses whinnied softly, making him think of Monty and the blood dripping from the horse's chest. Wade could still feel blood dripping down his own arm. He thought of the cougar kill.

"I have to do this," Wade told himself. He lifted his shoulders and strengthened his back. "I have to. Dad will hate me if Monty dies."

He pushed himself away from the fence and tested letting go. He wobbled to the right, which caused his bad arm to swing painfully. He cried out as the pain ran through the arm and back again. He forced himself to remain standing when his knees wanted to buckle.

Once his head cleared, Wade took a step, then another, and another. He tried to ignore the pain that shot through his body with every step. Staring at the ground, concentrating on the dirt, he took a few more steps. Pause, take a deep breath, three more steps, then pause again. He heard the horses and cows moving around. "For Monty…" He told himself and took three more steps. "For Monty…" He repeated and took three more.

Wade's head began to fog again. He couldn't shake his head without jerking the arm, so he took a couple deep breaths and let them out again. It didn't help.

"Just keep walking for Monty," He said out loud and took another step. He stopped and looked up to see where he was. The corral was still visible behind him. He wanted to cry. It was going to take him hours to get to the house at that pace.

"I have to," Wade told himself and took another step then stopped. He remembered the short cut trail he and his dad had ridden; it would make it faster to get back to the house. Wade slowly walked to the side of the road where he had seen the trail. Not really sure where it was, he just kept walking, hoping to run into it. Finally, he saw the gap in the trees.

He looked up the road. The shine from the moon lit a portion of the road in front of him and also made the top of the trees visible. He turned and looked down the trail. The moon's light couldn't reach the trail through the trees; it was pitch black. The trail had been wide enough for two horses and was in a straight line. He knew he could do it… but it was so scary.

Wade's legs began to shake. He needed to start moving again. Looking between the two paths and thinking of Monty's bloody chest, he turned left and walked into the darkness, continuing to walk three steps at a time. He tried to imagine the path that they had followed. He kept walking, his head got lighter, and felt his knees wobbling again.

"For Monty," He whispered and concentrated on one step at a time.

A wave of nausea ran through his stomach and up into his head making him dizzy; his feet began to feel heavier. Each step was slower…he barely had the strength to pick his feet up. They were dragging…making it that much harder to take another step. He knew he was going to fall so he stopped and tried deep breathing again. It didn't work. He tried another step but stumbled and fell to his knees. The broken arm jerked and the pain soared through him again; a cry of agony escaped.

Wade leaned forward and placed the good hand on the ground. His broken arm fell forward…hand dragging at his side. He tried crawling, but the movement of lifting the good arm, pushing it forward and dropping again to the ground caused even more pain. Laying on his stomach again he pushed with his feet and pulled with the good arm and was able to move forward. Wade remembered seeing army guys in the movies crawl that way with both arms.

"I can do it," He said out loud and continued to crawl forward until his right hand landed on a rock. He realized he was too far to the side so he angled himself differently and kept moving.

The pain in the broken arm was easier to bear this way instead of dangling at his side so he continued to crawl. He looked up and saw complete blackness, so he put his head down and continued to push and pull himself along the trail. He visualized Monty's bloody chest and the cougar kill to motivate him to keep crawling.

When he stopped to rest, he could hear breathing behind him. The fear rushed through his body again and he was about to scream when he felt the lick on his face. It was Bart. Wade wanted to cry in relief.

"Oh, Bart," He cried out loud.

Wade took a deep breath and continued to crawl. The dog walking along side of him seemed to give him a burst of energy. His left shoulder bumped into something and pain shot down his arm…his head swirled in fog and he thought he was going to pass out.

"I have to make it to the road." Wade told the dog. He looked up and had to blink twice. Seeing the tips of trees highlighted with the moonlit sky he knew he had to be getting close to the end of the trail. He took a deep breath and continued. His broken arm had gone numb and only noticed it when it hit a branch or rock.

"What do I do when I get there?" He asked Bart. Dad was going to hate him. He had let Bart out of the bunkhouse, he had promised not to fence walk and yet he did it again and broke that promise. He felt the heaviness in his heart as he realized how disappointed his dad would be. He had always told Wade that a man should always keep his promise. Yet he broke his promise to his dad.

Wade continued to crawl as his head grew lighter and his heart heavier. The worst thing was…he caused Monty to get hurt and he was now bleeding and could be prey for a bear or cougar.

Raindrops touched his cheek. What else could happen?

Wade continued to crawl and adjust to the path as he hit things along the way. The raindrops came faster and heavier while Bart walked quietly next to him.

His hand reached out and landed on gravel. He had made it to the road!

He looked up and could see the outline of the trees. Looking left, he could see the top of the barn. He was so close. Turning right toward the house and bunkhouse he continued to crawl.

More raindrops splattered on his face.

Wade's head was getting lower and lower to the ground. Each stretch of his hand was slower and slower until he couldn't get his arm to lift anymore. "I'm so close." Wade cried as his eyes began to close. "For Monty." He whispered and tried again, but his arm wouldn't move.

"I can't stop now." Trying again, nothing in his body moved. His eyes closed.

Wade could hear Bart barking beside him; barking over and over again. He tried again to open his eyes but they wouldn't open. The ground began to rumble but he had no idea what it was. In one last effort, Wade opened his eyes just enough to see lights coming at him.

They stopped just before reaching him and a limping figure was running towards him; it was Jessup.

Wade tried hard to say Monty but his mouth couldn't get the words out. Suddenly he felt a searing pain run up his arm and through his body as Jessup tried to move him. He cried out and everything went black.

******

Nobody had spoken while he told the story. Wade sat quietly and couldn't get brave enough to look at his dad. He was sure his dad hated him.

"Jessup started honking the horn to get our attention," His mom said. They were still sitting on the bench. Wade was tucked in his mother's arms and could see his dad across from him. Nora was wrapped in his dad's arms. "Bart was running frantically around you."

"We got you to the hospital as fast as possible," Nora added.

"You were so close to the house that we didn't even think Monty's injuries had anything to do with you," His mom continued. "The rain…then the wind started just after we loaded you in the truck. Jessup tried to follow your trail but he couldn't, so we had no way of knowing what you went through." She squeezed him tightly.

Wade kept his head down. His dad wasn't talking.

Wade turned and looked up at his mom's eyes. They were so dark…almost black…and there was pain…worry…fear…and love. He had scared his family…hurt them…broke his promise…from the bottom of his heart he spoke, "I'm sorry," He said it with such honesty that more tears sprung to her eyes.

He turned to Nora and looked into her eyes, "I'm sorry."

She wrapped her arms around him and hugged him. When she sat back, she held his hand tightly while the tears fell down her cheeks.

Wade still couldn't look at his dad…he knew the truth now…he was sure he hated him. Wade had caused Monty's injuries and promises were broken. He hadn't cried as he told the story but now, knowing he lost his dad, the tears streamed down his face and dripped onto his shirt. He didn't even try to wipe them away.

The four of them sat in silence for a long time until his mom reached out and gently touched the side of his dad's face, but he still didn't move, his eyes were looking across the pasture. Slowly, she moved out from behind Wade, kissed him on the top of the head and took Nora's hand.

"But Mom," Nora complained as she was led out of the island, leaving him and his dad alone.

Wade sat on the edge of the bench and stared at the ground. Even if he never spoke to him again, his dad needed to know that he was sorry for what happened to Monty.

He didn't look up but spoke as firmly as he could, "I'm sorry Dad, for breaking my promise…I promised I wouldn't fence walk and I broke that promise. I'm sorry for almost losing Bart and I am really sorry that Monty got hurt."

Wade stood and turned away to walk to the house.

"Wade," His dad's voice was so low Wade barely heard it. What was worse; he called him Wade, not Buddy. His heart started to hurt worse than it did all week. There was no painful lungs or panicked breathes, it was just a breaking heart. He took a deep sobbing breath that shook when he released it.

"Turn around," His dad said in a whispered voice. Wade did as he was told and turned around but he stared at the ground.

"Chin up and look at me."

Wade tried…he lifted his head but his eyes went closed because he didn't want to see the disappointment on his father's face.

"Wade, look at me."

With all his might, Wade forced his eyes open and looked at his dad.

He was still sitting on the bench so their heads were at the same height. His eyes were sparkling from tears that hadn't fallen. There was no disappointment in his eyes.

"You," He started, but his voice cracked from emotion. He stopped and started again. "You are the bravest and strongest young man. What you went through …to help Monty…incredible. The strength to put yourself through the pain, to go into the darkness, and fight to continue…." His voice broke and a tear fell.

Wade stared in disbelief. "You don't hate me?" His heart raced in hope and desperation.

"Hate you?" His dad sounded surprised. "Never."

Wade took a deep breath and let it out slowly.

"Buddy, I am so proud to be your dad." His arms spread out and Wade ran into them. He called him Buddy! He hugged his dad as tight as he could.

After a few minutes his dad finally spoke again; "I'm just glad you didn't murder anyone."

Wade giggled.

CHAPTER TWELVE

Wade walked to the barn. He didn't want to be there when his parents told everyone how he broke his arm.

All of the Tagger Herd stuck their heads over the stall doors. Wade smiled; it was the best sight ever. No one had fed them yet because they were called to the house as soon as they had put them in their stalls. He looked at his cast, looked at the horses, then looked at the wheelbarrow.

"I'll give it a try," He said out loud to the horses.

Ten minutes later, Wade finally got the hay into the wheelbarrow and slowly maneuvered it into the barn. He was just able to balance the handle with his casted hand to get a half load of hay at a time. He had broken into a sweat by the time the last horse was fed.

Grabbing a brush, he made his way to the stall with Rooster and Dollar. The horses had put on enough weight that the inside stall wasn't big enough for them to move around so the door to the outside section of their stall was left open. Which meant it was getting chilly.

"Wish I'd brought a coat," Wade told Rooster as he stepped into the stall and started brushing the horse's red hair.

"I brought you one."

Wade turned to see Nora, smiling and holding up a jacket.

"You're awesome." He grinned.

She stepped into the stall and they maneuvered the coat on him. His casted arm was left under the jacket, the empty sleeve dangled at his side which made them both smile.

"Did they tell everyone?" Wade asked.

"Jack and Reilly just got here, so they are now."

"I'm sorry, Nora."

"I know…but you're a lot braver than I am. I don't know that I could have run after Bart in the dark, let alone crawl with a broken arm."

Wade didn't answer. He didn't care if he ever talked about it again.

"You done talking about it?"

He nodded.

"OK."

Nora remained quiet and brushed Dollar while he brushed Rooster.

"They sure look better." Wade commented.

"All but Arcturus," She sighed. "He's losing weight."

"That's what Uncle Grayson said. He was going to talk to Nikki about it."

"She changed his supplement plan and we're going to take him in once a week to the clinic for a checkup."

Nora stepped out of the stall and returned with a bale of straw to drag into with them.

Wade smiled, she understood he needed to be with his horse…it could be the last night.

They both took a seat on the bale with Nora slipping an arm around his good one then leaned her head on his shoulder. They sat quietly watching Rooster eat.

Reilly appeared at the stall door then disappeared. He returned with two more bales and placed them next to theirs. He took a seat without saying anything. Sadie and Grace appeared next and sat with them.

No one spoke; they just watched the red horses eat.

Wade leaned his head on Nora's which was still on his shoulder. Reilly was on the other side of her. Sadie was cuddled into Wade's other side, with Grace next to her.

One person was missing…he felt his heart aching for her to be there. It wasn't right that they could be spending the last couple of hours with the horse and she wasn't there.

Then…she was. She appeared at the door, smiling at the five of them. Her blue eyes sparkled with pride and love. When she stepped through the door she was carrying blankets.

Sadie and Grace scooted over so Aunt Dru could sit next to him. They spread out the blankets over the top of all of them.

After a few minutes, she broke the silence.

"Well, it sounds like Jordan is going to only work part time in her job."

"She said she was only going to work Tuesday, Wednesday, and Thursday," Nora added.

"How come?" Wade asked.

"Seems like we have a bunch of horses and 5 kids that are going to be doing rodeos and horse shows," Aunt Dru answered.

"Is she nuts?" Grace laughed…the laugh that made everyone else laugh.

"I think she loves all of you and wants to spend more time with you. Helping you all fulfill your rodeo and horse show dreams will do that. She'll be scheduling your shows, making sure you're in the right clubs, and driving you to them…like your manager. It's going to be quite a challenge for her."

"She's a brave woman." Reilly chuckled.

Dollar turned in the stall and looked at the group on the straw bales and stared.

"I think he's confused," Wade smiled.

"Just imagine how you would feel if you woke up with him in your bedroom." Sadie giggled.

"I'd love that!" Wade laughed.

"How would you get him upstairs?" Nora asked, her eyes shining in amusement.

"Not so much that, as cleaning up after him…and having to haul it down the stairs." Grace laughed.

"I'd just throw it out the window." Wade grinned up at the amused eyes of his aunt.

"The guest room is underneath," She smiled at him. "I think the urine soaking through the floor might become an issue."

"I'd have done it over the summer." Sadie sighed. "Especially the first night, if they hadn't been so dirty."

"I can't believe how dirty we ALL were when we got home," Aunt Dru chuckled.

"Dad hosed off all my clothes outside before he threw them in the washer," Reilly grinned.

"Uncle Scott had to take all the trucks in twice to get the seats cleaned." Grace added with a laugh.

"We had to wash the horses twice to get all the mud off them." Sadie reminded them.

"They loved the baths." Wade nodded.

"They still do." Nora sighed with a smile.

"They love…the love you kids have given them." Aunt Dru said softly.

"You, too." Wade whispered.

She nodded and kissed the top of his head.

"I wish it was still summer so we could spend the night out here." Sadie said.

"Me, too." Wade nodded.

"I wish we could all go tomorrow." Nora whispered.

"But we can't." Reilly stood, walked to Rooster and lay is hands on his back.

Sadie stood and joined him…then Grace and Nora.

Tears sprung to Wade's eyes as his aunt helped him stand and unzipped his coat so his casted arm was free.

Then he walked to Rooster's front shoulders and laid his hand on the horse. Aunt Dru stood next to him and did the same.

Just as they had when Angel died, they each touched the horse and gave him their love.

******

"Can Reilly spend the night?" Wade asked Jack as they walked into the kitchen.

"Sure," Jack nodded. "Of course."

Wade tried to smile, but he just didn't feel it. Besides having to leave Rooster's stall, he had to walk in to the hugs and comments from the parents about his broken arm. He just nodded but didn't say anything when they mentioned it.

"It's ten o'clock now, so you all should be getting to bed," Aunt Leah told the kids as they walked in.

The girls headed up the stairs. They all turned back and looked at him.

"Good luck," Sadie said sadly. Wade nodded.

"Come on, I'll go up with you," Jack told him.

Wade followed Reilly up the stairs, Jack walked behind Wade with an arm on his back to support his climb up the steps.

After helping him change from his jeans to his sweat pants, Jack helped him crawl into Matt's big bed and place the pillow under his cast.

Jack looked over at Reilly, who was already tucked into Wade's bed, then back to Wade.

"I wish Reilly could go with you tomorrow," Jack told him.

"Me, too," The boys said in unison.

"But it wouldn't be fair to the other kids…and you'll have your parents there."

"Uncle Grayson and Aunt Dru, too." Wade nodded; then frowned. "Can you check on her before you leave?"

Jack looked at him in surprise.

"She's holding in how upset she is," Wade informed him. "She's got 'her poker face on', as Dad puts it."

"I promise, I will," Jack smiled reassuringly. "But let's get you guys to sleep so your birthday gets here."

Wade chuckled; "I forgot tomorrow was my birthday."

"The big double digit!" Reilly grinned.

"Ever wonder why the double digit one is so special?" Jack asked with a smile.

"Because you're closer to being a teenager," Reilly answered.

"Because I'm closer to being able to ride with the men on cattle roundups," Wade answered truthfully. "How old do I have to be?"

Jack shrugged. "I think Matt started when he was seventeen. He was a strong enough rider and had a good horse."

"Dollar will be a good horse but I need to grow more," Wade sighed.

"You'll start growing pretty soon," Jack assured him. "You'll end up going through a couple spurts."

"A spurt?" Wade looked at him in confusion. "That's a weird word."

"Like when I grew 4 inches one summer," Reilly nodded. "Then I grew three more the next year."

"You had two spurts?" Wade chuckled at the word. "I think I might need three or four to catch up."

"Well, hopefully you get some of Scott's height." Reilly smiled.

"Just another reason to hit the double digits," Jack smiled. "So you can start your growing spurts soon."

Wade nodded. He was the shortest kid in his class. Why did his mom have to be only five feet tall?

"OK, you boys get to sleep," Jack said and walked to the door.

Wade lay in the dark looking at the ceiling…thinking of his dad.

"Thank you, Reilly."

"For what?"

"Your first big brother advise."

"I'm glad it worked…but Wade?"

"Yeah?"

"You can always trust me. Don't hold things in like that anymore."

"I won't…if Mom and Dad don't hate me after that…I can't imagine they would hate me for anything else."

"Except murdering someone," Reilly chuckled.

"Yeah…'cept that."

Wade started to drift off to sleep…

"You'll call me, right?" Reilly said as he yawned.

"As soon as I know."

CHAPTER THIRTEEN

"This is no way to spend your tenth birthday," Wade thought as he moved his fingers around the coil of the lariat. It was his choice to have the surgery on his birthday and had said yes because he didn't want Rooster to hurt anymore, but now he just wished it was over.

He was in the back seat of the truck again, sitting between his parents. He was relieved that they were getting along now. Uncle Grayson was driving and Aunt Dru stared silently out the side window. Her Tagger Enterprises cap was pulled low over her eyes.

All the girls were crying when they said goodbye to Rooster. They didn't know whether the horse would come home again. Wade walked to Dollar and talked to him while the girls said goodbye. All the horses were standing at the fence wondering where Rooster was going and why they weren't going too. Libby was running and bucking… unhappy they took one of her horses.

They pulled into the university a little early so Wade took Rooster for a walk before they went into the big building. He walked over to the large oval arena and leaned into his big red horse.

"We went to the rodeo a couple weeks ago," He told the horse. "I sat and watched all the cowboys on their horses and dreamed of us chasing the cow down the arena and roping it in world record time. We'd win rodeo after rodeo and everyone would know us."

Wade ran his hand down the nose of the horse and rubbed under the rounded jaw. Rooster leaned into him…he seemed to know something was wrong.

"I don't want you to be in pain anymore Rooster," Wade tried to hold back the tears but it wasn't working; one escaped. He rubbed his cheek on the horses shoulder to wipe it off. "I'm supposed to be an adult while we're here, but I just feel like crying like a baby," He sniffed. "Why do you think your nose gets runny when you cry?" He asked the horse. The horse answered by nudging his hands for a treat.

"I know you're hungry," He ran his hand down the length of Rooster's neck. They weren't allowed to give him his morning hay since he was having surgery.

Wade looked underneath the horse's neck and saw there were people in white coats with his parents, Aunt Dru, and Uncle Grayson. To his surprise, Nikki and Matt were standing there too. They had driven over from their university which was only a half hour away.

"Look at that Rooster… they are worried about you too." He sighed.

"Wade?" He heard his mom call out.

"I guess it's time, boy," He turned the horse and started walking back to the adults.

Wade's heart began to hurt again. Each step became harder to take and he started slowing down. It could be his last walk with the horse and he wanted it to last longer. He stopped and Rooster came to a stop next to him, with the horse's nose bumping the cast.

Not ready to let the horse go, Wade turned his back on the building and the people waiting. He looked up at the horse; his throat was tight and his voice trembled when he spoke. His big brown eyes were even with the horse's eyes and he could see his reflection. "I know, if you don't come back out, that you will be in heaven and won't be hurting anymore." Rooster rubbed his head against his chest.

Wade took a deep breath and slowly let it out. "I had a dream the other night…well, it turned into a nightmare, but in the dream I was riding you at the ranch and we were running as fast as we could. We were so happy," He wrapped his good arm around the horse's neck and took a deep breath. He wanted to remember the smell of him. He looked up into the horse's big brown eye. "No matter what happens, Rooster, I will always ride you in my dreams," A tear slowly rolled down his cheek.

"Wade," It was his mom again. He stepped away from the horse and, without turning, handed her the rope. He wanted to remember Rooster like this, not walking into the strange building. As the horse walked by, he reached out and ran his hand down the length of him. His fingers fell away from the horse's hip…the last touch. His fingers instantly felt cold so he balled them into a fist.

Rooster's hoof beats moved away from him, each step, each sound, beating into Wade's heart. "I'll ride you in my dreams…." He whispered…the hoof beats slowly faded away.

"Do you want to go in with him?" It was Aunt Dru, her voice was low and shaky.

Wade shook his head and stared at the ground. She came up beside him and stood quietly next to him.

"Remember when we first found him?" Wade asked.

"Yes," Her voice was a whisper.

Wade looked over and saw her hand stretched out for his. Aunt Dru was there from the beginning and every day since. He took her hand and squeezed tightly…she understood how special Rooster was.

They walked, hand-in-hand, into the large brick building and sat next to the door where the lady told them the doctor would come out when the procedure was over.

They waited and waited.

For two hours, Wade sat and stared at the door. The lariat lay coiled in his lap. He gently ran his fingers over the ridges of the rope.

When the handle on the door began to twist, he sat up straight. Uncle Grayson and Aunt Dru were sitting next to him, pretending to read magazines, but they had been watching too and sat up. His parents, sitting across from them, quickly glanced over at Wade, then to the door.

It seemed like forever before the door actually opened.

"Come on," Wade whispered. He had promised to act like an adult if they brought him. He didn't think running over to the door, pulling it open, and yelling at the doctor would be what they considered acting like an adult. He took another deep breath and let it out. He gripped the lariat tightly.

Finally the door opened and the doctor came out. He nodded at them then turned back to say something to someone in the room. There was no indication whether the surgery was bad or good.

"Come on," Wade repeated; his eyes not moving from the doctor. His heart was beating so hard he thought everyone could hear it.

Finally the doctor walked over and sat in a chair across from them. Just as the veterinarian opened his mouth to speak, Wade lifted his good hand in the air; like parents did when they wanted to quiet down the kids.

The doctor stopped and looked at him in surprise. Wade didn't notice what the other adults did.

"I'm sorry if I'm rude," Trying hard to sound like an adult but without letting the doctor respond, he continued. "I don't understand all the long words that you say, and they kind of scare me," He admitted and took a deep nervous breath; his body was tingling in dread. "I just want to know if Rooster is alive."

The doctor turned his chair so he was directly facing Wade, giving him his full attention and looked him straight in the eyes. "Yes."

Wade fought hard to keep from crying and yelling, "Is he in pain?"

"Right now he is coming out from anesthesia," He paused, realizing he had used a long scary word. "He is waking up and his legs have pain killers in them."

"I had those for my arm," Wade told him. "Will he hurt when the pain killers go away?"

"He will for a couple days, but then it will slowly go away."

Wade's eyes opened wider. "You mean he won't be in pain anymore like he was before the surgery?"

The doctor shook his head. "No, we fixed him so his joints wouldn't hurt anymore."

Wade felt his body shiver in relief.

As Wade started to ask his next question, the doctor held up his hand. "His joints won't be in pain anymore, but that doesn't fix the knees and hocks completely."

"He will still walk weird?"

"Yes," The doctor glanced up at the adults. "But the joints won't be able to take the stress of heavy weight on him or hard work."

"Doctor?" Wade asked getting his attention back. "Will I be able to sit on him until I grow up?"

The veterinarian nodded, "But he can't be ridden strenuously."

Wade cocked his head to the side. "I don't know what that word means."

The doctor nodded again, "It means that you won't be able to do things like ride him up and down mountains or run in an arena. He will only be able to walk and maybe trot with a little weight on his back."

"So, while I'm a kid, I can ride him at a walk around the pasture?"

"Yes, there shouldn't be a problem with that," The vet smiled.

Wade lifted his lariat to his lap, "I can sit on him and practice my roping?"

The doctor grinned, understanding what Wade meant, "Yes."

Wade let out a long breath and felt the stress leave with it. "When can I see him?"

"In about 15 to 20 minutes."

Wade moved the lariat over to his casted arm and stretched his hand out to the doctor like his dad had taught him. The doctor took it and they shook hands.

"Thank you," Wade smiled. "I need to go outside for a few minutes so you can say all the long scary words to the adults now." Without looking at anyone, he turned quickly and walked through the large open lobby, with his boot heals hitting the ground hard and echoing throughout the room.

Once through the front doors, his pace quickened as he walked towards the truck and horse trailer. Moving behind the trailer he sat on the wheel well. He didn't want to be an adult anymore, he wanted to scream and yell like a kid.

He took a couple deep breaths to keep the tears away and started banging the rope against his legs to take his mind off the tears. Each time the rope hit his legs, his smile got bigger. Rooster wouldn't be in pain anymore. He would be fine. They would be training buddies and Dollar could be his competition horse. The three of them would be a perfect team. He jumped off the trailer and jumped in the air a couple times.

"Yes, yes, yes!" He yelled.

"Wade?" His dad's voice was on the other side of the truck.

Wade ran around the back of the horse trailer; his dad was jogging toward them. Wade ran, grinning all the way and jumped in his dad's embrace and they wrapped their arms around each other. Wade hugged his dad as tightly as the cast would allow.

His dad leaned back and grinned down. "He's OK," He whispered in relief. "And you came up with a great plan for him."

Wade beamed back, the happiness soaring through his body and out in his excited voice. "Can we go see him now? And I need to call Reilly."

CHAPTER FOURTEEN

Wade's eyes flickered open and he stared at the ceiling. *"It's my birthday party today."* He sang quietly. He looked over at the window and could tell it was early. Matt was snoring on the other bed which made Wade grin. Since Wade was in Matt's bed, his cousin was laying in the smaller bed with his feet dangling off the end. He came home for my birthday…just like he promised!

He lay quietly thinking of the afternoon with Rooster the day before. His parents let him stay with Rooster for hours so he could be there for the horse, like the horse was there for him. The WSU school attendants had given him a small birthday cake since it was his actual birthday. It was in the shape of a red horse! When it was time to go, his dad had to literally carry him away from Rooster.

Wade was listening to the quiet house trying to decide if anyone was up yet. Matt had opened the window to let the cool air in, so Wade could hear cars and trucks drive by on the road. There was no sound from the house, but he heard a truck slowing down by their gate. It had to be a truck…it was too loud for a car and was definitely a diesel truck!

He slid out of bed, stopped to make sure there was no dizziness then quickly ran to the window. It was a truck and horse trailer…and it wasn't just any truck and horse trailer! It was Jessup from the ranch!

"Jessup came for my birthday!" Wade yelled in his head. The cast over his hand and arm kept him from being able to pull on jeans. With his pajamas on, he pulled on his socks and grabbed his lariat. He snuck out of the room quietly so he didn't wake Matt.

He positioned his lariat over his shoulder then took off running down the long hallway and halfway to the steps, he jumped into a slide and slid on the wood floors to the top of the steps. The side banister stopped him. He giggled quietly to himself.

"Wade," He heard his dad behind him. Busted! His parents hated it when he did that.

Wade turned to see his dad standing at his bedroom door. It was slightly open and he was whispering something to his mom. He closed the door, then…took off running down the hallway, halfway to the steps he jumped into a slide and slid to the top of the steps and next to Wade. They grinned at each other.

Wade started laughing and had to cover his mouth with his free hand to keep from waking everyone.

He turned his back to Wade. "Hop on."

Wade giggled again and awkwardly climbed onto his dad's back. They both laughed quietly as his dad carried him down the steps, setting him down on the bottom step to help slide on Wade's boots. "We have to wait for your mom."

Wade stood at the base of the steps and waited for her, "Come on," He whispered impatiently.

Jessup's truck went by the side window; Wade turned to look out the back kitchen window in time to see it stop by the barn. He started hopping in excitement and looked back up the stairs in time to see his mom suddenly appearing at the top; she had come to a SLIDING stop, her dark hair flying over her face.

She looked down and grinned. With a finger to her lips she trotted down the steps. "Don't tell your father," She whispered and gave him a big hug. "Happy birthday, son."

Wade was laughing as they walked into the kitchen. His dad was already waiting for them with the back door open so Wade ran out the door without waiting for them, and ran to Jessup's truck. The older cowboy was just coming around the backside of the trailer as Wade reached him.

"Jessup!" Wade said excitedly. "You came for my birthday!"

"That I did, boy," Jessup smiled back at him. "You look much better than the last time I saw you."

A horse whinnied from inside the trailer. It started a round of whinnies from inside the barn and the pasture. Cora's colt, Libby and Kit had come running and were standing impatiently at the gate…waiting to see who came to visit.

"You brought a horse?" Wade looked up at him in confusion. "We have fourteen horses here!" Wade reminded him as his parents walked up next to them.

"Yeah, you got a herd here, but this isn't just any horse." Jessup smiled as he opened the gate to the trailer. The door swung towards Wade, and blocked his view as Jessup stepped in the trailer.

As he stepped around the trailer gate, Wade's eyes opened wide and he took a step back. It was Monty. His pulse quickened and his heart hurt. His hand went to his chest again.

A hand rested on his shoulder, "Are you OK?" His dad asked.

Wade nodded and silently watched the big grey horse step gracefully out of the trailer. The three horses in the pasture started whinnying and dancing. Monty just stood quietly and watched them; his head high and alert.

When Wade took a step towards the horse, Monty's head turned to look at him; his big gentle eyes taking in the whole scene. Wade didn't hesitate, he walked right up to the horse and ran his hand down the grey nose. He cupped the round jaw in his hand and massaged the underside. The horse leaned his head into Wade, letting him know he liked it. "How could I have been scared of you?" Wade whispered to him.

He turned to look at the horse's chest to see scrapes and scratches across it, but two large cuts stood out where the horse had rammed the fence. Wade softly ran his fingertips over the stitches where Jessup had sewn them closed.

His dad's hand stroked the horse's neck. "He'll be just fine, Wade."

Wade looked up at his dad, his big brown eyes shining, "He saved me."

"Yes, he did." His mom joined them in petting and thanking the horse that saved their son.

"Well," Jessup interrupted. "Let's get him tied up."

Jessup tied the horse to the side of the trailer.

"You want to ride him?" His dad asked.

"What?" Wade gasped, "You said he was too strong for me."

"He is, but there aren't any cows here. You can walk him around the small corral."

"Yes!" Wade grinned. What a way to start his birthday party day!

Wade stepped to the horses head and talked to Monty while they saddled him. He told him about Rooster.

"Ok," His dad said and Wade positioned himself next to the horse. Monty was too tall for him to get on without standing on something. Plus he couldn't pull himself up with a cast on his arm.

As his dad lifted him into the saddle, Wade saw something on the leather skirt of the saddle just in front of his left knee. He leaned over and looked at the imprint. "What's that?"

"Back in the 1800's they used silver dollars for payment," Jessup told him. "That there… is a dollar coin."

Wade grinned. "A dollar?" He laughed. "You put a dollar coin on your saddle?"

"Well, not really." Wade's dad said. "Look at the saddle, Buddy."

Wade looked at the saddle again. It was a brand new roping saddle and way too small for Jessup. He turned to his parents.

"Happy Birthday!" They grinned in unison.

"Wow!" Wade smiled then looked over at Jessup. "Dollar?" Then he realized what it was. "You put Dollar on my saddle!" He said excitedly.

"Look at the other side," Jessup said with a twinkle in his eye.

Wade turned…just in front of his right knee was a rooster. "Rooster!" Wade yelled with a laugh. "I have Dollar and Rooster on my saddle!"

******

It was just after lunch and Wade was waiting in the middle of the lawn where his mom told him to stand. Reilly, Grace, Sadie, and Nora were standing around him. Matt, Nikki, and Aunt Dru were standing to his left in front of Aunt Dru's truck…the door was open. A covered wheelbarrow was placed in front of them.

Jack, Uncle Grayson and Aunt Leah were standing behind Wade…another covered wheelbarrow was placed in front of them. To his right stood his parents; they were next to the open gate to the pasture. A covered wheelbarrow was in front of them too. The horses had been moved to the North pasture.

Wade looked at each of them, wondering what they were doing. He looked around for Cora and Jessup and found them standing on the porch of the house. They had a covered box in front of them.

"Now what?" Wade asked his aunt. She reached in the truck and turned on the radio, LOUD. The music boomed across the yard. It was his favorite song, Toby Keith singing 'I Should Have Been a Cowboy'.

Wade started laughing, his toe started tapping, and his hips started swinging to the music. All the kids had started dancing and so did the parents. Everyone was singing the song at the top of their lungs.

He turned to look at Cora just in time to see something red flying toward his head. He didn't have time to move and it hit him in the forehead. Water splashed all over and was accompanied by roaring laughter all around him.

He looked at Cora in shock. She had taken the cover off the box and was grabbing another water balloon.

Screams and laughter broke out as all the parents were throwing water balloons at the kids. The kids screamed in delight and ran for the wheelbarrows. Aunt Dru was the closest, so Wade ran for her. She handed him a balloon and he turned to throw but was hit in the chest with a blue balloon, water drenching him. He looked over and saw the culprit was Sadie. She laughed and grabbed another balloon.

Wade threw his balloon at Nikki and hit her in the back of the head. She squealed and turned to see who hit her. He looked up and saw dozens of colorful water balloons flying through the air. Wade laughed and watched Reilly hit Grace; Uncle Grayson hit Matt; Nora hit her dad; Jack hit Jessup; Aunt Leah hit Aunt Dru and it continued. He was picking up another balloon and getting ready to throw it when he heard Nora yell.

"No, Dad, No!" She was laughing and screaming. Their dad had picked her up and was carrying her to the horse's large round water trough. She kicked and hollered in fun as he dropped her in the trough. She fell with a splash, but stood up quickly. Her hair was drenched and clinging to her head and shoulders. Their dad roared in laughter until he was hit in the back of the head with a stream of water from the hose, held by his wife. Wade's mom was drenched from water balloons and had run for the hose when the water balloons ran out. Wade didn't think he could laugh any harder than he was already laughing.

His mom held the hose on his dad until he charged her and picked her up. The hose went flying as he turned and started walking back to the water trough that Nora was quickly crawling out of.

"Oh, no you don't!" His mom yelled. She circled her arms around his neck and held on tightly. Wade watched as his dad kissed her and was about to turn away when he saw her arms relax and she was quickly tossed in the air and down into the tank. Water splashed everywhere.

Wade was laughing so hard he couldn't stand anymore. He fell to the ground. "Well, maybe Dad isn't so boring after all."

THE TAGGER HERD

BOOK THREE

NIKKI TAGGER

CHAPTER ONE

Nikki, with Nora in the passenger's seat, pulled into the large parking lot of the veterinary clinic just in time for Arcturus' appointment. For the last two months, since the horse started losing weight, the trip had become a Wednesday afternoon routine. Before Nikki even put the truck in park, Nora was opening the door. It was her cousin's responsibility to unload the horse from the trailer and lead him to the scales. It wasn't just a routine for Nora and Nikki; it was for the horse, too. Arcturus knew exactly what was expected of him and calmly walked with Nora. Nikki smiled; even if the horse wasn't haltered, he would probably walk to the scales by himself.

Nikki walked behind Arcturus and Nora hoping that the horse hadn't lost more weight, but looking at the horse's hindquarters and sides as they entered the barn, there was no doubt. The scales confirmed he lost 8 pounds the last week. That was now 121 pounds since September of weight the horse couldn't afford to lose. For most horses, it wasn't a drastic amount, but for one of the Tagger herd, it was critical pounds they needed to regain their health.

All the other rescued horses were gaining each week. The carefully measured feed with supplements he received morning and night should be putting weight on him.

Dr. Mark walked out of his office and out to the examining area. The older man was wearing a baseball cap this time, instead of his usual cowboy hat. She wasn't much of a fan of mustaches but his was the exception. It just seemed part of him.

"How much?" He asked in his light southern drawl.

"Eight pounds," Nora answered. "Why isn't he gaining…why is he still losing?" Visibly upset, Nora gently stroked the black neck of the horse. Arcturus was busy looking at the other horses and mules in the corrals and stalls.

Dr. Mark shook his head with a sigh and looked to Nikki. "We can't just keep up the trial and error with changing his feed."

Nikki nodded. "The other horses have all gained the 100 pounds while Arcturus has lost it…he's 200 pounds behind them now." She looked at the veterinarian in concern. "I'd like to do some research. Maybe consult with WSU."

She sighed with relief when he nodded. She didn't want him to think she didn't have faith in him.

"I think that's a great idea. You're a smart young lady Nikki, I have no doubt you'll track down the issue," He turned to his office. "I've been reviewing some of my old journals. I have a gut feeling I've seen this before, but after 40 years of practice I can't remember when or where. I'll give them to you for your research."

Nikki was ecstatic. She loved looking through his journals and reading about his past. She followed him as Nora walked out into the parking lot with Arcturus; the sound of the horse's hoof beats echoed throughout the clinic; she loved that sound. Nikki greeted Marie, the assistant, as she entered the office. The older woman was putting the last of dozens of journals into a box.

"I was prepared," He smiled at her surprised expression. He plopped himself down behind his cluttered desk and slapped his hands on the arms of the chair. "I've been frustrated, too."

Nikki glanced down at the abundance of papers on the desk and a picture of the Tagger herd looked back up at her. It was the cover of the western magazine that had run an article on the horses. "Since that article came out, I've gained 25% in business and its growing and I'm shorthanded," He sighed. "Erik was hired by a clinic in California, so I've advertised for another fully licensed veterinarian to join us. I have a few interviews next week, but I am overwhelmed now."

Nikki looked in the box at all the leather journals and grinned, "I was just talking to Nora about how excited we were that school was out for a couple weeks for the holidays." She picked up a journal and opened it to look at all his hand written notes. "And here I am overjoyed to sit, read, and research through these books."

He chuckled. "Well at least it's something you're really interested in," He watched her thumb through the journals.

"Nikki?"

She pulled her eyes from the written notes and looked over at him.

"Why are you studying resort management in school?"

"We are considering building a Barn and Breakfast near The Stables."

"A what?"

"It's like a Bed and Breakfast except we also provide a small corral for customer's horses. People can bring their horse and ride the trails. Mom thought it would go over well when we had the clinics where the instructors work with the attendees' personal horses. People also like to take their horses on vacations, but have a hard time finding places to keep their horses near a hotel."

"That's a great idea. Dru has a great sense for business," He nodded while furrowing his brow, "I'd spend a weekend up there and ride myself."

"We'll hold you a room for the grand opening," Nikki laughed. "But why did you ask?"

"Are you set with that major or have you considered anything else?"

Nikki hesitated answering. She'd been thinking of nothing else but changing her major. The horses coming into her life have taken her into a new direction. She just didn't want to disappoint her mom.

"What were you thinking?" She asked him.

"Have you ever thought of studying animal nutrition in college?" He asked. "I know you liked working here, but not the standard veterinarian work. Working with the Tagger herd you've gained a unique experience in the program," He leaned forward when she didn't respond. "Look how excited you are about researching nutrition for Arcturus."

"It doesn't feel like work."

"That's the point!" He slapped the arm rests on his chair again.

She smiled at his enthusiasm. "I have considered changing to get back into the equine field. I love working with horses."

He stood as a customer came through the door and picked up one of the boxes. She took the other and they walked to the door. Nikki smiled and nodded to Marie as she followed the veterinarian to her truck.

"Do what you love to do and you don't work a day in your life," Dr. Mark told her. "I am just so overwhelmed with the amount of work here at the clinic… I knew you would do this. You've done a tremendous job with those horses and I have all the confidence that you will find out what's wrong with that black colt." He turned and looked at her as they placed the boxes in the back seat of the truck. "I wouldn't let you take these journals if I didn't."

Nikki shut the truck door and motioned for Nora to load the horse. She turned back to the veterinarian she had known most of her life. "Thank you. I've been thinking the same thing and to hear you say that just makes me want it more. I just need to discuss it with Mom."

He grinned at her. "I'm glad and have no doubt that Dru will support your decision," He started to walk away and yelled over his shoulder. "I'll hire you the day you graduate."

She laughed. "I'll take you up on that!"

******

"Mom, are you sure you're alright with this?" Nikki looked across the office desk at The Stables.

"Are you kidding? I've been thinking the same thing, but wanted you to make up your own mind," Her mother's blue eyes sparkled with happiness. "I'm glad Dr. Mark pushed the issue. Maybe you can get your classes changed by the time next semester starts."

"I've been anxious to look." Nikki took control of the computer and quickly signed onto her student account on the University's website.

"Do you think you should transfer over to WSU?" Her mom asked.

Nikki shrugged just as a text alert on her mother's phone echoed in the office.

Nikki looked over at her mom who gave a short laugh. Nikki knew that look on her mother's face, she'd seen it a number of times, "Another 111 text from Jack?"

"Poor guy," Her mother giggled and walked out the office door.

Nikki grabbed the mouse for the computer and clicked a few times and brought up the security video. Jack was in the round pen they used for training. Both Jack and a client were standing next to a horse. The customer, a lady, took a step towards Jack and he maneuvered himself to the opposite side of the horse. The client quickly followed.

Nikki giggled and watched the screen in fascination. She had really begun to enjoy watching the security feed in these situations. It should have been insulting since the video system was installed because of her infatuation with Jack. She was twelve when he started working at The Stables and in the next couple years had developed a major crush on him. By the time Nikki was 17, she was sure Jack was in love with her.

It was all in her head, but no one at the time could have convinced her of that. Jack was 35, but to her, that didn't make any difference. He was so handsome she couldn't help falling for him.

She wasn't the only one. Many of her friends were the same way. Nikki and her friends would flirt incessantly with him to the point Jack had finally talked to the Tagger Trio about it. Nikki couldn't figure out why she was never left alone with him; there was always someone with them and it frustrated her.

The worst situation was just two years before when they had a teenage girl that would continually reach out and touch him. After repeated warnings, they finally called her parents and explained that their daughter would be banned from the property if she didn't stop. The girl's parents were furious and threatened legal action. Once their attorney and the parents sat down and watched the video footage of the teenager continually advancing on him and, in one instance, nearly tackling him as he was walking into the tack room, the parents apologized and the girl was never seen at the property again.

Nikki's mother and uncles decided to protect Jack and Tagger Enterprises they would put a video system throughout the property. Once they started recording, they showed Nikki the video and pointed out how Jack was trying to be polite to her, but he wasn't interested; she was way too young. She was mortified at first that they all knew her feelings about him, but now at 20, she realized how patient he had been with her. Jack had never made her feel humiliated about the situation and now, Nikki considered him a great friend.

The 111 texting alert system was also put into place. When anyone felt uncomfortable with a client's advances, they would text someone on the property. That person was to react immediately and put themselves between the client and the person making the distress call. Nearly all of them had made the distress call, but no one more than Jack. He worked with more clients giving riding lessons or training the client's horse. As far as Nikki was concerned it was because, with every year that passed, he was just that much more handsome.

She watched the video feed and saw Jack nearly walk circles around the horse to get away from the client. Leaning in closer, her long dark hair fell across her face. She pulled out a hair tie from the desk drawer and captured it in a ponytail. Then she leaned back to the monitor and tried to see the client but she couldn't tell anything more than it was a woman.

She laughed softly as her mother stepped into the round pen and put herself in between Jack and the client. It didn't take Jack long to silently make his way out of the pen.

Within minutes, Jack appeared at the office door.

"She too much for you?" Nikki grinned, still watching the video feed of her mother and the client.

He tossed his jacket on a chair and walked into the storage room in the back where they kept the refrigerator. He came out with a large bottle of water. "She wasn't bad to start with," He sat across the desk from her and stretched out comfortably. "She was actually quite nice, but about half way through I adjusted her leg in the stirrup and she just went full on leech mode."

"Don't touch them, Jack!" Nikki laughed. "Trust me, I know. You have this Midas touch that turns women into liquid."

He laughed and rolled his eyes.

"No, I'm serious," She chuckled and exaggerated her tone. "Between those piercing blue eyes, dark hair, and those dimples, you're irresistible!"

Jack just shook his head. Nikki knew he didn't believe it.

"And how many 111 texts have you made since your winter break started?"

She had been on holiday break from college for just over a week, "Once or twice."

"Yeah, all those young cowboys trying to get to the beautiful maiden," He teased.

"Maiden!" She nearly choked on the coffee she had just sipped. "I don't think you've called me that one before."

"Well, I've called you just about everything else," He leaned forward to look at the video monitor. "I've got to come up with some new ones."

They watched her mom untie the horse and lead him out of the round pen they used for training. The client was not seen on the monitor.

"Jack," Nikki whispered. She had glanced out the window in the door and could see the client walking to the office. "Here she comes."

He nearly tripped on his chair in his hurry to get to the back room. The client just walked on by the office and out to the parking lot. She was walking so fast Nikki didn't even see what the woman looked like.

Nikki was laughing out loud when her mom walked in from outside and Jack returned from the back room with a sheepish look.

"You chicken!" Nikki laughed at him. Her mom quickly read the situation and joined the laughter.

"Yeah, yeah, yeah…" Jack grinned and glanced out the window to make sure the client had left, grabbed his coat and then headed back out the door to the round pen. "I'll make sure to come running next time one of your young cowboys come a calling."

"How bad was the infatuation?" Nikki asked after he had left.

"She asked if he was single, kids, AND his phone number."

Nikki just shook her head. They've had some interesting people but most don't ask for the phone numbers. "Wow, he was right, full on leech mode." Nikki nodded with a knowing look. "She'll call within the next 30 minutes for another appointment."

"I doubt it will take that long."

Nikki glanced down to the security video and watched Jack gathering the tack he had left in the pen.

"He is a great guy," Nikki said softly then looked up at her mom who was giving her a worried look. "No!" Nikki waved her hands. "I'm not back to that. I'm just saying he's a great guy."

She nodded with a sigh of relief, "Tagger Stables is very lucky to have him."

Once he put his supplies away, Jack joined them in the office.

"Dru, I haven't seen Rooster for a while, how is he doing?" Jack asked as he took the seat next to her.

Nikki remained behind the desk. She liked it when she looked like the boss.

Her mother smiled, the love for the horse shone in her expression. "He's doing great; more active than he was before the surgery. No trotting or galloping yet. We've been keeping him in the stalls and the smaller corral so he hasn't had the chance to be overly active. Wade checks on him in the mornings, as soon as he gets home from school and before bed. He insists he is the only one to move the horse from the corral to the stall."

"What about Christmas?" Nikki asked. "Grayson said something this morning about taking all the horses with us."

"All of them?" Jack asked.

Her mother nodded. "The kids don't want to be away from the horses for a full week. The longest any of them have been away was when Rooster was up at WSU. Besides, that way we don't have to find someone to take care of the horses here, too."

"I don't think we should be away from Arcturus very long either." Nikki added. "If there is a physical reason the horse is having issues, we don't want it to escalate while we're not here."

Jack and her mother nodded.

"Christmas is on a Thursday this year so we'll close The Stables the Monday before Christmas to the Friday after Christmas." Her mom said. Jack and Reilly joined the Tagger family for Christmas at the ranch and then they left for a week to visit their family in Texas. It was the only time his family and his late wife's family saw Reilly.

"I've already confirmed with Ann and Howard that they will take care of The Stables while we're gone." She continued, referring to the neighbors adjacent to the buildings. "We just need to leave them clear feeding instructions for each of the horses."

Jack nodded. "With the Tagger leased and rental horses at the ranch for the winter, we only have one stable with horses. Reilly and I winterized and shut down the other one yesterday."

They discussed the horses that were on the property and which had owners coming out and which didn't. They drew up schedules between the three of them to make sure The Stables always had a manager onsite while Jack took Reilly to Texas.

Nikki finished writing out the schedule and pinned it up on the bulletin board above the computer.

"You working on taking over my job?" Jack teased her.

"No!" She laughed. "It's all yours. Do you know how many upset clients we would have if we let you go?" She glanced down at his appointment book. "Especially one Elena Pelten...I think she enjoyed the session today and I'll bet she'll be calling for another appointment any minute now!"

"That's an appointment I'll pass on." Jack chuckled.

Nikki looked over at her mom. She wasn't laughing and was staring at her with an odd expression.

"What did you say her name was?" She asked.

"Elena Pelten," Nikki answered looking at the book then glanced up, her mother had turned and was looking out the window of the office. That was an unexpected reaction to a name Nikki hadn't heard before. Nikki turned to Jack. "Had you met or seen her before?"

"First time was today. I think she called for the appointment a couple days ago," He stood, and leaning over Nikki's shoulder, pointed in the book. "Yeah, right there. She talked with Matt and made the appointment over the phone. Two days ago."

"Jack?" The tone in her voice was odd and made both Nikki and Jack look up.

"Yeah?" He answered.

She didn't look at either of them; she was still staring out the window. "I need to talk with Nikki alone please."

Jack stood straight up. Nikki glanced up at him and shrugged her shoulders. She didn't have any idea what was happening.

"Dru…are you alright?" He asked.

She glanced up at him then to the floor. "Yes, I just need to talk with her for a few minutes."

"OK." Jack said then grabbed his coat and walked out the door; closing it behind him.

"What's going on?" Nikki asked her mom who had an odd look on her face.

She answered with the four words that no one, in any situation, wants to hear; "We need to talk."

CHAPTER TWO

Her mom sat in the chair opposite of Nikki and leaned her elbows on the desk. She opened her mouth to speak but nothing came out. Nikki was beginning to get worried. "Mom?"

"Just a second," She looked at the ground, then after a very quiet couple minutes, slowly raised her head and eyes to Nikki, whose stomach had begun to tighten in concern. "Do you remember when you were 12 and we discussed your biological mother and father?"

Nikki slowly nodded. She knew nothing of her birth mother and very little of her father; her mother's ex-husband, Nick. The hairs on the back of her neck stood up…this wasn't going to be good.

"You told me never to tell you anything unless you asked me to."

"I know…" Nikki nodded cautiously.

"I agreed with that, but I think that agreement was just broken."

"Why?"

"Although there isn't any mention of your mother's name in the adoption papers, Nick told me her name."

Nikki stared in shock. She didn't even know her mother knew anything about her birth mother. Nikki started to rise out of the chair, "I don't want to talk about this now! Why would you even bring this up now, out of the blue?"

"Sit down," Her mother said firmly. Something in the way she said it made Nikki lower herself back in the chair without argument.

"Elena Pelten is your birth mother's name." She stated bluntly and leaned back in the chair.

Nikki felt the shock run through her and tried to remember what she had seen of the woman on the video monitor…which was nothing more than black and white footage that was too far away to see anything clearly.

Nikki took a deep breath to settle her nerves then looked across the desk. "Do you think it's her?" She wasn't sure if she wanted the woman to be or not.

Her mother shrugged, "I don't know. Nick never mentioned anything about her except her name, and Elena isn't exactly a widely popular name around here. He also said she was 17 when she gave birth to you."

"Which would have been close to your age…" Nikki leaned forward in the chair, elbows resting on the desk. Her mother nodded.

"You talked to her and saw her," Nikki said softly. "What do you think?"

"I would say the age fits…dark hair and eyes…"

Nikki didn't know what to do or say. She wasn't really sure if she wanted to go down this path but, if the woman was there looking for her she wanted to be prepared. Nikki thought of something…

"Why would she need riding lessons? If she was with Nick, wouldn't she know how to ride?"

Her mom shook her head, "Not necessarily. Nick was a bull rider…besides, lots of the girls that run after rodeo cowboys don't have a clue how to ride and probably had never been around a horse."

"Buckle bunnies…" Nikki sighed. "So….what do we do?"

"It's up to you."

"Well, the question is; does she know? And if she does, what is she doing here?"

"There is also that possibility that she doesn't know."

"What are the odds that she doesn't know, but still ends up here, where we are?"

"I don't know. It's been twenty years. If she was truly looking for you, you'd think she would have found you by now. There are public records of my marriage to your father."

Nikki exhaled in disbelief; her mind was racing with the possibilities. "I, literally, NEVER think of her…this is so weird, Mom."

"I agree. In all the scenarios I thought of in the last twenty years of your birth mother showing up, this is not one of them. I haven't thought of her for years either."

Nikki leaned forward, chin on hand and looked at her mom. She was a beautiful woman with blue eyes and long blonde hair that flowed down her back. Normally, she had a Tagger Enterprises ball cap with the T3E logo holding her hair out of her face and would either be tied up in a ponytail or a braid down her back. But it was loose today and framed her face perfectly. She was slender and fit from being such a physically active person. Any man would be lucky to be with her.

"How come you're not dating?" Nikki asked.

Her mom looked at her in surprise, then shook her head and smiled.

"Where did that come from?"

Nikki shrugged.

"Well…how do you know I'm not dating?"

Nikki's jaw dropped in surprise and she sat straight up in the chair. "Are you?"

A shoulder shrugged, "Back to the issue at hand."

"You're not going to tell me?"

"If I ever have a relationship, that might have the potential of going somewhere, then I'll let everyone know," The answer was delivered with a mischievous smile. "Now, back to the issue at hand…"

Just as Nikki was going to tell her that she didn't know what to do, the phone rang.

Nikki answered it with a quick, "The Stables."

"Good morning," It was a female voice. "I was just there for a riding lesson and didn't have time to make another appointment." Nikki sat straight up in her chair again and looked at her mom with eyes wide. She pointed to the phone and her mother gave her a quizzical look.

"Let me check the appointment book," Nikki reached for the book. "Elena Pelten?" She asked staring at her mom, whose jaw dropped in surprise then spread to a wicked grin.

"Yes," The woman answered. "I was wondering if the trainer that I was just with had some time open tomorrow or the next day."

Nikki wanted to laugh out loud. Jack would kill her if she set up the appointment! But she really wanted more information about the woman.

"Let me put you on hold for a moment and check his schedule," Nikki quickly pushed the hold button, double checked that it did go on hold then looked up at her mom. "What do I do? She wants an appointment with Jack!"

Her mother leaned forward in the chair with a smile on her face. After a minute of silent deliberation she threw her hands in the air and nodded for Nikki to make the appointment.

Nikki made an 'oh my, he's going to kill me' face and reached for the hold button with a quick glance at Jack's schedule.

"Ms. Pelten?" Nikki smiled at her mother. "I'm sorry for keeping you on hold."

"That's fine. Does he have the time?"

"Yes ma'am, he has 11:00 tomorrow or 10:00 the next day."

"Tomorrow would work great."

"Would you like the same horse?" Nikki asked the standard question.

"The horse?" The woman paused making Nikki want to burst out in giggles. "Yes, yes, the same horse would be fine."

"Alright, I have you down for 11:00 tomorrow with Jack and Star." The woman agreed and hung up.

Nikki stared at the phone then slowly pushed the end button. She looked at her mom with wide, nervous eyes. "He's going to kill me!" She squealed.

"You're telling him!" She laughed and stood to open the door. "Call him in."

Nikki reached for the stable wide intercom system and called Jack to the office.

When he walked in the door, he stopped and looked at her mother. She smiled and motioned for him to have a seat as they both sat in the chairs across from Nikki.

"So, do I get in on the big secret now?" He asked.

Neither woman spoke.

"What?" He asked looking between the mother and daughter.

"I just booked an appointment with you for tomorrow at 11:00 with Elena Pelten." Nikki said quickly before she lost her courage. His expression didn't change, but his neck and face started to turn red.

He looked over at her mom then back to Nikki. Without saying a word he started to stand up. She looked at her mother with eyes pleading for help.

"Jack, please hear us out." Her mother said softly and looked up at him. He hesitated, then sat back down and looked between the two women.

Nikki looked at her mother again, which made Jack look at her too.

Turning in her chair so she was looking more direct to him, her mother sighed. She took a deep breath then blurted out, "Elena Pelten is Nikki's birth mother's name."

Jack's eyebrows shot up in surprise. He looked over at Nikki then back at her mom.

The two women sat quietly while he processed the information.

"Are you sure it's her?" He finally asked.

"No," She answered. "But she is the right age."

"So the name and age are the only thing you've got right now?" He asked looking between the two.

Both women nodded.

He leaned back in his chair and stared at her mom. "Are you OK?"

Nikki was stunned. She hadn't even thought about how this would affect her mother. She had only thought of herself. "Mom?"

She stared at Jack a moment then looked over at Nikki. "I'm fine," She answered. "If this would have happened while you were still a minor, then I'd have issues, but there isn't really anything the woman can do now."

"Mom," Nikki leaned forward on the desk. "It doesn't matter whether she is the woman that gave birth to me or not. YOU are my mother in every other way."

"I know, Sweetheart. I have no doubt about that," She paused. "It just brings your dad and his memories back into my life."

"Oh Mom, I am so sorry." Nikki wanted to cry. "Let's just drop this right now."

She shook her head and raised a hand. "It's here, and it's happening, so let's just deal with her."

"How?" Jack asked.

Nikki and Dru just smiled and looked back at him.

"That's why you booked the appointment tomorrow? To find out if it's her?" They nodded at the rhetorical question. "What do you want me to do during a riding lesson?"

"Just politely ask about her and her past." Nikki shrugged with a teasing smile.

"…while you're circling the horse trying to get away from her." Her mother chuckled.

Jack shook his head. "You two..." He leaned back in his chair to quietly assess the situation. "Alright, since you've already booked the appointment, I'll do it." He looked at both of them. "I wouldn't do this for ANYONE else. I'm not sure what information I can get from her during a riding lesson."

"You're charming…I'm sure she'll give you just about anything." Nikki grinned.

He just glared at her, which made both women giggle.

"There is one condition," Jack added.

"What?" They asked in unison.

"One of you has to be close by to intervene if she gets out of hand."

Nikki frowned and looked at her mom. She didn't want her mom to have to converse with the woman …just in case she was THE Elena Pelten.

"You look too much like your father," Her mom said. "Until we know whether she is…or isn't…or if she knows…or doesn't…then she shouldn't see you or Matt. Matt would really throw her for a loop, he looks identical to Nick."

"Are you sure Mom?" Nikki was starting to have second thoughts. "Maybe we should just forget it."

"I'm sure Jack would agree with that," She glanced over at him, but they couldn't read his expression. "Let's just do this tomorrow and go from there."

***

At 10:50 the next day Nikki watched the woman, who could possibly be her birth mother, drive into the parking lot. She glanced down at the security monitor and saw Jack and her true mother talking by the round pen. The horse and gear were ready.

Nikki held her breath as the woman walked toward the office, then exhaled as she passed by and headed straight for the corral and Jack.

She watched the monitor closely as Jack was shaking her hand. "Don't touch her!" Nikki shouted at the computer and laughed. The poor woman probably just melted inside. At least she was warm on a chilly day, Nikki chuckled to the empty room.

She couldn't see her mother, but was sure she was close by. The woman was now standing next to the horse and "tried" to step into the stirrup. Nikki could tell she didn't try very hard. The woman motioned for Jack to come over and help her. Nikki laughed out loud. Jack was probably silently cursing her at that point!

Instead of assisting the woman, he walked the horse over to the mounting block that was just outside the pen. Jack lifted it and positioned the block so the woman could step on it, then step into the stirrup of the saddle. Jack wouldn't have to touch her.

"Ooohh, smart man," Nikki smiled.

She sat back in her chair, stared at the monitor and watched silently as Jack proceeded to have the woman move the horse around the arena. The horse and rider seemed to be moving well together as the she followed Jack's instructions. Nikki was beginning to get nervous that Jack had changed his mind when he had them stop in the middle of the pen and he approached her. They stood quietly talking for almost five minutes; Nikki was watching the clock on the video feed. Jack was stroking the horse's neck as he was talking.

He said something that made the woman nod but Nikki couldn't see the woman well enough to see her facial reaction. Nikki sighed; they needed to get audio feed on these things too!

The rest of the appointment went without any stopping of the horse and rider. No more chats. Soon the woman slid down from the horse and stood quietly. There was no movement towards Jack, like the day before, so he wasn't being chased around the horse by her. There was no 111 call. Nikki leaned both elbows on the desk as she stared intently at the woman. She couldn't really tell any features about her from the camera angle.

At the end of the appointment, Jack reached out to shake the woman's hand. "Interesting," Nikki thought. The woman shook his hand with her right hand and brought the left hand up to touch his arm. That was an obvious gesture of flirtation and Jack didn't flinch.

"Oh, heck," Nikki was shocked. What had she started here?

Just as the woman turned to leave, the office door opened and her mom stepped inside.

"It's chilly out there," She slid out of her coat.

"But hot in the pen," Nikki sighed. "Could you hear them? Did he get any information?"

She shook her head. "I was too far away to hear the conversation in the middle."

To Nikki, that confirmed that her mother was watching as closely as she was.

A car started and Nikki turned to watch Elena Pelten drive out of the parking lot.

The door opened and Jack stepped into the office.

"Well?" They asked in unison.

He shook his head and grinned at Nikki. "As soon as I shook her hand, all I could hear was you yelling 'Don't touch her!'"

His face tinted red as the two women laughed.

"Did you find anything out?" Nikki asked him.

He took his coat off and sat in the chair across from her. "She's originally from Pendleton. She was just hired at the Red Lion Hotel as a sales manager. Looking for something to do, she saw The Stables ad in the flyer at the hotel. She thought riding lessons would be fun."

"Jack," Nikki asked patiently. "Is she or isn't she, THE Elena Pelten?"

"Well," He shrugged, "I know that Pelten is her maiden name."

Nikki's jaw dropped. "I hadn't thought about it being her married name."

"Anything else?" Her mom asked.

"Not really." He shook his head.

Nikki sighed in disappointment. She really thought they would have the answer today. "So, now what do we do?"

Jack shrugged, "I'll ask her more tomorrow."

Nikki sat up straight in her chair and looked at him hopefully. "She's coming back for another appointment?"

"No," Jack grinned. "I asked her out on a date."

"YOU WHAT?" Both women gasped.

CHAPTER THREE

Nikki closed the first journal from Dr. Mark's collection and laid it on The Homestead library table. She glanced around the room at the shelves filled with books and numerous magazines…nearly every horse, horse show, and rodeo magazine that was in publication.

To her left, along the wall, were three computers and monitors used by all the Tagger's for homework, games, and business. Cora used them for keeping records on the Tagger Enterprise's horses. To her right, by the windows looking out at the south pasture, were two long couches for curling up and reading. There were a number of chairs scattered around the long table where she had placed the books.

"Wow," She rubbed her tired eyes, "I think I need a break." The details in the journal were extensive. She had to follow closely to make sure she understood each one, but they were also mesmerizing. Dr. Mark's writings were thorough and entertaining.

Nikki walked through the quiet house and stepped out onto the back porch for fresh air. She was just in time to see Grayson lift the gate between the large north pasture and the small corral off its hinges. He placed the gate against the fence. To her left, the herd of horses lifted their heads at the clanging sound of the gate hitting the fence. After assessing the situation, most of the horses lowered their heads again determining there was no one going to feed them.

Eli, the buckskin, started walking towards her uncle. Nikki stuffed her hands in her jacket pockets and leaned against the house to wait and see what the horse was up to. Eli walked across the pasture and to the new opening that had been created. The horse sniffed the fence where the hinges were. Grayson had turned his back to the horse and was kneeling down digging into his tool box. The horse slowly walked up behind him.

Grayson stood slowly then dipped his head low and looked behind to see which horse was there and what it was doing. Eli lowered his head to the back of Grayson's boot. The horse sniffed, then slowly lifted his head to the knee and sniffed again. Grayson didn't move. Slowly the horse moved his way up to the back pocket where Grayson had just stuffed his work gloves. Eli sniffed the gloves then using just his lips pulled the gloves out. They dropped to the ground and the horse lowered his head again and sniffed them. He quickly bored of the gloves and raised his head to the back pocket again.

Grayson remained still as Eli lifted his head and sniffed the back of Grayson's neck. Nikki laughed softly. She'd had horses do that to her and knew the feeling of the horse's breath going across the skin. She shivered just thinking about it.

Her uncle continued to stand still as his cowboy hat became the next target of the horse. The horse tipped the hat with the end of his nose. When it didn't move, Eli used his lips again and pulled on the hat. A grin spread across Grayson's face as Nikki chuckled.

Eli gave up on the hat and placed his nose on her uncle's shoulder. He pushed his nose forward so most of his head was resting across Grayson's shoulder, then he did something that made Nikki laugh again; he tilted his head sideways and from the dipping of Grayson shoulder he pressed down. Grayson started chuckling. He waited for the horse to move, but it seemed to have made himself comfortable.

Finally, he reached up with his left hand and touched Eli's soft velvety muzzle. The horse tilted his head back up but remained across his shoulder. Her uncle turned to the horse and with a hand on each side of the horse's face, he rubbed his nose then moved up to his large round cheekbones and on up to his ears. The horse leaned into him, and he walked around the horse, rubbing him down his neck, across his ribs, back, and under his belly. The horse stood quietly taking in all the attention.

A whinny from the pasture made Eli lift his head and look out to the herd. With one more look at Grayson, the horse turned and walked back out to the rest of the horses. Grayson watched the horse walk off and when he turned he saw Nikki watching and waved.

Nikki waved and turned back into the house. She was glad she had witnessed that moment between Grayson and Eli. She knew it was special.

She glanced up at the clock as she walked through the kitchen, back to the library and Dr. Mark's journals. It was three o'clock; the kids would be arriving by bus soon. It was their last day of school before their winter break started.

Once they arrived, her studying would be interrupted. It also meant that Jack's date with Elena Pelten was only three hours away. Nikki sat back in her chair and stared out the window.

Did she really want to know if Jack's date was THE Elena Pelten? Between her mother and her uncles, she had never felt like she was missing anything in her life. Was she supposed to? She'd seen on television and in the movies all the people that had to have the reason that they were adopted.

When she was twelve, she had asked her mom for anything she knew about her birth parents. But it was only because a friend of hers had just found out she was adopted and had gone on a search for her birth parents. Nikki thought she should also try to search for her birth parents until she spoke with her mom, who was willing to give any information that Nikki wanted, but Nikki had changed her mind at the last second.

"Never mind, Mom," She had said innocently. "I'm happy now and don't want anything else coming into my world that would take away from this happiness." The logic of a twelve year old, Nikki mused. "Don't ever tell me anything unless I ask."

And her mother had kept her promise until yesterday. Nikki wished she could have seen the woman more clearly on the security video. She was now more curious about her than she had ever been. What portion of her looks did she get from Elena Pelten? Did she have any unique characteristics from her like Matt had from Nick, their birth father? She had seen pictures of Nick, from his rodeo days, so she knew Matt and herself looked a lot like him. Nick seemed to have dropped off the planet after leaving her with Dru and the Tagger family.

Nikki hadn't even thought of asking Jack or her mom what Elena Pelten looked like and neither had offered the information. And now Jack was going out with her mother's ex-husband's ex-girlfriend. Nikki shook her head. This had to be hard on her mother. Until Jack asked her mother how she was doing, she hadn't even considered her mother's feelings. How selfish was that!?

Nikki closed her eyes and tried to imagine Jack out on a date. He was such a charming man…when he wanted to be. After the years of trouble she gave him when she was younger, she couldn't imagine him doing something so unselfish for her and her mom.

"What a guy," Nikki muttered then heard footsteps walking down the hall. They signaled Cora walking to the backdoor to pick up the kids' backpacks that they always dropped off on the back porch as they made their way to the horses.

Nikki looked up at the clock and realized she had been sitting there for twenty minutes and hadn't opened the next journal. "I give up," She laughed and walked out the backdoor to hang with the kids and wait for her mom to arrive from The Stables.

She and Reilly arrived around 6:00, the same time Jack would be picking up Elena Pelten for their date. The family was gathered around the large dining room table when Nikki heard Reilly tell Grace that his dad was on a date. Nikki glanced over at her mom who was smiling and talking to Cora.

Matt, Grayson and Scott's heads turned quickly and Grayson asked Reilly what he said. Reilly happily repeated himself and proceeded to tell them how awesome his dad looked when he had left. He hadn't seen his dad dressed up like that in a long time.

Nikki's uncles and brother just stared at Reilly, then looked at each other and laughed.

"If only they knew," Nikki frowned. She glanced back at her mom who didn't seem to be listening to Reilly's conversation.

After dinner, Nikki walked into the living room with a hand over her nervous stomach and stared at the twinkling lights on the Christmas tree. She kept glancing at the clock on the wall. It was only 7:30. How long would he be? How long was appropriate to covertly interrogate someone and bring back information that may change her life forever?

Nikki stood in front of the tree and touched the ornament she had made in kindergarten for her mother. It was a blonde angel and a shorter brunette angel holding hands. To the little kindergartener it was a symbol of her and her mother…always together…always supporting each other. There was never a moment she didn't consider Dru as her mother. They had never hidden the fact that Dru didn't give birth to her but even when she was young and angry at her, Nikki never wavered…Dru was her mother.

This tree was full of ornaments the kids had made throughout the years. The other tree was in the no-media room and it was decorated in horses, cowboy hats, western stars, and anything else western the kids could find. The presents were placed under that tree until they were packed in boxes and taken to the ranch, where another tree would be waiting in the bunkhouse. It was family tradition to decorate that tree on Christmas Eve.

"You OK?" Her mom walked up behind her. Her long blonde hair was down again and the colorful lights from the Christmas tree reflected in it, changing its color from blue to red to green.

Nikki turned to her mom and could feel the tears start to well. The emotion was surprising. She hadn't realized she had been so affected by Elena appearing into their lives. Recognizing her turmoil, her mother opened her arms and Nikki gratefully stepped into the welcome embrace. "I'm sorry, Mom." Nikki whispered.

"You have nothing to be sorry about. None of this is your fault."

"I shouldn't have asked Jack to do this."

"You didn't ask Jack to take her on a date. That was his idea to help you. He wouldn't be doing it if he didn't think it was the right thing to do. Besides, I wouldn't let him do it if I didn't think it needed to be done."

Nikki leaned back and looked into her mother's eyes. They were so loving and understanding. "Mom, I want this to be over. I don't want her to be THE woman we think she is. Call Jack and tell him to come home." She said desperately.

She slowly shook her head and smiled with compassion. "Honey, it's too late for that. It's in motion and we can't stop it now."

"Can you call or text Jack and tell him to stop?" Nikki pleaded with her again.

"Honey, no," She answered, and squeezed tighter, "We find out one way or the other. You don't want to know the woman is in town and not know the answer. You can run into her at any time. Besides, Jack probably already knows."

Reilly and Wade ran through the living room toward the stairs that led to the bedrooms on the second level of the house.

"I want to be young, naïve, and innocent again." Nikki sighed.

"Me, too," Her mother giggled.

Lights flashed through the front window indicating someone had pulled up the driveway. Nikki knew it was Jack. Her stomached turned and she could feel dinner headed up the wrong way. She turned and looked at her mom. "How much money do you think it would take to bribe Jack to never tell us the answer?"

Her mom laughed with the Christmas lights reflecting in her blue eyes. "Well, you know Jack; he'd do whatever you want," She twisted Nikki around and gave her a gentle push, "Head out to the barn and I'll try to get Jack out there."

Since everyone was still in the dining room and kitchen, Nikki quickly went out the front door. There were windows on the outside walls of the dining room so she headed to her left, which was more concealed but meant she had to walk all the way around the huge house to get to the barn. By the time she walked through the small door into the barn her mom was walking out the backdoor with Jack right behind.

The horse's heads popped up from their stalls as she turned on the lights. That was the best sight ever.

"Hi everyone!" She called out. Harvey stuck her head out the stall opening and stretched out to her for attention. "Hello, Beautiful," Nikki ran her hand down the bay horse's nose and down the side of her face and neck. "You always make me feel so much better."

She smiled at the horse as Trooper left his hay and walked over for his share of the attention. She gladly gave him all he wanted. Equine therapy…always the best cure.

The small side door opened and her mother and Jack entered. Her mom was giggling and her eyes were laughing as she smiled at Nikki. "James Bond reporting, Agent Q."

Nikki laughed. She needed that. "What do you have to report Agent Bond?"

Jack just laughed as they took seats in the small office.

He took a deep breath and looked over at Nikki. "OK," He said seriously. "That was one of the most uncomfortable things I've ever done."

"I'm so sorry Jack," Nikki giggled nervously. "Was she back in leech mode?"

He shook his head. "I wish she was, but she was friendly and nice." He glanced between the two of them.

Her mom smiled and nodded in understanding. "Thanks for doing it this time." She said and he just nodded. "But what did you find out?"

He sighed then smiled. "Well on the previous episode, we knew her maiden name was Pelten and she grew up in Pendleton."

Nikki and her mom giggled. All three were trying to keep the humor going in what could be a terribly traumatic time.

"In this episode we find out that Elena Pelten loves steak and cheesecake, and doesn't like it when her date won't dance with her," He smiled. "And she had two kids."

"Had?" Nikki's heart skipped a beat and she forgot to breathe.

"She raised one," He paused and turned directly to Nikki, his blue eyes showing his concern. "When she was underage, she gave up her rights to a little girl at the insistence of her angry parents. She saw her once and can only remember she had a lot of black hair."

Nikki let the breath out slowly. "Wow." She was glad she was sitting, since her whole body started tingling in shock.

"You got that all out of her in two hours?" Her mother asked in surprise.

He turned to her and tipped his head to the side. "Did you forget? You keep telling me I'm charming." Then he flashed her a cheesy charming smile.

Nikki could feel the nervous giggle come out of her. She looked over at Jack. "Does she know I'm here?"

Feeling her brain start to go numb, she quickly glanced at her mom who was also looking at him curiously.

He shook his head. "I don't think so."

"But you're not sure?" Nikki asked him.

Again, he shook his head and leaned back in his chair. "After we talked about kids, she tried to get me to dance. When I refused, adamantly, she closed down and stopped talking about her personal life. Only talked about her work…which is really boring." He smirked at Nikki.

"Thank you, Jack." Nikki reached out and grasped his hand as he nodded.

Then Nikki turned to her mom; "What do we do now?"

Her mother shook her head and turned to Jack. "How did you leave it with her?"

"We had dinner at the hotel restaurant; she has a room there until she finds a place to live." He answered.

"Convenient." Her mom nodded, trying to look serious but with a devilish glint of humor in her eyes.

He ignored her and continued. "We left the restaurant and I headed for the front door. She asked if I had an open appointment time in the morning. Since I didn't know what to do, I said yes and set it at 10:00."

Nikki stood to walk back to Harvey and stroked her long neck to help her mind relax.

They had an opportunity but what to do? She was her birth mother, but did Elena know Nikki was there? If she didn't, should she just drop everything and avoid the woman when she came for appointments? If she did know, then why hadn't she tried to make contact with her? Either way, would it really even matter if the woman knew who she was? She wasn't a minor anymore, so there wasn't anything Elena Pelten could do.

Nikki continued to stroke the horse who was leaning into her and happily taking in all the attention. There was one thing that bothered her. If the woman knew, then why didn't she make contact? Again, it made no difference if the woman knew or didn't know about her. She had a great family and a happy life and, no matter what, the woman couldn't change that.

Nikki turned to her mother and Jack. They had stood quietly waiting for her to decide what to do. She knew they would help her.

"I think we just get it out there and let her know who I am." Nikki surprised them both with the decision. "That way we find out whether she knows or not, because it really doesn't matter."

Her mother stared at her for a moment in surprise. "OK….and how do you plan on doing that? Just come out and tell her? How do you know she'll believe you?"

"Matt." Nikki answered; her co-conspirators nodded.

CHAPTER FOUR

Nikki paced her bedroom floor. She had told her mother and Jack that she wanted to talk to Matt alone, and then walked straight to the guest bedroom she used when she was home from college. They were going to send Matt to her. Nikki didn't want anyone else to notice how anxious she was so she had avoided everyone by coming in the side door of the house, which was right next to her bedroom door.

She heard a knock on the door and quickly pulled it open. She did it so fast that she startled him.

"What the heck, Sis?" He laughed as he walked in. She quickly shut the door. He looked at her in confusion, "Mom said you needed to talk to me about something."

She nodded with a smile and jumped up on her bed to sit cross legged in the middle.

"That important?" He said as he took off his boots and crawled on the bed to sit cross legged in front of her. Since they were little, this was how they always discussed important things. It was their discussion pose and how they solved all the world's problems.

Nikki watched him carefully, noticing how relaxed and happy he was. She knew Matt would do this for her if she asked. The concern was whether to ask. Maybe they shouldn't do this. Just let things ride out until Elena made a move…or not.

"How long are you going to just sit there and stare at me?" He chuckled; his brownish green eyes looked highly amused.

Nikki laughed nervously. "Sorry, lost in thought."

"What's the world's problem this time?"

"Last week you took a riding appointment, for Jack, for a woman called Elena Pelten." She started.

He shrugged. "Yeah, I remember…so?"

"She's my birth mother." Nikki said bluntly.

It was his turn to stare at her in surprise. "Seriously?" His voice raised two octaves.

She nodded and spent the next half hour telling him about the last three days.

"Jack went out on a date with your birth mother?" He shook his head in amazement.

"Only to see if he could get information from her that would prove she actually was my birth mother. He really didn't like it," She sighed. "He's too honest of a guy, so it must have been hard for him."

"Depends…what does she look like?" Matt grinned with a roguish glint in his eyes.

"Matt!" Nikki rolled her eyes.

"Yeah, bad joke…so, now what are you going to do?" He moved from the cross legged position and leaned against the wall instead. He stretched his long legs out in front of him. At 18…19 in just a few weeks, he stood just over six feet tall with broad shoulders like Grayson. His looks came from their dad, but his height came from his mom's family. He wore a Tagger Enterprises T3E baseball cap and a dark green shirt that made his brown eyes turn a dark hazel color. Thankfully his jeans seemed to be clean on her white bedspread.

"Just let her know who I am." She answered.

"You're going to walk up to a total stranger and say 'Hi, I'm the daughter you gave up twenty years ago'?"

Nikki giggled. "No," She hesitated, not sure how to ask him to help.

He leaned his head back. "Well, if I were you, I'd want me to innocently introduce myself to her so she would think of Nick; a way to begin the connection."

She nodded; surprised at how fast he figured it out. "Once that happens, we thought she should see the herd picture with our names. If she sees you and thinks of Nick, then she will see my name as Nikki. I resemble Nick, so hopefully she'll figure it out on her own. Mom only changed my last name on the birth certificate, so Elena had to be the one that named me."

"Once she does, she'll make contact with you and you'll confirm." He finished.

"That way she figures it out herself. We think it would be easier than coldly approaching her."

Matt nodded. "Seems like the easiest way."

"Then you'll do it?" She asked nervously.

"Sis," He gave her a concerned look. "If this is truly what you want, then I'll do it."

Nikki nodded. "I've thought about it for the last couple days," She sighed. "It needs to be out, one way or another. I don't want to spend every minute looking around for her wondering if I'm going to run into her. I'd rather make contact and just get it over with, but I want to do it in the easiest way for her." She shrugged. "It's the only thing I can think of."

"What about Nick?" He asked her with a frown.

"What about him?" She asked in surprise.

"Are you thinking she'll lead to him?"

"Absolutely not," She replied. "If she knew where he was, then she'd already know where I am."

Matt looked out the window to his left. She twisted her head around and lifted her shoulders then dropped them to relax the tension in the muscles. The stress in her shoulders released.

After a few minutes he looked back at her. "I have no desire, wish, or need to see or hear about him."

"I agree," Nikki nodded. "He knows where we both are. If he wanted to see us he would have contacted us a long time ago….he's had almost 19 years. I have no intentions of going down that road."

She reached out and grabbed his arm. "Matt, the only reason this came up at all is because she showed up, not that I was searching for her. It's only about her. I love my life and have had no inclination to search for either of them. Mom is Mom and no one else could even come close."

"She is a one and only," He smiled back at her.

"That she is."

"How is she taking all this?"

"She's been pretty calm," Nikki answered truthfully. "She said if it happened while I was a minor she would be concerned, but now, there isn't anything the woman could do to change our relationship. It's not like she could try and take me away from here."

Matt nodded. "OK, so what's your plan for her seeing me?"

******

The next morning at 9:45, Nikki stood in the office looking at the herd picture. It was taken in the south pasture of The Homestead after Rooster returned home from the surgery at WSU. Libby and Kit were in the picture and so was Monty; he was there healing from the wounds on his chest. It showed all 15 horses and the Taggers with extended family; all 15 of them.

It was a large picture so every face was clear and distinct. For those people that didn't know the Taggers, there was a listing of names below the print. There was a matching picture in the hallway outside the library at The Homestead, minus the names. The hallway was lined in numerous pictures of the kids and family as they grew.

Nikki leaned closer to the picture and looked at her and Matt's faces…she could easily tell it was them. She turned and looked around the room, then smiled as an idea formed. She searched the desk for the magazine article about the herd, then quickly flipped through the pages and found the one she was looking for. It was a photo of her standing with Matt; Trooper and Harvey were on each side of them.

"Perfect." Nikki said out loud.

"What's perfect?" Her mom's voice came from behind. Nikki turned, smiled, and lifted the picture.

"You're right…perfect. I'll make sure it's blocked from view until Matt shows up," She glanced out the window. "Just in time."

Nikki turned to look out the large office window that faced the parking lot and road. Elena's car was pulling into a space close to the front so Nikki stepped away from the window so she couldn't be seen. Her mom reached over…ready to hit the intercom. Once Elena opened her door and climbed out, she hit the intercom button, "Jack and Matt, please come to the office."

"She's looking around at the buildings…" Her Mom updated her. "Now she's waving."

She would have seen Jack come from the behind the office after hearing his cue to move. Matt would wait until they were in the office, then come in.

"And here she comes."

With heart racing, Nikki quickly moved to the back room so she wouldn't be seen. What would Elena do when she saw Matt? Or the picture in the magazine? Her knees were weak. She looked around to find something to sit on that was close enough she could hear everything.

She heard the outside door open.

"Sorry about this," Jack said.

"No problem," Elena's voice answered, there was a little country twang in her voice that caught Nikki by surprise. Where would she have developed that? Certainly not in Idaho or Oregon, "…as long as it's warm in here."

"Hi, Elena," Nikki heard her mother say.

"Dru…isn't it?" Elena's voice was sweet.

"Yes, I hope you don't mind, I need to clarify an order, and I'm not sure if Matt or Jack placed it."

"Invoice?" Jack asked. There was silence as Nikki presumed Jack was pretending to read the invoice.

Her heart jumped and she held her breath when she heard the outside door open again. This was so insane! Nikki rolled her eyes to the ceiling just thinking how ridiculous this charade was.

"Need something, Mom?" Matt's voice reached her.

"Hello ma'am," Matt greeted Elena. There was no answer. She wished she could see the woman's face! How was she reacting?

"I took the order, Mom," Matt said. "It should have been 10 boxes, not 100. I hope they didn't send that many."

"No, they called to confirm the high number. Thanks." She answered.

"Jack, can you help me for a minute before your appointment? I hope you don't mind ma'am." Matt said; still no words from Elena.

"You can wait in here where it's warm if you'd like," Jack said.

There was no answer, but she heard footsteps and the door close. Did she go out or stay in? Nikki's heart was racing…her palms moist. She tried hard not to breathe too loudly so she wouldn't be heard.

"That's a picture of the horses that our family rescued last year," She heard her mom say. There was paper shuffling. "And of course the entire family plus a few."

No words from Elena.

"Here's the article in the magazine that came out too. It turned out well so the family was pretty excited about it."

No words from Elena.

Nikki's legs started shaking. She laid her hands over her knees to calm them then leaned towards the door to hear anything.

A chair scraped across the floor.

"Elena?" Her mother said.

"Would you please tell Jack that I forgot I had another appointment and I couldn't stay?" Elena's voice was calmer than Nikki expected and the country twang was gone. The door opened and closed quickly without letting her mother answer.

"It's clear," Her mom called out.

Nikki stood with shaking knees. She took a couple deep breathes and walked into the office. Her mom was watching Elena climb into her car. They heard the engine start and the car pulled out of the parking lot.

"Mom?" Nikki's voice was shaking. "What happened?"

She turned to her with eyebrows raised in surprise. She didn't have time to speak as the door opened and Jack and Matt rushed in.

"Well? That answers that." Matt looked over at his sister.

"What do you mean?" Nikki asked as their eyes met.

"She froze and stared at Matt," Jack answered. "Like she'd seen a ghost."

"I need to sit!" Nikki grabbed the closest chair and quickly sat down. Her mother sat behind the desk and Jack in the chair next to her. Matt leaned against the door.

"Did she say anything after we left?" Matt asked.

"Not a word," Her mom answered. "She stared at the herd picture. Then when I handed her the article with Matt and Nikki's faces and names on it, she stared at it for about thirty seconds then excused herself."

"Her voice sounded calm." Nikki looked at her mom.

"That's what I thought." She nodded and leaned back in the chair, a look of confusion on her face.

"She knew who I was," Matt stated.

"Without a doubt," Jack agreed.

"So she knows I'm her daughter, and I'm here, and she just left?" Nikki was still shocked. Jack reached over and took her hand for support.

"Honey," Her mom leaned forward and Nikki looked up. "We don't know her well enough to know how she acts when she's surprised. She may need time to process it, and then come back and make contact."

Nikki nodded, knowing her mother was just trying to help, but the fact was, it did sting that the woman had left so quickly.

"What did you want her to do?" Matt asked.

Nikki looked up at him and lifted her shoulders in a slow shrug. "Part of me wanted at least a reaction. The other part of me wants her to just go away and never see her again."

They were silent as Nikki overcame her shock.

She looked up at them. "Thanks." She didn't know what else to say. They all went so far against who they were, to pull off this charade.

"Let's just get back to work." Nikki stood.

The rest of the day passed with no word from Elena.

******

The next day, Sunday, she read Dr. Mark's journals and watched football with the family. Nikki did everything she could to keep from thinking of Elena and what her reaction meant. She helped pack presents into boxes and load them into the truck for an early Monday morning departure to the ranch for their Christmas vacation.

The kids' enthusiasm and energy about Christmas and spending five days at the ranch helped lift her mood. Her thoughts about Elena began to subside. As the trucks and trailers pulled out of The Homestead driveway Monday morning, Nikki had decided that Elena was now in the past and she would only look to the future.

CHAPTER FIVE

Nikki gripped the handles as tightly as possible. The engine started with a loud rumble. The louder the engine roared, the tighter the arms around her waist squeezed.

"I don't know about this!" Nikki heard from behind her.

Nikki adjusted her gloved hands one more time and gripped tightly as she felt the jerk that propelled them forward. Snow flew in her face and over her head. A scream from behind made Nikki laugh. The snowmobile, driven by Matt, gained speed as it turned in a large circle. The force of the turn threatened to throw her from the sled being pulled by the machine. Grace's hands gripped tighter as their screams of laughter grew louder.

Nikki could hear Matt laughing over the roar of the engine and snow splattered against her goggles making it hard to see. They hit a bump causing her and Grace to rise a couple inches. When she landed back on the sled, Nikki held on tighter and lowered her body as far as she could. She was bound and determined that Matt wasn't going to get her to come off.

They were flying fast over a straight stretch, so Nikki quickly released a hand and wiped away the snow from her goggles. Matt was headed back to the bump that nearly dislodged them earlier.

"Hold on!" She yelled at Grace.

They hit the bump going faster than the first time, propelling them higher into the air. She felt Grace's hands lose their grip from around her, and when the sled hit the ground, she was gone. Nikki turned in time to see Grace fly to the side and land in the powdery snow. Nikki laughed which allowed snow to fly into her mouth. She coughed and gagged on the snow and laughter.

She knew he was going around to hit the bump again. Matt managed to dislodge Grace, but he wasn't going to get her to come off! Her hands began to hurt from holding the handles so tightly. Crouching lower, Nikki watched Matt turn the machine. The engine roared even louder. She pulled herself down onto the sled as it hit the bump; her body lifted; she tried to hold on but the force from the jump caused her hands to fly free from the handles. She saw sky, then ground, then sky, then nothing but snow. She was laughing so hard, snow went up her nose and mouth as she landed face first.

The engine decreased in power and Matt's laughter increased in volume. The crowd on the sidelines matched his laughter. She slowly stood and looked up at her brother.

"You should have seen yourself fly!" He yelled from the machine.

Suddenly, she felt arms come around her and push her forward into the snow. Grace's mischievous giggles told her who the culprit was. Nikki turned, grabbed the teenager, and rolled on top of her. Grace squealed louder as Nikki stuffed snow into the girl's jacket in revenge.

Matt pulled the snowmobile up next to them. Nikki stood quickly, ran at him and tried to push him off the machine. He braced himself, and even with Grace's help they couldn't get him off. She stood back, smiling at the grin on her brother's face; he slowly shook his head, "Never gonna happen, Sis!"

She gave up that futile attempt and climbed on the machine behind him. Grace quickly jumped on the sled and Matt drove them back to the crowd. For the next two hours they played in the snow; sleds, snowmobiles, horses, and snowball fights. They all returned to the bunkhouse exhausted and hungry. It was Christmas Eve and the snow had started falling again.

******

Nikki sat on her bunk bed with a large bowl of steak stew and watched her family. Wade and Sadie were already fighting to stay awake. Cora, Jessup, Jack, Grace and Reilly were playing cards at the corner table, laughing and joking. Nora was sitting with her parents, Jordan and Scott, retelling her best snow story; one that they had already seen first-hand.

Grayson and Leah were standing by the large window looking out at the falling snow. It was a Christmas Eve tradition for them. Arms wrapped around each other's waist; they were swaying to the Christmas music playing throughout the room. They looked happy and content.

"That's the type of love I want," Nikki thought as she watched them.

Matt made his way down the aisle and sat down on her bunk bed next to her. "I think that was the best snow day we've had in years."

Nikki nodded. "Best Christmas tree, too." She looked to the end of the room to the tree twinkling and lighting up the room. They had all spent the day before creating one ornament each to decorate the tree; even the parents had joined in. The floor had disappeared under the mass of presents placed under the tree.

Nikki leaned her head on her brother's shoulder and looked around the room at the happy faces; one was missing. "Where's Mom?" She lifted her head back up and looked around.

"I don't know, I thought she was playing cards."

She was about to stand when the door opened and her mother stepped in carrying three gift bags.

Wade and Sadie jumped up and ran to her. "More presents!" The 10 year olds were chanting.

"Who are they for?" Sadie asked excitedly.

"Well," her Aunt Dru smiled down at her. "This blue one is for all you kids, from Grayson and Leah."

"All of us?" Wade asked in confusion.

She grinned at him. "And this green one is from Scott and Jordan, to all you kids."

"That's a pretty small bag for all of us." Sadie looked concerned.

"And this little red bag is filled with my gifts to all of you kids." She laughed at their shocked but excited faces.

"Oh, I can't wait!" Sadie bounced excitedly, causing her long blond pony tails to fly up and down.

******

Christmas morning, after all the other presents were open and everyone was settled back around the tree and relaxing on the bunk beds, Jordan picked up the bag from her and Scott. She took out a small wrapped present for each of the kids and told them not to open it until she said go. Then, they opened them all at once. The kids stared in dismay when they saw the work gloves in the package.

"Gloves?" Sadie asked in shock. She looked up at her Uncle Scott for an explanation.

He nodded with a grin. "Those are for the arena you're all going to help build at The Homestead…behind the horse barn would be a good place. All the panels will be delivered New Year's weekend and if the weather holds up, you'll be riding in it by that Sunday night."

Shouts of excitement rang throughout the room. All the kids and adults were excited. The kids would have a new place to practice their gaming and roping events without having to share The Stables arena with clients.

Leah handed out the gifts from the next bag, and again they were all opened at the same time…again the confusion as they pulled out a hammer.

"A hammer?" Wade looked up at his dad and mom. He looked around and saw all the kids got one. "We don't need hammers for putting panels together."

Nikki laughed at their confusion.

"Well that's true, but you're still going to need it." Grayson grinned.

"For what?" Nora asked.

"Well, we have 14 horses at The Homestead and only 6 stalls, so it seems it's time you all build an addition to the barn."

Again the excitement ran through the room.

Her mother picked up her bag for the kids and sat on the floor in the middle of them and handed each of them a very small narrow box.

The kids sat quietly looking at the small gifts. "We'll start with the youngest first, so Sadie, you can open yours first."

Sadie quickly unwrapped the box and threw the lid off in excitement. She sat and stared at the box a moment, before she raised her confused eyes to her aunt.

"Pick it up," Her aunt told her with a chuckle. There was a clasp that held together a tassel of black horse hair.

"It's a tassel to decorate your bridle or saddle." Sadie explained to the family watching her.

"It's made of tail hair from Little Ghost," Her Aunt Dru smiled warmly. Sadie's eyes opened wide, "And, it also includes hair from Angel's tail."

Sadie threw her arms around her and squeezed tightly, tears glistening in her eyes.

"It'll be my good luck charm." Wade grinned while running his fingers through the horse hair on his tassel of Rooster, Dollar's and Angel's hair.

The rest of the kids opened their boxes according to age, which left Nikki for last. It wasn't a tassel for her; it was a beautiful black horsehair bracelet with a silver charm in the shape of an N. Now, when she was off to college, she would always have part of Harvey with her. She smiled at her mom. What a wonderful, personal gift.

Her mom took a seat between Nikki and Matt, while Scott stood to hand out a special gift.

The Tagger Trio siblings didn't buy each other gifts. Each Christmas they took turns purchasing something fun for the three of them and sometimes the spouses were included. Last year, Grayson had purchased three large remote control helicopters that they flew all over the ranch and The Homestead. The year before, Dru had purchased them, and her sister-in-laws, all tickets to the Watershed Concert at The Gorge in Washington. They watched over a dozen country singers during the weekend's massive event.

Scott stood in the middle of the room with a small gift bag in his hand. He grinned at his brother and sister. "Well," He started. "It was tough trying to beat the last gifts you two gave, but I think I've done it." All the kids watched excitedly.

He reached in the small bag and pulled out a tube and threw it at Grayson, then one to his sister.

"Sunscreen?" Leah looked at him worriedly.

"You're going to need it where we're going." Scott teased.

"And that is…?" Grayson asked.

"Well, there is one more thing before I tell you that." Scott grinned and looked over at Nikki. "With Jessup at the ranch, and

Cora at The Homestead, I asked Nikki if she would cover The Stables so Jack could go with us." He threw a tube of sunscreen at a surprised Jack.

"Is this a good thing?" Jack grinned at Nikki. She nodded excitedly.

"We're going on a four day, white water rafting trip in July!" Scott announced and handed each of the adults a flyer showing the adventure.

Grayson and Leah looked up at Scott and grinned. "Nice!" Grayson agreed.

"Awesome, Dad!" Reilly exclaimed and looked over his dad's shoulder at the pictures.

Nikki grinned at her mother who was shaking her head at her. "Young lady! You sure can keep a secret."

As the kids went off to play with their new gifts, the adults reviewed the flyers and already started planning the summer vacation.

The remainder of the day passed quietly, with Wade's new train set the big hit of the day. They created new paths for it to trek across the bunkhouse floor. It didn't stop until late that night, as the lights of the bunkhouse and ranch were turned off.

Nikki lay quietly listening to her family settling in for the night. What a perfect Christmas…content with life, she closed her eyes…oblivious to the train wreck headed her way.

CHAPTER SIX

Nikki rolled over onto her side to see who was already awake. She loved the bunkhouse; it was fun to stay in the same room as everyone else; even when they snored. Jack and Reilly were already gone. They were headed to Texas to visit family and had a plane to catch. Of course Grayson and Scott were awake and sitting quietly in the kitchen area talking. The smell of coffee finally reached her, which meant they had just woken up. She looked around the room. They were the only three awake.

She slid out of bed and waved to them. Retrieving clothes from the dresser, she made her way to the bathroom. It was a large room since they used it as a changing room too. She ran a brush through her hair and pulled it back into a high ponytail then placed a wide winter headband over her ears. When she left the room the men had moved outside, a steaming cup of coffee in their hands. She grabbed her boots and coat and joined them.

"You're up early." Scott hugged her.

"I love quiet mornings in the mountains." She smiled.

"Brisk, fresh air and a new layer of snow." Grayson said. "What's not to love?"

"Are the horses at the barn?" Nikki asked. In the mountains, they pastured together in a large corral that adjoined the barn.

Both men shrugged and followed her as she made her way through the fresh snow.

Most of the horses were huddled together in the corner of the pasture. There were a few walking through the corral, pawing at the snow to see if they could find grass to eat. Buttercup's head came up and she whinnied when she saw them. It caused a round of whinnies from the others and they all headed to the stalls that were built into the side of the barn.

Nikki and her uncles pitched flakes of hay into the stalls. All the horses pushed at each other with their noses as they aimed for the stall they wanted. A light fog was created from each breath. Monty and the other ranch horses were in another corral, so her uncles used the pitchforks and carried the hay to their feeders.

Nikki climbed the fence and watched the Tagger Herd. Arcturus was in one of the stalls closest to her. The little black colt seemed to have more energy than he did at The Homestead. His eyes were more alert and his energy increased as he warned Scarecrow and Little Ghost to stay away from his food. They had only been there a couple days but it was such a remarkable attitude difference.

"Arcturus looks better," Came a voice from behind. Nikki turned to see Sadie climbing up the fence next to her. Her long pig tails swinging across her back and a wide winter headband covering her ears.

"You're up early."

"I like the mornings here in the mountains." Sadie answered; her gaze on the horses.

Nikki smiled. She'd just said the same thing to her uncles.

"Look at how big Little Ghost's butt is getting," Sadie pointed.

"He looks all quarter horse, doesn't he?" Nikki agreed.

"Dad's gonna train him for my roping horse," Sadie said excitedly. "Aunt Dru said I could use Kit for my barrel horse." She turned to Nikki. "Are you going to train Harvey for anything?"

"Can you keep a secret?" Nikki asked her blonde little cousin.

"Of course!" She said seriously. "But don't tell anything to Nora, she doesn't keep secrets."

Nikki nodded. "Good to know."

"So what's your secret?" Sadie asked.

"Matt and I have discussed team penning together."

"Oh how fun! Don't you need three people though?"

"Yes, we do," Nikki smiled. The girl knew a lot about her horse events for a ten year old. The girl was a wizard when it came to learning; especially math and anything horses. Sadie read all the time and seemed to remember everything.

"Who's gonna be your third?"

Nikki shrugged. "Not sure yet. We want to work with Harvey and Trooper to check their cow sense."

"I'm so excited about getting them trained," Sadie told her. "And now with the arena at home! I can't wait! That was the most awesome Christmas present. I'll never want to leave it. I've been practicing on my roping, too."

Nikki laughed, Sadie's enthusiasm was infectious.

"I was more into showing, like Nora." Nikki told her cousin. "I wasn't into gaming but I think roping would have been fun too."

"You can still learn," Sadie turned her pretty blue eyes towards her. "You're not too old."

Nikki giggled. "College is taking a lot of my time, plus working at The Stables. If we team pen, I won't have much time for anything else."

Sadie nodded in understanding. She blew air out and saw her breath in the cold air. "That's cool." She giggled and did it again. Nikki joined her and made Sadie giggle even more. Her giggling caught the attention of the feeding horses and a few heads popped up; including Little Ghost. Sadie looked at him and sighed.

"What?" Nikki asked her.

"I just like looking at him," Sadie admitted with love shining in her eyes.

Nikki laughed and hugged her cousin. "I feel the same way about Harvey."

Their conversation was interrupted by the bunkhouse door opening and a loud Wade shouting good morning. Everyone, that had still been sleeping in the bunkhouse, made their way out the door and into the fresh air.

"Mom said we have to get ready to go home." Wade ran up to them with the snow crunching under his boots.

"It's supposed to snow more, so they want to get home before we get stuck." Nora said running up behind him.

"I wouldn't mind getting stuck." Nikki smiled at Sadie.

"Me either." Sadie agreed with a grin.

They left an hour later with presents packed away safely in the trailer tack room. Nikki sat next to her mom on the way home.

"This is always the weirdest week at The Stables." Nikki said. "I always miss Jack and Reilly when they're gone. Grace is such a different person when Reilly's not here."

"She's more withdrawn…like a part of her is missing." She agreed. "But they'll be back Tuesday night."

"Are we still going to the New Year's party at the Fair Building?"

"It's one of the few events where we all go, even Matt decided to go with us this year."

"Is Cora coming with us? She doesn't seem to get out much."

Her mother shook her head. "She doesn't like big crowds and offered to watch the kids."

"Well I hope the next five days go fast." Nikki sighed.

******

Five days later, Nikki was thinking how fast those days had passed by. Jack and Reilly arrived home and all was good again.

She stood in front of the mirror trying to decide if she should put her hair up or let it flow loose. The party was pretty informal so she had on black jeans, a pretty pink top and would be wearing the new black western jacket that her mother had given her for Christmas. She lifted the hair up then let it fall around her shoulders. She nodded to herself and smiled; it would be down and more casual.

The door to the room was open and her mother walked through. Her long blonde hair was cascading down loose with big curls. "Mom! You look beautiful." Nikki grinned.

"Well, at least we match in clothes tonight." She laughed as she stood next to her and looked in the mirror. Nikki agreed. Her dark hair and brown eyes were a contrast to her mother's light blonde hair and pale blue eyes. She was also in black jeans, a black jacket and her shirt was a lighter pink than Nikki's and made her blue eyes stand out.

"Should I go put my pink top on too?" Matt teased as he walked through the door. He was in black jeans too, but was wearing a dark green long sleeve shirt. It made his eyes look green instead of brown.

Their mother giggled softly, "We could make it the Tagger Enterprises uniform."

"Just not gonna happen!" Scott informed them from the doorway. "So let's go!"

They all laughed and walked to the back door.

The party was well underway when they arrived. Nikki was excited to see friends from high school and college. For the next couple hours she hugged dozens of past friends and clients of The Stables. She smiled so much her face was hurting.

"Having fun?" Jack asked as he came up next to her. The girls she was talking to made a 'wow' face, giggled, and walked away to leave Nikki alone with the handsome man.

"Seriously, Jack," Nikki rolled her eyes. "We keep being seen together and people are going to talk."

He shrugged with a roguish grin, "Let them talk."

She just shook her head. "Have you seen Matt? Is he having fun?"

"You know Matt; he's probably out back with some pretty little thing."

"Pretty little thing, Jack?" Nikki shook her head and giggled at his phrase.

"Is young maiden better?" He teased.

"No!" Nikki laughed, "That's worse!"

She looked around trying to find her brother. Nikki spotted her mother and right behind her was Matt…no… her head tilted sideways in confusion. He looked like Matt; but he was older. Shock ran through her and her heart nearly stopped when Nikki realized who was standing behind her mother.

CHAPTER SEVEN

Nikki felt like she was frozen in place. She stared at her birth father standing behind her mother like it was a dream; a nightmare. Slowly her arm raised and her hand grabbed at Jack's arm. He turned…looked at her then followed her gaze. She heard his intake of breath. Even to him, it was obvious who the man was standing behind her mom. Jack turned and looked at Nikki and she slowly turned to him. Her eyes registered the horror that her mother would turn and come face-to-face with her ex-husband.

Nikki felt like she was in slow motion as she started walking towards her mother. Just beyond her, Nikki saw Matt. Matt! How was he going to react to his father being there? She had sworn this would only involve Elena. Nikki tried to walk faster, but she felt like she was walking through cement. Her eyes moved from her father, to her mother, then to her brother. When she was within fifteen feet of Matt, his head turned slowly and his eyes connected with hers. He could tell something was wrong and his head tilted slightly and his mouth formed the word "what". Her eyes pled forgiveness from him; she stretched out her right hand. Just as their hands touched and her hand slid into his, her eyes moved to look at their father then back to Matt. Matt had followed her gaze and his expression changed from confusion to shock. Then his expression changed to concern as he turned back to her. Matt's grip tightened around her hand.

Just as Nikki's mind was screaming for her mother, she felt her mother's hand slip into hers and the pressure of her squeeze. Still in slow motion, Nikki turned around to look at her mother and saw her staring at Nick; Jack was there staring at him, too. Nikki turned back to Matt who was looking past her to their mother. Behind Matt, were Grayson and Scott making their way to the group with looks of shock and concern on their faces. Nikki turned again and not only saw Nick, but even though she hadn't seen her, she knew it was Elena that stepped out from behind of him.

The eight of them stood in a silent hurricane of emotions. Nick was staring at Matt as Nikki gaped at Elena who was staring back at her in wonder. Then suddenly, Nikki felt the jerk on her arm as Matt had turned away from the group and was pulling her with him. Nikki's hand instinctively tightened on her mother's and she was pulled along as well. Matt's pace quickened as they made their way through the crowd and towards the exit. Nikki turned and looked past her mother. Scott, Grayson, and Jack had stepped in between them and her birth parents to block the attempt to follow their exit.

Matt busted through the exit in the back corner of the building and without a word headed for his truck. None of them spoke as they quickly loaded into the front seat and Matt started the engine and drove away from the building. Nikki's heart was racing as she sat between her brother and mother. She was holding her mother's hand tightly. Half way between the fair building and The Homestead was the rodeo grounds. Not wanting to go home yet, Matt turned into the driveway to the indoor arena, then drove to an area behind the building so they would be unseen from the road.

His hand was shaking as he reached down to turn the key and shut off the truck. They sat quietly drowning in their own thoughts. Matt's hand came down on hers and he squeezed tightly. Nikki looked up to see he was staring out the side window of the truck into the darkness. She turned to her mother who had her eyes closed, her right hand resting over them. Tears were sliding down her cheeks. Nikki felt her own tears of guilt build and begin to fall.

It was Matt that finally spoke; "I don't think I've been this shocked since I found out how Wade broke his arm and what he went through to get Monty help."

"I'm so sorry." Nikki cried. Both her brother and mother squeezed her hands.

"It wasn't your fault, Nikki." Matt turned to her then glanced up at his mother. "There is no way we could have known that Elena knew where Nick was and that she would bring him here."

"But you didn't want to see him," She sniffed.

"But that doesn't stop them from wanting to see us." Matt rationalized. He stared at their mother for a moment. "Are you OK, Mom?" She nodded, but didn't say anything. Her hand dropped from her face, but she turned and stared out the side window of the truck; her chin resting on her right hand. There was something about staring into the darkness that helped clear the mind.

All three of their phones started ringing and all three reached down to decline the calls. Within minutes their phones alerted them of text messages. Their mother lifted her phone and Matt and Nikki watched as she typed 'Give us time' then turned off the phone. Matt and Nikki turned their phones off.

"So what do we do next year to top this New Year's Eve party?" Matt chuckled in an attempt to break the tension.

Their mother giggled, which made Nikki relax a little. She lifted her shoulders and twisted her neck around, trying to make the tension leave.

"Well," her mother started. "I don't think there are any more ex-husbands or long lost parent's out there." She turned to them, "Unless there's something you two haven't told me."

The three of them laughed awkwardly.

"No ex-wife here." Matt smiled.

"No ex-husband here." Nikki added.

"And I only gave birth once, and wed once, so we're good there." Their mom sighed.

"Well, that just means next year doesn't have a chance over this year's party." Matt concluded.

Nikki stared ahead of her and tried to imagine what was happening back at the party.

"Why do you think they waited so long between when Elena left to now?" Matt asked.

"I imagine they had families to spend Christmas with and then came here," Her mom answered.

Nikki had forgotten that Elena had another child. Was it a boy or girl? What about Nick? Was he married, have kids, or were his own parents still alive? Where was he living?

"To be honest," She started hesitantly. "Now that I've seen both of them, I'm curious about them."

"I'd be worried if you weren't." Her mom replied.

"Matt?" Nikki turned to her brother.

He nodded. "It was like looking in the mirror, of the future. You always said he looked like me, but even in the pictures I've seen, I didn't realize how much…it was still a bit…bizarre." He looked across the truck at his mother. "You OK?" He asked again.

"Yeah," She sat up taller in the seat. "I think the shock has worn off. To be honest," She hesitated. "It was like someone slapped me."

"Oh, Mom!" Nikki cried.

Her mom squeezed her hand and smiled. "It's OK, really it is. The shock is over now. I'm just numb and like you, a little curious." She reached across Nikki and grasped Matt's hand. Nikki laid hers over the top of theirs.

"Why would Elena bring Nick?" Matt frowned.

"They can't be back together if Elena went out with Jack." Nikki added.

"I'm curious about them, but I'm not worried about them." Her mom frowned. "I am concerned about Jack, Scott, and Grayson. They have to be worried sick about us."

"Jordan and Leah, too." Nikki added.

Matt turned to them. "I don't need this like you two do. You need closure. That door was never open for me, so there is no closure needed with me. Does that make sense?" They both nodded. "I'll go with you…if you want to go see them…but I'm there for you, not him."

Her mother squeezed her hand which made Nikki look at her. "There isn't anything either of them can do to take you away."

"I know, Mom." Nikki smiled. "And there is nothing they can say or do to change how I feel about you, Scott, or Grayson."

"I have a morbid curiosity just to find out why they are here." Matt smirked. "Why did she go get him? What's the connection there?"

"As much as I didn't think about them before," Nikki looked up at her brother. "I'm just as curious about them now." She turned to her mother. "Are you OK with seeing them again?"

She nodded. "The shock has worn off."

Matt reached down and turned on his phone. It sounded like an alarm going off from all the messages. "Twelve," he said; without reading them, he typed into the phone.

TEXT TO GRAYSON: Where are they?

Within seconds he had an answer back.

"They're still at the party." He looked up at their mom. "Where do you want to meet them?"

"I don't want them at the house," Nikki added quickly. It felt like it would be too much of an intrusion on her life. "I just want them to answer a couple questions, then, go away," She added truthfully with a nervous giggle.

Her mom nodded, but added, "You know it won't be that easy."

Nikki took a deep breath and let it out slowly. "As long as the three of us face them together, I think I'm OK." She turned to Matt.

"I keep asking myself why this had to happen." Matt frowned. "What caused Elena to pick up that flyer to Tagger Stables and make that one phone call that has created this chain reaction," He sighed and looked up at his mom. "So what do you want to do?"

"We get it over with tonight, no delaying." She answered and they quickly agreed. "But where?" They looked at each other without any answers.

Matt's phone alerted them to another message. He glanced down, "Elena has offered a meeting room at the hotel to talk."

Nikki looked up at her brother then her mother. "Is it odd that I hope for a room with two exits so I don't feel blocked in?"

"Claustrophobic and trapped!" Matt agreed, and sent a message back stating they agreed and would meet them in the hotel lobby. He turned the truck back on. As he turned around and headed for the road he said; "Let's just get this over with."

CHAPTER EIGHT

They drove into the packed parking lot of the Red Lion. The two bars in the hotel were full of New Year's Eve revelers.

Matt pulled his truck in next to Grayson's then they sat quietly looking at the hotel.

"I think I'm going to be sick." Nikki closed her eyes.

"We don't have to do this," Her mom reminded her.

Nikki opened her eyes and looked at her mom. "Yeah, I think we do."

She nodded at Nikki and reached for the door handle.

Jack, Grayson, and Scott were standing in the lobby when they walked through the doors. No sign of Leah and Jordan. People celebrating the New Year were scattered around them laughing and joking.

Nikki smiled nervously at her uncles. The both gave her a quick hug. Jack did, too.

"They're down the hall there, third door on your right." Grayson pointed down the hallway.

Nikki followed her mother who was walking with long determined strides; she really wanted this over! When she walked through the door, Elena and Nick were standing at the back of the room. Elena looked like a mouse in the corner. Her hair was brunette, like Nikki's, and was straight, stopping just before her shoulders. Her eyes were darker than Nikki's, but they highlighted a pretty face. Elena smiled hopefully at Nikki, then glanced up at Nick. That was confusing…why would she look at him? What was the connection?

Nick stood quietly waiting for them to enter. This was the first time Nikki had a chance to actually look at her birth father. He was shorter than Matt but not by much. Matt was broader in the shoulders but Nick looked trim and muscular. His dark brown hair was longer than she expected, just touching the collar of his black shirt. His brownish green eyes watched his ex-wife as she walked to the side of the room to his left. Nikki was close behind her.

The room wasn't small, but it wasn't overly large either. The men walked in behind them and moved to the left. Scott and Grayson leaned against the edge of a table that was pushed into the corner. Jack stood next to them. Matt was the last into the room and he closed the door to block out any interruption from the partiers.

Nikki was shocked when Matt took ten steps directly up to their father. Nick took a deep breath and let it out slowly. They stood just feet apart and stared at each other.

Matt spoke first, with a calm and confident tone that was way beyond his 18 years; "I just want you to know that I don't want or need you in my life." There was no reaction from Nick. "I have two men behind me that have raised me, as their own son, and I consider them the only fathers I need." Nick nodded without looking away. "I am only here to support my sister and my mother who you abandoned and they need closure." Again Nick nodded; a flicker of respect in his eyes. "I will not allow you to disrespect them." Matt added.

As Matt turned away from Nick, the older man spoke; "I loved your mother."

Matt turned, and Nikki was as shocked as everyone else in the room when his right fist went flying towards Nick's face; his full weight and forward movement behind the throw. Nick didn't have time to react before Matt's fist hit him just below his left eye, connecting with full impact on the cheekbone. Their mother and

Elena both cried out as Nick landed on the floor. Matt took a step forward as Nick looked up at him from the ground.

Nikki didn't know what to do. She glanced at her mom who was staring at Matt in shock. They had never seen a violent side to Matt. Nikki turned to her uncles. They had taken a step towards Matt; Jack at their side. Without looking, Matt held out a hand to stop their movement.

Nick slowly stood, his hand touching the cut under his eye and wiping away the small trickle of blood. He said nothing.

"Telling ME you loved my mother was disrespectful to her and my sister." Matt's voice was controlled anger. "No man, that truly loves a woman, would abandon her when she was pregnant, or abandon a two-year-old scared little girl, with a family he barely knew."

Nick stiffened his back, trying to match Matt's height. He couldn't.

"I will give you that one," Nick said of the punch. "No more." Nikki knew it was a veiled warning. He didn't seem to care that there were three other men in the room backing Matt up. Nor did he seem to remember that they were there as his eyes never left Matt's.

"DO NOT disrespect them!" Matt responded, matching the veiled threat.

Nick nodded. "I'll rephrase it so you understand what I was trying to say."

Matt had started to turn away but turned back to Nick. Nikki cringed in anticipation of another punch but he didn't lift his arm. She was amazed that Nick didn't flinch even though he too thought another punch was coming.

Matt stood quietly, threatening with his eyes. "She's standing right there," Matt pointed to his mother. "Try your explanation on her."

Matt started to turn again when Nick spoke. "Matt," Matt stopped and looked back. Nikki realized, with shock, that it was the first time either she or Matt had heard him speak his son's name. "There are three men behind you." With that, Nick turned and looked at his ex-wife, ending their conversation.

Matt walked towards his uncles who had sat back down on the edge of the table. They moved in opposite directions so Matt could sit between them. Once he sat, Matt looked over at Jack who turned to him. They nodded to each other then turned back to the room.

Her mother had taken a step forward, so Nikki couldn't see her face, but her voice was calm, yet cold. "I'll take Matt's example on this and just state it bluntly… I am here for MY daughter." Nikki felt the tears spring up in her eyes at the possessive tone. "I never thought or hoped to see you again." Nick's eyes narrowed very slightly.

Nick turned to indicate his full attention was on her mother, who was tall enough in her boots that her blue eyes were even with his dark eyes. They only stood a few feet apart.

"I hoped to have this conversation just between us," Nick started, he was met with silence. He sighed. "I have spent a lot of time over the years trying to understand what I did…I don't *ever* talk to *anyone* about my personal life or feelings," Still no response from anyone in the room. "But I believe you deserve to know the complete truth…you, Matt, and Nikki."

He turned and took a drink off the table behind him. She hadn't noticed it before. He swallowed half the drink, then picked up a napkin and wiped another drip of blood from the cut. He kept the drink and napkin in his hand and turned back to his ex-wife. He hadn't looked at anyone else in the room.

"When we met, I didn't tell you how I was raised," He stated and she slowly shook her head. He took a deep breath. "I lived in New Mexico on the side of the road in a small hut of a house with my parents; no brothers or sisters. My father didn't like or want to work, so he didn't. My mother had a hard time keeping a job. We were a true example of dirt poor.

"When I was 16, a friend bet me $50 that I couldn't stay on a bull out in the middle of a field. I won and he gave me the fifty bucks. It was the most money I had ever seen. I took that fifty to the closest rodeo and entered the bull riding. I borrowed the gear and won a hundred bucks, so I entered the next rodeo. I stuck with bulls because I couldn't afford a horse or trailer. I bummed rides until I could afford a small car to get me from rodeo to rodeo. It steam rolled from there and I never looked back. It was two years before I saw my mother again. My father was dead." He paused and cleared his throat.

"When I was 18, I met a young buckle bunny at the Pendleton Roundup. She went on the road with me and before long she was pregnant, and I found out she was only 17 and had run away from home." He paused but didn't divert his gaze from her mother. Nikki looked behind him at Elena; she was staring at the back of his head. Nikki couldn't read her expression.

"I took her home in the spring when I found out. A couple months later, I was back at the Pendleton Roundup. After I rode my last bull and walked behind the chutes, there were two men in suits handing me papers to sign stating the baby was mine. I did, because it was… she was." He rolled his neck and shrugged his shoulders to loosen the tension. He then dabbed the cut again. "Once the papers were signed, a woman walked out from behind them and I was handed a car seat in one hand and a bag of stuff in the other. I had no clue what all the stuff was, but when I looked down in the car seat there was a baby. When I looked up again, they were gone." His voice was tired and strained from the memory.

"I literally stood there for fifteen minutes wondering what happened. Pretty soon, everyone had left the area and I was standing there, alone, with a four day old baby girl." He drank the rest of the drink, walked it to the table and slowly placed the glass down. He returned to his position in front of her mother. Nikki stood silently, mesmerized by his story. No one else had spoken and he wondered if they were as stunned, too.

"I thought they were insane," He continued.

"My parents wanted to punish us," Elena said quietly from behind him. "In their minds, handing you the baby was the worse that they could do to you and it would make you stop riding."

Nick continued as if she hadn't spoken. "I did the only thing I could think to do…I headed down to my mother. Along the way, I had to figure out how to feed her and change her diaper. I drove straight through, only stopping for gas. I was terrified." He paused; his ex-wife said nothing. "I left her there and went back on the road to earn money the only way I knew how, riding more bulls. I sent almost all the money to my mother to take care of her. A little over a year later, I met the most beautiful blue-eyed blonde barrel racer I had ever seen. I fell head over heels in love. We traveled from rodeo to rodeo together and within three months we were married." He paused again. "Then I met her family."

Nikki saw was her mother's head tilt to the side in confusion. "My family?"

Nick nodded solemnly. "They were loving, supportive, and to me…smothering." He sighed, his eyes never left hers. "I was used to being alone and here were these people wanting me to live with them, work on their ranch, stay in their big house, and drive their fancy trucks."

"Sounds awful." Her mother said coldly.

He nodded and his lip went up in a smirk. He dabbed the cut for the last time as it had finally quit bleeding.

"To me, it was." He tucked the napkin in his jean pocket. "I had never been around that…EVER…I didn't know how to handle it. I tried for months, but each day I felt even more controlled and overwhelmed." She started to say something but he shook his head and raised his hand slowly to stop her. "It wasn't your family, Dru, it was me," He grunted. "I know that many a man has broken up with a girl with the 'It's me and not you' crap but this time it is true."

He paused, when she didn't respond he continued, "When I told you I needed to leave, I was going to ask you to come with me. I still wanted you and wanted to be with you…I loved you." He took a deep breath and exhaled slowly. "When you said you were pregnant, I freaked out…thinking of those terrifying days with the baby…I ran out as fast as I could." He dropped his gaze to the floor then slowly looked back up to his silent ex-wife. "I can give you every excuse in the world, but they're just that…excuses."

He glanced past her mom and over at Nikki. "I hit every rodeo I could and drank every bottle that I could find. I'd just hit 21 so it wasn't that hard." He paused, took a deep breath and exhaled slowly. "When I woke up from the haze, I thought of you with my mother, living in the dirt house she called home. I didn't want you growing up like I did; I wanted you to have what Dru had. I drove straight to my mom's house, picked you up and loaded you in my car. My mother was having a fit, scratched the hell out of me, but it didn't matter. I met with an attorney as soon as I got to town. Had the papers drawn up and then brought you to Dru."

When he stopped, her mother cut in; "You said your mother insisted you bring her here to be raised with her brother."

He looked back to her, shaking his head. "She didn't know about Matt and I wanted her to sound better than she was…like she was a caring person and thought more of Nikki then she did of the money I was sending her." There was silence in the room. "I saved as much money as I could and purchased an airline ticket to Australia. I was there for 17 years; until I came back last summer."

"What made you come back?" Her mother asked.

"Nikki and Matt," He said flatly, glancing over at Nikki. "I was at a friend's house just outside of Sydney and they showed me a story about a herd of rescued horses in the States…in Idaho. You can imagine what a surprise that was."

He stepped back to the table and leaned against it similar to her uncle's stance. Nikki touched her mom's arm and pulled her back. She had listened quietly, now it was her turn.

Nikki took a step forward and glanced between her birth mother and her birth father. She had never even thought of a moment like this. The image of the two of them together…in front of her…she didn't believe it would or could have ever happened.

Nick watched her, his expression calm…and tired. When she didn't speak, he spread his arms out to his sides; "Ask me anything you want. I won't lie or try to cover anything up, makes no sense at this point."

Nikki had gone from shock, to fear, to anger, and now she was at an eerie calm. She hadn't analyzed the story he told her yet. She didn't doubt the truth of it, but had more questions.

"Did you ever think of me…of us?" she asked him.

"Every day."

"Why didn't you call?"

"I didn't want to interrupt the wonderful life you were living."

"Did you know about the accident that killed my grandparents and great grandparents?"

"Not until last year."

"Would it have made a difference?"

"I doubt it."

"Why?"

"There comes a time that every man or woman has to be honest with who they really are. Mine came when I was honest with the fact that I shouldn't be a father."

"Why?"

"I didn't know how to be one and I couldn't handle the THOUGHT of the responsibility; let alone the responsibility itself. The time I spent taking you to my mother was the most terrified I'd ever been; worse than any bull I'd ever faced."

"Do you have any other kids?"

"No," He paused and rephrased; "Not that I know of, but they would have to be older than Matt."

"Why?"

"After I dropped you off and knew the choice I made, I had a vasectomy so I didn't screw up anyone else's life."

"Did you ever get married?"

"No, they either wanted or had kids and I couldn't handle that…I still have a hard time being around kids." He smirked with a slight shrug.

"You said you came back last summer."

"I did."

"If you came back for us, why didn't you come here? Where did you go?"

"I started working for a stock contractor down by Boise."

"Why didn't you come here?"

"Same reason as before, I didn't want to interrupt your life. For some reason, Boise was close enough."

"Why?"

"I don't know. Australia was too far…Boise was close enough."

"Did you ever try to find out how we were?"

"Every day since last summer when I saw the report, then the articles in the newspapers and magazines. I've been on Facebook every day looking for more pictures," He paused. "I was right."

"About what?"

"Leaving you with Dru and disappearing, so you could have a good life."

Nikki thought that one over. "You're probably right," She agreed.

"I know I am."

She bent her head around and lifted her shoulders, then dropped them. The tension released. It dawned on her that she did the exact same movements he did a few minutes ago.

"You've known where we were, so why today? Why come here tonight at the party?"

Nick glanced over at Elena then back to Nikki. He didn't have to say anything. Nikki turned to Elena.

"When I saw Matt at The Stables I knew he was Nick's, it was quite obvious. It was like going back 20 years." She glanced over at Matt. He hadn't moved and just stared back at her with an unreadable expression. "When I saw your group picture and saw your name, the name I gave you…and your resemblance to Matt, I knew you were my daughter," She took in a breath. "I had just seen my daughter for the first time in 20 years."

Elena stepped forward but stopped when Nikki made no motion and didn't respond to the word 'daughter'.

"I knew some of the old cowboys that knew how to contact Nick. I reached out and they told me where he was." She glanced at Nick. "I called him and told him I found you and I was going to tell you who I was."

Nikki turned to him. "She didn't know anything," He explained. "So I told her not to contact you until I got here. I drove up from

Boise and arrived this afternoon. Elena insisted we show up at the party tonight." He glared over at Elena, "Not my choice, but she was going with or without me."

There was no emotion between the two of them…Nick didn't seem to even like her…so why did she bring him here?

Nikki turned to Elena. "Why tonight?"

"I'd waited long enough." She answered meekly.

Nikki stared at her a moment then realized how tired she was. She needed to finish asking questions so they could leave and end this bizarre day.

"Do I have a brother or a sister?" She asked Elena.

"What?" Elena asked in surprise.

"You said you had two kids, but only raised one." As soon as she said the words Nikki realized what she'd done and unintentionally looked at Jack. He raised his eyebrows…he knew too.

Elena turned to Jack. "You knew who I was?"

"Not exactly," Nikki's mother stepped up next to her daughter. "Nick had told me your name. When I heard it after the first appointment, we asked him to find out if it was you and if you knew who we were."

Nick cleared his throat and stood. "Nikki," He glanced over at Matt. "Do either of you have any other questions for me?" Matt shook his head, so Nick looked back at Nikki. "I'm exhausted… mentally and physically, and half buzzed, so now is the time to ask." When she shook her head, he looked at her mom again. She shook her head.

"If you think of anything, I will be here for the next couple days, in room 414, and then I'll be gone." He headed for the door but stopped half way and turned back. "Dru?" Everyone in the room looked over at him. "I'm sorry that I couldn't explain it to you better back then. I really didn't understand it and didn't know how," His eyes looked sorrowful. "I am sorry for leaving you like that, but I will never apologize for leaving Nikki with you and getting out of Matt's life. It was the only right thing I've done in my entire life."

Nikki turned to her mother, who didn't respond; he turned and walked out without another word.

"Nikki?" Elena took a hesitant step to her.

Nikki felt every muscle in her body screaming of exhaustion. She turned tired eyes to her birth mother. There was nothing she wanted to say until she could process the whole evening. Nick's story was heart wrenching and she needed time before she heard more.

Nikki shook her head.

Elena nodded and slowly made her way out the door.

They were finally alone. She glanced at her mother who was still staring out the door Nick and Elena had just walked through. The men slowly stood and walked towards them.

The sound of the New Year's revelers was louder now that the door was open.

"And just think," Matt said. They all turned to him. "I was actually looking forward to tonight!"

Nikki heard her mother chuckle, which made her sigh in relief mixed with a slight giggle. The men nodded and agreed.

Her mom turned, smiled, walked up to her and cupped both sides of her face in her hands. Her blue eyes were sparkling as she leaned in and kissed Nikki on the forehead. Matt wrapped his arms around them and squeezed tightly just as they heard the New Year's countdown.

CHAPTER NINE

Nikki's eyes fluttered open, but she quickly closed them to hide away from the light streaming through the windows. Curiosity got the best of her and she reluctantly opened one eye to look at the clock; 7:10 in the morning. Six hours of sleep wasn't bad. She'd had less at college. Rolling onto her back she allowed her eyes to open and stare at the ceiling.

Nick's story played back in her head. She believed every word of it. Like he said, there was no reason to lie.

Fifty bucks had made his whole world change. He pulled himself out of a dirt hut and traveled all over the country for rodeos and then to Australia for seventeen years. That had to say something about the person he is…didn't it?

Nikki flipped back onto her stomach and buried her face into the pillow.

How terrifying would it have been to be handed a four day old baby when you've never been around one before? They are so tiny and helpless! Learning how to change the diaper is one thing…but how did he feed her?

Nikki turned her head enough to look at the picture on the bedside table of herself, Matt and their mom. It was taken in October, at college during one of their Friday night dinners. A friend of Matt's was enrolled in photography classes and had taken the picture for them. The fall colors on the campus were spectacular and she and her mom were throwing leaves in the air at Matt. So cliché, but she loved it…the three of them were so happy… and they still were. No matter what happened the night before…it didn't change their happiness.

She'd been fortunate in life, and knew it…and it was because of Nick's decision to take her to Dru and Matt. He wanted a good life for her…not the life he had. Isn't that what every father wants for their child? A better life than what they had?

When he had left the room saying he would be gone in a couple days, her stomach turned. How, in just a couple hours, could she have gone from not wanting him in her life or even thinking of him *at all*, to not wanting him to leave? She just wanted a chance to…? Nikki flung herself onto her back and stared at the ceiling.

"Wanted what? A chance for what?" She said out loud.

When the room didn't answer, she sighed. The whole night was odd…but something…something was nagging at her.

"What's bothering me?" She spoke to the ceiling again. She had ridden back to The Homestead with her mom and Matt, so they could discuss the evening's events. But they hadn't spoken a word until they said goodnight and headed to their different rooms. For Matt it was the couch in the living room since Reilly was sleeping in his bed.

Matt….she smiled thinking of how he had stood up for her and her mother. She'd never seen anyone get punched, let alone her brother throwing the punch. The shock in the room was evident. I bet he was even shocked, she giggled, then sighed loudly. There was something about the confrontation that seemed wrong.

Her mom was quiet most of the time listening to Nick's story. From her questions and her expression after it was over, it seemed like she believed Nick too. She would be the one person in the room that would know, other than Nick himself.

Scott, Grayson, and Jack had stood in the back, ready to pounce at any moment, Nikki smiled.

Matt was strong, confident, and defended her and their mother.

That left Elena. The mouse in the corner. She had been quiet…almost too quiet. Nick had glared at her twice and didn't speak a word to her…there was no love lost between the two of them. Nikki sat up in bed and realized that was the problem. If it was her daughter she hadn't seen for twenty years, she wouldn't have been a mouse and let Nick's story take over the night. There was no doubt that she WAS Elena's daughter, but there was something that just didn't fit.

It was Elena…something about her wasn't right.

Nikki looked around the room. The bed was sitting in a corner with a window next to the headboard and one at the foot. She pulled up her comforter, wrapped it around herself and sat cross-legged at the end of the bed looking out the window. Her long dark hair flowed in tangles down her back in contrast to the white material.

Nikki saw the horse herd was making their way out into the pasture. The grass had gone dormant, so they were just wandering around hoping to find something to nibble. It was just exercise after being in their stalls all night. Cora's colt, Libby and Kit would be in the North pasture so in the south pasture she saw the entire Tagger herd walk by…except Arcturus. She leaned as far forward as possible to peer through the window in the direction the horses were walking. Finally Arcturus appeared. He was walking very slowly.

They had seen a significant improvement in the horse while they were at the ranch. She had thought it was just the excitement of the new environment, but now Nikki was wondering if it wasn't something *in* the environment.

She heard a knock on the door and turned. Matt stuck his head in, grinned, stepped in and shut the door. As if they were kids again, he jumped up high and plopped on her bed.

"What's up, Sis?"

She laughed and shook her head.

"You're in a good mood."

"I think I am," He chuckled and looked past her to the horses. "What are you doing?"

She turned and pointed out Arcturus and the change in him since they had arrived back.

"You think it's something in the pasture that's making him sick?" He asked. He leaned closer. "None of the other horses seem any different."

"I know," She was frustrated. "I'm going to hit Dr. Mark's books today."

"I'll help."

"With both of us…" A movement from the horses caught her attention. It was Eli. His head had gone up and he started walking back towards the barn. The other horses ignored him.

"It has to be Grayson," Nikki giggled. She leaned forward again to check, but couldn't see him.

"What's Grayson?" Matt looked in the same direction. Finally Grayson appeared by the horse's water trough.

"I can't see from here!" Nikki squealed and threw the comforter off. "Come on!" She yelled at Matt and he followed her as she left the room and ran down the hallway of the house.

"What are you doing?" Matt laughed.

She came to a quick stop and turned into the living room and jumped on the couch that still had his blankets across it. The long sofa ran the length of the wide window. They leaned on the back of it with their feet dangling off the cushions.

"Watch Eli," She quickly told him what she had seen a couple days before.

"What are you two doing?" It was her mom. Nikki waved her over and they made room between them so she could kneel on the couch too. They were all three still in their pajamas.

Eli walked straight towards Grayson who had turned his back on the horse and was unhooking the hose from the water faucet that emptied into the trough. Even though the temperature had dropped and it was cold out, Grayson took off his gloves and placed them in his back pocket.

"He's playing with him!" Nikki laughed.

The three on the couch watched the horse walk non-stop, straight to the back of Grayson and lower his head to the gloves. Grayson didn't move. The horse quickly, using his lips, pulled the gloves from Grayson's pocket and let them fall to the ground. Grayson grinned and the group on the couch laughed. Eli lowered his head to the ground and picked up one of the gloves. He bounced his head which made the glove wave in the air; another round of giggles from the couch.

With glove in mouth, Eli turned and walked away from Grayson who turned, picked up the one glove from the ground and followed the horse. They couldn't hear if he said anything but the horse kept walking so Grayson had to jog to catch up with the horse. Eli stopped and he pulled the glove from the horse's mouth and placed them back in his pocket and turned to walk away. Eli swung his head around and grabbed at the gloves, but missed. Grayson continued to walk as Eli turned and followed. Just as Grayson made it back to the water trough, Eli was close enough and pulled the gloves out again and let them drop to the ground. That made Grayson turn to the horse with his hands on his hips. Horse and man stood staring at each other. The crowd on the couch laughed.

Eli took a step forward and pushed his nose into Grayson's chest, causing him take a step back.

"If he isn't careful, that horse will push him in." Nikki's mom giggled.

Grayson held his ground and the horse took another step forward and slowly leaned his head into Grayson's shoulder and lifted his arm with his nose. Eli's head remained tucked into Grayson's side. The group on the couch silently watched as Grayson rubbed down the horse.

"Wow." Matt laughed.

"Exactly." Nikki smiled.

"I think Grayson has a friend." Their mom added.

They continued to lean across the back of the couch and watch Eli get his attention.

"I thought you two would still be in bed sleeping." Their mom said.

Nikki shook her head, "I was watching Arcturus when Matt came in the room."

Her mom stared at her then turned and looked at Matt; he was still staring out the window.

"No discussions about Nick?" She asked in bewilderment.

There it was! Nikki turned to her mother. "Isn't it funny how last night was about Nick and not Elena?"

Matt looked surprised, then nodded. "Most the time I forgot she was there."

"Exactly!" Nikki replied.

"I agree." Her mom said and leaned back.

"I couldn't figure out this morning what was bothering me until I realized that little fact." Nikki turned to face them. "If it was my daughter, that was taken away from me when I was under age, standing in front of me I wouldn't let anyone get in my way of making contact with her."

"So….what now?" Matt asked.

"I'll support any decision you two make," Their mom quickly added.

"I believed every word he said." Nikki admitted. Her mom nodded.

Matt hesitated, "I did, too."

Nikki looked at her mother then over to Matt. "I believe he truly thinks he did the right thing when it comes to Matt and I," She took her mother's hand. "I woke up thinking about it. I've had a great life because he brought me here. So how can I say he didn't make the right decision?"

"There are so many different possibilities of how things would have been different if he had stayed," Her mom frowned. "But bringing you to my family…I would have to agree… if he couldn't stay…at least he brought you to us."

"So…when he said, 'It isn't you, it's me'…he was telling the truth because he wanted Nikki to have what you had." Matt pointed out to their mother.

"I know," She smiled up at him and looked over at Nikki. "No matter what was right for him or for me…he did right by you."

Nikki took a deep breath, trying to get the courage to tell them what she was thinking earlier.

"Just spit it out," Her mother smiled.

Nikki looked at Matt with worried eyes. "I don't want him to disappear again."

Matt turned to look out the window, his eyes distant.

Nikki sat on the back of the couch with her feet resting on the cushions; she laid her hand over Matt's and noticed the red marks and swollen knuckles where he had connected with Nick's cheekbone. "I created this mess when I asked Jack to talk with her, and you into greeting her."

Matt turned to her but didn't say a word. His face was unreadable.

"We have answers," She paused then thought of Elena. "Well, we have the answers from Nick. So we can let him disappear and never have to talk to him again." He rolled his lips into a grimace and moved them side to side. "Or we extend a hand and see where it leads." Still silence. Nikki glanced at her mother then back at Matt. "I will make the decision on Elena, obviously. You make the decision about Nick and I will stand behind it." She finished talking and waited for him to answer.

Matt looked over at their mother pensively and she quickly spoke, "I'm behind you no matter what."

Matt turned back to Nikki and looked at her thoughtfully. "This is what you really want?"

Nikki inhaled deeply, thought of Nick's story…the fact that he came here…asking for nothing but to tell his story to her mom and them…*making sure* they had the truth, she exhaled sharply. She nodded, "I think we'd regret it if we didn't give him a chance."

"A chance for what?" Matt asked, his eyes narrowing slightly.

"I don't know." She answered truthfully staring straight into his brownish green eyes. "I just know…I don't want him to disappear."

He matched her stare and must have decided she was sure about what she wanted. "We play it out then." He said and pulled his phone out of his pocket, looked up the hotel on the internet then dialed, "Room 414 please."

Matt stared out the front window as he waited. Nikki turned and saw that Eli had returned to the herd and Grayson was nowhere to be seen.

"Nick. Matt." There was a pause. Nikki could barely hear that Nick was talking. She had no idea what he was saying and when she looked at Matt, his expression gave no hint. After Nick's voice stopped, Matt continued with a matter-of-fact tone that hid the nerves she could see in his eyes. "O.K., thanks, I'll let her know. We're having a load of panels delivered tomorrow to build a roping arena. We could use an extra hand if you're available."

There was silence; Nikki couldn't hear Nick's voice. Her hand went to her stomach as a knot formed… butterflies dive bombing around it. Her palms grew moist from anticipation…what if he said no?

Matt continued when there wasn't an answer. "Not at The Stables but behind our house." There was an answer this time and Nikki saw Matt's eyes close. In disappointment or relief? They opened, but he continued to look out the window. "They'll be dropping them off around 7:30." Another pause as Nick spoke. "There's a ranch supply store a mile up the road from you on your left hand side." Another pause as Nick spoke. "Do you know where we are?" A short answer then Matt gave him the address and directions. "OK, we'll see you in the morning."

Matt lowered his phone and pushed the end button with a shaky hand. He let a long slow breath out then looked over at Nikki. He nodded.

She breathed in a couple shaky breathes then reached for the phone. "My turn I guess."

Matt lowered the phone out of her reach. "When he answered, Nick said to watch out for Elena."

"Why?" Nikki asked in surprise.

Matt shook his head. "He said she was up to something and he didn't know what it was, but it wouldn't be good for the either of us."

Nikki nodded. "OK, I will. I'll have dinner with her and see what I can get out of her."

Matt and her mother both shook their heads.

"It's safer in crowds Nikki," Her mother said. "Until we know what she wants."

Nikki wiggled her head and lifted her shoulder to release her tension. Inwardly she smiled at the image of Nick doing the same thing the night before. "Now that she knows who you are, I don't think she'll be open to talk with you there, Mom."

Her mom looked up at Matt. "I don't know how well she'll take to you being there either."

"There's really only one choice." Nikki looked between them.

"Jack." They said in unison.

"He's done so much already." Nikki sighed. "I hate asking him to do anything else."

"This time she knows the truth, so it isn't the same." Matt pointed out.

"You're not facing her alone," Her mother told her. "Call Jack and tell him you want to meet her at The Stables. He doesn't have to be in the conversation, but he has to be near, at least watching on the security monitors. I don't think he'll have a problem with that."

Nikki nodded. She knew it was the right decision but hated to include Jack again.

"Just something to think about," Their mother said as she slid off the couch. She looked at both of them. "The first thing Nick does when he's back in your life…is try and protect you." She turned and walked away as Matt and Nikki looked at each other in silence.

CHAPTER TEN

"Do you have any idea what we're looking for?" Matt asked her from across the library table.

They had quickly showered, dressed and then met in the room to research Arcturus' weight loss. New Year's was a day off from work at The Homestead. It was also Jordan and Scott's anniversary. The family would be sleeping in, watching TV, and just generally relaxing. And per the happy couple, they would feast on pizzas and watch movies all evening.

Nikki and Matt swore they wouldn't stop looking through the journals and internet sites until they came up with a plan for Arcturus.

Nikki shook her head. "I know it's in here," She said. Then corrected her statement; "I HOPE it's in here."

"OK, let's start from the beginning," He stood and leaned his back on the bookshelf relaxing. "I'll do quick-fire and you answer as fast as you can."

Nikki smiled. That was how they worked together at college; they had started it in grade school. It was part of why her questioning Nick went so fast the night before.

She nodded; he started.

"When did you first meet the patient?"

"September."

He cocked his head to her and repeated the question. "When did you first meet the horse?"

She smiled. "June"

"What condition was the horse in?"

"Near starvation."

"Internally."

"Digestive issues, parasites, dehydration."

"Externally."

"Hair loss, scrapes."

"Bare skin?"

"Minimal."

"Initial response to treatment."

"Satisfactory."

"More."

"Weight gain, return of hair loss, hydration returned to normal levels."

"Current concern."

"Weight loss."

"When did it start?"

"September."

"Was there change to diet?"

"No."

Matt hesitated letting her rethink her answer.

"Less natural grass, increased dry alfalfa, supplement ration remained the same."

"Any other horses having issues with the feed?"

"No."

"Dental issues in change of grazing to feeder?"

Nikki hesitated. Matt waited.

"We floated the teeth to make sure they were level with no sharp points and checked for damage caused by the starvation."

"Abscesses?"

Nikki stared at him for a moment and broke their quick-fire. "Would they last that long?"

Matt shrugged and they both moved to the computers. Each started searching on different computers.

"Do you think he would let us look in his mouth?" Matt asked.

Nikki shrugged, "Let's go try it. I have a tooth mirror in the barn office."

They quickly put on boots and coats. "Go down to the pasture or bring him to the barn?" He asked.

Nikki hesitated. "Let's bring him to the barn and out of the wind."

Ten minutes later they had the black colt in the barn. Within minutes Nora and Sadie were joining them.

"What are you doing?" Nora asked as she crawled on one of the benches so she was close to her horse.

They explained as they tried to open the horse's mouth.

Both girls laughed at their attempts.

"He likes applesauce," Nora told them; then giggled. "Put your hand in applesauce."

Matt and Nikki looked at each other and shrugged. Sadie ran to the house to get a jar.

"You try running up the inside of the jaw gently. See if you can feel anything," Matt told Nikki. She dipped her hand in the applesauce and then slowly moved her fingers between the horse's lips. Arcturus mouthed her hand, but was patient and let her feel along the gums. Matt took the mirror and looked in the back of the mouth the best he could. The two girls were laughing at their feeble attempts.

"You know this works a lot better when you have the proper equipment," He chuckled.

Nikki laughed. "We'll have to talk Dr. Mark into giving us a key to his clinic so we can play."

Nikki couldn't feel anything wrong. After cleaning her arm, she stepped back and watched the horse lick applesauce from Nora's fingers. Nora's eyes were bright with love when she looked at the horse.

"Round two," Matt said. "Maybe it will help if we're looking at him."

Nikki nodded and stared at the horse.

"Dental issues when changed from grazing to dry feed?" He repeated the last question.

"Initial review, while looking like idiots, no, intensive review postponed until proper equipment can be used."

"Environment change?"

"No."

"What about when we went to the ranch?" Sadie, the wizard, asked. "That's an environment change."

"Yes," Nikki smiled as she changed her answer.

"Did the condition improve or worsen?"

"Improvement when changed, condition reappeared when the horse was returned to initial environment."

"Was feed different?"

"No."

"It's not an internal issue." Matt broke the pattern again.

"It's an external issue." Nikki agreed excitedly. They had finally narrowed the problem. "Something he's touching or is touching him."

They turned to the girls who were brushing the thick winter hair of the horse.

"Are you using anything different on him?" Nikki asked.

"Like what?" Nora asked and stopped brushing to look at them.

"Fly spray, conditioner, new brushes or tack." Matt answered.

"I brush him every day, same brush for months." Nora answered. "We haven't used fly spray since his winter coat grew."

That's it! Nikki grabbed at Matt's arm.

"What?" He asked.

"It's his winter coat," Nikki grinned.

"His winter coat is making him lose weight?" He shook his head and looked at her like she was crazy.

"It's the only thing that changed." Nikki answered and ran a hand down the thick hair on the horse's neck.

"He went from the stall to the ranch corral." He reminded her, then paused… his eyes widened. "There has to be something in his stall that is getting in his hair and staying there now because it's longer due to the winter coat. How does that cause weight loss?"

"It's not just weight loss." Nikki explained. "This morning I noticed he was the last one to get out to the pasture. He was walking slower. I don't know if he's lethargic as a symptom or just slow because he's not feeling well."

"What's lethargic?" Nora asked.

"Lacks energy, tired, or sluggish." Sadie said off-handedly as she combed out Arcturus' mane.

"Then why didn't you just say that?" Nora asked Nikki.

Nikki chuckled at Sadie's wizardry for a ten year old, Nora's matter-of-fact manner, and the roll of Matt's eyes at them.

She moved the horse's hair and looked at the skin. She turned to her brother. "It looks irritated."

Matt turned back to Nora, "Let me see the brush." She handed it to them, then followed him and Nikki into the office. Arcturus had found the plastic jar of applesauce and was licking what he could as it moved in circles.

They pounded the brush on white paper to see what came out of the brush.

There was a bit of dirt and the hair, but barely visible were black flakes. They looked closer but couldn't tell what it was. Matt used the camera on his phone and took a picture then enlarged it.

"I can't tell, can you?" Matt asked. Nikki shook her head.

"Why would he have problems and the other horses don't?" Nora asked.

Nikki turned and looked at her then back at Arcturus. Then she remembered something she had read in Dr. Mark's journals. "I think I know."

"Want to share?" Matt asked.

"Allergies," She said. Matt nodded with a smile.

"Allergies?" Nora asked.

"Remember that Reilly is allergic to the medicine penicillin?" Matt asked, and the two girls nodded. "But no one else is."

"So Arcturus is allergic to something, but all the other horses are OK." Sadie pointed out.

"Yes," Nikki said, "Now we have to find out what." They walked through the barn looking at anything that would touch the horse and would have little black flecks.

Nikki walked into Arcturus' stall and instantly sunk into the bedding. She knelt down and cupped the bedding in her hand to look closely at the curled wood shavings, but she couldn't see any little black flecks...the ones in the brush were so tiny.

"Matt? Can you bring me a clean piece of paper?" She called out. Matt and the girls showed up at the stall door. Arcturus was right behind them; the horse put his head down and sniffed at the paper.

Nikki dropped a handful of the bedding onto the paper then picked off the larger pieces until the tiny black flakes were visible. She stood and showed them to the group.

"What are they?" Nora asked, her brown eyes wide in curiosity.

"Well, we'll have to figure that one out, but first we need to get them off Arcturus." She looked around. "Nora, get him into the washroom. Sadie, get the shampoo and brushes ready. Matt, you work on getting this building warmed up. I'll gather as many towels as possible to get him dry."

An hour later, Arcturus was enjoying his unexpected towel rub down. Grace had joined the two younger girls; they were laughing and giggling about putting curlers in the horse's mane and tail. Arcturus was enjoying every minute of it.

Scott and Grayson joined them and created a makeshift stall for Arcturus in the hay barn. It was one place they knew the bedding had never been used. Scarecrow, his stable mate, was put into the barn with him to keep him calm. To make sure she didn't transfer any of the flecks to Arcturus, she was bathed too and enjoyed her rub down as much as Arcturus had.

Jordan and Leah drove to Dr. Mark's clinic and met him to get allergy medication for the horse.

Nikki and Matt headed back to the internet and the journals.

Nikki glanced up at the clock. "Only an hour left, then I have to head out."

Matt nodded. "Which journal?"

"I'm pretty sure I saw something in either the second or third."

They each took one of the thick leather journals and curled up on the couches in front of the large open window.

"These are interesting," Matt mumbled about a half hour in. "I find myself just reading and not paying attention to the detail."

"I did, too. He should publish them," She answered without looking up. Then she came across the story she was looking for. "Black Walnut," She said and sat up in her chair. "It's toxic to horses, it can cause depression, lethargy, laminitis, swelling, increased temperature, and so forth."

"Arcturus doesn't have all those." Matt reminded her.

"Maybe there was just enough to irritate but not to be fully toxic," She was still reading the paragraph. "The one Dr. Mark treated had all these symptoms…it was in his bedding." She paused and looked up at him. "…it died."

"Well, that's not happening. So they used black walnut in the bedding?" Matt walked over to the internet and started searching the brand maker of the bedding. He started to nod, "In a recalled batch they had found black walnut specks. They didn't know how they got into the bedding because they didn't use it."

Nikki was sitting in the chair next to him, elbow on arm rest, chin in hand, looking at her brother. He leaned back in his chair and smiled at her, "You did it."

"We'll know in the morning," She corrected him. Thinking of Nick being there in the morning, made the butterflies in her stomach come to life again. Then there was the meeting with Elena. She glanced at the clock. "I have to go. Tell Mom what we discovered and find out where that bedding came from. Maybe not all the bedding is contaminated."

They stood and walked to each other for a brother and sister bear hug. "I love you, Little Brother."

"Back at ya, Big Sis."

"I won't be long," She said as she walked out of the room.

CHAPTER ELEVEN

Nikki arrived fifteen minutes early and Elena's car was already there. She saw a small cloud of smoke coming from the back of the car. The woman was waiting in her car and not going in to visit with Jack. "Interesting…" Nikki frowned as she pulled in next to the car.

The door to Elena's car opened as Nikki climbed out of her truck and they met at the front of the vehicles. Elena had a hopeful expression as she reached out to touch Nikki's arm. Nikki was touched by the small gesture. She wasn't as tall as Nikki but she was very slender, almost too slender. Her large dark eyes seemed too large for her dainty face.

"I was so happy to get your call," Elena said. "But I was surprised you wanted to meet here."

Nikki started walking toward the office, but stopped when Elena didn't follow. "Is something wrong?"

Elena hesitantly looked at the office. "Jack…"

Nikki nodded but didn't really understand. "We can talk in the stable with the horses."

As they walked toward the first stable building, Elena would stuff her hands in her pockets then pull them out quickly and twist them together.

Nikki opened the stable door and they stepped out of the winter weather into a slightly warmer environment. The horses quickly came to their stall doors and stuck out their heads to see who came in and could possibly feed them. Nikki smiled at their curiosity. Elena looked around the room but not at the horses. She was looking up and around the walls of the building.

"Are you looking for something?" Nikki asked. What an odd way to start the conversation.

"Oh, no," Elena smiled innocently. "I was just looking over this beautiful building. I can't believe how large it is, and there are two!"

Nikki smiled. She heard that statement from most the people that walked through the building the first time.

They went to each of the horses and Nikki reached out to each and gave them attention. Elena kept her hands in her pockets.

"Do they all belong to the Taggers?" Elena asked.

Nikki shook her head, a little confused at the line of questioning. "Only a few here, there are more at the ranch."

Elena's eyebrows raised in surprise. "How many?"

Nikki hesitated at the odd question, then gave a general answer. "About a dozen or so." Since she did the paperwork for Tagger Enterprises with her mom, she knew exactly how many horses the company owned. She didn't feel comfortable sharing the information with Elena, but she didn't know why.

Nikki walked up to Star, the horse Elena had ridden at both appointments. Elena had no reaction to the gelding and continued to walk. An uneasy feeling started to form in Nikki's stomach. It seemed like an odd reaction toward a horse she had ridden twice.

"Can we sit a minute?" Elena asked. "It's comfortable in here."

"It's one of my favorite places," Nikki smiled. "Even when it's just cleaning stalls."

"They make YOU clean the stalls?" Elena looked at her in surprise.

"Of course," Nikki laughed as she stepped into the tack room to retrieve a couple chairs. "We all take our turns cleaning."

Elena followed her. Even though she didn't need it to see the chairs, Elena switched on the lights. There were rows of horse bridles on both sides of the walls. Saddles were placed on racks just below them. Numerous saddle pads and blankets were hung on racks in the back of the room. Miscellaneous tack was hung on any free space on the walls. A few were Tagger Enterprises tack, but most belonged to the clients.

"Wow," Elena exclaimed with her eyes opened wide.

Nikki felt the uneasy feeling again. Elena walked through the tack room; her hand reached out and touched a few of the more ornate saddles and up to the bridles.

Nikki pursed her lips and twisted them side to side, and bit the inside of her lip. Shouldn't SHE be the center of Elena's attention and not the building, horses, and tack?

Elena turned and looked at her. "There's just so much."

Nikki didn't know what to say, so she just nodded and pulled the chairs out of the room; hoping it would signal Elena to leave the room. She sighed internally when the woman walked out. Nikki quickly turned off the light and shut the door. That was odd.

As much as she wanted to leave the building, Nikki placed the chairs in the center aisle and sat in the chair opposite her birth mother.

Elena's smile was brilliant. She seemed happier than she did when they first walked into the barn. "I was so surprised to see Matt the other day. He looks so much like his father!"

Nikki tried to smile back, "I'm not really sure what to say."

"Don't worry, Honey, we have time to learn about each other now." She smiled sweetly.

Nikki leaned back in her chair and stuffed her hands in her pockets and found her phone. She kept the phone hidden in her hand as she pulled it from the pocket and pushed the buttons to make it record. Having used it for recording lectures in college, she could do it quickly and without looking. Then she put on the toughest, brave face she could muster.

Nikki nodded with an uneasy feeling. "I know it probably isn't pleasant, but can you tell me what happened when I was born?"

Elena smiled, which Nikki thought was odd. "Getting right to it," She sighed. "OK, Nick and I met at the Pendleton Roundup in September and then I found out I was pregnant the next spring. He found out I was seventeen when I ran away with him, so he took me back to my parents." She sounded rehearsed. She looked at Nikki with sad eyes. "When you were born, I saw you for only a few minutes," She sighed dramatically. "My parents made me sign the papers to give you up to Nick."

"You said last night that they were trying to punish him." With her mind processing Elena's story, Nikki leaned toward her.

Elena nodded. "I didn't know about the story Nick told last night," She sighed again, finally looking Nikki in the eye. "Do you think he was telling the truth?"

Nikki nodded, "I don't think he has a reason to lie."

Elena shrugged and leaned back in her chair. Her eyes darted around the stable again.

"Why did you call him?" Nikki asked.

Elena sat up again and leaned towards her. "I thought I needed him to prove who I was. I didn't know that Dru knew my name."

"Did you ever look for me?" Nikki asked.

Elena looked her in the eye and smiled, a sweet smile…that didn't quite feel right. "Of course, Honey. But I didn't know where to look. I thought they had adopted you out to strangers, especially after I saw Nick at the rodeos without you."

That was a surprise! "Did you ever talk to him at the rodeos?"

"No," Elena hesitated. "I was still pretty young and in shock from them taking you from me."

That odd feeling was back as Nikki watched the woman look around the building. Only once or twice had she looked her in the eye. Her answers were either rehearsed or flippant.

Nikki didn't believe anything the woman said, so she decided to push for the truth and find out why she was there…it obviously wasn't for Nikki.

"Why didn't you come to The Stables to see me? Why go to the New Year's Eve party and bring Nick?"

Elena smiled sweetly. "I wanted to meet you and he wanted to do it in a public place."

"He said you wanted to." Nikki pushed.

"He lied, Honey." Elena smiled and waved her hand. "He does that."

Nikki took a deep breath and let it out. The woman hadn't seen him for 20 years so how would she know?

"It would have been nice to do it before the party," Elena sighed and Nikki looked at her in confusion. "So I could have gone to the party with you…and meet your friends."

And there it was, Nikki thought…Elena wanted to be publically connected to the Tagger family. But why?

She decided to change the subject. "You told Jack that you had two kids and raised one."

"Oh that!" Elena's smile turned into an accusing grin. "You were pretty tricky on that one; using that hunk of a man," She laughed. "I was pretty surprised last night when I heard that…maybe we do have something in common."

Nikki was confused. "I don't understand."

Elena laughed and waved her hand again. "Sometimes you have to stretch the truth a few directions to get what you want."

Nikki was stunned as she watched Elena stand and walk around the stable aisle. "You have it good here," She finally said. "He evidently did the right thing by dropping you off with the Taggers…they seem well-off…"

Nikki felt her blood go cold and her nervousness eased. That statement confirmed the fact that Elena wasn't there for Nikki. She wanted nothing from this woman beside the truth as to why she was there. She decided to play Elena's game and see what she was up to.

"I think he did," She finally said. "I did figure one thing out so far."

"About what?" Elena asked with a too bright smile.

Nikki rose so she would be eye to eye with the woman.

"Well, the way I calculate it, you met Nick in September when you were seventeen."

Elena nodded, "I was young… but he just swept me off my feet…he was…"

"You gave birth to me right before the Pendleton rodeo the next summer." Nikki interrupted the fairytale the woman was about to spin.

Elena started to say something then stopped; raising her eyebrows in surprise at Nikki.

"I'm twenty *and* a college student." Nikki said firmly. "I can do math. The Pendleton rodeo is in the middle of September…every year." Elena's eyes squinted slightly. Nikki continued; "Which means you were eighteen when you gave birth to me and they couldn't have taken me away from you."

Only the sound of the horses moving in their stalls could be heard in the barn as the women stared each other down.

"You said they made you sign over the papers to give me to Nick…then you said you didn't know where to look for me."

Elena didn't react, not a muscle twitched.

Nikki decided to push things a little more. "Like you said, we have something in common."

Elena didn't say anything but just continued to stare at her with no expression.

Nikki continued. "So, I'm guessing you were the one who wanted to punish Nick and had me dropped off at the rodeo with him."

Elena just continued to stare.

Nikki forced a twisted smile. "Pretty devious…I don't think I would have thought of that one."

Elena's stare narrowed slightly… a hint of a smile appeared.

That worked…Nikki got braver. "I've done a few devious things in my time," Nikki lied. "But that one is really good."

Elena's smile turned into a grin.

"I'm guessing if you knew I was a Tagger, you would have been here a long time ago."

Elena again looked surprised but didn't say anything.

"So you didn't know I was here until you saw Matt and the picture in the magazine. Then you knew it was me."

Elena nodded.

"Then you took a couple days to do some research on the family."

Again a nod.

"I understand all that," Nikki said with a devilish grin. "It's what I would have done," She leaned against one of the stalls to make it look like she was relaxed; which she wasn't…her legs were shaking and was surprised Elena didn't notice. "I don't understand why you would bring Nick into this; seems he was a wild card."

Elena turned to face Nikki, "Part of the research was about what happened after the attorney's dropped you off with him." Elena smirked. "I found out that he had abandoned you…and it was with a brother."

"That must have been a surprise." Nikki said to keep her talking.

"I thought it helped when I learned he abandoned *two* of you." She began pacing slowly.

"Helped?"

Elena smiled deviously. "I brought him in to be the bad guy and show me as the victim."

Nikki's stomached turned. "Everyone thought I was ripped from your arms…you WERE the victim."

Elena stared again, this time with a frown, knowing she made a huge mistake. "How do we fix that?"

Nikki slowly shook her head…fix what? And for what?

"Last night was odd…the ambush at the party didn't set well…with anyone…so I'm not sure we can."

Elena sat back down in the chair and stretched her legs out in front of her. She was relaxed; which meant she believed this charade.

"How do I work back into their good graces?" Elena looked up at her. "You're firmly in with them. Give me an idea."

Nikki was stunned. The woman didn't consider her a Tagger.

"What do you want from them?" Nikki asked as calmly as she could.

"Anything and everything…" Elena stared at her feet. "I'm tired of just skimping by…I want to live the good life."

"You didn't get married?" Nikki asked.

"I did, but he took the kid and left a long time ago."

Nikki felt numb from all the lies. She had told Jack that she raised her other child…now that was a lie too.

"Where are they?" Did she have a brother or sister? She wanted to ask, but didn't want to stop Elena from answering her questions.

Elena shrugged. She rose again and started pacing with more energy. "Tell me about Jack."

Nikki internally screamed in frustration at the change of topic. "What about him?" She said coolly.

"You and he ever get together?"

"No." Nikki answered firmly.

"Good. That would have been awkward." Elena chuckled.

"Awkward?"

"If I went after him," Elena said with that fake sweet smile.

Nikki shook her head. "Not an option."

Elena nodded with a sigh and shrug of the shoulders, "Yeah, the date didn't go that well, even if he was there just to get information from me." She stopped pacing and seemed in deep thought. She finally looked up at Nikki. "Are you willing to help me out?"

"How?"

"Can you get money from the Taggers?" She asked hopefully.

Nikki shook her head. "No, I don't have access to any money."

"I read in the article that you were handling all the donations. You can't get any of that?"

"The donations have died off." Nikki answered. The donations had died off but the donation account was still quite high from the amount that came in right after the horse rescue was published. It would be used for the horse's veterinarian needs.

Nikki's stomach ached just listening to the woman. She was willing to take money away from the horses, who Nikki loved as family members.

Elena started pacing again, deep in thought. "Well, Jack is the key then."

When Elena wasn't looking, Nikki glanced down at her phone. It was still recording.

"Jack's a pretty popular guy." Nikki told her.

Elena nodded. "That's good…that'll help."

"With what?"

Elena's grin was wicked this time. "When I had my first appointment with him, he was very physically aggressive towards me."

Nikki felt like her blood turned cold. She tried hard to keep her face calm…the poker face she had seen her mother use so many time.

"I can get to them through his harassment," She stopped and looked at Nikki. "All you have to do is back me up. Tell the police that you saw him harassing me and I'm sure the Taggers will settle with a big payout…to keep it out of the papers."

"Then what?"

Elena shrugged, "We'll have to see," She turned to Nikki and smiled. "Why don't you come with me?"

Nikki looked at her in amazement. "What? Where?"

"Mother and daughter team on the road." Elena looked excited. "I'm young enough; I can pass as your sister."

Nikki didn't know whether to laugh or cry. This woman was delusional. "What would we do?"

"We could go back out on the road; from rodeo to rodeo! It was fun. It'll make me feel young again." With her eyes shining in excitement, Elena reached out and touched her arm; Nikki tried hard not to flinch away from her. "It will take us some time to get the money from the Taggers, so you'll have to stay with them for a little longer. Maybe you can find a way to get some money from them on the side."

Nikki nodded and pressed her lips together, wiggling them from side to side. How could Elena think that she would follow that insane plan? Was she delusional enough to think that Nikki would turn her back on the family they raised her for the last 18 years…for her? The mother that abandoned her…endangered her…gave her away like she was nothing…?

She'd had enough and didn't care if Elena saw her. She checked the phone to make sure it had recorded everything that was just said.

Nikki sent a 111 text to Jack. Within seconds of the message going, Jack opened the side door of the building and walked in. He must have been standing outside the door the whole time.

Elena was visibly startled when he walked up to them.

"You OK?" He asked Nikki with a concerned expression.

"Yes," Nikki nodded gratefully. She looked over at Elena, the woman was staring at her in disbelief.

Nikki turned to Elena and lifted her phone. "Everything you said in here is recorded," Elena's jaw dropped in shock. "As long and thoroughly as you stared at this building, I'm surprised you didn't notice the little boxes up there. They're video monitors and they are all over The Stables. I have this recording and the videos of your rides here, so there is proof that Jack did not harass you in any way. It also details your plans of extortion," Nikki took a step toward her. The woman took a step back, a flicker of fear in her eye. "No matter what you seem to think, I am a Tagger and I am nothing like you!"

Nikki took another step towards her birth mother; all her fear and frustration coming out of her as she spoke. "What you did by dropping off a four-day-old baby with someone that couldn't provide for them is disgusting. You are a cold-hearted monster. You are not my mother. You were only the woman that gave birth to me!" As Nikki took another step forward, Elena took two steps toward the door. "You are going to leave this place and NEVER return. If you ever come back, I will forward this recording to the sheriff and let them throw you in jail where you belong." Her voice started to shake from anger.

Elena stood frozen in place, her eyes wide and in shock. Nikki grabbed her arm firmly and dragged her to the door. Jack had reached the door first and held it open for her. Nikki pushed the fear stricken woman out the door. "Get out of my life!"

CHAPTER TWELVE

Elena ran to her car and sped through the parking lot and down the road. Nikki stood silently as the car disappeared into the night and hoped she would never see the woman again. Once the lights disappeared, Nikki felt a tug on her arm as Jack pulled her back into the building and closed the door. She didn't look at him, she stared at the floor. While she had spoken to Elena she had been strong and confident. Now…she felt like a little girl who wanted her mom.

Nikki took a deep breath and slowly let it out. Then she started to shake and felt a sob making its way through her body. Just as she felt like she was going to lose control, Jack wrapped his arms around her and pulled her into a hug. His strength and compassion made her begin to cry. Soon her whole body was shaking from the sobs. He said nothing, just held her tightly, resting his chin on top of her head.

Nikki let the tears flow; she wanted all the frustration, fear, anger, and disgust out of her. When the tears finally started to stop, Nikki began to relax. She could feel one of Jack's arms come out from behind her, but the other held on tightly.

"Yeah?" Jack said. He was talking on his phone. She hadn't heard it ring. "It's over, Elena's gone." He paused, listening to the person on the other line. "No, stay there, we'll close down here and meet you there." Again a pause. "She's fine…or will be…she's a strong young lady."

Nikki chuckled into his chest; she didn't feel very strong at the moment.

"We'll be there…OK." His armed lowered as he ended the call.

Nikki relaxed and stepped back. She started giggling when she looked at his shirt. There was a large wet area with mascara, eye shadow, and makeup covering the front of his shirt. She looked up at him. He was looking down at his shirt then to her.

Jack laughed, his blue eyes sparkling, "If you think my shirt is bad….you should see your face."

Nikki instinctively reached up and tried to wipe away what was left of her makeup.

It made him laugh harder. He grabbed her shoulders and turned her to the door. "It's going to take a whole lot more than that; like a wash cloth and some water. Luckily, I have extra shirts here. We'll clean up and wipe away all the remnants of the last ten minutes." He opened the door for her. "You walk out of here a stronger more confident woman, Nikki Tagger, and I'm very proud to know you." He closed the door.

******

Nikki checked the recording on her phone as they drove back to The Homestead. Everything was loud and clear. She turned it off quickly since she didn't want to hear it again. She glanced over at Jack who had insisted he drive her, they could retrieve her truck in the morning. He had changed his shirt and she'd freshened her makeup so, like he said, they had wiped away the remnants of her breakdown.

She laid her phone on the seat between them. "I'm going to go to the barn and check on Arcturus and love on Harvey."

"Equine therapy..." Jack smiled in understanding.

"It's important you all listen to this."

"Are you sure?" He glanced at her in concern.

"You need to know what she had planned."

"Did she know who you were when she made the first appointment?"

"No."

They rode the rest of the way in silence.

When Jack pulled to a stop, she slid out of his truck and headed for the hay barn where Arcturus and Scarecrow were penned. They were both lying in their makeshift stall, so she turned off the light and headed for the barn.

She flipped the switch to light up the dark barn, which caused all the horse's heads to pop up over their stall doors. That was one of the best sights ever and helped lift her spirits. She walked down the aisle and greeted each horse, then walked back to Harvey and Trooper's stall and opened their door. They quickly stepped out and headed down to the other horses. Grabbing a pitchfork she busied herself cleaning out their used bedding.

She found more bedding that wasn't the contaminated brand of wood shavings and spread out a new layer over the floor of the stall. She quickly checked on Harvey and Trooper. They were down visiting with Cooper and Rufio.

She turned back to the stall and kicked around the bedding with her boot then sat against the back of the stall against the door that led to the outside and waited.

She heard the distinctive sound of dogs trotting along the cement floor and saw Mavis and Bart pass by. They stopped and turned back to the opening. When they saw her, they quickly joined her on the stall floor.

Nikki sat cross-legged and Mavis crawled up onto her lap, their normal relaxing position. Bart lay down next to her, leaning against her leg. Nikki stroked Mavis down her back and rubbed Bart's neck and ears. Their warmth and love made her feel better. There was something to be said about canine therapy too, she smiled.

The small side door opened and she could hear footsteps walk in; lots of them.

Nikki looked up in time to see her mother start to walk by. She stopped, and turned her head to look at Nikki. A smile spread across her face when she saw her daughter sitting quietly in the horse's stall; the dogs comforting her. Without hesitation she walked in and sat next to Nikki.

Matt, Scott, Grayson, and Jack walked in behind her and they all took a seat around the stall. Bart's head went up when he saw Matt. He rose and walked to Matt only to fall on his back and present his tummy for Matt to scratch…which he did.

"You listen to it?" Nikki asked her mom.

"We did," She answered and took her hand, squeezing tightly. "You OK?"

"A little stronger and more confident." Nikki smiled over at Jack who returned her smile. "I can't believe that woman is family." She rolled her eyes in disbelief.

"Family is in your heart, not your blood." Her mother reminded her. "I'm not really sure what to say, except I was floored when I heard she was responsible for having you dropped off at the rodeo with Nick. The extortion part didn't surprise any of us…her actions, since the beginning just were…off." She turned to her daughter. "You played your part very well…makes me worried for all the 'excuses' you gave me when you were a teenager."

Nikki chuckled, "I can honestly say I have never lied like that before in my entire 20 years."

"Well, I have," Matt chuckled, which made everyone turn and look at him in surprise and disbelief. "Wait!" Matt looked around in feigned shock. "Did I say that out loud?"

They all started laughing and their mom picked up stall bedding and threw it at him. Nikki felt the stress and tension start to ease from her muscles.

She looked at her mom in concern. "Mom, are you OK with everything that's happened the last twenty-four hours?"

"Yes," She answered firmly and looked at her daughter with a serious expression. "No matter what happens during a relationship…when one person leaves, the person left behind always wonders what's wrong with them…how they drove that person away. I've played my relationship with Nick over and over in my head for years. I didn't know what happened and why he left…but after last night, I have the answer." Everyone was quiet in the stall. They could hear Trooper and Harvey's hoof beats echo throughout the building. "When it was just Nick and I, everything was great, just like he said," She smiled warmly. "Looking back now and learning of his past, I understand why he left. I was so encompassed in a strong family atmosphere, that I couldn't imagine anyone not being raised in the same way. Learning of how he was raised, so different than my upbringing, I now understand why he brought you to me."

Nikki leaned her head back on the wall. "I can't imagine what Nick went through those first couple days."

"I had a happy family around me to help raise the two of you. The first time I changed Matt's diapers, I had your grandmother on one side and your great-grandmother on the other. I was scared to even touch him because he was so small, but they were there to help and teach me. Well, for about nine months." She looked over at her brothers. "Then I had Grayson and Scott to help."

"Help?" Scott chuckled. "Honestly, once they were gone, we were all three scared of the two of you! Raising a nine-month-old and a three-year-old, we had no idea what we were doing."

"We relied on Andy and Clara a number of times." Grayson added about their ranch neighbors. "But in the middle of the night, when a nine-month-old is screaming for no apparent reason, it can literally bring three inexperienced adults to tears."

"Let alone the diaper issue," Scott laughed. "I've seen Grayson handle anything and everything that has come out of a cow or horse, but the day Matt decided to use his diaper contents to decorate his crib? I thought Grayson was going to lose it." Everyone laughed.

"They were just dry heaves," Grayson defended himself with a chuckle.

"For the first year, Scott and Grayson refused to take both of you at the same time. Even when I would head out to the barn, I would take Nikki and one of them would take Matt. And then there was the day, when you were four," She said to Nikki. "We were at a horse auction. Grayson lost a bid for a horse he wanted and swore. You said the same word but three times louder and it echoed. The whole room stopped and stared at this beautiful little girl with long dark curls saying a word like that! We nearly died right there on the spot."

"Which is when we put the 'dang' rule into effect..." Grayson laughed. "No curse words around kids...'dang' was the only one anyone could say..." With a chuckle and a raised brow, "And through the years...we've managed to say that word in many different tones."

"By the time Grayson married Leah, and Grace was born, we were teaching Leah how to take care of babies," Scott said. "By the time Sadie was born, we were old pros." He chuckled then looked over at Nikki. "It was because we had each other, that we could make it through," He paused. "Grayson and I rode in the rodeos with Dru and Nick; spent a lot of time with them. Then we worked side-by-side with Nick at the ranch. We had no idea what his past was like."

"When he said he didn't talk about his past...it wasn't just now. Looking back, he didn't talk about it then either...ever." Grayson spoke, looking between Nikki and Matt. "It doesn't excuse what he did, but it does make it easier to understand."

Nikki nodded and glanced at Matt who was staring at Bart. The dog had rolled back over and was now allowing Matt full access to his ears to scratch. She looked around at the family she had around her, which included Jack. How would it be if she had gone through the scene with Elena tonight and not had all of them to come back to?

What would it be like to not have that family support? To be alone in the world when things were tough…she didn't want to know.

"Nikki?" She looked up at Jack. "Thank you." She smiled and nodded.

"This has been a tough twenty four hours," Nikki glanced at all of them. "I'm tired and ready for bed."

They heard hoof beats again slowly approaching the stall. Harvey walked to the door and stopped abruptly when she saw all the people in her stall.

"I think she's ready for bed too." Nikki laughed.

CHAPTER THIRTEEN

Nikki moved the tractor closer to the flatbed truck that held the fencing panels. Scott and Grayson lifted the panels from the flatbed and placed them on the two long prongs that stuck out in front of the tractor. She backed the tractor and turned to cross the newly plowed field to drop them off with Matt and Nick. They unloaded them and stood them up for Jordan and Leah to hook the panels together. Reilly and Grace held the panels, tools and supplies for the women. Once unloaded, Nikki went back and Scott and Grayson loaded the tractor again; they had a great routine and the arena was going together faster than expected.

As Scott and Grayson were loading the tractor with more panels, Nikki stood and stretched to see if she could see Arcturus in the north pasture. She heard a banging and looked down. Grayson had hit the front of the tractor to get her attention and motioned for her to shutdown the tractor. She did.

"What?"

"Go check on him. We can take a break." Grayson waved her away.

Without hesitation, she jumped from the tractor and headed for the barn.

Nikki had jumped out of bed at six that morning to see how Arcturus was doing. She was shocked to see Nora and Sadie were already up and putting on their coats. They giggled when they saw her and pointed behind her. Matt had crawled off the couch and was standing behind her. They all headed out to the barn together.

As they pulled open the door to the hay barn they were greeted with a couple loud whinnies. Sadie ran to the switch and flooded the barn with light. It shone on two beautiful horses standing at their gate anxiously awaiting their morning feed. Arcturus was just as energetic as Scarecrow.

"Yeah!" Both girls ran to the horses.

"That's the most energy he's had since we were at the ranch." Matt smiled at his sister.

Nikki smiled back. "Finger's crossed." She ran a gloved hand down the horse's nose. "Let's keep them separate from the other horses this morning. Mom said if it worked, she and the kids would clean the barn while we put the arena together."

And now, Sadie and Nora walked out of the barn they had been cleaning, and followed Nikki from the tractor to the pasture. They climbed the fence together and watched Arcturus and Scarecrow grazing quietly.

"Whistle Nikki," Nora grinned at her.

Nikki put fingers to her lips and both girls covered their ears and laughed. Nikki whistled her famous, loudest whistle contest, whistle. Scarecrow and Arcturus' heads instantly rose, and to the delight of the fence watchers, began trotting up to them. Arcturus kept up with Scarecrow.

Once the horses arrived, both girls began loving and talking to them. Their eyes just shined; horses and girls.

Nikki saw Nick walking up to her. She hadn't talked to him since he arrived. Concerned how he was going to be able to handle being around the kids, Matt and the men had met him at his truck and taken him straight up to show him the project and start work.

No one had spoken about Nick's black eye and the cut underneath it, until Wade saw him.

"What happened to your eye?" The ten year old asked him.

"I ran into the past." Nick answered calmly.

Wade looked at him in confusion then continued. "I broke my arm."

"How did you do that?"

Wade hesitated then smiled roguishly at the new adult. "Being stupid."

Nick laughed. "Well, I've done that a number of times, too."

And now, Nick was walking up to her and the girls, "Scarecrow and Arcturus?" He asked the girls.

"Yes!" Sadie grinned. "This one is Scarecrow." She said rubbing the palomino's forehead.

"And this is Arcturus!" Nora hugged the horse's nose. "They're mine."

Sadie's grin faded as she turned to the palomino. Nikki glanced up at Nick, he had noticed it, too. His shoulders seemed tight and tense. She'd never known anyone that had issues being around kids but from the tension radiating from him she knew it was true.

"I've seen them and you two on the computer." Nick told them.

Sadie turned back to him and smiled. "Aunt Jordan and my mom always post pictures for everyone. People see them all over the world."

Nick nodded and leaned against the fence. "I saw them in Australia."

The girls' eyes opened wide. "Australia!" They said in unison.

"I lived there for 17 years." He answered.

"You look like Matt." Sadie smiled, her blue eyes curious.

Nick chuckled, "I would like to think he looks like me."

Both girls were quiet while they figured out what he said then Sadie started laughing. "That's funny."

Nick's shoulders lowered as the stress of talking to the girls eased.

A truck slowed down on the road and turned into the driveway. It was carrying the second supply of panels and the chute that would be used for running the cattle into the arena.

"Back to the barn girls," Nikki said and gave the horses one last pat before turning away. The girls quickly ran out ahead of them.

"That wasn't too bad." Nikki smiled.

Nick shook his head, "Scott told me to talk to them like they were adults….just without the swear words."

Nikki chuckled, "If you have any problems at all, let me know," They were only a couple yards from the crowd so she turned to him and looked into his eyes and whispered, "I don't want you to disappear again." She turned before she could see his reaction and climbed back onto the tractor with shaky legs.

The remainder of the arena was completed quickly so they took a break for lunch, which Cora brought out to the barns. Grayson built a fire in the fire pit so they could stay warm. Nikki watched Sadie walk up to Nick, who was leaning against the trailer between Matt and Scott.

She stopped and looked up at Matt, then Nick, and grinned. "Yep, Matt looks more like you, than you look like him." She continued walking.

Nick and Matt looked up at Nikki and laughed. How amazing is that? Forty-eight hours earlier she would have never dreamed of a moment her brother and father would be standing next to each other and laughing.

After lunch, the chute and runs were installed. Nikki and the kids went down to get the horses and bring them into the arena so they could see their new hangout and get used to it. The horses pranced excitedly by them as they neared the arena. Everyone was gathered near the chute as the horses were released from their lead ropes and allowed to check out the arena on their own. Trooper moved out quickly and got Rufio and Arcturus trotting behind him. Soon, nearly all the horses were running and bucking.

Nikki was watching Arcturus, when she heard Wade give out a huge "Yeehaw!". She turned to look and he was jumping excitedly and pointing at Rooster. "Dad, look at Rooster! He's trotting!" He ran to his dad and jumped in his arms so Scott could put him on the top of the chute for a better view of his horse. "Dad! Dad! Do you see?" Wade's voice was full of wonder.

"I do, Buddy." Scott laughed.

Nikki smiled as Wade watched his horse. His eyes were wide in excitement and the grin couldn't be any bigger.

"Ah, Dad…I knew he could do it." Wade bent down and hugged his dad around the neck; his eyes never leaving the red horse. Scott's eyes were glistening and Jordan wiped away a tear of relief and happiness.

Nick leaned in closer to Nikki; "You'll have to tell me that story."

"At dinner tomorrow night?" She said without looking at him. She felt her heart suddenly racing. She wanted him to say yes so bad she thought he could see her shaking.

"Sounds good, you'll have to pick the place." He said quietly.

She nodded. Her nerves kept her from talking. She would also let him know about her meeting with Elena.

Suddenly a clanging sound rang out and echoed through the property.

"What the heck is that?" Grayson looked around for the cause of the sound.

Jordan and Leah started laughing.

"Dinner's ready!" Leah laughed. "Cora bought herself a dinner bell to get everyone in from the arena."

As the group made their way down towards the house, Matt and Nikki walked with Nick. Sadie came up beside him and looked up.

"What's up?" He asked with a relaxed smile.

"Do you have a hammer?" She asked, her big blue eyes looking serious.

He didn't answer for a minute, but finally said, "I believe I do."

"All us kids got hammers for Christmas so we could help make a bigger barn and more stalls for the horses." She told him excitedly.

"Then why would you need my hammer?" Nick slowed his pace, so she didn't have to walk so fast next to him. Good move, Nikki smiled.

Sadie continued, "You worked pretty darn good today," she said. "You should bring your hammer and help us build the barn. It will be fun."

Nick didn't answer. He just kept walking.

Nikki didn't know what to say. She was glad her hands were in her pockets so no one could see them shaking. Did he want to or not? She couldn't tell; her stomach began to ache.

Sadie finally looked up to him, to see if he was going to answer. Her long braid was swinging back and forth under her T3E cap.

"I think if he can't find his, then we'll have plenty of extra ones he can use." Matt gave him the opening to say yes.

Nick took a few more steps then looked down to Sadie. "You make sure that Matt and Nikki let me know when you're ready to start building and I promise I'll bring my hammer and help."

Sadie grinned and ran ahead of the three.

As they neared the house, Nick veered towards his truck. He stopped by the door and looked between Nikki and Matt then to the very large house.

"We understand," Nikki said, thankful her voice didn't shake. Being outside with everyone was very different than being in an enclosed house with all the people and chatter. Besides, the size of The Homestead could be very intimidating.

"One step at a time," Matt added standing next to her.

Nikki looked at Matt, then Nick, and nodded; her throat had suddenly constricted with emotion so she couldn't speak.

Matt turned to Nick and spoke for both of them. "We don't know where this is going…." The men were looking eye to eye to each other. Nick nodded, his expression unreadable. "But we would like the past to remain in the past and only move forward and just see where it goes."

Nick looked between Nikki and Matt, he started to say something then stopped. When he didn't speak again, she understood that the emotion was too much for him to speak, too. She stretched her right hand to him to shake on the future. He looked down at her hand and smiled. His hand came out of his jacket and firmly gripped hers then to Matt's outstretched hand.

CHAPTER FOURTEEN

Nikki stared at the picture of the pretty brunette on Nick's phone. Her hair was a little darker than Nikki's and her jaw line more sleek and elegant. The smile that highlighted her face didn't seem to reach into her eyes; which seemed a little sad.

Nikki looked up at Nick and Matt as they sat across the restaurant table.

"She's in Montana and her name is Josey. Elena named her after her favorite barrel racer," Nick chuckled. "Considering Elena's never competed, I thought it was a strange choice."

"How did you find her?" Nikki asked, as she stared at the phone looking for any resemblance to either her or Elena.

"Same people that Elena used to track me down," He grinned. "…figured it was only fair since she never answered you about a brother or sister."

Nikki glanced over at Matt. When he nodded she looked back at Nick. "I met with Elena the other night."

Nick's eyebrows shot up in surprise. "How did that go?"

Nikki shook her head. "Not well." She briefly outlined for him the attempted extortion, he shook his head.

"I knew she was up to something, but didn't think it would be so drastic." He commented.

"I asked her to tell me about my birth." He looked at her with interest. Nikki took a deep breath and continued. "When she finished her story, I confronted her with the fact that she was eighteen when she gave birth to me."

"Really?" His eyebrows shot up in surprise again. "She told me she was seventeen."

Nikki shook her head. "Elena admitted she was the one that signed the papers and had the attorney's drop me off with you at the rodeo. She was the one that wanted to punish you, not her parents."

Nick looked at her in disbelief; "I never saw that in her when we were together. She didn't seem that evil or damaged," He sat quietly a moment, reflecting on the past then looked back up at her. "Where is she now?"

Matt chuckled and Nikki smiled. "She's gone." Nick looked between the two, knowing there was more to the story but was fine not knowing.

"Can I send it to myself?" She asked Nick about the picture of her half-sister Josey.

He casually nodded, but as she pushed the button to go to the home page, he turned quickly and reached for the phone. She pulled it away from him as she saw the reason why he wanted it. His wallpaper on the phone was the picture of her, Matt, Harvey, and Trooper taken from the Tagger Herd's magazine article. She giggled and looked up at his exasperated expression. She turned the phone to Matt so he could see it.

"I was thinking you wanted it back, because there would be a little hottie on it." She teased.

He chuckled and leaned back in his chair. Ignoring her comment he replied; "Would you mind putting in your phone numbers?"

"Of course, and I'll call myself so I have your number." She glanced up and he nodded.

"So what do you want to do?" Matt asked.

"About what?" She said as she typed in her phone number.

"Josey," Matt answered.

Nikki concentrated on pushing the numbers while her mind was trying to figure out what she wanted to do.

She put the phone down and looked back up at the two men. Both were relaxing comfortably in their chairs watching her. She was still amazed at how much they looked alike.

"I find myself wanting to say that I don't want to interrupt her life if she's happy." She tilted her head and looked at Nick. She began to understand his actions a little bit more.

******

Two hours later she and Matt were making their way up the driveway of The Homestead. He headed for the couch and Nikki headed out to the barn to check on Arcturus. She was exhausted. The barn light was on already and she started to open the small door when she saw her mother and Jack standing in front of Arcturus' stall. They must have come out to check on the horse too.

Nikki sighed, and decided she was too tired and didn't want to answer questions about the dinner, so she began to turn away when she saw Jack reach out and take her mother's hand…Nikki froze. He lifted the hand towards his lips and very intimately kissed the inside of her wrist while they stared into each other's sparkling eyes. The eyes of love, Nikki realized. She was stunned.

As she reached for the door, a hand gripped her arm and pulled her away. She turned her stunned eyes and saw Scott.

"What the…" She started to say as he dragged her towards the house.

"You didn't see a thing." He told her as they stopped in the middle of the driveway.

"You knew?" She was in total shock.

"I don't know anything." He smiled.

"How long has this not been going on?" She asked playing his word game.

"The night before Rooster's surgery; after everyone found out how Wade broke his arm."

Nikki stared in disbelief, "I expected you to say for years."

He shook his head. "They should have been together for years. Grayson and I were secretly wishing they would, but it finally took the emotional draining she was going through for it to happen."

"I can't believe this. How did you find out? Does she know you know?"

He looked over at the barn. "If they come out, we met here as soon as you drove in." Nikki nodded. "She was pretty upset after I told her about Wade, and the possibility of losing Rooster was pretty hard on her, too." He tucked his hands into his coat pockets. "Grayson and I got up early the morning of the surgery; we wanted to get up before Wade. We walked down the steps and they were asleep on the couch. We woke them up before the kids came down."

"Does anyone else know?"

Again, he shook his head. "Not our story to tell."

"Jordan and Leah?"

"Not even them." He paused and looked directly at her. "Like I said, this is not our story to tell. They need to play it out between the two of them."

"Why?" She was confused. Everyone would be so happy, like she finally realized she was.

"Reilly."

"What? Reilly?" She didn't understand.

"What if everyone knew about the relationship and it didn't work out?" He looked concerned. "How bad would that be for everyone? Especially Grace and Reilly. If Jack were to leave, so would Reilly."

She was stunned. Tears stung at her eyes just thinking of Reilly leaving, and Jack. She nodded and looked back at the barn. "I understand," She whispered turning back to him.

"If it's just the two of them, Grayson and I, then things can be worked out without them leaving."

"The look on their faces and in their eyes just now..." Nikki still couldn't believe it. "Wow...," She didn't know what else to say. Then her mind reviewed the last ten days.

Her jaw dropped and eyes widened. He tilted his head in confusion.

"My mother sent the man she loves out on a date with her ex-husbands, ex-girlfriend."

Scott chuckled and nodded. "We thought that one was pretty good."

"For me!" Again she felt the tears in her eyes.

"Now that's love!" He laughed.

"And the other night with Nick...." She shook her head again. "I cannot believe I've been around them all this time and had no clue," She smiled disbelievingly at him. "They hid it so well."

"They've been hiding it from each other for seven years." Scott reminded her.

Nikki was amazed. "You know what Wade would say?"

Scott nodded with a grin. "The horses came into our lives for a reason, and this must have been the reason for Dru and Jack. I've thought of that many times." He looked beyond her to the barn. "Here they come, so..."

"I won't say anything."

"Nikki!" Her mom called as they got close, so Nikki fixed a natural smile on her face and turned to her. Both of them had their hands buried in their coat pockets. No sign of the love she had seen on their faces. Wow, I don't want to play poker with them, Nikki laughed to herself.

"How was dinner?" Her mom smiled. It was a true smile, not one hiding concern about her being with her father.

"Long story, and it's too cold out here to go through it." She answered calmly.

They walked into the house to see Matt's plan of going to sleep had been postponed as the entire family was playing Twister. They had moved the furniture around in the large living room to clear the floor. Four Twister mats had been taped together and looked like a new rug with large multi-colored circles.

Matt was already in the middle of the board, bent over backwards with a hand on yellow and a foot on blue. He grinned over at her when he saw her. Leah, Grace, Reilly and Nora were also awkwardly wrapped around each other and Matt as they placed their hands and feet in their called on spots.

Nikki laughed and quickly ran forward to join the fun.

THE TAGGER HERD

BOOK FOUR

SADIE TAGGER

CHAPTER ONE

Sadie stood at the large window in the dining room and looked at the lights of Lewiston twinkling in the darkness. Occasionally a car would drive by and she'd follow the lights as far as she could until they disappeared around a corner. Today was the first day of spring break and they were headed to the ranch for branding. She'd woken early and couldn't stand to lie in bed any longer. Being careful not to wake Nora and Grace, she had made her way downstairs. The clock said it was 4:59 a.m.

She checked her hair again to make sure it was pulled tight in the pony tail. She'd have the braid all week while riding and branding, so today was pony tail day. She swung her head back and forth feeling the hair slide across her back. She'd have to find a hat to wear like Aunt Dru always did.

A clicking noise echoed in the dark kitchen; Sadie turned to look. The automatic coffee maker had turned on which meant her dad's alarm clock would be going off, too. He always timed it so his coffee would be ready when he came down the stairs. She leaned against the window and quietly waited.

She heard the first footsteps and looked up at the ceiling. Right over the top of her was Aunt Dru's room, over the kitchen was her parent's room but she couldn't tell which room the footsteps were coming from. Still looking at the ceiling, she followed the footsteps with her eyes as they made their way down the hall and to the stairway. Whoever it was would come out of the stairway right beside the dining room arch-way.

She waited…her dad stepped from the stairwell and into the kitchen. She didn't say anything, she just smiled and watched as he open the cupboard for a coffee mug and set it down on the counter. He was dressed in jeans and a dark blue long sleeve shirt; a red sweat bandana was tied around his neck. No hat yet. Sadie agreed with Wade, their dads looked like they came from a western movie.

More footsteps and she looked toward the steps again. This time it was her mother. Her dad grinned at his wife and put out an arm inviting her in for an embrace. Without a word, she stepped into his arms and he kissed her. Sadie's eyebrows went up. It wasn't just a regular everyday kiss; it was a movie kiss! His hands lay on each side of her face then slowly made their way to her back to pull her in closer. Her mom's arms wrapped around him, hands clenched his shirt. He dipped her to the side, nearly to the ground and a soft giggle escaped her mom.

Sadie was about to yell when Aunt Dru came down the stairway. "Oh, get a room you two!" She teased. They rose from the dip and the kiss stopped as her mom stepped away from her dad, both her parents were grinning.

Sadie laughed, which caused all three of them to turn surprised eyes to her.

Aunt Dru made a face at her; "Ewww, you had to witness that too?" …and she continued walking to the back door.

"Yeah, ewww get a room." She said to her laughing parents. She copied her aunt, even though she didn't quite understand why her aunt would say that since they had a room upstairs.

Their coats and boots were in a large open closet by the back door. She followed her aunt and watched her slide on a denim jacket and a Tagger Enterprises T3E baseball cap. Sadie looked around to see if there was a cap for her but they were all used and dirty. Aunt Dru reached high on a shelf and pulled down a small box and pulled out a brand new cap that matched her own. With a knowing smile she helped Sadie put it on with the ponytail through the back, just like hers.

"Mini-me today?" Aunt Dru asked with a grin.

"Yep," Sadie giggled. She loved the game they played. Most people said that Sadie looked enough like her aunt that she could be her daughter. The long matching pale blonde ponytails and the blue eyes added to it.

"OK then," Aunt Dru looked around, "We need a denim jacket for you."

Sadie shook her head. "I grew out of mine."

"Well, there's one right here." She pulled one off a peg.

"That's Nora's. I don't think she would like me wearing it."

"Well," She opened the coat for Sadie to slide in, "If she complains, send her to me. When we get back, you and I'll go get you a new one."

Sadie was so happy at the possibility of going shopping with her aunt that she slid the coat on without thinking about how mad Nora was going to be. Nora was always mad if she wore something of hers. Her cousin was twelve to her ten, but Sadie was taller. That seemed to make Nora mad, too.

"Boots next," Sadie smiled. They sat on the bench and slid on their boots then stood and looked at each other.

"Mini-me success!" Aunt Dru declared.

Sadie put out her hand for a high-five and her aunt slapped it with a chuckle.

As they walked out the back door and headed for the new enlarged barn, Sadie noticed the only thing different was her aunt's light blue shirt sticking out of the jacket. Sadie had on a white one. She thought about running in the house and changing the shirt quickly, but the idea of Nora seeing her with the jacket on made her follow her aunt to the truck instead.

The stock trailers were already hitched to the trucks so Sadie unhooked the back door of the trailer and they turned towards the barn.

"Who should go first?" Aunt Dru asked.

"Not Little Ghost," Sadie answered. "If he goes in first here, then he's last out at the ranch and I'll have to wait longer for him."

"Smart girl," Aunt Dru chuckled. "So who's first and has to wait longer at the ranch?"

"Well, if Scarecrow and Arcturus go in first, then I have time to tie up Little Ghost and go back and help Nora with her horses."

"Good thinking, that's nice of you."

Sadie didn't say anything, but she always tried to find a way to help with Scarecrow.

They loaded half the horses in the stock trailer hooked to Aunt Dru's truck, then the other half in the trailer hooked to her dad's.

"Think they have any coffee left for me?" Aunt Dru looked up at the house that was now lit with most of the lights in the house.

Sadie shrugged. She didn't want to go in the house and face Nora.

Her aunt climbed up into the back of her truck, sat on the silver tool box and leaned against the cab. She didn't know what they were doing, but Sadie followed and then matched her aunt's position.

"What are we doing?"

"Enjoying the quiet morning before the commotion of the week starts," Aunt Dru smiled and looked up. "Not many stars."

"Probably a cloudy day," Sadie nodded. It was the last Saturday in March. They would be at the ranch for nine days. "But it's still warm."

Her aunt nodded.

They watched the figures in the house pass by the windows.

"Sadie?"

"Uh, huh?"

"Scarecrow."

Sadie turned to her aunt. "What about her?"

"I noticed you like her."

Sadie didn't know what to say. She had been trying to keep it a secret, and didn't think anyone knew so she didn't answer.

"How about Little Ghost?"

Sadie sat straight up and turned to her aunt with wide eyes. "Oh, I love Little Ghost. He's awesome! I just love being with him, looking at him and I love coming home from school so I can see him. Even though I love school and learning, I have such a hard time just staying there! We're going to be great roping partners."

Her aunt smiled. "And I can't wait to see you two competing. I'll be at every rodeo I can."

"I can't wait until they get trained. Dad said they are healthy enough now we can start after spring branding, so it should be when we get back."

"You've been doing well at barrels with Kit this winter. You'll be able to go to more this summer since Jordan's helping."

"Grace has, too. I'm glad we can share…but she is Nikki's horse."

Sadie looked up at her aunt…maybe she would understand what's bothering her.

"Go ahead," Her aunt encouraged her. "This conversation is just between the two of us. I promise…just spit it out."

Sadie took a deep breath and said out loud the one thing she had been holding in for months. "It's really hard having only one horse while all the other kids have two, and I feel bad because that means I'm disrespecting Angel and I really, really wish he was here, because of him and not just because I want two horses." She took a deep breath and sighed loudly. She looked up at her aunt hoping she didn't hate her for saying such an awful thing.

Her aunt was frowning, but it was a comforting frown. "Keep going."

"What?"

"There's one more sentence to that, so say it and get it out."

Her aunt was so smart…Sadie took a deep breath and let it out slowly…her shoulders drooped. "I want Scarecrow for my barrel horse, but I don't want Nora to have only one horse and feel as bad as I have."

They sat quietly a minute.

"Does it feel better saying it out loud?" Her aunt smiled. Sadie looked back up at her understanding eyes and realized it did.

"Yeah."

"Does Nora know?"

"No, and even if she did I don't think she'd care."

"Why?"

"She doesn't like having to give me stuff."

"Well, Scarecrow isn't really hers to give or keep."

Sadie shook her head. "I don't want her to have only one horse though."

"Do you think it's possible she only wants one horse? She's still using Libby for horse shows until Arcturus is ready."

"She keeps talking about all the possibilities with Scarecrow like western pleasure. She just wants to show, but I think Scarecrow is built for running and racing."

Aunt Dru nodded; "I agree."

Sadie smiled proudly that her aunt agreed with her. "I've been doing research on the best horse conformation and even their blood lines. Scarecrow's is perfect."

"Conformation and bloodlines, that's all?"

Sadie grinned and shook her head.

The back door opened and they turned to see her dad walk out the door with two cups of coffee.

"Looks like special delivery," Aunt Dru winked at her.

Before her dad got too close, Sadie turned quickly, "I just love Scarecrow and she is beautiful and so sweet. I want to be with her all the time."

"What are you two up to?" He handed his sister a cup.

Aunt Dru smelled the coffee and smiled before taking a sip. It did smell good, but the one time Sadie had tasted it, it tasted awful.

"We're sitting and enjoying the beautiful peaceful morning," Aunt Dru said but didn't make any attempt to get up.

"It's nice out here in the dark," Sadie told him; his blue eyes crinkled into a smile. "The house looks so pretty in the dark with all the lights on."

"Looks like a big electricity bill to me," He teased and looked at the trailers. "Both loaded already?"

"That's what happens when you have good help," Aunt Dru said over her coffee.

"And that she is." Her dad patted her leg. Sadie grinned; she loved to do the work, but liked it when they appreciated it too.

"All the branding supplies are either at the ranch or loaded in the trucks last night. Cora has some refrigerator items to go, then we're ready. You ladies took care of getting this herd ready; I'll go get the other herd out the door."

Sadie laughed, "Good luck, Dad." She watched him walk towards the house.

"Sadie," Aunt Dru said. "The best way to approach this problem is to come up with a solution first, before talking to people about it. Does that make sense?"

"Kind of…" Sadie nodded. "I need to figure out how to get Nora a second horse before I ask for Scarecrow."

"Or see if she's just happy with Arcturus and Libby."

"She wouldn't tell me."

"Then, you'll have to come up with an offer she can't refuse."

Sadie's eyes opened wide in confusion, "How do I do that?"

Aunt Dru shrugged and stood up as the family starting exiting out the back door and the lights started going off.

"Think about it. You're pretty smart, our family wizard, so I'm sure you'll come up with something."

"Will you help?" Sadie asked hopefully.

"If you come up with something, talk to me first and I'll give you my opinion before you move forward with it." Aunt Dru stepped over the tailgate and hopped to the ground. She waited until Sadie was on the ground then turned to climb in the driver's seat.

"That's my jacket!" Sadie heard Nora behind her. She turned and her cousin was standing with her hands on her hips accusingly.

"Aunt Dru said I could wear it," Sadie said nervously. She hated making Nora mad, she could be so mean.

"Well, I didn't say it." Nora put out her hand, expecting Sadie to take it off.

Aunt Jordan walked up beside her daughter and quickly grabbed Nora's arm and lowered it to her side. "That, young lady, is extremely rude. There's no problem with her wearing that jacket."

Nora glared at Sadie. "She only wants to wear it so she can look like Aunt Dru."

"Seriously Nora," Aunt Jordan laughed. "Who wouldn't want to look like Dru?"

Sadie giggled and headed for the truck Nora wouldn't be in.

CHAPTER TWO

Sadie could hear a clicking sound and knew it was the coffee maker starting. Her eyes were still closed and she was enjoying the cool air on her face but also the warmth of the blankets over her body. She always gave herself a few minutes of peace before she got up. The smell of the coffee spread through the room.

Sadie turned her head and finally opened her eyes. It was still dark outside. She glanced around the bunkhouse to see if anyone else was awake. No one was moving. She moved closer to the edge of the bed and looked at the lower bunk. No one was there. Usually Nikki slept there, but she and Matt were at college and wouldn't make it until Thursday. She heard a noise and looked up. Uncle Scott was sitting up on the edge of his bed. Aunt Jordan had her back to him and it looked like she was still sleeping. Uncle Scott leaned back towards her and whispered in her ear. Sadie heard a low giggle.

She grinned and sat up so they knew she was awake. Uncle Scott looked up and smiled. He rose, walked over, and turned his back to her. She slid down off the bed and onto him for a piggyback ride then giggled quietly as he walked to the kitchen table and dropped her onto a chair. Her dad walked up behind them and kissed the top of her head.

"I can't believe how early you get up, Sadie girl," He said and sat in the chair.

"I can't wait to get the day started," She smiled.

Uncle Scott put a coffee cup full of milk in front of her and one full of coffee in front of her dad. He then sat in the chair on the other side of her. Sadie held her cup of milk and listened to the men talk about the day of rounding up the cows. Why would anyone want to sleep and miss moments like these? Today they were gathering all the cows that were spread throughout Dry Creek Valley. Tomorrow was branding day!

"Wade and I are ten this year," She reminded them. "Do we get to help roundup now?" She looked over at her dad with hopeful eyes.

He put his fingers to his lips, to keep her quiet, then nodded his head with a twinkle in his eye. She felt the excitement run through her and had to quickly put the cup down so she didn't spill it. She grinned up at her dad, then over to Uncle Scott.

"Yeah, Wade's going to be pretty excited too," Her uncle smiled.

"About what?" Aunt Dru asked as she walked by and headed for the coffee maker.

"We were just reminded that we have two new roundup riders this year," Sadie's dad told her.

Aunt Dru brought the coffee pot over and filled her brothers' coffee cups then held it up to see if Sadie wanted some. Sadie giggled and shook her head. Her aunt slid in the chair across the table.

"Leah, Grace, and Sadie can go up Wolf Pass. Jordan, Nora, and Wade can head up Gypsy Gulch?" She recommended.

Sadie smiled, that way she wouldn't have to be around Nora all day!

Sadie listened excitedly while they planned out all the routes the riders would take to surround the cows and push them up to the large spring branding pasture. The areas that she and Wade were riding had the easiest trails with no steep and rocky hillsides.

She looked out the window and saw the mountains were starting to brighten, which meant the sun was coming up.

"Well, you going to help with the horses?" Aunt Dru asked as she rose from the table and put her cup in the sink. She didn't have to ask again, as Sadie ran back to grab her clothes and get ready for the day.

******

An hour later, Sadie was standing on the side of the road holding the reins of the ranch pony, Milo. The little red gelding had been the horse she had ridden for the last couple of years. He was easy to saddle and bridle, but he didn't like to leave the barn without the other horses.

"Sadie Anne, you've just about outgrown that horse," Her mom declared.

"I know! I barely have to lift my foot to get to the stirrup." Sadie leaned down to play with Mavis. She was a good cow dog that listened well to commands on when to go after a cow and when to back off. Her dad said a good cow dog was invaluable to a cattle ranch. As far as Sadie was concerned, that made Mavis and Bart invaluable.

"It's a good thing your dad's training Little Ghost in the next couple weeks," Her mom smiled. "You'll be riding him for late branding."

"Oh, MOM! I can't wait!" Sadie grinned while watching her mom step up onto the horse.

"How long before we meet up with everyone?" Grace asked as she swung herself up in the saddle.

"They should be at Trail's End by now," She answered. "It'll take them about a half hour to get to the bottom and start pushing them out of the valley. It'll take them another hour to move them up and out, unless they have problems."

"It'll only take us a half hour to reach the top of the valley," Grace guessed.

"Then we help push them down the road to the big corrals." Sadie confirmed the words her dad said that morning.

"That gives us girls an hour of riding together before we meet up with everyone." Her mom said.

"It's been a long time since we rode with just the three of us," Grace smiled.

"Just enough time for a good story," Sadie looked over at Grace for her agreement. Grace nodded with a smile.

"What would you like to hear about?" Her mom easily relented.

Sadie thought quickly about seeing her parents kissing in the kitchen and giggled. "How did you and Dad meet?"

"I've told you girls that story," She smiled.

"You just said you met at college," Grace reminded her. "How did you actually meet? When did you first see each other?"

Their mom, who was riding between them, didn't say anything.

"Mom?" Sadie asked.

"Is it that embarrassing?" Grace nervously teased.

Their mom just shook her head slowly.

"I was going to college up at U of I, just like your dad," She started. "I didn't see him my first year there but on the first day of my second year, I was sitting with a friend of mine, and we saw this really good looking guy sitting at the front of the class."

"Dad?" Sadie asked.

Her mom smiled at her and nodded. "Tall, blonde, muscular, and a great smile when he debated with the professor." Her eyes twinkled. "So we decided the second day, we would sit down where he was sitting. Just before the class started he wasn't in the front row. We looked around the room, thinking he sat somewhere else but he came in just as the professor was closing the door."

"Did he sit by you?" Grace asked.

Her mom nodded. "He came in and sat just a couple seats down from us," She glanced at each of her girls. "He turned, looked me right in the eye, and winked."

"Oh my gosh, did you swoon?" Sadie giggled but her smile faded when she saw the look on her mother's face.

"I did when it happened," She looked at the girls again. "I fell in love with him, that very moment."

"Did he ask you out on a date?" Grace asked; excited to hear the story she'd never heard before.

Her mom shook her head slowly, "A few minutes later, the professor pulled him out of class and told him about the accident that killed his parents and grandparents."

Both girls gasped. The story went from very happy, to very sad so quickly that Sadie didn't know what to say. She stayed quiet and just waited for Grace or her mom to speak.

Sadie looked over at Grace. She was looking straight ahead with a sad expression.

Their mom continued with the story, "He returned to class the next week, but I stayed up in the back of the room for the rest of the semester."

"Why?" Grace asked.

"I knew he needed some time to himself and his family before he would need a girlfriend," She smiled at both of them. "The wait was worth it."

Sadie matched her mother's smile. "When did you talk to him next?"

"The next March, when he came back from spring break; he had a really dark and ugly black eye. It covered half his face it was so big."

Sadie's eyebrows went up in surprise. "How did he get hurt?"

Her mother chuckled softly, "I wondered the same thing. So, when I saw him climb out of his truck one morning, I walked right up to him and asked him."

"Were you nervous?" Grace asked.

"Did he recognize you from when he winked at you?" Sadie asked.

Their mom sighed, "For some reason, I wasn't nervous," She answered Grace. "I think it was because I felt I already knew him from that one wink," She turned to Sadie. "Yes, he did recognize me."

"So how did he get hurt?" Sadie asked.

"Branding," She answered. "It was their first branding without their parents and grandparents and all three of them were trying to do too much and he got hurt."

"Did a cow kick him?" Sadie had seen the men get kicked by a mad momma cow, but none ended with a black eye.

"No, it was one of the young horses he was training. With so much work, he should have been using an experienced horse. The young horse he had chosen to ride spooked when a scared calf ran underneath its belly. The horse spun around and smashed your dad's face against a tree."

"OH! Ouch!" Sadie cried out…she reached up and touched the side of her face. "That had to hurt."

Their mom nodded.

"Did he ask you out after you saw him at the truck?" Grace asked.

"Yes, he did," She smiled; her eyes bright and happy. "He said he wouldn't tell me unless it was over dinner that night."

"Ooooohhhh…" Grace sung. "That was smooth."

Sadie looked up at her mom and smiled, "So, if he didn't smash his face on the tree and get all bruised; would you be together today?"

Her mom glanced over with a shine in her eyes. "I would like to think that we were meant to be together and we would have found each other one way or another."

"Except for the part where he smashes his face into a tree, and all our grandparents dying, it's kind of a romantic story," Grace said with a confused tilt to her head. "I'm not sure if I'm supposed to laugh or cry."

Their mom laughed softly, "I've never heard it put that way." She looked between her two daughters and explained, "But that's why we haven't told you the whole story before."

Grace turned and looked at Sadie, then their mother. "Kind of glad you didn't," She smiled. Sadie felt the same way.

As Sadie was trying to think of what to say, a couple of deer walked out in front of them. "Oh, Mom, look!" She whispered.

They rode quietly past the deer so they didn't run away. Although she had seen deer all her life, it was still fun to see them.

The rest of the ride they talked about friends and school.

They were the first ones to reach their destination, so they rode to the edge of the mountain to see if the riders were near. Dry Creek Valley opened up below them, wide and majestic.

"Over there!" Sadie said excitedly as she pointed to their left. A small herd of cows, with little calves running next to them, were slowly making their way to the top of the hill. Behind them were two riders. "It looks like Dad and Reilly."

To her right, suddenly appearing out of a row of trees was another herd of cows. Sadie waited patiently to see which riders were pushing them and would also appear out of the trees. There were two riders that came out of the trees; one below the cows and one above. "It's Aunt Dru and Jack." She announced.

Just as the cows from the left and right, merged into one large herd in the middle they could see the largest herd of cows down at the bottom of the valley. The riders were too far away to recognize, but the only riders missing were Uncle Scott and Jessup. Sadie squinted her eyes and looked down; there were three riders pushing the cows at the bottom. She was about to ask her mom who the other rider was, when she heard a yell.

"Howdy partners!"

Without looking, Sadie knew it was Wade. She turned with a grin to yell back at him but she saw Nora first, and the smile faded. Nora and her mom were pushing a cow and a calf onto the road. Nora and Wade had pushed a cow and Nora wasn't going to let Sadie hear the end of it.

Sadie did her best to ignore Nora and looked over at Wade. His grin was ear to ear. "Did you have fun?"

Wade rode right up to her and blocked Nora from coming closer.

"I saw the cow and calf first," He told her. "They were in a bunch of trees, so Mom sent Bart in after her. It's soooo cool to watch the dogs!"

Sadie nodded and watched as Mavis and Bart greeted each other. They sniffed each other then walked over next to her mom's horse and lay down; their tongues hanging out of their panting mouths and what seemed to be smiles on their faces.

"I love watching Dad ride in with the herd." Wade grinned and walked his horse to the top of the valley. He sat quietly watching with an 'I want to be there' look on his face.

Sadie saw Nora coming towards her and quickly pulled her reins to the right and moved closer to Wade so he would be between them again.

"Spread out and back up kids," Aunt Jordan yelled at them. "We need the cows to come up this way and onto the road so they know where they are going. If you stay there, you'll spook them into another direction. Stay along the trees so they don't try to dart into them."

Wade and Sadie quickly moved their horses over towards their mothers. The sound of the cows mooing, reached them long before the cows did. The first cow that appeared saw them and stopped. She was big and black, with a small red calf next to her. He was trying to nurse on her. The black cow stared at them a minute, then looked behind her to see if there was another trail to walk. The flood of cows behind her started her walking again, but not before the cow let out a long bellowing moo that made Wade and Sadie laugh.

The cow's little calf, that was trying to nurse, gave up and ran ahead of his mom…he stopped abruptly when he saw all the riders. He turned his head and stared at Sadie and Wade with big curious brown eyes.

"Moo cow!" Sadie yelled at him. The cows were so loud, and so many, that she could barely hear anything else. The big black cow pushed her little calf with her nose to get him walking again.

Sadie and Wade looked at each other and smiled.

"I love this!" Sadie yelled.

"Me, too!" Wade yelled back.

CHAPTER THREE

As they walked next to the cows, Sadie watched the back of her mom. She had explained that their job was to make sure the cows kept moving and didn't go into the trees. Sadie tried to look like she was calm and had done all this before so no one would know how she was excited and scared at the same time. Her horse, Milo, was walking calmly. A cow tried to take off into the trees between her and her mom, but Milo trotted forward, stuck out his nose, and laid his ears back along his head to look menacing to the cow. It worked, and the cow ran back into the herd.

"Good job, Milo!" She yelled at him and reached down to stroke his long red neck.

Sadie looked across the herd and saw Wade. He had his cowboy hat on and his chaps, which protected them from the long thorny bushes they had to ride through. He was slapping his lariat against his leg and yelling at the cows to keep them moving. He looked just like one of the kids from his favorite movie, *The Cowboys*.

She was watching Wade so intently that she didn't realize her mom had stopped and was waiting for her.

"Sadie!"

Sadie jumped and turned, but before her mom could speak she yelled back; "Mom! Look at Wade! Do you have a camera?" It was a picture that would be perfect in their hallway at home.

Her mom glanced over at him and smiled. She leaned back and reached into the saddle bags and pulled out the camera. She pointed the camera at Wade and then the other kids, then finally at Sadie, who smiled happily.

As she put the camera back, her mom yelled. "I was going to ask if you were having fun, but I think I know the answer."

She grinned and nodded; her mom moved back up the herd. Sadie turned in time to see Aunt Dru in a slow gallop riding up behind her; far enough from the herd she didn't scare them. She was riding Libby and they looked great together; like they were part of each other. They stopped next to her.

"Hey, Mini-me!" She greeted her. Sadie grinned back.

"You need a bigger horse!" Her aunt yelled at her over the noise of the herd. Sadie nodded.

Aunt Dru continued to her mother. They rode and spoke together for a few minutes, and then her mom turned her horse around and headed towards Sadie. When she was close enough, she leaned in and yelled, "I'm going back to ride with your dad, just follow Aunt Dru." Then she kicked her horse into a gallop.

Sadie turned to watch her mom gallop back to her dad who was waiting at the back of the herd. Sadie smiled and wished she had the camera so she could take a picture of her parents riding together.

She followed her aunt until they reached their destination. The branding corrals were just ahead of them and the cows seemed to know exactly where to go. They slowly walked into the large pasture. Aunt Dru rode to the side and stopped next to a fence, so Sadie rode Milo up next to her. They smiled at each other and watched the rest of the herd file into the pasture.

Slowly, all the riders came in and lined up next to the fence with them. When Nora started riding towards Sadie, Wade moved in between them. He turned his horse so he was facing out to the cows. Nora frowned at him then turned her horse away.

Sadie was surprised to see Matt and Nikki's father, Nick, riding with Jessup. He must have been the third rider at the bottom of the valley. She hadn't seen him since they finished building the addition onto the barn. He had been there every day working next to Nikki and Matt.

Nick turned and looked over towards her so she waved and smiled at him. He waved and smiled back. He was still pretty quiet when he was around the kids, but he was getting better.

Her parents were the last ones into the enclosure; her dad stepped off his horse to close the gate. In the distance behind him, Sadie saw something move. He turned and looked too, then lifted a hand to his mouth. She heard his voice through Aunt Dru's walkie-talkie but couldn't tell what was said, but it made her aunt smile.

Aunt Dru pushed Libby into motion and she turned to the group of riders. "Reilly and Grace!" She yelled over the cows. They turned and Aunt Dru motioned for them to go back to the gate. Then she turned to Nora and made the motion to her. Sadie held her breath and knew Wade was holding in his, too. She nearly jumped, when her aunt turned to her and Wade and made the same motion. Wade turned quickly to Sadie with a grin then kicked his horse forward.

Sadie could feel the excitement running through her. She rode past Aunt Dru, who grinned but didn't follow them. Sadie and Wade trotted back to the gate together.

When they were closer to the gate, she saw five cows with calves in the distance. She rode between Wade and Grace then stopped and waited. All the kids were looking at her dad excitedly.

"OK, you five are going out to get them." He informed them. "Grace, Nora, and Wade go to the left and ride out wide to the side and come in behind them. Reilly and Sadie go to the right and do the same thing. When you meet up in the back, create a V behind them with Grace in the back, then Wade and Sadie to each side of her.

Reilly and Nora you'll be on point towards the front. Make sure you don't get too close and confuse them. They should just come right into the pasture."

All the kids nodded excitedly.

"Reilly!" Her dad called out and the teenager sat up straighter. "You take care of Sadie."

Reilly nodded, "Of course, sir!"

"Go get 'em." Her dad yelled.

The kids took off in a trot in the direction he told them.

Sadie trotted right behind Reilly. Milo had to break into a gallop a couple times to stay up with his horse. He led them off to the side, far enough the cows only watched them and didn't try to run back down the road in the wrong direction.

Reilly turned to her, "If you get scared just get Milo behind me."

She nodded in nervous anticipation.

Once they met in the back with Grace, Wade, and Nora, they followed her dad's directions and they split apart and started pushing the cows in the direction of the pasture. Sadie was relieved to see the cows start walking the right way with their calves trotting next to them.

There were four black cows and one dark red cow. The red cow kept looking at her and Milo, then down to her calf. Anytime the calf would stop, his mom would push him forward with her nose. Sadie made sure she stayed a good distance from her, but not too far the cow could get past her.

She looked up in time to see one of the black cows start running for the trees instead of the pasture; the calf following close behind her. Reilly took off in a trot to push her back. Sadie frowned nervously and bit at her bottom lip when he started to get too far away. She turned to look at Grace…then the red cow turned towards her. Milo put his ears back and pushed his nose at her to make her go back, but she didn't. Sadie lowered her heels in the stirrups and balanced herself in the saddle. She held the saddle horn with one hand and the reins with the other. She lowered the reins towards Milo's neck, like she had seen her dad do when he worked with cows.

Suddenly, the cow came running to her left and tried to make into the trees. Milo cut in front of the cow and it stopped, but it tried running the other direction. Milo's front legs came up off the ground as he jumped in the direction the cow tried to move. Sadie felt her body thrust in the same direction, but she was balanced in her saddle and held her seat. She felt calm even though her heart was racing. The cow tried the other direction and Milo jumped back with his front legs and trotted forward blocking her path. Again Sadie felt the thrust, but she stayed calm. The cow stopped again and moved back the other way. Milo did the blocking move again; this time his head was low, ears pinned back, and looked menacingly at the cow.

When the cow stopped, Milo stopped. Sadie stared intently at the cow and could feel the tension in Milo's body as they waited for the cow's next move. Both Sadie and Milo relaxed when the cow turned and ran back to the rest of the small herd that had kept moving.

"Way to go Sadie!" Grace yelled from beside her.

Sadie turned and smiled, "That was fun!" Her heart was racing. She had never had as much fun as feeling Milo under her, working the cow.

Sadie turned to check where the herd and Reilly were. To her surprise, she saw her dad had started to ride toward them but had stopped and was waiting. He must have been worried. She took a deep breath but she was ready to burst from the excitement. Milo trotted up closer to the herd.

Reilly turned to her, "Nice job, Sadie!"

"It was all Milo," She said breathlessly.

"But you stayed on! That was awesome! You looked like a professional!" Reilly told her with a big proud smile.

Reilly's comment made her sit higher in the saddle. She turned back to the cows and watched them walk into the pasture.

As the cows started through the gate opening, the five riders met and rode into the pasture together. Her mother had the camera up…another picture for the wall.

Sadie could still feel the happiness in her as Wade greeted her excitedly. "That was cool, Sadie!"

She looked over at her parents who were watching with pride in their eyes. She loved that!

As they rode up to the rest of the riders, she saw Nick. He smiled at her and put his hand to the tip of his hat and bent his head to her. She'd seen that in the movies but no one had ever done that to her before…it made her laugh.

Nothing was going to ruin this happiness, even when she saw Nora riding towards her. Suddenly, Wade was between them again. Nora turned and moved over to her parents.

Sadie looked at Wade, who had glanced over at Nora, then back to her. "Sometimes I do that just to piss her off." He told Sadie with a mischievous grin.

Sadie nearly fell off her horse laughing.

CHAPTER FOUR

The next morning, Sadie climbed on the fence at the corrals and threw a leg over the top. She balanced as she settled herself on the top of the large corner post. She kept her feet firmly on the top of the fence. Wade climbed up next to her and did the same thing, but he sat on the top of the fence, his lariat looped over his shoulder. They both looked out over the sea of cows that filled the corral.

"How much older do we have to be to help with branding?" Sadie yelled towards Wade. The sound of the cows mooing was deafening.

"I don't know," Wade shrugged and yelled back. "It's a good day for it though. It's not raining and it's not too cold."

Their mothers were the riders pushing a group of cows and calves into the big pen which was causing the cows to call out. Their dads were on the ground separating the cows into one corral and their calves into another. Nick was opening and closing the gate as the calves were walked into the small corral and made sure they didn't escape when they pushed in another calf. Jessup was at the branding table preparing the supplies. Their neighbor Andy's sons would be there soon to help when the branding started.

They sat quietly, watching the adults work the cows. Wade looked behind her then up to her. Sadie didn't have to turn around to know Nora was walking up behind them. She climbed up the fence and sat next to Sadie. She was wearing the denim jacket that Aunt Dru had let Sadie wear.

"Milo did a good job with that red cow," Nora smiled sweetly.

"Yes, he did," Sadie agreed, knowing that Nora was pointing out the horse did the work and Sadie didn't.

"Mom and Dad said I could help this year. I'm going to load the ear tag things for Reilly and Grace." Nora said proudly.

Neither Wade nor Sadie responded to her; they were both watching the cows and riders.

"What are you guys going to do?" Nora asked.

Sadie finally turned to her. "Same as you did last year."

"I guess you'll have to do that next year too," Nora smiled sweetly and climbed down the fence.

Once Nora had walked away, Sadie turned to Wade. "Why is she so mean?"

Wade shrugged and sat quietly watching everyone, but them, work. Sadie sighed.

It took another half hour for the first group of calves to be separated from their moms. Sadie climbed down from the fence and Wade followed.

"Where are you going?" Wade asked.

"I'm thirsty," She answered and walked over to the coolers. As she opened the cooler and handed Wade a bottle of water, she heard a loud whistle. Both she and Wade looked around for the source. Nick motioned for them to bring him a bottle.

"His whistle is as loud as Nikki's," Wade yelled at her.

Sadie grabbed a bottle and they ran over to the fence and handed one up to him. "What are you two doing?" He opened the bottle and drank the whole thing.

"We're just watching," Wade answered and took the empty bottle from him.

"Want to help?" Nick asked.

Sadie and Wade both nodded excitedly.

"I'll be right back," He grinned down at the pair and turned his horse around. Wade and Sadie both quickly climbed the fence and watched him ride over to Jessup. The foreman nodded and glanced over at the two of them. He motioned Nick towards Sadie's dad. Nick trotted his horse over to him and leaned in to talk over the cows. A grin spread across her dad's face as he nodded while glancing up to Sadie and Wade. They began riding to them.

"They're coming over here!" Wade shouted at Sadie.

Sadie felt the excitement build at the thought that they may be able to help with branding.

The men rode to them and moved their horses parallel with the fence.

"Nick said you two want to help," Her dad smiled at them.

Sadie and Waded nodded excitedly.

"Can you count?" Her dad teased them.

"Yes, Dad!" Sadie rolled her eyes at him.

"Climb on," He told his daughter. He didn't have to ask her twice. Sadie was on behind him before he could change his mind. She turned and saw Wade climb on behind Nick. Wade's grin was as big as hers.

Sadie wrapped her arms around her dad's waist and looked around him. Her hips rocked with the motion of the horse they were riding. He took her to the gate where all the calves were being held.

"Climb up there." He helped her step off the horse and onto the gate post. He made sure she was firmly on the post before he let her go. He reached in his jacket pocket and pulled out a pen and paper.

"We need a good count on how many calves we brand today," He yelled over the mooing cows while handing her the pen and paper. "Every time one of the calves is taken out, you make a mark on this piece of paper." He showed her how he wanted them tracked. "Wade is going to count on the other side as they are released back to find their mothers," Sadie nodded. "Jessup is going to work the gate for the first half, then Jordan will do the second half. Sometimes it gets confusing so if you have a question you ask one of them. OK?"

"OK Dad!" She smiled up at him. She was so excited to help. He grinned back; his blue eyes sparkling under the rim of his cowboy hat.

"Do not get down for any reason when there are riders and cows out here. I don't want you getting run over," He told her firmly. She nodded again as he left.

Sadie looked down at the calves in the pen. Some were standing around and a few had lain down along the side of the corral. When this group were branded and released, more cows and calves from the big corral would be separated and branding would start again.

Jessup came up next to her and patted her leg. "Good for you, Sadie girl." He smiled up at her then moved over to open the gate for the first rider to come in and rope a calf. As Aunt Dru threw her rope, caught the back legs of one of the black calves, and drug him out of the pen, Sadie made a mark on her paper.

Fifty marks later they took a break. Nick came up to her and she climbed on the back of his horse. When they reached the branding table and coolers, Nick gave her his arm and helped her slide off. She looked up at him and thanked him. He smiled then stepped off the horse.

Sadie turned in time to see Wade running up to her, "How many did you count?" Wade yelled. "I got 50!"

"Me, too!" Sadie said excitedly. She looked around at everyone else. They were all smiling and joking. Nora was sitting on the far side, quietly looking out to the cows. She looked lonely, so Sadie turned to Wade and pointed to his sister. He nodded and they walked over to her.

"Are you having fun?" Sadie asked her.

Nora nodded but didn't say anything.

"It looked like everything was flowing good," Wade told her. "Reilly and Grace never had an empty ear tag thing." He always forgot the word applicator.

Nora stood, looked at both of them, and walked away without a word.

"I guess we're not good enough for her." Wade shrugged and walked back to the group.

Sadie followed him and not really understanding what was wrong with Nora.

They had lunch when Sadie reached 150 marks, Wade had 149. Their parents said that was close enough.

When she reached 200 marks they took another break. Wade had 199. They were still only one calf off.

At 250 marks they continued to brand without stopping. Sadie could tell the group was getting tired; as tired as her butt was from sitting on the fence.

Jessup switched places with her mom so he would be riding and roping the calves and she would work the gate next to Wade.

Sadie counted the calves remaining. "TEN!" she yelled. When Aunt Dru drug the next calf out she yelled "NINE!" They all smiled at her countdown. Pretty soon she yelled "FIVE!" and heard whooping come from the group.

"THREE!" She yelled as loud as she could while laughing. There was more whooping from the crowd.

"TWO!" …as Aunt Dru pulled one from the corral.

"ONE!" …as Jessup pulled the second to last one out.

Sadie and Aunt Dru grinned at each other as she roped the last calf…it had been a long day since she had roped the first one.

"ZERO!" Sadie hollered as she made the last mark on her paper. Aunt Jordan helped her down from the fence and they turned to watch the final calf trot out of the corral with the T3E brand on his side.

Everyone was so tired they just sat and leaned on anything they could; grins decorated their faces. Uncle Scott opened the cooler of beer for the adults and soda for the kids. Once everyone had a drink in their hands, the beverage was raised in the air for a salute. As Sadie was told, this was a family tradition ever since the Tagger Trio were kids. They raised the drinks and yelled "To ranch life!"

Sadie smiled; there would be another branding in June to catch all the calves that didn't get rounded up and branded this time. She would be on Little Ghost!

The tack was pulled from the horses and they were placed in the pen for the night. A large amount of hay and water was placed with the horses and each was given grain to revitalize them for the next day.

All the cows and calves would be left in the pasture just outside of the branding corrals overnight so mothers could find their babies. Then, the next morning, they would be pushing the herd out to spring pasture.

"I love this." Sadie thought to herself as she helped clean up. There was nothing better than riding all week at the ranch.

It was dark before they had everything cleaned up, put away, and taken back to the ranch. Cora had a huge feast for everyone. Not too long after dinner was done; the bunkhouse was full of sound asleep cowboys and cowgirls.

CHAPTER FIVE

"Sadie, what do you want to do?" Her dad asked again.

Sadie stared up at him with anxious eyes; she wasn't sure what to do. It was either go on a ride with Reilly and Grace to shut gates in Dry Creek Valley or go with the rest of the group to push the herd to spring pasture. She wanted to do both!

"Do you want me to choose for you?" He laughed at her.

"Yes!" She whined with a giggle.

"OK, you're headed with Reilly and Grace," He turned her around and pushed her towards the smaller trailer.

He followed her to the truck and trailer where Reilly was getting ready to get in the driver's seat. He had been driving at the ranch for the last six months since he received his drivers' permit. They loaded Milo and her saddle into the trailer.

"Take it easy on the turns," He told Reilly. "Don't get in a hurry, we've got all day." Her dad opened the door for Sadie who quickly crawled in next to Grace. "Leave the truck at the bottom and ride up to the top to the corrals. We'll pick you up there and drive you back down to your truck."

Her dad leaned onto the window. "Reilly, these are my girls in here," He said with a serious tone. "You take care of them and don't let them get hurt."

"I won't sir," Reilly assured him. "I'll be careful and bring them back safe."

As her dad turned away, Reilly called out to him. "Grayson? Thank you for trusting me." They nodded to each other and Reilly started the truck and drove to Dry Creek Valley.

Sadie was the first to step up into the saddle and onto Milo. She had made sure her saddle bags had her lunch and plenty of water. They didn't have any of the dogs because they were with the cattle herd.

"Come on you two," Sadie grinned. "What's taking you so long?"

They climbed on their horses at the same time. Sadie shook her head and rolled her eyes. The two did everything together…so much they always seemed in perfect unison.

The first gate that needed closed was quite a distance away so they started out at a trot. Once they closed that gate, they settled into a comfortable walk down the road.

Milo was smaller than the other two horses so Sadie was constantly behind them and usually trotting to catch up. She began daydreaming about riding Little Ghost for the late branding in June. He was one of the biggest of the Tagger Herd and wouldn't have a problem keeping up with anyone! She couldn't wait.

She was looking out into the valley when she saw something move. Out here it could be a mountain lion or a bear, so she kicked Milo into a trot to catch up with Grace and Reilly. As they rode, she kept watching the spot but she didn't see anything move again. She started daydreaming about Little Ghost and roping and started to lag behind the dynamic duo again. Sadie looked over to the same place she'd seen the movement and there was another black flicker. She sat straight up in the saddle and stared at it. It was too dark for a mountain lion…it was too small for a bear unless it was a cub. If it was a cub, then momma bear would be around and dangerous. Her heart began to race.

She kicked her horse into a trot to catch up with the duo again. Grace and Reilly were chatting about school and their friends. Sadie didn't want to interrupt until she was sure she really saw something so she just kept staring at the spot. Her eyes moved around the valley for anything bigger.

There was nothing moving besides the three of them. The spot moved again. This time Sadie stopped Milo and watched. She looked down at her red horse to see what his reaction was. Her dad had taught her to pay attention to the horse, because he has better ears then hers. If it was a bear cub, Milo would be spooked and his ears would twitch wildly and his body would tense. Milo was standing still with his head towards the other horses that were getting too far away from him. He whinnied out to his departing friends. Sadie looked around for anything else moving…there was nothing. Curious, she turned Milo off the road and towards the black spot.

It moved again…it was black for sure, so she looked around for a momma bear. Her heart started pounding but she kept moving closer. There was still no stress from Milo except his attention to the horses moving away from him. She nudged him to get closer; they were only thirty feet from the spot.

She saw a flicker of black that made her pulse soar, and then the head of a baby calf rose up!

"Oh, no!" Sadie cried out and kicked Milo into a trot.

"Sadie!" Reilly yelled from behind her and glanced back to see him and Grace galloping towards her. "What are you doing? Get back here!"

"There's a calf out here!" She yelled as she stopped Milo. She quickly jumped from the horse and made her way to the calf.

The completely black calf was curled up on the ground, his head high in curiosity. Sadie lowered herself to crawl to the calf so she didn't scare it.

"Hi Baby." She spoke softly. The calf stood and walked over to her. "You must be scared and lonely." She told him while running her hand down its back.

Grace and Reilly stepped off their horses and came up to the two of them.

"Man, I can't believe he made it out here all night by himself." Reilly bent down and started petting the calf, too. He touched Sadie's arm making her look up at him. "Sadie, don't ever do that again," His expression was true concern. "I would never forgive myself if anything happened to you."

Sadie was surprised and instantly felt bad for scaring him. "OK, Reilly, I won't."

"And there's the fact that Dad would kill you." Grace laughed her 'life is good' laugh as she joined in.

"Yeah, and there's that." Reilly smiled.

Grace glanced underneath the calf. "It's a girl!" She announced.

The calf let out a little cry and nuzzled all three of them looking for something to eat.

"We need to take her with us," Sadie looked up at Reilly.

"I agree," He answered and looked back at the horses then back to Sadie, "Get back on Milo and we'll lay her across the saddle in front of you."

"Really?" Sadie asked excitedly and quickly climbed on Milo.

The calf kicked as Reilly wrapped his arms around it and stood. "Help!" He looked over at Grace who was giggling at him. She stepped in front of him and wrapped her arms around the calf too; it was sandwiched between them. They slowly made their way next to Sadie and Milo.

"This is the only time, all week, that I'm glad Milo is so short," Sadie laughed as they tried to place the calf in front of her. She grabbed the front legs to help pull them across in front of her. The calf was scared, cried out, and kicked but missed hitting any of them. Milo didn't move as they wrestled with the calf. Once the calf was balanced in front of her, it relaxed and lay quietly.

Sadie grinned down at Grace and Reilly. "This is cool. Wade is going to be so jealous!" She laughed.

The rest of the ride was slow since Sadie couldn't trot. Grace and Reilly had to keep slowing down and waiting for her this time.

"When we get to the top of the valley we'll stop and let her down for a little while," Reilly said. "We'll have lunch, too."

All the gates were closed, lunch eaten, legs stretched, and the calf placed in front of her again. The only thing they had left was a long walk to the corrals.

She adjusted the calf in front of her. It wasn't very big, but it was heavy enough to make her legs ache but she wasn't going to complain. She stroked the calf's head and ears; talking softy so it wouldn't be scared. The calf's hair was sleek, black and wavy.

She could see the corrals ahead of them with trucks, trailers, and people around them.

"I think they're waiting for us," Grace laughed.

"They're probably wondering what the heck was taking us so long," Reilly chuckled.

"Well, Dad did say to take our time." Sadie added with a grin.

As they approached the corrals, Wade ran to Sadie. He was excited to see the calf and, like Sadie predicted, was jealous.

"You look like those pictures on the cards we see at the store!" He grinned at her. "Or even in the magazines!"

Her parents were walking towards her.

"What did you find?" Her dad asked her then lifted the calf off her lap. She quickly crawled off her horse.

"I'll take Milo," Reilly took her reins.

Sadie smiled, "Thanks, Reilly," Then quickly followed her dad who was walking the calf to the back of his truck.

"Can I ride in the back of the truck with him on the way to the barn?" Sadie pleaded as she climbed over the tail gate.

"I don't see a problem with that," He waited until Sadie was settled on the floor of the truck and positioned the calf in front of her. "Where did you find her?"

"At the bottom of the valley," She answered.

Grace and Reilly climbed into the back of the truck, too.

When they arrived at the ranch, the calf was carried into the barn with Sadie following closely behind.

"Find Jessup and see if he has any milk replacer. If not, we'll go find a cow with a full bag and milk her out." Her dad instructed.

"OK, Dad." Sadie ran to find Jessup and the supplement bottle with long nipple for the calf to drink. Jessup instructed Sadie how to prepare the bottle then she excitedly headed out to the barn and calf.

She held the bottle for the calf and her dad held its body against his side as they tried to feed him. They were both laughing at the attempts of the calf to drink from the nipple the first time. The calf's long tongue would dart in and out and around the nipple, not understanding it needed the nipple in her mouth. Her dad's hand was covered with milk and the calf's saliva.

"Hold the bottle in one arm and the nipple in the other hand." He instructed her. "Now, as I open her mouth from the side, you slide the nipple straight in the front. I'll try to keep her mouth closed around it so she can't spit it out again."

Sadie did exactly what he said and it worked! The calf finally figured it out and sucked on the nipple for the milk. They laughed as the calf kept bouncing its head up and down as it drank. By the time the bottle was empty, they were both covered in milk.

Wade had been watching and laughing. Nora walked up behind him and watched but didn't say anything.

"What are we going to do with her, Dad?" Sadie asked once the calf was done drinking. Wade and Nora had made a big straw bed in the corner of the barn, but the calf was walking around checking everything out. When the calf got scared, she'd jump back and turn to look at them.

"Well," He sat on a bale of hay and Sadie quickly sat on his knee. He wrapped his arms around her and they watched as Nora and Wade knelt on the ground and tried to get the calf to come over to them. "I don't remember seeing a cow without a calf yesterday, but it would be easy to miss. We'll have to keep her at the barn and feed her. She's going to have to be fed at least four times a day to start. If we leave her here, that puts the burden all on Jessup since he doesn't have any more orphaned calves right now."

"Can we take her home Uncle Grayson?" Wade asked hopefully.

Sadie turned excited eyes to her dad, "Please?"

He nodded. "It'll be a lot easier for all you kids to take turns then Jessup do it by himself." He smiled at his daughter. "You did a good thing by finding her Sadie. You didn't just save her, but all the babies she'll have in the future."

Sadie hugged her dad, "I want to call her Dusty."

CHAPTER SIX

Sadie finally stepped out of the barn and away from a sleeping Dusty. She looked around but didn't see anyone. Wade and Nora had left with their parents and gone…somewhere.

It was late in the afternoon and the sun had finally come out from behind the clouds and was shining down on the ranch. She felt the warmth of it touch her face and started walking towards the bunkhouse when she saw Little Ghost in the pasture and changed her path to him.

She climbed over the fence and walked past Arcturus and Trooper, then Buttercup, and Cooper. She stopped and stroked each of their noses before she continued. Rufio and Eli were at the far side of the corral. They were standing, but their heads were down and their eyes were closed. The warm sunshine had made them sleepy. She glanced around the back of the barn and saw Dollar and Rooster laying flat out in the sunshine. Their legs were stretched out in front of them. Behind Dollar and Rooster, Harvey and Scarecrow were lying down on their sides; their legs curled under them.

It was a lazy afternoon for the Tagger herd. In a couple months, they would be tired from their ride instead of the sunshine.

Little Ghost had seen her coming and watched her approach. When she was close enough, he lowered his head and stretched his nose out to see if she had any treats. Sadie had learned months before not to bring treats into the pasture. Once the first horse received the treats, all of the rest of them would come trotting over and try to get some too. It quickly became dangerous.

"Sorry, not today," She whispered to him, as she rubbed the soft velvety spot on the end of his nose. Her hand slowly moved up to just under his eye. He always closed his eyes and leaned into her when she rubbed him there. She rest her forehead on the side of his head and breathed in the smell of him. It was wonderful…she closed her eyes. They stood quietly together taking in the attention from each other, along with the warm sunshine.

Her mind went back to the months in the stall the summer before. The night Angel died was heartbreaking. The hardest part was walking back into the stall after Angel was removed…it was so empty. She had walked to the back corner, leaned against the back wall and cried. When hoof beats had echoed in the barn she turned to see her dad walking Little Ghost back into the stall. She rushed to the horse and from that point they had become nearly inseparable.

She had fallen asleep cradled in her dad's arms. When her eyes opened during the night; her dad was still holding her while he slept. Little Ghost had lain down next to them, his nose out just close enough that Sadie could reach out and stroke the fine velvety hairs while she fell back to sleep.

The rest of the summer was spent with just the two of them in the stall. She couldn't count the amount of times she had brushed the horse. She came up with whatever games she could and treats for him when he would do a trick.

A noise behind her made Sadie open her eyes. It was Mavis and Bart making their way through the corral. She watched them trot off then turned her attention back to the beautiful grey horse. She started walking around him, rubbing him down like she always saw her dad do with horses. Her hand went up and under the long black mane her dad had jokingly threatened to cut off or thin it if she didn't keep it brushed. Sadie loved his mane because it would wildly fly around as he ran and played in the pasture. His long black tail, which she combed every day, would flow behind. His coat wasn't completely grey. It was polka dotted with a lighter color.

Sadie had read every horse book she could find.   In the library at The Homestead she had a whole section of the bookshelf filled with the books. She read them over and over. Many of them she had read to her horse in the stalls the summer before. Little Ghost's grey and white mottled coloring was called dappling. Palominos could also be dappled but Scarecrow was pure golden; pure sweetness.

Sadie walked around Little Ghost until she came across the scars on his side from the broken feeder in his stall where they found him. Her finger followed the track of the small scars towards the top of his belly. The longest ran from his withers down to the top of his leg. They were still pretty ugly and Jessup told her they would fade a little more over time. They would always be visible but Sadie didn't care.

The scars would be in front of the saddle so they wouldn't be bothered by it when she rode. Sadie knew every scar by heart. One night, she had drawn them on a piece of canvas and hung it on her bedroom wall. One long line…two sideways lines…and a couple small ones. Only Reilly had guessed what it was. The horse tassel Christmas gift that Aunt Dru had given her, with Angel and Little Ghost's hair, hung from a peg next to it. The tassel would be placed on Little Ghost's bridle once she started riding him.

Sadie turned away from the scars and ran her hand up and across his back from his withers to the base of his tail. The backbone was completely covered with muscle and fat. He was totally different from when they found him starving in Cora's barn. He looked healthy now. She went back to the front of the horse and up the side of his neck without the mane. It was high and arched…very masculine.

"I can't wait to see you shed out this summer Little Ghost," She whispered to him. He turned his head to her, touching his nose to her hip, then he closed his eyes. This was his way of asking her to keep rubbing…so she did for another half hour.

As she turned away from Little Ghost, Sadie glanced over to Scarecrow who had stood. The horse stretched her neck up and leaned back to stretch her front legs. The palomino was so beautiful and sweet…Sadie adored her.

With a sigh, she headed for the gate until she noticed Libby, Kit and Cora's Zippo colt playing in the next corral. She climbed up on the fence so she was standing on the bottom rail then crossed her arms over the top rail. She rest her chin on her hands and watched the three playing.

Sadie heard footsteps behind her but didn't move; she was enjoying the horses and the warm sunshine. The person came up from behind and encircled her waist with their arms and squeezed tightly. Aunt Dru leaned her chin onto Sadie's shoulder so they were cheek to cheek. They watched the horses for a few minutes before her aunt spoke.

"Seeing you out here made me think of my mother."

"Why?"

"Because I used to come out here and do the very same thing; stand on the fence and watch the horses play. Of course, it was Nan and Jet playing instead of their offspring," She sighed. "My mom would watch me watching the horses."

"Do you miss her?"

"Every day."

"What do you miss the most?"

"Her voice."

"I think I would miss my mom's laugh."

"Except for when she laughs so hard she snorts!"

Sadie could feel her aunt giggling.

"Dad can really get her going sometimes," Sadie agreed with a grin.

"Some of my best memories are out here with the horses and my parents. This pasture used to be my arena."

"You lived here your whole life?"

"Yep, and so did my dad."

"Wow."

"His dad's dad; your great-great-great grandfather came here when your great-great grandfather was a teenager."

"What were their names?"

"Mathew Tagger, Anderson Tagger, Mathew Tagger again, then the three of us."

"And Grandma's name was Anne, just like us?" Sadie Anne said to her Aunt Drusilla Anne.

"Yep."

"Someday, I'll have a daughter and call her Leah Anne." Sadie smiled at the thought.

"I think that's a great idea." Aunt Dru squeezed her tightly.

Cora's colt playfully reared up over Kit, then came down to stand perfectly still, head held high in the air arching his neck. He seemed to lift his face to the sun, his dark red coat reflecting the light.

"He's magnificent," Sadie said in awe.

"One of the most beautiful horses I've ever seen," Her aunt agreed. "It's a good thing he's gelded…I'd be tempted to keep him as a stud."

"Nora should show him," Sadie said. "They would look great together."

Aunt Dru stepped out from behind her and leaned on the fence. She turned and smiled. "Is that what you've been thinking…on how to get Scarecrow?"

Sadie looked at her in surprise. "I didn't really think of that," She said honestly. "It just popped into my head just now." She looked out at the horse then back to her aunt. "Even if I don't get Scarecrow, she should still show him. If Cora would agree."

As if the horse knew they were talking about him, he turned his head and looked at them. His ears twitched back and forth then he reared up again. When he came down, he lowered his head and chased after Kit, who took off at a gallop to get away from the red colt.

"I agree," Aunt Dru leaned her arms on the fence and rest her chin on top, just like Sadie.

"So now what?" Sadie asked.

"Well…let's keep the idea between the two of us for now. Matt and Nikki will be here tomorrow and we'll have a group meeting about all the horses." She looked as Sadie. "Just between us?"

Sadie nodded and stepped down from the fence.

As they turned to walk back to the house, Sadie took her aunt's hand.

Spring break at the ranch, getting to help with the cattle roundup, chasing the red cow, getting to help with branding, and finding the little calf; it was the best week of her life, Sadie thought with a smile.

And then it went bad…

CHAPTER SEVEN

It was absolutely the worse day she had ever had in her life, Sadie thought angrily as she walked to the back of the trucks and trailers. She hated Nora, absolutely hated her. Her mom always told her that hate was too strong of a word and it wasn't a good word. Right now, Sadie didn't care. It was the EXACT word that explained how she felt about her cousin.

First there was Dusty….Sadie had awoken early in the morning to feed the calf. She and Jessup had fixed the supplement and put the full bottle in the bunkhouse refrigerator the night before. She even used the ladder to climb down her bunk, instead of just climbing down the side because it was quieter and she wouldn't wake anyone. Tip-toeing across the floor, she was anticipating watching the calf try to drink again. Just the thought of it made her giggle inside.

Sadie pulled open the door…and the bottle was gone. She turned and looked in the sink and on the counter to see if she had left it out. No, it wasn't there. There was no other place it could have been, unless someone already took it out to the barn.

"Maybe Dad…" She slowly walked through the bunkhouse towards the door. But there, in his bed, curled up with her mom, was her dad. Sadie quickly turned and looked at all the beds, all the adults but Matt and Nikki, who hadn't arrived yet, were in their beds.

Dancing on tip-toes, she looked at the upper bunks. She could barely make out if anyone was there or not. Giving up, she decided to head out to the barn. Anticipating being up early, she had slept in her jeans and shirt so all she had to do was grab her boots and the closest jacket to the door.

As quietly as she could, she opened and closed the door. There was a large light that lit the area between all the buildings. She quickly ran out to the barn, frowning at the hint of a light coming from inside the barn. They don't keep a light on in the barn. She took hesitant steps as she approached the building; quickly looking back for reinforcements from the bunkhouse, but the light was still off.

Still determined to find out what happened to the bottle, and make a new one if needed, she kept walking towards the barn door. There were two large double doors that the adults would open wide when they worked inside shoeing or loading the hay in the barn. But Sadie headed for the small side door which was easier to get through and would lead her right to Dusty.

Finally reaching the door, she flipped up the lever and pulled it open expecting to see a very hungry calf inside. Instead, she saw Nora. Her cousin was kneeling next to the calf holding the now, almost empty bottle. Sadie felt her back stiffen and her jaw clench.

"What are you doing?" She asked, in a very controlled rising anger as she stepped through the door.

Nora turned surprised eyes to her, then she smiled sweetly. The sweet smile that Sadie disliked because it always meant Nora was getting away with something.

"Feeding, Dusty," Nora said in her sweet little voice. She continued to hold the bottle for the calf…that had milk all over its head.

"Who said you could feed her? She's mine to feed this morning." Sadie walked right up to her and tried to take the bottle.

Nora pulled it away from her. Not understanding what was happening, the calf took a step towards Nora, trying to get back at the bottle. Nora roughly pushed the calf away, which made the anger switch in Sadie flip.

"Get away from her!" Sadie yelled at her cousin and stepped in between the two.

"The milk is gone anyway," Nora threw the bottle on the ground. "Uncle Grayson said we would share feeding the calf."

"You NEVER get up this early, Nora!" Sadie turned to her cousin with her hands on her hips.

"I haven't had a reason to before...I did this time," Nora yelled. "The calf was hungry so I fed it."

"You only came out here to piss me off!" Sadie yelled back.

"Sadie!" Her dad's voice reached her and her head jerked up to see him walking through the side door. "What's going on?" He walked up between the two girls.

"I came out to feed Dusty and she got mad at me," Nora pouted, which made the hairs on the back of Sadie's neck rise and the anger inside grow.

Her dad turned and looked at her with tight lips and narrowed eyes. Sadie's anger nearly boiled over...now she was in trouble with her dad! Sadie looked down and watched as the calf tried to nurse on the empty bottle that was lying on the ground.

"Go back to the bunkhouse Nora," Was all her dad said. Watching Nora leave, he turned to Sadie.

"What's going on, Sadie Girl?" He hadn't moved and still looked upset with her.

"I got up to feed Dusty and the bottle I put in the fridge last night was gone. So I came out here and found Nora feeding her."

He sighed. "All the kids will be taking turns feeding her, Sadie."

Sadie turned frustrated eyes up at her dad. Why did he have to take Nora's side?

"I fixed the bottle with Jessup, while she just WATCHED. Then she WATCHED me put it in the bunkhouse fridge, knowing I was getting up early to feed." Sadie stopped and took in a deep angry breath. "She NEVER gets up this early! She only did it to make me mad."

"You're right, she doesn't get up early, but you don't know she did it to make you mad. She was probably just excited about feeding the calf too. She didn't get a chance to last night." He was trying to calm her down but it wasn't working.

He was defending Nora! Sadie reached down and grabbed the bottle from the confused calf. "And now she left the bottle so I would have to clean and refill it to get it ready for the next feeding."

Sadie's hand was shaking from anger as she reached down to pet the calf who had given up trying to feed.

"Give me the bottle," He held out a hand for it. "I'll make sure she takes care of it properly."

Sadie hesitantly gave it back to him. As mad as she was at Nora for not doing the job, Sadie actually liked preparing the bottle. But she wasn't going to backtrack on her argument.

He stood silently watching her pet the calf until Sadie finally looked up at him.

"She doesn't always do things just to piss you off," he said calmly.

Sadie rolled her lips together tightly and glared at him. He was defending Nora again. She didn't respond…she just knelt down to pet the calf.

She heard him sigh then turn to leave. "We're getting an early start to Andy's this morning to help him with his branding, so get yourself and Milo ready to go."

Sadie watched him walk out then glanced down at Dusty. The calf had a full stomach and was now tired and ready for a nap. It laid down in the corner and curled up to sleep.

Sadie stomped out the door.

******

First the calf, and then THE HAT!

In the short time she was in the barn, everyone had woken in the house and in the bunkhouse. Reilly and Grace already had their horses and were walking to the stock trailers to load them. Wade was stepping out of the ranch house with his saddle bag supplies. Cora prepared something for everyone's saddle bag; water, snacks, and something for a light lunch if they didn't make it to the big lunch that Andy's daughter-in-laws would be providing.

Sadie walked to the house to get her saddle bag supplies, thanked Cora, and then headed out to get Milo. Supplies put in the saddle bags; she haltered Milo and helped load him in the trailer. One last trip to the bunkhouse to get the hat Aunt Dru gave her, use the restroom, and then she'd be ready to go.

When she stepped into the bunkhouse no one was there. Sadie immediately looked for her hat and found it up on her bed and set it down on the shelves by the door as she stepped into the bathroom. When she came out of the bathroom the hat was gone. She looked around on the floor and behind all the coats that still hung on the wall. It wasn't there. Anxiety rose; how could it be gone? It was right there. She did the search again, repeating everything she had just done.

Grace stepped in the door. "Come on they're waiting for you."

"I'm looking for my Tagger Enterprises hat that Aunt Dru gave me," Sadie nearly cried.

"The blue one?"

Sadie looked at her sister and could tell she knew something. "Where is it?"

Grace stared at her a minute, before she hesitantly answered, "Nora has it on."

Her head was going to explode, the angry switch flipped again. Grace quickly stepped into the bunkhouse and shut the door.

"Calm down, Sadie."

"I just put it down for a second!" Her breathing started to quicken from the anger. "How could she get it that fast?" She stomped her booted foot.

"Calm down. We'll find you another one." Grace started looking.

"She doesn't even wear baseball caps!" Sadie yelled.

"Uncle Scott told her to come in and get a hat," Grace said, trying to calm her down. "It was probably the first one she saw."

"She knows it was mine!" Sadie argued.

"And you wore her coat," Grace reminded her. "She probably thought you were already in the truck and wasn't going to wear it."

Sadie took a deep breath and let it out slowly. Now Grace was defending Nora!

"What other hats do you have here? You have to have one," Grace reminded her.

Sadie walked past her sister and to her bed. She crawled up and grabbed her cowboy hat that was hanging from the wall. She shoved it on her head and without another word walked out the door with Grace following.

Half way to the trucks, Sadie stopped and looked up at Grace.

"What?" Her older sister asked.

"Watch her face, and then tell me again she didn't know what she was doing." Sadie said and stomped her way to her dad's truck. It was the details…they needed to pay more attention to the details!

When she crawled in the truck and shut the door, she leaned against it and stared out the window. She had to stop the anger before she got in trouble. The best way was not to talk to anyone until her anger subsided.

"Cowboy hat day?" Her mom said from the front seat.

"SOMEONE took my cap!" She spit out. It was the only words she said on the short ride to Andy's branding corrals.

Sadie dropped down out of the truck, and without looking at anyone, went to the back of the trailer that held Milo. She kept her head down so she wouldn't see Nora wearing her hat and get madder. She patiently waited for Milo.

By the time Milo was out of the horse trailer, her dad had placed her saddle and gear next to the trailer. She concentrated on getting the horse ready…her gaze did not wander from Milo. She used the front of her cowboy hat to hide her face from anyone looking at her. The last thing was the cinch. She got it as tight as she could and waited for her dad to come check it. That was their routine.

She saw his boots approaching her and stepped to the side so he could check on the saddle and cinch.

He pulled up on the cinch and it barely moved. "Good job, Sadie Girl," He said as he tightened the cinch. She nodded her head and watched his boots turn to her, but she didn't look up.

"You look good in that hat, Sadie." He said and turned away. She watched his boots. He was just trying to make her feel better, but she was still mad at him for defending Nora.

Milo stood quietly while she put a boot in the stirrup, reached for the saddle horn and with a push from the foot on the ground she easily lifted into the saddle. Still blocking her face with her hat, she walked to the other horses and found Grace. She turned Milo away from the group so she could lift her gaze out to the mountain range.

The sun had risen as they arrived and now the light was reaching all the distant mountains. If she wasn't in such a bad mood, she would have enjoyed the morning.

"You're right," Grace said to her.

"About what?" Sadie asked without moving her gaze from the mountains.

"She keeps looking over here at you," Grace chuckled. "I think you not looking at her is getting to her."

The group started moving and Sadie didn't have to encourage Milo to go, he just moved as the group did.

Milo was a comfortable walker. She just rocked her body with his steps and the movement started to make her relax.

By the time they reached the first herd of cows, the tension in her body had decreased and she looked around at the group of people. When her eyes reached Nora, she looked at her cousin and stared…in bewilderment…

"She's not wearing it," Sadie looked over at Grace.

Her sister nodded sheepishly. "Just as we started moving, she took it off and threw it back at the trucks."

Sadie's back stiffened, all the tension rising in the muscles in her body. She started to talk but her sister stopped her.

"I didn't tell you because I didn't want you to yell again," Grace put a hand up. "Keep your cool while we're here. Be respectful of Andy and his family."

Sadie frowned at her sister and nodded, it was the right thing to do. She would just ignore Nora all day and get her hat when she got back to the trucks.

Andy's family didn't have as many calves to brand as the Taggers, so the day went by fast and they were done early.

Sadie had spent most of the day with Andy and his grandson. Andy's knees were bad and he walked with two crutches, but he got around fairly well. Lots of practice, he had joked with Sadie. She and Wade had taken turns giving Andy's grandson rides on Milo.

Nora was helping her mom and dad on the other side of the corral, so Sadie didn't have a problem ignoring her.

******

The calf, the hat, and then THE HORSE…

Nora walked over and did the final straw that made Sadie so mad she was sure she had steam coming out her ears.

As Nora and her parents walked up to Andy, Sadie was helping his grandson step off of Milo.

Sadie glanced over at Nora, just as her cousin turned to Uncle Scott and Aunt Jordan. "Everyone keeps saying that Milo is too small for Sadie now, but he would be perfect for Andy's grandson," Nora said sweetly.

The blood froze in Sadie's veins and she nearly dropped the grandson in question.

Sadie's eyes slowly went up to her uncle and aunt to see what their reactions were. They were a bit stunned, she decided. Maybe that was good.

"Really?" The grandson had overheard the comment. "I could have Milo for my own?"

Blood frozen… now heart stopped. Sadie looked down at the excited face of the young boy she had enjoyed all day…and suddenly hated him.

Her feet felt glued to the ground; she tried, but couldn't move from the cascading events that unfolded in front of her.

The grandson had run to Andy as excited as could be…Andy looked surprised at Uncle Scott and Aunt Jordan who were still stunned and had no idea what to say. Then Sadie's dad and mom walked up behind them.

"Great day," Her dad smiled. "What's going on here?"

Nora turned quickly to him. "They were discussing giving Milo to Andy's grandson since Sadie's too big."

To her horror, Sadie's father and mother smiled. They looked over at her and didn't recognize the emotional turmoil their daughter was in, and then, her dad said the worst possible thing at that moment.

"I think that's a great idea, Sadie." He looked over at the grandson. "Milo would be perfect for him. We don't have anyone smaller than Sadie and Wade, better for him here than using him at The Stables."

"Oh, YES!" Yelled the grandson who hugged his still stunned grandfather and happily ran over to Sadie and Milo.

Sadie slowly turned her gaze to the happy little boy…who was now stroking the face of his red horse named Milo.

Sadie's dazed eyes turned back to the small group. Andy, Uncle Scott and Aunt Jordan were looking at her in bewilderment. Her eyes lifted to her parents, who suddenly realized that it had not been what Sadie wanted. Their eyes instantly filled with regret and shock.

She didn't know what to do as she looked down at the young boy who was so happy to have his own horse. Sadie could remember the feeling like it was just yesterday…because her first horse was Milo. Tears started to sting the back of her eyes; she blinked hard to make them go away.

Hiding her face again with her hat, she reached over for the grandson's hand. There was no stopping this now; she couldn't say no even if they let her. She wouldn't break this little boy's heart like hers was now shattering.

"Well, let's give you another ride on your new horse," She managed to say with a shaking voice. Helping the little boy up onto her saddle, she turned and walked the boy around the horse corral. Once she was far enough away from the speechless group, and when the grandson couldn't see her, she let the tears fall.

CHAPTER EIGHT

They rode the horses back to the truck and trailers. Sadie was quiet as she rode. She no longer needed the rocking of Milo's footsteps to relax her; she was numb inside and didn't feel anything.

Grace and Reilly both tried to talk to her, but she ignored them and kept her gaze down in front of her.

As they got closer to the trucks she started looking for her hat. "Where was it?" She asked Grace.

"It was by the front tire of Uncle Scott's truck," Grace answered and was helping her look. "I don't see it."

Sadie didn't care what Nora thought, she jumped down off of Milo and pulled him to the front of the truck. There was no hat on the ground. She knelt down and looked under the truck; nothing. She turned and looked up at Grace who had stepped off her horse and came over to help.

"Sadie, look." She turned, her sister was pointing to the ground. There were animal tracks everywhere. Since Andy's sons used their own dogs for the roundup, Mavis and Bart were still at the ranch.

"Coyotes?" Sadie asked her sister with dread.

"Yeah, looks like they came to see what they could find and took your hat." Grace cautiously answered, "Don't freak out and yell again."

Sadie felt the tension and anger start at her feet and slowly rise throughout her whole body. She was sure the pressure behind her eyes was going to make them pop out.

"You're turning red," Grace whispered to her. "Stop before you explode."

"What's going on?" They heard their mother behind them. "What are you looking for?"

Sadie raised her eyes to her mother, then to Grace, hoping her sister would answer.

"Sadie's Tagger Enterprises hat," Grace said softly. "Nora threw it here as we left and it looks like coyotes took off with it."

To the sisters' surprise, their mother's hand came up and covered her suddenly closed eyes. Her lips tensed into a frown and she let out a long stressed breath. "We'll deal with this when we get back to the ranch." She turned and walked away from them.

Grace looked down at her sister, shrugged, and followed their mother.

Sadie stood there, staring after them. The anger had started to make her shake. Now her mother was mad at her. First her dad this morning, then Grace sticking up for her too; Nora was slowly tearing her apart, one family member at a time.

She walked Milo to the trailer and tied him. She took his saddle off then climbed into the tack room of the trailer and put her saddle away. She grabbed a brush and began brushing Milo for the last time.

Aunt Dru, Jack, and Nick were still helping push Andy's cows into their spring pasture so everyone was waiting for them to return.

Sadie ignored everyone that came up to tie their horses and put their tack away. The anger was beginning to eat away at her and she knew she would explode if she said anything.

"Nora, put your saddle away," Uncle Scott said from the other side of the trailer where their horses were tied.

Sadie took a mane brush and started working through Milo's hair. She normally didn't do it now, but she didn't have anything better to do.

"Nora, put your saddle away," She heard again.

She kept brushing, each stroke getting firmer and firmer; she was getting angrier with each mention of Nora's name.

Sadie looked up and over the horse's back and saw the three riders trotting in. Everyone had stepped to the front to wait for them.

"Nora, I'm not going to tell you again. Put your saddle away!" Uncle Scott said again.

Sadie lowered her arms; they were getting tired of the angry brushing.

Nora walked around the front of the trailer and looked back at her. She smiled sweetly, then turned and walked to the front of the trucks with everyone else.

The switch flipped and Sadie blew up. She stepped away from Milo and kicked the ground. She needed to walk. She took off with as long as strides as she could, and when she reached the last truck, which was Nick's, she turned and walked up the other side. No one was there; they were all up in front but Nora's saddle was still sitting on the ground next to her horse.

Sadie could hardly stand it. He had told her three times! Nora was getting away with everything!

Dusty, her hat, Milo, and now this! With each step towards the saddle, Sadie got madder at her cousin. She hated her! No matter what her mother said about the word, she hated her cousin at that moment. As she got closer to the saddle, she looked to the side of the road. There was an embankment that led to the rocky mountain hillside with a small ravine of brush and trees.

When Sadie's angry strides finally got her even with the saddle, she reached down with both hands and with all the fury and frustration racing through her body, she threw the saddle as high and far as she could. It disappeared into the brush and Sadie kept walking without looking back.

She rode back to the ranch with her parents and Grace. They rode in complete silence. Sadie was glad it wasn't very far back to the Tagger ranch house…until she envisioned the saddle flying through the air…then her stomach started to hurt.

***

Sadie walked slowly up to the horse trailer. Uncle Scott had climbed into the tack room of the trailer and was handing everyone their gear. Wade and Grace were in front of her and Reilly and Nora were behind her, waiting.

Uncle Scott helped Wade balance his saddle and pad in his arms. The bridle was tied over the saddle horn with the breast collar and cinch straps looped over so they didn't drag on the ground and trip him.

The same procedure was completed for Grace and she walked towards the barn. All gear would be put in the barn tonight. Tomorrow was a day off of riding for almost everyone so the horses could rest.

Sadie stepped next to the trailer and looked up at her uncle. He smiled down at her then turned into the trailer to get her gear. She felt the first pain of guilt. How could he smile at her when she threw his daughter's saddle into the ravine? Sadie felt like she was going to throw up.

"You OK?" Her uncle looked at her in concern.

"Yes," She tried to smile up at him as he lowered the saddle and pad into her arms. He made sure the cinches, breast collar, and stirrups were up. "Off you go, Little Lady," He winked at her. She felt the pain in her stomach again.

Sadie was halfway to the barn when she heard it. The words cut through her like a dagger of guilt.

"Nora! Where's your saddle?" It was Uncle Scott.

"It's in the trailer." Nora responded.

"No. It's not." He argued.

Sadie kept walking…hoping to get far enough away not to hear them.

"Dad, I don't know where it is," Nora told him.

Sadie walked faster; nearly running into the back of Grace.

"Slow down, Sadie," Grace said over her shoulder.

"But Dad…" Was the last thing Sadie heard from Nora as she stepped into the barn. She made as much noise as she could while hanging the saddle on its rack to drown out any more of the conversation.

"What's up with you?" Reilly said from behind her.

"Nothing…" She said and headed out the door as fast as she could and walked to the back corrals… away from the trailers.

She turned and nearly ran to the back of the barn, then turned the corner so no one could see her. She fell to the ground, pulling her knees up to her chin and wrapped her arms around them.

"What did I do?" Sadie yelled at herself in her head. "Why did I do that?"

Stomach pains started shooting through her. Her skin felt moist; like when she had the flu.

Then, she heard them again.

"I told you at least three times to put your saddle away," Uncle Scott said.

"I don't know what happened to it, Dad," Nora sounded like she was crying.

"Nick was in the last truck. If it was in the road he would have seen it."

"Maybe it's in the wrong trailer," Nora cried.

"Go look," He ordered her.

Sadie leaned her head back against the barn. Why? Why? Why? Why? She kept asking herself.

She was surprised at how scared she was, but she didn't feel like she needed to cry. Maybe it was because she was still mad at Nora? Listening to Nora and Uncle Scott made Sadie even more angry… but it was Sadie's fault now…not Nora's…now she was just confused.

"What do I do now?" Sadie asked herself. She needed to get up and get back to everyone before they found out she was gone. She stood quickly before she changed her mind and turned around the corner of the barn.

Nora was at the trailers with her parents. Hands on hips, Uncle Scott was glaring down at his daughter.

Sadie walked too fast towards the house and slowed herself down trying to act natural. I can't do this! She cried out in her head. This is awful! Her heart was racing.

She opened the door of the house quickly and closed the door to hide from the scene outside. It wasn't dinner time yet, but Cora had baked a special surprise for them. Sadie paused, took a deep breath, and walked into the kitchen where everyone was gathered eating apple pie and homemade vanilla ice cream.

Cora handed Sadie a plate and she quickly walked through the kitchen and into the dining room. She found Wade and sat next to him. Neither spoke as they ate their food. When Wade was done, he looked over at Sadie. Her dish was almost full.

"Aren't you hungry?" Wade asked her.

"Not too much," Sadie told him. Her guilt pains were soaring through her stomach. The first bite had hit her stomach and nearly came back.

"Do you want mine?"

"Do you really have to ask?" Wade giggled and they traded plates.

Sadie stood and walked back to the kitchen. She tried to look through the door to see where Nora was, but all she could see were the trailers. Handing her plate back to Cora, she smiled politely and thanked her.

"Wow, that was fast," Cora chuckled. "Did you get enough? There is more."

"No thanks, it was very good, Cora." Sadie smiled. "Do you need help cleaning up?" Sadie needed something to do to keep her mind busy.

Cora looked around, which made Sadie look around. The kitchen was spotless. "I baked last night and cleaned up breakfast after everyone left this morning."

"Then what did you do?" Sadie asked curiously.

"Well, I went out and played with my colt, did some computer updating on the ranch horses, fed the calf a couple times, and then read a bit." Cora answered.

"How come you don't come with us?"

"Well, I don't know," Cora chuckled. "I guess I could have since everything was done. I could have come over in between calf feedings."

"Maybe at late branding I can help you get everything ready before hand and you can come help. Andy's daughter-in-laws prepares all the food the night before and put stuff in coolers. She serves lunch out of her horse trailer." Sadie looked up at Cora. "I would help you prepare and get things ready at lunch time so you can come with us."

"Sadie," Cora shook her head at her. "You are the nicest young lady I've ever met."

Sadie's heart dropped…she knew that wasn't true anymore, but she tried hard to keep the smile on her face. "Is that a yes?" Sadie asked.

"Let me talk it over with the Trio and see what they think," She nodded. "I think I would enjoy helping out."

Sadie headed for the door as soon as she could. Uncle Scott and Nora were walking into the house. Opening the door for them, she stepped backwards so they could walk through first.

"Thanks, Sadie," Her uncle said and walked into the kitchen.

Nora turned and glared at her as she walked through.

Sadie nearly ran for the bunkhouse and climbed up into her bed. She lay as flat and as still as possible.

"I can't do this," She whispered to herself. Her head began to hurt and her pulse was racing. "I think I'm going to explode." Her stomach was still hurting.

The door to the bunkhouse opened. Sadie tried to sink farther into the bed and just disappear.

"You aren't getting pie and ice cream until we find your saddle, and I don't need it around my waist. Now sit down." It was Aunt Jordan.

"Mom, I don't know what to say. I don't know where it is." Nora pleaded.

"Did you put it in the horse trailer?"

"It should be in there."

"Did you put it in the horse trailer?"

"Mom, you just asked me that."

"Did you put it in the horse trailer?"

Silence.

Sadie felt like throwing up. Why did this happen? Why did she throw the saddle? Her eyes started to hurt more from the pressure behind them.

"Did you put it in the horse trailer?" Aunt Jordan repeated again. Each time she said it her voice was lower and firmer. Sadie knew she was getting angry.

"Mom!" Nora cried out. "You just…"

"Nora Cheyenne Tagger…answer yes or no, nothing else."

The middle name…that was bad…Nora didn't answer.

"Nora, one more time, did you put it in the horse trailer?" Aunt Jordan's voice was eerily calm. Sadie had never heard her like that before. "Yes or no."

"No," Nora finally answered.

"Alright then," Aunt Jordan exhaled. "Do you know what happened to it?"

"No. It was behind the truck. I put the saddle pad and bridle away then forgot the saddle."

"Your dad told you at least three times to put the saddle away. You didn't remember then?"

"I don't know what happened," Nora continued to try and worm her way out of trouble.

"Nora, if we can't find the saddle, we have to buy a new one."

Sadie's heart sunk and felt the dagger of guilt stab her in the gut again. Having to replace the saddle had never crossed her mind. They cost a lot of money. Again, the pressure behind her eyes made her squint. Her hand lay over her stomach, trying to calm the turmoil inside her.

"I don't know what to do," Nora whimpered.

Sadie couldn't take it. The anger she felt for Nora was still there, but the guilt was overwhelming. Now, Aunt Jordan and Uncle Scott were going to have to buy her a new saddle and they would hate Sadie for that. Her hands began to shake. How can people do this? This was the worst feeling ever. Anger, fear, guilt, and misery swirled and stabbed in her stomach. She couldn't even throw up to get rid of it. She knew what she had to do…

"I did it!" Sadie sat straight up and yelled. She looked down at Aunt Jordan, expecting anger…but she wasn't there…neither was

Nora. Sadie glanced around the bunkhouse. No one was there. She had confessed to an empty room. She fell back on the bed.

"Why?" She said out loud. "I just can't take this stress."

She slowly rolled over and slid down off the bed and sat on the lower bunk. She had to tell them she threw the saddle into the ravine.

Sadie rose and walked slowly to the door. Her boots felt like they were full of lead and they drug on the floor as she walked. At the door, she grabbed the handle and slowly turned it. The door felt full of lead, too. She stepped through and down the first couple steps.

"Sadie! There you are." It was her mom standing over by the barn.

Sadie looked around and didn't see anyone else, "Were you looking for me?" She asked.

"Come into the barn," She yelled and turned into the building.

Sadie hesitated. Everyone would be in the barn. She didn't want to admit her guilt in front of everyone, just to her mom and dad. They could tell Aunt Jordan and Uncle Scott so she didn't have to see their anger and disappointment.

Having no other choice, Sadie walked towards the barn in her lead filled boots.

It was worse than she thought….it was a family meeting. Literally everyone was there including Cora, Jessup, and Nick!

As she walked in the room, she looked for Wade, he was the safest to sit with. He moved over on the bale of straw to make room for her.

"OK, now that we're all here," Uncle Scott started. "Everyone knows we've been looking for Nora's saddle. It didn't just disappear. Can everyone think back to what they were doing when we got to the trailers? Did anyone see Nora's saddle at the back of my truck?"

"I saw it," Reilly admitted. "But you were telling Nora to put it away, so I left it there."

Everyone else said the same thing. Except Sadie; she didn't say anything because she didn't want to lie again. She also didn't want to admit her guilt in front of everyone so she looked down at the ground.

"Maybe it ended up in one of Andy's trailers," Grace suggested.

"Sadie," It was her dad and the sound of his voice made her feel ill again. She took a deep breath and looked up at him. "Did you see the saddle?" She nodded slowly. "Do you know what happened to it?"

This was it, all she had to do was say yes and it would be all over with…but the punishment…just say yes, she told herself. Out of the corner of her eye she saw Nora, then to Sadie's surprise, she looked right over her dad's right ear, so she wasn't looking in his eyes, and said, "No."

Sadie hesitated then looked over at Wade. He was playing with his lariat again, running his finger around the coil. She silently watched his finger and tried to tune out the rest of the conversation.

She did it again…she lied. How could she do it again? She was coming out to tell the truth. She lied again!

As Wade stood, so did she without looking at anyone else. Wade turned to her, "Let's go check on Dusty."

CHAPTER NINE

Sadie lay on top of the bed, as close to the edge as she could get. On her stomach, head resting on her arm, she looked around the dark room. They had been in bed for hours, but she couldn't sleep even though she was exhausted.

Her eyes moved down to see Nikki in the bed below her. She and Matt arrived right after the family meeting. Sadie and Wade had stayed in the barn with Dusty until dinner, then quickly went back to the barn until bedtime so she didn't have to talk to anyone else. She didn't even go out and see Little Ghost.

There were little lights on the coffee pot, microwave, and the cell phone chargers that illuminated the small kitchen area. The light outside the main door lit up the other side of the room. The middle of the room was the darkest and that was where Sadie was laying.

Tomorrow was the big horse meeting where they would talk about what was best for each of the horses. To test how cowy the horses were some of the adults were going to get a dozen yearling heifers and bring them to the fall branding corrals. They would then put a couple of the Tagger herd in with the cows, a few at a time, so the horses could interact with the cows. Afterwards, they would have the meeting.

Sadie flipped over onto her back. She knew Aunt Dru was going to work on getting her Scarecrow, but now Sadie wasn't sure that was the right thing. Taking the saddle and throwing it into the ravine was basically stealing the saddle from Nora. So she lay in bed as a liar and thief. Two things she never, ever, thought she would be. She didn't deserve Scarecrow. She didn't deserve Little Ghost. She didn't deserve anything.

She rolled over and faced the wall. She was still mad at Nora but knew the best thing for Cora's colt was Nora to show him. With Nora's talent and the colt's looks they could win just about any show. In a couple years, when both were more experienced, they would be unbeatable. Sadie was sure of that.

She rolled over onto her stomach and realized she had been there for hours feeling guilty and nauseous. Lying to her dad was worse than throwing the saddle into the ravine. She couldn't imagine how he would feel when he found out she lied.

Uncle Scott and Aunt Jordan were going to be upset, too. They were going to have to replace the saddle.

Then she got an idea. She flipped over onto her back.

"Sadie, quit moving or I'm going to tie you down," She heard Nikki's voice from below her.

"Sorry," Sadie whispered.

The one thing that Sadie could do was get the saddle back. Maybe the disappointment from her dad wouldn't be so bad. He could be a little happy that she made the effort to right the wrong and the saddle wouldn't have to be replaced.

She started to roll again then froze and lay back down; Nikki's threat fresh in her mind.

Andy's corrals weren't that far away from the Tagger ranch house. The ravine was only about a half hour ride away. So it would take her an hour. She could do that easily on Milo; even by herself. After Wade's accident they had all promised they wouldn't sneak out of the bunkhouse at night. She wouldn't be breaking that promise, because it would be daylight.

Just after daylight, her dad would be going down to get the cows. They would have to round up the cows, load them, and then haul them back. So, she could get to the ravine and back before he found out.

Anyone left in the bunkhouse would still be sleeping or they would think she went with her dad. She could be there and back before anyone realized it. For the rest of the night she lay quietly perfecting her plan and mapping out the road from the ranch house to the ravine. She had ridden it before many times when they went on trail rides.

She heard a ticking noise in the distance and opened her eyes. She had fallen asleep somewhere in the night while making her plans. The smell of coffee would be next, which meant her dad would be up at any second. She laid perfectly still, waiting.

It didn't take long; the smell of the coffee reached her just as the sound of someone getting out of bed did. Keeping her eyes closed, so they wouldn't know she was awake, footsteps walked past her bed and into the kitchen and then a couple more sets of footsteps. Sadie worked hard on keeping her breathing soft and slow while she patiently waited for them to leave the room. Her heart was beating fast.

Finally, they walked past her again and out the door. She flipped over on her stomach and looked around the room. No one was moving. Bart and Mavis were curled up at the foot of Nikki and Matt's beds. She slid over the side of the bed, careful not to wake Nikki or disturb Mavis, then made her way down to the bathroom, grabbing her clothes on the way. When she stepped back out of the bathroom, she looked around to make sure no one else was awake. No one moved.

She slid on her boots and looked at the jackets lined up on the wall of pegs. The only one that fit her was Nora's denim jacket. She grabbed it and her cowboy hat, then, as quietly as she could, turned the door knob. She looked into the bunkhouse one more time…no one moved so she stepped out and closed the door.

The sound of the truck starting made her freeze next to the door. She turned slowly and looked in their direction. The truck was beginning to move. She waited until it was out of sight before turning and running to the barn and Milo.

Sadie had the horse saddled faster than she ever had before; thankful that he was easy to bridle. She kept the halter on underneath the bridle. She would have to lead him away from the barn and it was better to lead with the halter than with the bridle.

Her plan was to drop down behind the barn so if Milo whinnied as they were leaving it would sound like the other horses.

She checked her saddle bags; they still had a few granola bars in them but no water. She checked everyone else's bags and excitedly found two full bottles. Then she saw a lariat on the wall. She didn't know why she would need it but grabbed it anyway. She was good to go.

Sadie led Milo out the back of the barn and headed along the corral. The Tagger Herd came running to the side and kept pace with them. To keep them quiet, she talked to them as they walked.

When they passed the last corner post and kept moving, the herd whinnied a few times then turned back to the barn. She led Milo down the mountain in case he let out another whinny. The sound would be lost into the mountains and not up to the bunkhouse.

She walked, leading Milo, until he quit trying to head back to the barn. Once she stepped into the stirrup and swung her leg over the saddle they were ready to go. Her nervous energy fed his excitement. She headed down the road at a trot.

The sun was up enough to lighten the hillside and road, but there was no sun beaming down on her. The wind was chilly but her energy kept her warm.

Sadie was nervous about riding out on the road and mountainside alone, but she was more scared about not making it back in time and getting caught.

As she trotted down the road she felt the fresh air on her face and finally felt like she was doing something right, even if her parents would say it was totally wrong.

Two more turns and one long stretch, Sadie told herself. Just as she came around the first corner a dozen deer suddenly lifted their heads and stared at her. Milo didn't flinch but Sadie's heart did. She was working hard on not thinking about the bears and mountain lions she had seen at the ranch. Milo would be able to smell them and would let her know if they were near.

She took a few deep breathes to calm her nerves and kept Milo moving. According to her calculations she was ahead of her timeline. She hadn't planned on trotting so much but Milo was handling it well. He could rest when she got there and was recovering the saddle from the ravine.

Around the second corner, Sadie prepared herself for another herd of deer but none were there. Her heart started racing. To the left, the trees ended and opened up to flat treeless grass land. To her right, the road dropped off to treeless mountain side. She could see her destination in the far distance; the ravine that held brush and a couple trees that dropped off to the bare mountain.

Sadie slowed Milo down to a walk to judge his breathing just like her dad had taught her. He was breathing fast but not hard. She started trotting again. The sooner she got back the better.

She quickly looked behind, but saw nothing but the road and trees she had just passed.

The ravine was getting closer. Her excitement got the best of her and she kicked Milo into a gallop. He didn't hesitate and took off. Her heart was racing, knowing her destination was near. She quickly glanced behind again and thought she saw something so she pulled up the reins and made Milo stop. Pushing the reins against his neck she turned him to look in the direction they had just come; nothing moved.

"It's my imagination playing tricks on me." Sadie told Milo as they began to trot again.

Relief ran through her as she finally reached the ravine. Looking around she realized there was nowhere to tie him up at the road like she had planned. There was nothing but dirt and rocks where they were. The trees were too far away.

"You'll have to go down with me." She told the horse. Removing the lead rope from the saddle she hooked it to the halter and led the horse off the side of the road equal to where she thought the saddle may be.

Gripping the lead rope tightly she walked into the brush and trees as far as the rope would let her before she finally saw the saddle. It didn't drop all the way to the ground it was stuck half way in a small tree.

"Dang it, Milo," She mumbled. That was unexpected. Now what?

If she could crawl underneath the brush, she might be able to reach the saddle; *IF* she could get directly under it. She led Milo farther down the hillside until she found a strong branch that she could tie him to. If he got away, he would run the full distance home…without her. She would have to carry the saddle and would be caught by everyone.

As she tied the horse on the branch, she looked him square in the eye. "Don't leave. Stay put, please!" She rubbed his nose a few times then walked back up to the brush that led to the stuck saddle.

She took off her cowboy hat and set it aside, then, crawling on the ground, she slowly made her way into the brush. Small branches stuck out and grabbed her hair and jacket. She had to keep reaching up and releasing her hair from the sticks. Part way in, the brush turned into one of the thorn bushes.

"Dang it…" She muttered. The thorns were at least an inch long and really hurt when they dug into the skin. They easily penetrated jeans. That's why they always wore chaps on their legs when they rode. She was going to have to go around the dangerous bush.

She crawled in about half way and looked up, just a couple more feet and she could reach it. It was hard to stand up, but a stirrup had dropped far enough she could reach it. When she pulled, the saddle didn't move. She looped her arm all the way through the stirrup and lifted her feet off the ground. Even with her full weight the saddle wouldn't budge.

She was going to need Milo's strength too, so she quickly retraced her path. The horse was standing quietly where she left him.

Relief ran through her as she realized that the lariat was exactly what she needed to reach the saddle.

"We gotta hurry, Milo," She said and placed the loop of the lariat around the saddle horn, tightening it as best she could. He wouldn't leave if he felt the tension on the saddle. Stretching out the lariat as she crawled, she made her way back to the saddle. All the while hoping it was long enough. She stood again and could easily reach the stirrup. She sighed in relief!

Sadie quickly ran the end of the rope through the stirrup and tied a knot. Dropping back down to crawl out, she felt the jacket get caught on something. In a hurry, she yanked hard to get it loose and heard the denim rip. Her heart sunk. Now she had ruined Nora's jacket. She let out a big sigh and, telling herself to worry about it later, continued to crawl.

As she made her way out of the brush, she looked up to see Milo staring at her. She stroked his nose then whispered softly. "Alright

Milo, here we go." She made the horse backup until the lariat pulled tight. "Please hold," She muttered and made the horse back up more. He started to balk as the pressure got too tight. She kept pushing him back.

Finally, she heard a crack of brush and the tension on the line decreased.

"Keep going Milo, you can do this." She turned him, so he was facing away from the saddle and could use his full strength.

Again there was the crack and pops and she turned in time to see the saddle appear out of the brush. A huge sigh of relief escaped her.

Sadie ran back to it and her heart sunk again. There were deep scratches across the whole seat of the saddle. The leather skirt in the back had a long deep gouge. She'd never thought about it getting damaged. Now she wondered if she should take it back or not.

Was a damaged saddle better than no saddle? Sadie guessed yes.

She left it hooked to the rope so she could have Milo pull it up to the road.

Sadie led the horse up the hill and turned to watch the saddle. As soon as they reached the top, Milo's head went up and he looked around. She did a quick glance to see what he was looking at and couldn't see anything. She was in a hurry, so she turned back to her mission. She led him down the road until the saddle appeared over the hillside.

She held onto the reins and unhooked the lead rope from the halter and looped it onto the horn of Nora's damaged saddle. Holding the end of the rope, she stepped in the stirrup and mounted her horse. Then, she pulled up on the rope to lift the saddle next to her. For the second time that week, she was thankful that Milo was short. Looping the rope around her own saddle horn, she secured Nora's saddle to hers. She coiled the lariat and attached it to the other side of the saddle.

Sadie kicked Milo into a walk to make sure everything was going to hold. The saddle dug into her leg but she didn't have a choice; she needed to start moving.

She took off at a trot and tried to get her mind off the horn digging into her leg.

Milo would need no directions; he knew how to get home.

As she rode, she looked down at the leather. There were some deep scratches that would never come out. She guessed they came from the thorn bush. The gouge would be from a limb of the brush or tree where it broke through.

Sadie's excitement began to drain from her. This wasn't what she had expected. In her plans, she was going to return the saddle as good as new. That was supposed to help with the guilt, but this didn't. The damage to the saddle made it worse and the rip in Nora's jacket doubled the disappointment. She reached under her arm where the jacket was ripped. The tear was all the way down the side. The jacket was ruined.

Sadie sighed; there was nothing she could do about it now.

When she neared the house again, she dropped down the side of the mountain that led to the back of the barn. The herd of horses met her again and walked next to them at the fence. Sadie dropped the saddle at the back of the barn and slid off of Milo. She quickly took off his tack.

She glanced into the barn to make sure no one was there. It was quiet; no sign of anyone. She led Milo in and quickly brushed him to remove the signs of sweat on him. She grabbed a towel and wiped him down, then led him to his corral hoping he would roll and the dirt would cover the wet hair.

She headed to the back of the barn and grabbed her saddle and put it to the tack room. Then returned for Nora's damaged one. What to do with it? She couldn't just give it back and admit what she did now that it was damaged. Not knowing what else to do she put it in the tack room where it should have been all along.

Sadie glanced down at Dusty to see if she had eaten. The calf was sleeping, it didn't seem to care about the noise she had created returning Milo and the tack.

Peeking out the side door, she saw no one moving so she slid out and headed for …she stopped. What's she supposed to do now? She hadn't thought of that.

If someone saw her out here there would be no doubt when they found the saddle that she had something to do with it.

How was she going to get out of this?

CHAPTER TEN

Sadie realized Mavis and Bart weren't outside. The first thing anyone did when they woke up in the bunkhouse was to let the two dogs out. She had seen them when she left so she knew they weren't with the group collecting cows.

She could take the two dogs down to the fall branding corrals and wait for everyone to arrive. They might even be there by the time she made it. If she was that far away from the barn, they wouldn't think she had anything to do with the saddle's return.

Taking the chance the dogs were still in the bunkhouse she quickly hurried to the door and quietly turned the knob. Once the door was open far enough, she saw Mavis' head appear. Sadie breathed a sigh of relief and let the two dogs out.

Without hesitation, she took off running down the road towards the big corner that led to the corrals. Mavis and Bart were running excitedly around her. When she turned the corner she stopped to relax her breathing since her heart was racing from the fear of getting caught and the run. There was no one at the corrals yet so she took off running again. Mavis and Bart realized where she was going and took off in front of her.

When she arrived, she looked down at her shirt and pants and tried to wipe away all the dirt from crawling into the brush. She took off the ripped jacket and placed it over the top rail next to the loading chute. Hopefully, Nora would ignore it and not see the tear.

There was water in the trough, so she quickly washed her face and hands of all the dirt from the crawl and ride. She tried to smooth out her shredded braid with water then placed her hat on her head to hide the messy hair. Then she heard them…the truck and trailer were almost back.

Sadie made her way to the gate by the road and opened it in preparation for unloading the cows. Aunt Dru's truck appeared and Sadie waved when she saw her. Her stomach hurt from the stress of wondering if she was going to get away with the mission.

"Oh, I hate this," Sadie whispered to herself as her aunt backed the trailer full of cows up to the gate.

Her dad appeared at the back of the trailer to help.

"You're up early again," He commented as he opened the back of the trailer.

Sadie didn't say anything. She just stepped back and crawled on the fence to watch the cows make their way into the corrals.

She felt the dagger of guilt plunging into her stomach and the pressure in her head made her eyes hurt. The longer she sat there, watching the adults unload the cows, the worse she felt. She climbed down from the fence and walked the length of the corral so she was on the opposite side of the trailers. Stepping up on the bottom rail, she leaned her arms over the top.

Sadie watched the cows as her stomach churned and her heart saddened at what she did. She was supposed to feel better after retrieving the saddle but she felt worse. Her eyes locked onto a rock in the corral and she stood there staring at it. All she could hear were the cows mooing. She was in a remorseful daze.

She felt her hat being lifted off her head but didn't even jump even though it startled her; she was that numb. Glancing over, she saw her Aunt Dru set her cowboy hat on the post and reach over and place a new blue Tagger Enterprises hat on Sadie's head. Her braid was pulled out the back hole.

Sadie leaned her head to the side and looked up at her aunt. "Thank you," She said loud enough to be heard over the cows.

"You feeling OK?" Her aunt leaned against the fence. Her eyes reflected her concern.

Sadie shook her head. Finally something honest, she sighed.

"Get up too early?"

Sadie didn't reply, she just turned back to the cows feeling the depression and fear take over. This was her chance to confess, but now she didn't want to see the disappointment on their faces because she damaged Nora's saddle and ripped her coat. She leaned her chin on her hands and wondered what to do.

Aunt Dru turned and walked away without a word. Sadie watched her walk all the way back to the trailers.

"I should have told her…too late now," She looked back at the stock trailers.

She saw the parade of horses appear on the road. All of the Tagger Herd was there. Her mom was walking Little Ghost. Sadie climbed down off the fence and walked to meet up with them.

The herd had been across the fence from cows before but never in the same corral. Sadie had been looking forward to testing the cow sense of the horses but now she just felt numb.

The herd filled the side corral and the cows the back corral. Nick and Jessup pushed half the cows into the front corral. Matt and Nikki led Trooper and Harvey in with the small herd and let them go. The horses stared at the cows, then slowly approached them.

Trooper snorted then pawed at the ground. Harvey pranced next to him excitedly. After a few minutes of smelling the cows and snorting at them, Trooper laid his ears back and pushed at them with his nose. Harvey still continued to dance until one of the cows mistakenly walked towards her and she whipped around and quickly kicked out at the cow; just barely missing it. Both reactions from the horses were positive…it's what they were looking for.

"Catch 'em up." Sadie's dad told a pleased Matt and Nikki.

The next in the pen were Rufio and Cooper. Both horses walked excitedly to the cows and started pushing them around with their noses and an angry look in their eyes. With smiles, Jack and Reilly quickly caught them so the next set of horses could be let loose.

Sadie held onto Little Ghost's lead rope tightly. She turned her face into his neck to keep from watching Nora and Uncle Scott walk Scarecrow and Arcturus into the corral. She heard everyone chuckle. Peeking around her grey horse's head she saw Scarecrow eating what grass she could find and Arcturus prancing excitedly through the cows…he didn't like them at all. Arcturus scared a cow into Scarecrow's direction…the palomino filly turned her butt to the cow and threatened to kick…while still eating. Giggles erupted from Nora. Sadie felt the resentment for her cousin build inside her again.

Nick and Jessup quickly moved the herd of cows to another corral and pushed in the other half of the herd.

Eli and Buttercup were next. Eli walked right over to Sadie's dad and stood quietly watching the cows. Everyone erupted in laughter. Sadie could almost muster a half chuckle at the darn horse.

Buttercup walked tentatively up to the cows, then backed up quickly. Gaining a little courage she walked closer and snorted at them. All the cows jumped back, which made Buttercup jump back. Her legs spread wide apart, she was ready to flee at any moment. The cream colored horse looked back at the buckskin, as if looking for help. Eli stood quietly next to his human.

"You have a friend, Grayson," Uncle Scott laughed.

Her dad stroked the horse's neck, then he led him out of the corral. Grace quickly reassured her horse that everything was OK and led Buttercup out of the pen and away from the scary cows.

Little Ghost and Cora's colt were next. Sadie walked her grey horse into the corral. When she stopped, she leaned in and whispered in his ear, "Go show them who's boss."

Sadie unhooked the lead rope from the halter and stepped away from the horse. He turned his head and looked at her. She swung the rope in the direction of the cows. The grey horse turned and walked past Cora's colt that just stood quietly staring at the cows.

Sadie quickly admired the stance and look of the colt, then turned her attention to Little Ghost. The horse walked straight up to the cows and snorted at them. The small herd turned away from the intruder, only to have the intruder jump at them and block the direction they had tried to run. The group around the corral let out a round of gasps. Sadie watched silently, a glimmer of pride rose in her.

As the cows headed in the other direction, Little Ghost trotted beside them and lowered his head to stop them and pushed them the other way. The horse stopped and watched them for a moment, then when the cows moved too far away, he quickly ran over at the lead cow and scared it back the other way. The grey horse was herding the cows around the corral, without any direction from anyone. It reminded Sadie of Milo and the red cow.

Sadie was amazed at her beautiful Little Ghost and so was everyone else. She took a few long strides into the corral then yelled his name, "Little Ghost!" He stopped, turned and looked at her, then with a buck and a swift kick towards the cows he trotted up to her; pushing her shoulder with his nose. She leaned her head against his and stroked the curve of his jaw. "Good boy," She whispered to him, closing her eyes and momentarily blocking out everyone around them.

Sadie smiled politely to everyone as they expressed their astonishment. She clicked the lead rope back onto the halter so she could lead her remarkable horse out of the corral. Cora led her colt out behind her.

She stepped out and past Wade, who was waiting with Dollar. Rooster was tied up to the fence watching the commotion. He wouldn't be taking a turn; they didn't want to take the chance he would hurt his legs.

"That was awesome!" Wade grinned at her. Sadie forced a smile at him and turned to watch him walk his red horse into the corral.

Little Ghost stood at attention and watched Dollar, too. Sadie leaned against him and hoped the red horse would interact with the cows also. He did. The horse walked up and through the cows sniffing and snorting at the herd; making them run back and forth. The horse just walked curiously around the cows. Wade turned and smiled back at his dad. That was a good sign, Dollar wouldn't be afraid of the cows he would be chasing in the future.

Her cousin turned further around and looked at Sadie. He grinned at her, then turned back and yelled his horses name like Sadie had done with Little Ghost.

"Dollar!"

Dollar just kept sniffing and snorting at the cows.

Wade shrugged and headed out to get his horse. Uncle Scott stopped him and took the lead rope. Wade watched his dad wander through the cows and catch Dollar. After leading the horse through the cows, his dad handed him the lead rope and Wade stroked his horse's nose and praised him as they left the corral.

"Take them back up to the barn corral and we'll meet after lunch." Aunt Dru yelled to the kids and everyone turned to follow her directions.

Sadie walked the other way.

"Where are you going?" Her mom asked as Sadie walked past her.

"My cowboy hat is on the other side. I forgot to grab it," Sadie answered and kept walking.

Little Ghost walked patiently beside her as she rounded the corner and headed to the hat. She wished she could just keep going…a walk in the meadow with Little Ghost…she really needed that. Instead, she grabbed the hat and returned. Everyone but her mom had left.

They walked quietly a moment before her mother spoke.

"That was an impressive little show Little Ghost put on."

Sadie nodded. She knew she should be enjoying the moment, but the depression and anxiety of the morning was making her stomach turn. When they got back to the barns someone might find the saddle in the tack room and the thought of it made her want to throw up. Her neck and back hurt from the stress.

This was the moment she was waiting for. She should tell her mother everything since they were alone but wanting to have a few moments of normalcy she reached out and grabbed her mom's hand as they walked down the road. Her mom on one side and Little Ghost on the other, Sadie took a deep breath and enjoyed the moment. It would be gone soon enough.

CHAPTER ELEVEN

Her mom walked into the house to help Cora with lunch, as Sadie walked Little Ghost back out to the corrals. The other kids had let their horses loose and were sitting on the fence talking excitedly about the results of their "cow test".

Matt held the gate open for her as she walked through. His hand came out and stroked the horse as they made their way into the corral. "He did great Sadie and your calling to him was just the kicker." Matt chuckled looking down at her.

Sadie stopped and smiled politely at him. "Thanks," Her voice was low and bland.

Matt cocked his head to the side, confused at her lack of enthusiasm. "What's wrong?"

She stared at him, finally realizing she could tell him. He would understand doing stupid things…he was only 19…close to being a kid.

"I did something stupid," She pleaded with her eyes for him to understand. "I got really mad and …."

She saw Nora walking up to them. She quickly closed her mouth and gritted her teeth as the cousin's sweet smile hit her like a slap in her face.

"Did you see Scarecrow?" Nora laughed. "She didn't care about the cows until they tried to get her food!"

Sadie glanced up at Matt; he was still watching her. She shook her head and walked away from Nora.

As she slid the halter off the grey horse's head, the images of his dance with the calves in the corral played in her mind. He truly was a great horse. A horse that a liar and a thief didn't deserve. The pains shot through her stomach again and they made their way to her heart. She watched him walk away and join the other horses. Her eyes went to the golden Scarecrow. She didn't deserve her either.

"That was fun," Nora said walking up next to her. Sadie was taller than Nora so when Sadie turned to her, she looked down into her cousin's dark eyes.

Sadie's mind went back to the day before; the calf, the hat, and Milo. The anger started rising in her. It was Nora's fault she no longer deserved the horses. If she hadn't been so mean, then Sadie wouldn't have been so angry and thrown the saddle.

"Why do you look so mad?" Nora asked her innocently. "That was fun and Scarecrow was hilarious."

Sadie looked down at the pain in her hand and realized she was squeezing the rope so hard it hurt. The best thing to do was leave, quickly, so she did just that.

"What is your problem?" Nora asked as Sadie walked away.

Sadie kept walking until she got to the house. She knew she couldn't get away with not going in and having lunch, so she stepped through the door.

"It's in the tack room?" She heard Nikki ask in surprise.

Sadie's blood ran cold…they found it.

"Yeah," Matt answered. "No clue how it got there, scratches all across it like it had a battle with a cat."

Sadie forced herself to walk up to Cora and take the plate she was holding out for her.

"What now?" Nikki asked.

Matt shrugged and they walked into the dining room. Sadie walked numbly to the table, knowing she was going to have to listen to questions about the saddle.

To her surprise, as she set her plate down and slid in the chair, Nick walked over and sat next to her.

"Little Ghost did great," He smiled at her.

She forced a smile and nodded.

"How long have you been calling him like he was a puppy?" He teased. His brownish green eyes twinkled and made her feel a little better.

Sadie was surprised when a giggle escaped her.

"I started that in the stall last year when it was just the two of us. Then, when he started out in the pasture, he came to me, too," She explained. "I wouldn't give him a treat unless he walked over to me when I called him."

"Ah…so there was a trick," He laughed. "That's a pretty smart horse when he can learn like that. You could have a trick horse in the rodeo."

Sadie shook her head. "I'd rather ride and rope with him."

"I've seen you out practicing in the arena; you're getting pretty good for your age. I'm not much of a roper," Nick admitted.

Sadie looked at him in surprise. "Really?"

Nick pointed at himself, "Bull rider," and Sadie giggled again. "Most bull riders don't rope the bull….and if they do…they're…."

"Crazy?" Sadie finished his sentence with a grin.

He grinned back. "That's more polite than what I was going to say, so we'll stick with crazy."

She took tentative bites of her lunch as Nick told her about the trick horses he'd seen at the rodeos when he was bull riding. It was a nice break from the stressful morning.

Unfortunately, it ended way too soon as her Aunt Dru yelled out to the kids to meet her in the bunkhouse.

"Sounds like it's time for you to head out." Nick rose and glanced down at her. "It was a pleasure talking to you, young lady." He smiled and turned away.

Sadie hesitated, then slowly rose and walked into the kitchen to put away her plate.

Grace walked up behind her and pushed her through the kitchen and out the door. "Let's go!"

Aunt Dru made sure all the kids from Nikki down to Sadie were in the room plus Cora, Aunt Jordan, and Sadie's mother before she closed the door. She took a chair and sat in the aisle while everyone else made themselves comfortable sitting on the beds. Sadie and her mom sat at the end of Nikki's bed with Matt and Grace playfully pushing at each other in front of her on his bed.

"Well, that was a fun little experiment this morning wasn't it?" Aunt Dru grinned at everyone. They all agreed with smiles. "We all know what we're here for; to make sure the right horse is with the right person and the right activity." They all nodded. "Anyone want to start?"

Sadie looked at the ground. As excited as she was for this day to happen, it was here, and she dreaded the whole thing. She quickly glanced up at Aunt Dru, who was looking around the crowd and stopped on her. Sadie looked back down again. Every fiber inside her wanted to get up and leave.

"Dad and I are going to share Eli," Grace started. "He'll use him here and he'll be my backup roping horse."

Aunt Dru smiled. "I think Eli had more of a say on that one."

"Dollar did good with the cows," Waded added excitedly. "He's my roping horse. Sadie, Nora, and I will be sharing Rooster as a practice horse. He can stand or walk while we practice throwing a rope off him."

Aunt Dru smiled. "He's going to do a great job at that." Everyone nodded.

"Anyone else have any changes they suggest?" Aunt Dru said and Sadie knew she was talking to her but kept her eyes down. She knew she should answer but she just couldn't get herself to do it.

"Sadie," Her aunt prompted her.

Sadie looked at her aunt who was waiting patiently; her eyes calm but determined. Instead of looking at Nora, Sadie turned to Cora. "I…Aunt Dru and I were watching the horses the other day…" She hesitated then did what was best for the horse and Cora. "Your colt is magnificent," Cora smiled and nodded, "I was thinking that Nora should be showing him."

Sadie heard Nora's intake of breath.

Cora looked at her in surprise then turned to Nora. "Would you be interested?"

"YES!" Nora cried out. "Oh YES! He would be awesome!"

Sadie looked back down at the ground with her cousin's happy words stabbing her in the heart.

"I can use him for showing, Arcturus for English and Scarecrow for Western competitions," Nora nearly yelled in her excitement.

Sadie closed her eyes at the greed of her cousin. It flipped her angry switch. In a flash, everything from the moment she saw Nora feeding Dusty to her giving away Milo ran through her head and she jumped up and spun to her cousin.

"Are you freaking kidding me!?" Sadie exploded.

"Sadie!" Aunt Dru and her mother both admonished her.

"You are a horrible selfish bully!" Sadie snarled; the anger taking over again. Nora looked at her in shock, her eyes wide and mouth dropped open.

Sadie felt her arm being tugged by her mother, but yanked it out of her grip. She felt the fire coursing through her body.

"Sadie!" Her mother grabbed her again and sat her down.

Sadie's whole body was stiff from anger; the pressure behind her eyes was intense.

Once she made sure Sadie was going to remain quiet, her aunt spoke.

"Nora, you are not going to have three horses," She stated flatly. Aunt Dru's voice was firm, yet calm. Sadie couldn't tell if she was upset at her or Nora.

"OK…" Nora said hesitantly. "Cora's colt for showing and …Scarecrow for western pleasure and trail."

Sadie gritted her teeth and her hands where clenched in a tight fist…her body shaking. Nora knew she wanted Scarecrow and she was intent on keeping the horse from her. Even after Sadie suggested she use Cora's colt!

Sadie tried to stand but her mother held her down and leaned in and harshly whispered in her ear. "Don't say a word!"

Sadie's chest was heaving angrily.

"Nora, why would you choose Scarecrow over Arcturus?" Aunt Jordan asked.

"I like Scarecrow," Nora said hesitantly.

"And you don't like Arcturus?" Her mother responded raising her voice slightly.

"Of course I do," Nora answered. "It's…it's too hard." She whined.

Sadie tried to stand again but again her mother held her down so she turned slowly to her cousin and glared at her. If she could throw something at her, she would.

Nora didn't look at Sadie. She just stared at her mother.

"Scarecrow is built for barrel racing. Don't you think she would be best as a racer for Sadie and Arcturus for your horse shows?" Aunt Jordan asked.

"Sadie has Kit," Nora stated flatly.

This time, when Sadie stood, her mother loosened her grip and let her go.

She walked passed Aunt Dru, who also didn't make a move to stop her. Even when she heard Aunt Jordan call out to her, Sadie didn't stop.

Once through the door, she walked with the longest stride she could make. With every step the anger, guilt, disgust with herself and Nora ran through her. She was done with horses. As a thief and a liar she didn't deserve them. Neither did Nora.

She walked past the barn where Uncle Scott was shoeing Monty. Her dad, Nick, Jessup, and Jack were watching. They were all laughing. She barely looked at them and continued to walk down the road. Her dad's voice reached her, but she didn't know if he was just talking to the group of men or talking to her. It didn't matter…she wasn't stopping. She needed to get away from everyone before she exploded again. The large corral was on her right and the shortcut path to the fall branding corrals was on her left. She turned left.

"Sadie Anne Tagger, stop right now!" She heard her mother behind her but she kept walking, even when she heard her mother's running footsteps behind her.

"Sadie!" It was her dad. Her stride grew faster and longer. It didn't take long before his hand was on her arm pulling her to a stop and twisting her so she faced him.

She kept her eyes calm, the guilt from tossing the saddle, then damaging it, and anger at Nora had made her numb. She stared at him blankly.

"What is going on?" He looked up at her mom, who had finally caught up with them.

Her mother paused a moment while she caught her breath. "We were discussing the horses and what would be best for them. The discussion about Scarecrow started and didn't go as expected," She bent over so she was eye level to Sadie. "I'm sorry, Sadie," Her mom said. "But after you walked out, Aunt Jordan agreed that Scarecrow would go to you as a barrel horse."

Sadie looked at her numbly and didn't answer. She felt as if every muscle in her body was trying to go to sleep, her brain trying to shut down.

"Sadie?" Her dad knelt beside her. "Isn't that what you wanted?"

She didn't say anything. The emotions of the last couple days and the stressful ride that morning was just too much. Her body tingled and eyes burned from the stress.

"Sadie, talk to us," Her dad ordered.

She said nothing. She just stared at him.

He sighed and looked over at her mom who just shrugged. They stood at the same time and each grabbed one of her hands and drug her back to the bunkhouse. She said nothing; she just let them pull her along.

They took her inside the bunkhouse. Everyone had left except her mom, dad, and Aunt Dru, who was sitting at the table.

"So what happened exactly?" Her dad asked. Sadie had been watching them. When he spoke, she turned her head and looked out the window. Her mind shut off to what they were saying. She didn't want to hear it or relive it.

"Sadie!"

She turned to her father. "Your idea with Nora showing Cora's colt was perfect. Both Cora and Nora are very happy."

Nora is happy….twist the dagger through her heart…she turned back to the window and blocked out their voices. Fine… Nora could have all of them, Sadie was done with horses.

Maybe she should just get rid of all of her riding stuff. She had no more plans on using them. She could get into sports like her friends at school had been wanting. They wanted her to play volleyball because she was so tall.

"Sadie; look at me." Sadie turned her head but her eyes were so tired she couldn't focus on her mother's face. "I know you're angry at Nora, but you need to stop this. Talk to us."

Nothing…that's what Sadie wanted. She wanted to say nothing, hear nothing, be nothing; she just wanted nothing. Her head went down and she stared at the floor.

She felt her arm being grabbed then lifted. She didn't even look to see who was dragging her again. It really didn't matter.

They walked through the bunkhouse and out to the corrals; to the herd of horses. They were taking her to her torture. Her eyes remained staring at the ground. She heard the gate open and the arm drug her out to the corral. Horse hooves passed her by….she knew each horse by their legs and hooves. Buttercup, Dollar, Eli, Rufio, and then they stopped at Little Ghost. She said nothing, she didn't look up. She no longer deserved him. She would never ride him. Nora could have him, too. But then again, he is scarred, so she probably wouldn't want him. Maybe Wade would want him.

The arm pulled her again and they stopped at Scarecrow. She would know her legs anywhere…it didn't matter. She wasn't going to ride her; she was going to be a volleyball player.

She felt a finger under her chin, which raised her face to look at the beautiful blonde horse. The horse turned to her and pushed Sadie's shoulder with her nose. It felt like they stabbed her heart. She pushed down against the finger and won; her gaze went back to the ground. The arm holding her dropped, letting her free; she instantly started walking across the corral. It was sloped downhill so her strides seemed longer than ever. She didn't hear anyone following her.

Sadie made her way past all the horses without looking at them and climbed the fence. Once over the fence she kept walking down the hill. There wasn't anything there except more hill side. At the bottom was the river. She really didn't think it was a good idea to walk all the way to the river, because she would have to walk up hill and she hated walking up hill. Just as she decided to turn left and head back to the trail leading to the branding corrals, she heard more running footsteps and an arm wrapped around her waist. She was turned and thrown over someone's shoulder.

How funny was it that she recognized the person carrying her by their butt? Matt was the youngest, which is probably why they sent him after her. His shoulder dug into her stomach which hurt, but she was so numb from her emotions she didn't cry. Her braid bobbed around her head. She could see the tip of it every other step.

When they finally made it to the top of the hill, she heard people talking but couldn't make out what they were saying. It seemed the blood was rushing through her ears and it was loud.

She watched the ground pass and finally figured out that they were headed to the barn. They were taking her to Dusty. She felt her heart sink. Dusty….another knife turned in her heart. They continued their emotional torture.

Matt bent over and Sadie felt her feet touch the ground. She bent backwards to stand up and he knelt down next to her.

"What's going on?" He asked. "You were telling me something about being stupid…finish Sadie…tell me."

Sadie stared at his eyes. Today they looked brown because he was wearing a brown shirt. Sometimes they were really green. Nick's eyes did the same thing. So he got his eye color from Nick, Sadie thought.

She wondered what it was like not to have your actual dad around. She loved her dad, and knew he would always be there for her. *I wonder if he'll go to my volleyball games.*

Matt leaned forward and kissed her on the forehead. He never did that! Why would he do it now when she was emotionally dead inside? She sighed when he stood and walked away.

Sadie stood there waiting for them to take her somewhere else. She had no intentions of looking at or playing with Dusty. She was a symbol of her guilt. When no one touched her, Sadie turned and walked out of the barn.

"Where to now?" She heard her mother say as she walked alongside.

Sadie didn't know; she just walked. She couldn't remember what time of day it was or how long she would have to walk before she could go to bed and forget about horses and calves. It was time to think about volleyball.

She noticed she was walking next to the bunkhouse. She didn't care what time it was… she was just so tired. She had barely slept at all and it had been a long day. Her whole body wanted to lie down and have this day over with….her last day of horses.

She walked up to the door of the bunkhouse, opened it and pushed the door behind her; she didn't want anyone in there with her, but someone caught the door and followed her in; probably her mother. She bent over, took her boots off and placed them properly next to the wall like her parents always told her to do. She turned, walked to the bunk and climbed the ladder to her bed. She crawled under the covers, jeans and all, and rolled over facing the wall. She closed her eyes, hoping to fall asleep quickly.

She didn't. She lay quietly as people came in and out, not knowing if her mother was still there or not. She finally gave up and rolled onto her back and stared at the ceiling. Her moving must have been seen as she heard someone climbing the ladder. It had to be a kid because the parents didn't need the ladder to see her.

"Sadie." It was Nora…

Daggers! Why her? Sadie didn't answer; she didn't even let Nora know she heard her. Why would Nora think that Sadie would want to talk to her now?

"Cora said I could give the colt a new name…a barn name." Nora said and continued to jammer about all the names she was thinking about. Sadie rolled back over and stared at the wall.…emotional torture. Why couldn't she just fall asleep and make her cousin go away?

"That's enough, Nora." Sadie heard Aunt Jordan say and then heard Nora climb back down the ladder.

Fingers touched the top of her head and played with her braid. "Honey, I know she seems to be mean to you every once in a while," Her Aunt said. "But she really does love you."

I doubt that, Sadie thought.

"It was very nice of you to suggest Cora's colt as Nora's show horse and I'm sorry she was so stubborn when it came to Scarecrow." Aunt Jordan added.

Daggers! Sadie closed her eyes and wished her aunt would go away. Eventually she did, and Sadie listened to her footsteps walk down the length of the bunkhouse and the door open and close.

She turned on her back again and stared at the ceiling. She didn't think that volleyball was in the spring, it must start in the fall. Maybe she should play beach volleyball through the summer and learn the rules.

The door opened again and she heard boots hit the ground hard. It was a man.

"Sadie!" It was her dad.

She said nothing and stared at the ceiling.

"This is getting old very quickly," He told her. "It's only two o'clock and you're not lying in bed all day."

When she didn't reply, she felt his hands grab her leg and arm and drag her to the side of the bed. He picked her up and stood her up on the ground then bent, grabbed her hand and pulled her through the bunkhouse.

His hand was really warm, but he was squeezing way too hard and it hurt a little. Now was the punishment… then she realized they were walking back to the barn.

Milo was there. DAGGERS! She screamed in her head, and tried to pull her hand out of her dad's. He gripped tighter and wouldn't let go.

"I know you're not happy about him leaving, but it's best for him," He said sympathetically. "None of us like the way it happened, but it's the best thing for Milo. He'll like ranch life better than working at The Stables." He walked her to a bale of straw along the barn wall and motioned for her to sit down. He then sat down next to her. "We have to think of what's best for him."

Sadie stared at the ground remembering the look on Nora's face when she said it. She looked so….pleased with herself. It didn't matter that it was best for Milo; she knew Andy's grandson adored Milo and would take care of him. It mattered that it was Nora that suggested it. Sadie just knew she only did it to hurt her.

"Sadie, talk to me, tell me what's going on in that head of yours," He slid off the bale and knelt in front of her. Using his finger tip, he lifted her chin up so she had to look him in the eye. He was pleading with his eyes. She knew she should tell him, but she was so numb, so tired of it all, and didn't want to discuss it like he would make her. She just stayed quiet.

"Honey," He whispered softly, "You have to tell me so I can help you. Is it just Nora and Scarecrow?"

Sadie didn't flinch. She just stared at him.

"Sadie girl, talk to me," He said again. She couldn't look in his pleading eyes anymore, so she closed her eyes.

Her dad sighed and stood up. "Don't leave this bale until I say you can," He told her softly and walked back to Milo.

She lifted her eyes enough to see he was going to work on Milo's shoes then lowered them again. Her last ride on Milo would be to go get the saddle. Her last ride on him was…as a liar and a thief. She wanted to cry, but there were no tears waiting to get out. There was no nauseous stomach, no pressure behind her eyes causing a headache; there was nothing. She was totally dead inside.

Sadie didn't know how long she sat there staring at the ground. She knew she had long enough to remember nearly every step of the ride to get the saddle. Even if it was for a bad reason, it was still going to be her last ride on Milo.

She heard her dad walk Milo out of the barn and looked up. No one else was there, but she didn't move. She had no intention of going against what he said. Pretty soon, she heard another horse walking towards the barn. Her dad walked in leading Libby. He glanced over at her and smiled. "Will you talk to me now?" He asked. She lowered her eyes again and watched their hooves and feet move around.

She needed to escape in her mind, so she started to think about staying in the saddle while Milo worked the big red cow. Legs walked in front of her and she felt the person sit down on the bale next to her. From the size of the legs, she knew it was a man. She felt like her lungs collapse. It was the last person she wanted to see.

Without lifting her eyes up, she moved herself back on the bale farther and brought her knees to her chest. Wrapping her arms around her legs and burying her face into her knees, she tried to become as small as possible. She closed her eyes and started screaming in her head so she couldn't hear the men talk. She made her mind think of volleyball and pictured her friends from school playing. What would they think of her playing? What did the uniforms look like? What was it like to ride in the bus to a game out of town? Question after question was silently asked and answered to keep from listening.

Sadie barely felt Nick stand and didn't move when he left. She knew he was nervous about talking to kids, yet he sat with her at lunch…and was so nice. She didn't want him knowing she was a liar and a thief.

She sighed inside. How could she get herself into a mess like this? Even if she did return the saddle, it was still scarred. She couldn't even blame Nora anymore. It was her own fault she couldn't control her anger. There was no one else to blame.

Sadie lifted her head and opened her eyes. Libby wasn't there, neither was her dad. In fact, no one was there. She glanced around and couldn't see anyone. Looking through the open double doors of the barn, she could see it was getting dark outside but the light was on in the barn. She wished it was off.

She sighed again, this time out loud. The weight of the guilt and the long day made her tired. The effects of the stress made her eyelids so heavy she could barely keep them open. She leaned over, resting her head on the straw where Nick had been sitting. Curling her knees to her chest, her heavy, shame-filled eyes closed.

Sadie felt something touch her face and barely got her eyes open enough to see her dad kneeling next to her, brushing her bangs off her forehead. His eyes looked so sad.

"You're breaking my heart, baby girl," He whispered to her. She didn't respond; she was numb. "But when you're ready to talk, I'll be here for you."

He picked her up and cradled her in his arms. She felt the strength of his arms and the warmth of his body. She didn't know why, but it didn't comfort her, it made her feel more tired. She closed her eyes again as he walked her out of the barn.

CHAPTER TWELVE

It was light outside when Sadie woke. She rolled over to the side of the bed and looked down. Nikki wasn't there. Her eyes searched the room. No one was there. She was the last person out of bed. That hadn't happened… ever.

She rolled out of bed and slid onto Nikki's bunk. She was wearing sweatpants and a t-shirt. Someone, probably her mom, had changed her clothes last night. She found fresh clothes and went into the bathroom to change.

Sadie walked out of the bunkhouse and looked around. There was no one in sight. They were probably all in the house having breakfast. She didn't want to see anyone, so even though she was hungry she headed for the barn instead.

Dusty was wandering around her little stall when she arrived. Grabbing the pitchfork, Sadie cleaned up the soiled straw and then added more clean straw. The calf quickly bedded down and curled up comfortably.

Walking out the back she looked over and saw Little Ghost headed away from the stalls of the barn. He must have gotten his fill of hay. Retracing her steps through the barn she hesitantly stepped into the tack room. The saddle was there…just where she had put it. Her fingers traced the scratches and the long gouge on the back skirt. It was such a stressful journey to retrieve it, the horrible meeting where she yelled at Nora, and then the shutdown of all of her senses. Her dad's pleading eyes saddened her heart and she felt the guilt start to weigh her down again.

It was time, Sadie thought. She needed to tell what happened. When she turned, her eyes landed on the carrier that had all the brushes, combs, and bottles of mane de-tangler. First she would brush out Little Ghost, in case they banned her from him as punishment.

Halter and lead rope in hand, Sadie made her way out to the horses and led Little Ghost out of the corral. Last time she tried to brush him in the corral, all the horses had swarmed her wanting to be brushed. It became dangerous real quick.

Once Little Ghost was tied up outside the corral, she retrieved all the grooming supplies. She brushed him from head to hoof, then pulled out the mane comb. By the time she was done, his mane and tail were shiny and sleek. The horse looked great. Rufio walked up on the other side of the fence. Sadie looked at him and thought, why not? She made her way to the tack room and within minutes had Rufio tied up next to Little Ghost.

Once Rufio was shiny and sleek she spied Harvey. As she tied Harvey up next to Rufio, she saw her dad stepping out of the ranch house and walking for the barn. She grabbed the brush and stroked it down Harvey's neck. Pretty soon her dad was leading Eli towards her. Without saying anything, he tied the buckskin to the fence next to Harvey. He grabbed a brush from the bucket.

Sadie made her way to the opposite side of the horse so she was facing her dad with the two horses in between.

"How are you feeling this morning?" He asked her without actually looking at her.

Sadie tried to smile. "Better."

"There's that voice that I love," He smiled. "Just woke up this morning thinking you'd brush out the whole herd?"

Sadie didn't stop brushing, "I'm delaying," She said honestly.

"Delaying what?" He didn't stop brushing either.

She knew he had to be done brushing that side of Eli, but continued to brush it so he was facing her.

Taking a deep breath, she spit out the words before she could change her mind. "Telling you that I threw Nora's saddle off the road and into the ravine the other day."

Sadie stared at the brush as she slid it across Harvey's back. She couldn't see him, so she slowly rose until she was on her tip toes and her eyes were just over the top of the horse's back. His arms were crossed over Eli's back and he was leaning against the horse looking at her. Her hand froze, the brush rested against the horses hip.

He didn't look angry, but she couldn't tell what the expression was so she lowered back down to the ground and moved the brush across Harvey's side and quickly continued.

"I don't know how it happened…I didn't plan it…I was just so angry at her that I didn't even think. Dusty…my hat…then Milo…I had listened to Uncle Scott tell her over and over to put it away …then when I was walking by it…it made me angry…and before I knew it, it was flying through the air." It was easier to talk when she was brushing. It felt like she was telling Harvey instead of her dad.

She stopped brushing and slowly rose on her tip toes again to see him. He was still leaning against Eli, watching her. She still couldn't tell if he was mad or not.

"I was really, really, really, mad at her." Sadie looked him straight in the eye.

"I know," Was all he said.

Sadie's jaw dropped in shock. Did he really just say that? "What?"

He walked around Eli so he was only one horse away and she didn't have to stand on her tip toes to see him. He leaned his back against the horse, who just stood there patiently. "I knew you did something with the saddle."

Sadie didn't know what to say. He knew but he didn't punish her? Maybe he didn't know for that long.

"How long have you known?" She stepped backwards and bumped against Rufio.

"Since the first time you said you didn't know what happened to it."

"You've known all along?" She asked in disbelief.

"Yes."

"Why didn't you do something?"

"I was waiting for you to tell the truth," He smiled. "I didn't think it would take this long."

She frowned and exhaled sharply. "Why didn't you just tell me you knew? Why didn't you punish me?"

"Because we wanted to see how far you would take this."

"We?"

"Yeah…pretty much everyone but the kids."

Sadie was stunned. "They all knew?"

He looked at her with a smile, "Sadie, you don't lie very well and this was so far past who you are that we were all shocked. We all tried to give you a chance to tell us, but you just kept silent."

"So you knew even before I went and got it…" She tilted her head.

"We were watching you every step of the way."

"What?" Her eyes widened in disbelief.

"Your mother saw you leave the bunkhouse and head to the barn. Once she saw you saddling Milo she texted me to come back. While Dru brought me back over by the fall corrals, she saddled a couple horses," He grinned at her expression. "We followed you the whole way… staying in the trees," Then he chuckled. "We were surprised you didn't see us when you came back over the edge of the road with the saddle. You were down there so long we thought you were hurt and were riding to you." He chuckled again. "We were only about 50 yards from you and had to duck behind some brush so you didn't see us."

"Dad! Why did you do that?" Sadie had started to get mad at them.

"Because you needed to play it out yourself."

"What?"

"You needed to work the guilt and anger out for yourself…we couldn't do that for you." He leaned back and crossed his legs at the ankles. "Besides, we couldn't have punished you any better than how you were punishing yourself."

"That was awful, Dad." She admitted.

"It looked it."

"Well," She frowned at him. "Don't do that again."

He chuckled at her; "Well don't do anything that you deserve it."

"I agree." Sadie jumped when she heard her mother's voice behind her. She turned and saw her mom leading Cooper and her sister leading Buttercup.

"Oh, Mom," Sadie said sadly. When she got close enough she stepped into her mother's warm embrace. "I am so sorry," She squeezed tightly.

Grace stopped at the back of Eli, her dad stepped around next to her.

"This has been one weird week." Grace shook her head.

"Agreed," Her dad nodded.

Sadie turned in her mom's arms, so her back was to her mom and she was facing her dad and sister.

"Everything was going so good. Then it went really bad." Sadie frowned. "But you all got angry with me, and it was all Nora's fault."

"I was not mad at you," He rested his arm up on Eli's rump and looked down at her. "She was just anxious to feed Dusty, and you got a little carried away."

"Well, it's my bad, on the hat thing," Grace confessed. "I talked to Nora. She had no idea that it was your hat. Uncle Scott told her to get any hat she could find, so she grabbed the first one she saw. When she saw you with your cowboy hat on, she was shocked and realized it was yours. She took it off so you didn't have to see it all day." Grace added with an ironic chuckle. "The coyote thing was just a weird accident."

"When did I get mad at you?" Her mother asked.

"When we were looking for the hat," Sadie said. "You put your hand over your eyes and walked away…that's what you do when you're mad at us."

"Oh, Sadie," Her mother squeezed her. "I'm sorry, Honey. I wasn't mad AT you; I was frustrated that everything was happening TO you." She stepped around her daughter so she could see into her eyes. "You have to understand how terrible we felt for giving your horse away, in front of you, without discussing it with you first." She paused and looked back at her dad then back to her. "We felt awful, Honey."

"Scott, Jordan, and Andy were just as horrified," He added. "We've all had to let go of our first horse. We know how hard it is and knew how upset you were. You handled it well with Andy's grandson."

"Scott and Jordan talked to Nora about it. She wasn't trying to be mean…she saw you playing with Milo and Andy's grandson all day and figured no one had thought about it so she said it out loud, unfortunately in front of the little boy who instantly got excited about it."

Sadie sighed; she didn't think she would ever believe that Nora didn't do it on purpose.

"You do need to apologize to Nora about the outburst yesterday," Her mother stated.

Sadie's eyes opened wide in shock.

"For the outburst, and for what you did to her saddle," Her dad added.

Sadie turned her eyes to Harvey. The horse was standing patiently, her eyes nearly closed. Just past her, she could see Scarecrow in the corral.

"What?" Her dad asked.

"I don't deserve Scarecrow," She said sadly.

"Why not?" Her parents said in unison.

"Throwing the saddle in anger, lying to you and treating everyone so badly. Nick…last night when he sat down, I was so rude to him…and everyone else. I don't deserve either of the horses." She looked down at the ground.

"Sadie girl," he said with a quiet laugh. "You are one of the most deserving people I've ever known. You are up earlier than anyone else when there's work to be done. You helped Dru load all the horses to come up here, before any of the other kids were even out of bed." He shook his head at her. "The misery you put yourself through the last 24 hours, because you lied, shows you deserve that horse. If you had gone on, without a second thought after throwing the saddle and lying, then I would agree with you."

"Nobody deserves these horses more than you Sadie," Grace added.

Her mother squeezed her. "I agree."

"The saddle is back, even though it's scratched up pretty good. You'll take some saddle soap and conditioner to it and see what you can do to fix it the best you can." He said and Sadie nodded.

"But that isn't all…I tore her jacket, too," She confessed.

"Sadie, when was the last time you saw her wear that jacket?" Her dad asked.

Sadie frowned, she really hadn't thought about that. Maybe Nora didn't like the jacket; she just didn't want Sadie wearing it.

"She always wears the pink jacket," Her dad continued. "She thinks it looks better with her hair."

Sadie smiled on that one. "How do you know that?"

"I have ears!" He laughed. "Haven't you noticed she talks all the time?" He paused. "Except for yesterday, you talk all the time, too." He grinned at her and she smiled back. "I know that Nora likes to wear dark brown, blue, and sometimes red depending on her mood and you like to wear pink and brown because you like the colors with your hair, too. And you like light blue because it looks so good on Dru that it should look good on you." He smiled but continued. "You like black fingernail polish because you can't see the dirt underneath it. Nora likes red fingernail polish because it's a flashy color and it makes her look like a model." He laughed and tilted his head at her. "In fact, I probably know more of the words from all the Selena Gomez and Taylor Swift songs, than the two of you put together!"

Sadie and Grace giggled. They did play them all the time when they were in the trucks. She just never thought of her dad listening to them while he was driving them around. In fact, she never thought of him even being there at all!

They all laughed.

Sadie's back relaxed and the pressure in her head was gone.

"Now what?" Sadie glanced between her parents.

Her mother stood and her dad glanced out at the rest of the horses.

"Let's get them all brushed out," He glanced at his daughters and smiled, "We might as well put the saddles on them while we have them all caught up."

"Really?" Sadie and Grace cried out.

"Catch 'em up." He handed Grace his brush. "I'll go talk to Scott and Dru."

He started to walk towards the house.

"Daddy?" Sadie stopped him. When he turned, she ran up to him and threw her arms around his waist. "I am so sorry for everything."

He leaned down and hugged her back, then grabbing her shoulders he pushed her back, and knelt in front of her.

"Don't ever shutdown again, Sadie girl." He ordered, "Yesterday was terrible; I don't ever want to see you like that again. You talk to us when it gets tough, OK?"

Sadie thought of how sad his eyes were the night before when he picked her up off the bale of straw. She never wanted to see that again. "Never again, Daddy." She leaned forward and kissed his cheek. "I love you."

"Dang girl," He said standing up. He looked at her then up at his other daughter and his wife. "You three girls just tear at my heart." He quickly turned and nearly ran to the house.

CHAPTER THIRTEEN

All the horses were brushed and tied outside the corral. Sadie turned and smiled at Wade. He was leading Rooster into the corral with Aunt Jordan leading Dollar.

They all agreed that Rooster had gone through the most to get to this point, so he and Wade would go first.

He was so excited, Wade was nearly dancing as he walked.

Everyone else was lined up outside the fence with the rest of the Tagger herd.

Rooster walked to the saddle Uncle Scott was holding, and sniffed curiously. Then he checked out the saddle pad. The pad was brought up next to him and rubbed down his side. Rooster didn't care. By the time Uncle Scott was done rubbing the horse down with the pad, Rooster looked like he was sleeping. It was placed on his back and Uncle Scott picked up the saddle and gently laid it on top of the pad. Rooster's eyes finally opened and he slowly turned his head and looked at the saddle. Scott tightened the front cinch, Rooster stood quietly.

Then he walked him around the corral with Rooster not caring about the saddle.

"Wade," He turned to his son.

"Yeah, Dad?" Wade was grinning.

"Come here."

Wade didn't hesitate and walked quickly to his dad expecting to take the lead rope. When he got close enough his dad moved to Rooster's side.

"Step up," Uncle Scott said to his shocked son.

"What?" Wade's voice went high pitched which made everyone laugh.

"I trust him; he won't do anything to hurt you." Uncle Scott grinned at his son.

Wade walked up to Rooster's side and stood frozen.

"What's the matter?" Scott asked him.

"I'm afraid of hurting him," Wade looked up at his dad.

"Well, I don't think you weigh 80 pounds. That's not going to hurt him." Scott assured his son. "I wouldn't tell you to get on him if I thought you would."

Wade smiled and turned back to Rooster. He couldn't reach the stirrup so his dad put his hands together to make a step and Wade placed his left foot into them. Uncle Scott lifted his son up onto Rooster for the first time. Rooster didn't move. Father and son grinned at each other.

Sadie looked at her cousin in awe. It was so weird seeing someone on top of Rooster. It made her think of Rooster as a working horse instead of a pet horse. She turned her eyes to look if everyone else saw it too….they did. Aunt Dru had tears in her eyes. Aunt Jordan was wiping tears away. There were smiles and grins from everyone including Jessup, Cora and Nick.

Sadie stepped up on the bottom rail of the fence and leaned over the top rail. As her uncle started walking Rooster around the corral he veered close to Sadie. She held up her hand and high-fived Wade as he walked by. She looked back at Little Ghost and felt the excitement run through her.

Sadie glanced over at Scarecrow who was at the end of the line. Grace had brushed the palomino instead of Sadie. She couldn't grasp the fact that Scarecrow was hers and had kept a distance from the horse.

Uncle Scott caught Wade as he slid off of Rooster and the same procedure was repeated for Dollar. Again, Sadie and Wade high-fived as he passed by.

"Who's next?" Uncle Scott turned as he walked Dollar and Wade led Rooster out the gate.

Everyone raised their hands but Sadie.

Jack and Reilly walked Rufio and Cooper into the corral.

Rufio, the roan, sidestepped a couple times when Reilly lifted the saddle pad, but settled down quickly. He again sidestepped when the saddle cinch was tightened.

"You want to try it or wait?" Jack asked Reilly.

"Oh, I'll try it," Reilly grinned at his dad, bouncing excitedly, his heels rising just inches.

"Stop bouncing and go slow." Jack chuckled at his son. "Step up a couple times but don't swing your leg over. Just up and down a couple times."

Reilly did as he was told. Rufio sidestepped the first time, but Reilly remained in the stirrup. When the horse stopped, Reilly stepped down. The second step up and Rufio didn't move.

"My heart is racing!" Reilly said excitedly to his dad.

Jack grinned as Reilly repeated the step up and down until his dad nodded at him, then he swung his leg over and sat on his roan for the first time.

Sadie had been holding her breath! She finally let it out when Jack started walking him around. As he walked by, Reilly winked down at her and Sadie grinned back.

As Reilly stepped off of Rufio, Aunt Dru walked Cooper over to him. He quickly grabbed the rope for the black gelding and smiled at her. He turned back to his dad.

"Your turn, Dad," Reilly motioned for his dad to get on.

Jack nodded and stepped up to the horse with the pad and saddle. Cooper retreated from the equipment. Both Reilly and Jack talked soothingly to the horse and Jack ran his hand down the horse's neck calming him. After a minute, Cooper relaxed enough for the saddle pad to be rubbed over his body. After a few minutes, Cooper's head lowered and he relaxed.

Jack placed the saddle on him and waited for the horse to relax again before cinching it tight. Cooper groaned but didn't move.

Reilly nodded at his dad and braced himself as Jack stepped up into the stirrup. Cooper sidestepped and backed up, but Jack held his position on the horse. Once Cooper stopped Jack stepped down. They repeated the steps until Cooper stopped moving. Then he slowly moved his leg over the horse and sat quietly. Cooper backup up until he hit the fence. Reilly held on tightly and talked to the horse trying to sooth him.

Sadie saw her dad and Uncle Scott start to walk into the corral to help, but the horse finally relaxed and stepped up to Reilly. He leaned his head into Reilly's shoulder as if asking for comfort. Reilly whispered to him but kept his eyes on his dad.

"It's OK," Jack told him. "Just step to his side and walk around."

Reilly did as he was told and Cooper stepped out next to him, calmly following Reilly's lead. After a couple times around the corral, Reilly stopped and Jack carefully stepped down from the saddle.

Sadie heard everyone around her finally exhale.

Jack stroked the horse's neck and Reilly started bouncing. Jack wrapped his arm around his son's neck and they laughed together as they walked out of the corral.

Next was Nora.

Sadie stepped down off the fence and moved closer to her grey horse. She watched her cousin happily get lifted onto Arcturus' back and be led around. Arcturus was a perfect gentleman and didn't seem to worry too much about being ridden. Nora leaned forward and stroked the black horse's neck as they walked. The look on her face was…just…astounding.   She looked absolutely blissful.

Then it was time for Cora's colt. As the magnificent horse was led into the corral, Sadie couldn't help but take a step to the fence and watch him.

Nora had not even looked at her while she was on Arcturus, but as soon as the colt came into the arena Nora turned and started looking at the family. As soon as she saw Sadie, she walked over to her.

Sadie was shocked and a little worried what Nora was doing. She had apologized to her cousin, and the girls had stiffly shook hands as Nora accepted her apology. Sadie had even offered to trade her saddles since they were the same size, but Nora refused.

Now, as her cousin approached her with a determined look on her face, Sadie stepped back to Little Ghost.

Nora finally reached the fence and looked Sadie in the eye. "I can't decide on Coco, short for Cora's Colt, or Isaiah. What do you think?"

Sadie stared at her in shock. It took her a moment to realize that Nora was serious.

"He's a magnificent horse," Sadie stammered. "He needs a strong name like Isaiah."

"Then, Isaiah it is," Nora smiled at her cousin …her good smile…not the sweet smile, and walked back to the gelding that Uncle Scott was holding.

Sadie watched in amazement as her uncle moved the saddle pad over and around the horse. The big red bay gelding stood perfectly and didn't move. He did lower his head to sniff the equipment, then turned his head back to try and bite the stirrup when the cinch was tightened.

Sadie stepped back up onto the fence and watched as Nora was lifted onto the horse for the first time. In her heart, Sadie knew that Nora and this stunning horse, Isaiah, were going to be champions together. She could feel the tears sting at the back of her eyes. They looked like they were made for each other.

"Wow…." Escaped her as she watched her cousin move around the arena.

"I agree," Cora whispered behind her. She reached over and placed her hand over Sadie's. "Thank you, Sadie."

Sadie turned and looked into Cora's eyes….the older woman had seen it too.

Sadie nodded and turned her eyes back to her cousin.

Once Nora was done, Grace and their dad walked Buttercup and Eli into the corral.

Buttercup was first and the beautiful cream colored filly stood perfectly still as the saddle pad and saddle were placed on her. Grace stepped into the saddle and looked down at their dad.

"I'm so excited…" She grinned down at him.

Buttercup didn't just walk around the corral, she pranced.

"I don't want to stop!" Grace cried out when her dad came to a halt.

"I think Matt, Nikki, and Sadie would argue with you on that." He laughed at her.

Grace stepped off the horse and took the rope from her dad. She started to walk out of the corral.

"Are you forgetting something?" He called out to her.

Grace turned and shook her head, "Seriously, Dad. I think you and Eli can handle this by yourself." She grinned and left the corral.

Grace walked up next to Sadie and the sisters watched their dad and his soul-mate horse. The buckskin had complete faith in his human and didn't flinch at the pad or the saddle. When he stepped up and into the saddle the horse turned and looked at him. He didn't move.

They could hear their dad talking to the horse, but no one could hear what was being said. In moments, the horse took a few steps forward. He only had a halter and lead rope, but Sadie knew that her dad was in complete control. Again, her dad spoke, and the horse moved forward again. Then he stepped down off the horse and the horse's head came around for attention. His human gave it to him, then lead him out of the corral to the grins and jokes from the crowd.

Matt and Nikki were next. Hand in hand, Dru and Nikki walked into the corral leading Harvey. Matt stepped into the corral and hesitated. He turned and looked at the row of family standing next to the fence. His eyes stopped on Nick.

Matt asked Nick to hold Trooper for him and his father stepped quickly from the fence and walked to Matt's side. Matt handed him the lead rope and they walked together to the center of the corral.

"That's got to be a weird feeling for Dru," Sadie heard her dad say behind her. She turned to look at who he was talking to. It was Uncle Scott and Jack. They were nodding and watching the four people in the corral. She had nearly forgotten that her aunt and Nick were once married. Sadie turned back...details... she didn't remember, *ever*, seeing the four of them alone together before.

Saddle pads and saddles were introduced to the horses and placed in position.

Nikki turned to her brother, "Together?" She smiled. Matt grinned and nodded.

At the count of three, they both stepped into the stirrup and swung their legs over their horses. Trooper didn't move, but Harvey took a step backwards. Aunt Dru held tightly and talked to the big brown horse to keep her calm. Once the horse settled down, Aunt Dru and Nick walked them around the corral in opposite directions.

Sadie could feel the excitement start running through her. It was her turn next. Her heart started pounding as she turned to Little Ghost and stroked his neck.

"It's our turn," She whispered to him and stepped him backward and headed for the gate.

Matt, Nikki, Aunt Dru and Nick smiled at her as she patiently watched them walk out of the corral.

She took a deep breath to calm her nerves and stepped into the corral. Little Ghost followed her calmly. Her dad was waiting for her, smiling proudly.

Little Ghost, her future roping horse, rubbed his nose on her shoulder as her dad introduced him to the pad and saddle. She giggled at him and played with his ears.

"I don't think we have any worries with him." Her dad grinned down at her.

"No, he'll be a perfect gentleman." Sadie smiled at her horse and ran her hand down the length of his neck, stopping at the scar. She traced it lightly with her fingertip from the withers to the top of his leg. Her dad was right; the scar was just in front of the saddle. She traced the scar one more time, then stepped to his side. Her dad didn't create a step with his hands; instead he picked her up by the waist and set her on top of the horse. He stepped back to the horse's head, holding the lead rope firmly.

Sadie looked down at the horse's neck and head. What a bizarre feeling to be on top of him…she had dreamt of this moment…couldn't wait for it to happen…and now it was here…her heart soared. Leaning down, she stroked the horse's neck again.

"Ready?" Her dad asked.

Sadie nodded and her dad stepped forward. She felt Little Ghost move under her for the first time and the grin spread across her face. Her whole body tingled with excitement.

She rested her hands on each side of the saddle horn and moved her hips along with the horse's gate. It felt so natural. She leaned forward and took in a deep breath of her beautiful grey horse.

"I'm in love, Dad," She giggled softly. Her dad turned and smiled.

As they walked along the fence and approached the lineup of horses and people, she searched for Wade. He had climbed the fence and was waiting for the high-five. She laughed and slapped his hand as they walked by.

After two laps around her dad walked back to the center and helped her down.

Sadie quickly stepped around to the front of the horse and wrapped her arms around his neck. The grey lowered his head and leaned into her back…the special horse hug. She felt warm and happy inside.

"You have to let him go." Her dad had leaned down and whispered in her ear. She quickly turned and wrapped her arms around her dad. He happily returned her embrace.

Stepping back, he looked down at her. "Stay here and I'll be right back."

Sadie held her breath. She knew what he was doing….he was switching horses…he was going to bring in Scarecrow. She shifted her weight from one foot to the other as she watched her dad and mom switch lead ropes. Her heart was racing and she felt her skin go moist from the anxiety racing through her heart.

Tears sprung to her eyes as she stared at the big beautiful golden palomino walking toward her. The horse's head was up high looking around alertly.

Sadie took a step back…the excitement was so strong inside her, she almost felt like running away.

"You OK?" Her dad whispered as he approached.

Sadie nodded and shook her head at the same time….she wasn't sure if she was OK or not.

He chuckled at her, his blue eyes twinkling.

The horse stopped just a few feet away. Sadie slowly lifted her hand and reached out to touch Scarecrow's nose. The horse stretched out for more attention, so she ran her hand up the flat part of her nose and up between her eyes. She took a hesitant step forward and the horse placed her nose in the crook of her neck; her breath ran down Sadie's back and she shivered; enjoying the warmth of it. She turned her face into the horse, closed her eyes and breathed in...her body tingled…her heart soared… heaven.

"Sadie," Her dad whispered again.

Her eyes opened and she looked up at him; her eyes peaceful and happy.

She nodded and watched as he introduced the pad and saddle to Scarecrow. The horse's head lifted excitedly but she didn't move.

Once the cinch was tightened he turned back to her, "I don't have to ask if you're happy."

Still entranced in Scarecrow's love, she slowly shook her head; she felt like she was in a dream.

He touched the side of her face; his hand was warm and the love radiated from his eyes.

"It's time," She whispered and stepped to the side of the horse.

Her dad's hands encircled her waist. Just as he tightened to lift her, she stopped him.

"Wait…" Her hands went to his and he loosened his grip.

"Are you OK?" He asked in concern.

Sadie grinned up into his face as her hand went over her chest. "My heart skipped a beat…just needed to recover."

He chuckled softly. She could have sworn she saw tears in his eyes before he stood. "I love you, Baby Girl," He whispered as he lifted her onto her horse.

Sadie felt her legs touch the saddle and her feet naturally slide into the stirrups. Her hands would normally reach for the reins, this time they went on each side of the horse's neck. The big golden neck with the full blonde mane stretched out in front of her. Scarecrow turned and looked up at her. She smiled down into the horse's big round brown eyes. They were so soft and gentle…Sadie knew she could trust this horse with her life.

"OK, Dad," She whispered looking up at him.

Her dad stepped forward and Scarecrow followed. She held her breath as she felt Scarecrow move under her for the first time.

Sadie matched her breathing to Scarecrows steps, so she would remember to exhale.

She finally looked up and saw the row of family and horses in front of her. The Tagger Herd…humans and horses.

Sadie searched for Wade again, but instead she saw Reilly had climbed the fence. His grin was as wide as hers, his blue eyes shining. As she approached he called out to her. "Vegas baby!"

Sadie reached down and touched Scarecrow's golden neck then looked back at him. The National Finals Rodeo in Las Vegas….yeah, someday, she grinned.

THE TAGGER HERD

BOOK FIVE

REILLY MORGAN

CHAPTER ONE

Text from Grace: Do you have it all written down

Text from Reilly: Yes, six things

Text from Grace: Don't forget the ranch one

Text from Reilly: Did forget will add

Text from Grace: Think Jack will go for it

Text from Reilly: Hope so

Text from Grace: Where is he

Text from Reilly: Downstairs fixing breakfast

Text from Grace: You only have 20 minutes

Text from Reilly: I know

Text from Grace: Then say goodbye and go do it!

Text from Reilly: Goodbye

Text from Grace: See you in 30! Fingers crossed!

Reilly quickly wrote down the ranch item on his list and checked over all the information. It looked good to him. Man, he hoped his dad was in a good mood this morning.

He quickly looked around his bedroom for a shirt, grabbed the first one he saw and slid it on quickly. Other than his boots, which were downstairs, he was ready for school. He opened the door and looked over at his dad's bedroom door. There were only three doors upstairs; a small storage room and the two bedrooms. They each had a bathroom in their own room so they didn't have to share. His dad's door was open, so it confirmed what he said to Grace, his dad was downstairs.

List in hand, Reilly skipped down the stairs which led into the small dining room and kitchen. He glanced around, didn't see his dad, but breakfast was sitting on the table. Ignoring it for now, he walked into the living room and found his dad looking out the large window. It was his usual morning check on The Stables. Their house had a bird's eye view of the property and buildings. Both of them had the habit of looking over the area as soon as they got up.

"Morning, Dad."

"Morning, Son."

It was their usually boring morning greeting.

Reilly hesitated, glanced down at his list, then took a deep breath and started.

"Dad, schools almost out for the summer."

"Yep."

"And I was thinking that to be more helpful to everyone, it might be…" Reilly paused briefly, then told himself to just say it. "It might be helpful if I had my own truck."

He simply nodded. "I agree."

Reilly hesitated, he wasn't expecting that. "You do?"

Walking past him, his dad headed into the kitchen. "You got your license a couple months ago. I'm surprised you haven't asked before." He sat at the table and scooped a large spoonful of bacon and cheese omelet.

Reilly quickly joined him and sat in his usual chair but ignored the plate of food. "Well, I drove all the time with you and then up at the ranch."

"So now you're ready for your own."

"Yeah," Reilly glanced at the list on the table.

"Do you want to read them to me?"

"What?"

"Isn't that a list of reasons you should have your own truck?" He pointed to the list.

Reilly grinned, "Yeah, Gracie and I have been working on it for days now."

"How many reasons?"

"Six…no, seven."

"It took you DAYS to come up with a whole seven reasons?" His blue eyes lit up with humor and his dimples deepened.

Reilly just smiled. "Yeah….you want to hear them?"

"Just the last one." He finished the breakfast and took his plate to the sink.

"Just the last one?"

"That's usually the one that you're really stretching for a reason, and is usually the most entertaining." He chuckled and sat back at the table, stretching his legs out.

"Well, it says Grayson trusted me enough to drive Grace and Sadie, plus the horses, to Dry Creek Valley to ride and shut the gates."

He glanced back up and saw his dad looking at him with an impressed smile.

"That's a good one. You and Grace did good on that one." He teased.

"Does it help?" Reilly looked at him hopefully. The whole conversation wasn't what he expected, but it sounded positive.

"Didn't hurt." He stood and headed for the door.

"Dad…!" Reilly quickly shoveled as much food in his mouth as he could and took the plate to the sink. He knew Cora would have extra breakfast at the Tagger place. He quickly checked to make sure nothing was left on the table and, stuffing the list in his pocket, ran out the door.

He climbed into the passenger side of his dad's truck, buckled his seat belt, and looked over at him anxiously. "Well?"

They started moving down the sloped driveway. When the truck reached the end and connected with the side road, he stopped and looked over at Reilly.

"This weekend is Memorial Day, so you have three days off."

"Yeah, but we're headed up to get the leased horses from the ranch tomorrow, aren't we?"

"We'll head up early in the morning. Nikki is taking care of The Stables." The truck started moving again. They were headed to The Homestead, where Reilly always met up with Grace to catch the bus or a ride with one of her family members into school.

"When are we coming back?" Reilly asked.

"Depends on the horses. We're riding them to get them ready for clients. It could take a day or two."

Reilly waited for him to answer the question. He knew better than to keep asking, he would answer when he was ready. It was a habit his dad had that drove him crazy!

Finally, as they turned off onto the main road, which led to the Tagger's place, he spoke. "You only have a half day of school today so I'm thinking it might work if I picked you up at school and we started looking this afternoon."

Reilly's heart started to race. "Really, Dad?"

"Yes." He grinned back at Reilly. "I just have one request."

"What's that?"

"Nothing against Grace, but I would like it to be just the two of us."

"No problem," Reilly had been thinking the same thing but didn't want to hurt Grace's feelings. She had worked hard helping him put the list together so he'd felt bad about not wanting her to go with them. Now he can say it was his dad's fault. He loved spending time with just him and his dad. He felt himself bouncing on the seat. Such a weird habit he had since he was little.

"Have you been looking on the internet?"

Reilly nodded. The rest of the way he told him about all the trucks he and Grace had looked at.

When the truck pulled up to the end of the Tagger driveway, Reilly slid out, landing on the ground with an energetic bounce. He looked back as his dad.

"Thanks Dad. I can't wait."

"I'm excited, too. I'll go online today and look at the trucks you mentioned but don't get your hopes up on a big truck."

Reilly was about to shut the door but hesitated. What did he mean?

"We have plenty of big trucks for pulling. For your first truck we'll be looking for smaller, like a Ranger or a Tacoma."

Reilly nodded, he wasn't going to argue, he was getting a truck! "Sounds good, I'll meet you after school."

"Try to pay attention in school." His dad yelled as the door closed. They both knew he wouldn't be able to.

Reilly watched as he turned the truck around and headed back to The Stables. He grinned, his dad wouldn't have to make this morning drive anymore; it was one of the things he and Grace had put on the list. Reilly turned and started running up the driveway. He couldn't wait to tell everyone about getting his own truck!

******

Reilly smiled over at Grace, waved and crawled into his dad's truck. Grace was stepping onto the bus.

He looked up at his grinning dad. "It feels like I just crawled out of this truck."

"Glad your morning went fast." He started the truck. "I got to shovel stalls all morning."

Reilly's eyes widened in surprise, they had hired a new stall cleaner just a couple days before. "What happened?"

"He didn't show up. Which means we're going to have to clean stalls in the morning before we leave."

"No problem, Dad," Reilly said cheerfully, hoping to make him feel better. "What about Sunday and Monday?"

"It's all Nikki's," He chuckled. "I'll call the second person on the list when I get back Tuesday, so let's not worry about it now. We should be concentrating on a truck right now."

"Oh yeah…" Reilly started bouncing again.

"I may need a new one soon, if you don't stop bouncing."

"I can't help it Dad, I don't know how to hold it in."

"Well I feel sorry for Rufio and Cooper when you start roping. They're going to need back massages after every competition."

Reilly laughed. "Or a chiropractor!"

"Was Grace upset?"

"Nah…Dru saved our butts. She's taking her up to Moscow for something, I think dinner with Nikki and Matt."

"Saved OUR butts?" He asked with a raised brow.

Reilly grinned mischievously. "Yeah, I didn't want her mad at me, so I was going to blame you, but since Dru's taking her we're both saved."

They laughed as they pulled into the first car lot.

Three car lots later, Reilly started to get discouraged. His dad said no to every truck he'd picked out so far. They were too expensive, no air conditioner, to old, brakes squeaked, too many miles, too much work needed, and Reilly's favorite; it's too dang ugly.

"Do you want to stop for lunch?"

Reilly sighed. He was hungry. Maybe food would give him the energy to keep looking. Just as he was about to say yes, he spotted THE truck. He sat up in the seat so he could see it better.

"Dad, over there!" He pointed and glanced over. To his relief, he'd seen it too and was driving over.

"Most important thing is…" His dad said as he pulled in next to the truck. "…you have to like looking at it day after day after day." It made Reilly laugh again. "And that, Son, is a dang good looking truck."

"Yeah, it's awesome. What a great metallic blue!" He slid out of the truck and walked towards the back to meet up with his dad. "It's a Tacoma too, just like you said we were looking for." Reilly could barely contain his excitement.

There was no body damage, mileage was low, it had the extra access cab behind the main seats, tires were good, and had a bed liner for the back. He just knew this was the one!

As his dad talked to the salesman, Reilly opened the driver's door and looked in; his heart just racing with anticipation.

"Get in," He heard from behind him and didn't need to be told again.

Reilly ran his hand around the steering wheel, across the dash, and over the seats. To his surprise, his dad opened the passenger side door and slid in. He dangled a set of keys in front of him.

"Yeah, oh, Dad!" The bouncing started again.

"It's not a done deal yet. Let's test drive it first."

An hour later, Reilly was pulling out of the car lot in his new truck. It was going to take hours to get the grin off his face; if not days. Buying the truck was one of the highlights of his fifteen years!

He had set the mirrors, seats, and, most importantly, the radio while his dad was doing the paperwork. When he came out of the building, he gave Reilly the 'thumbs up' and Reilly turned the key, grinned at the sound of the motor and happily headed to The Homestead to show off his knew bridge to independence!

After spending the rest of the day with the Taggers, Reilly drove into his driveway late in the evening with his dad following. As they stepped out of their trucks, they caught each other's eye and grinned.

"That's a nice looking truck flying down the road," His dad teased.

"Right on the speed limit the whole way," Reilly assured him.

Even though the sun had gone down and the sky was dark, they sat in the lawn chairs on the porch that attached to the side of the house. It had a clear view to The Stables, but more importantly, they could see Reilly's truck shining in the moonlight.

His dad went over all the rules again, which Reilly happily listened to. He wasn't arguing because he had a new truck. It was worth it!

As he talked, Reilly's mind went back to the signing the paperwork.

"Dad?" He said, after he'd stopped reciting the rules.

"Yeah?"

"Can I ask you something I wouldn't normally ever talk to you about?"

"You can talk to me about anything." He said with a tilt of the head.

Reilly hesitated.

"Just spit it out."

"OK, Dru." Reilly laughed at Dru's usual comment. Then he took a deep breath and spit it out. "When you did the paperwork, you just wrote a check instead of taking out a loan like most other people." He looked over to see if he was upset.

"We've never talked money before."

Reilly just shook his head. He never thought about money. Between The Stables and the ranch he had everything he wanted, except the truck…so NOW he had everything he wanted. But everything belonged to the Taggers. He had no idea about his dad's financial status.

"Well," He had taken off his boots and stretched out his legs in front of them. It was a warm night, a slight breeze, and lots of stars. Reilly thought he looked totally relaxed and content. "I guess, in case something happens to me, you should know what to expect."

"Nothing's happening to you." Reilly stated firmly. Just the thought of his dad not being there made him ill. He didn't have a mom…not having a dad was too much.

 "When your mother passed away, I put the money from her life insurance into a fund for you." Reilly looked at him in surprise…he had no idea. "It's to be used for your first vehicle but now that's taken care of. It's also for your college and for your wedding."

Reilly's jaw dropped.

His dad looked at him with a slight smile. "Those were the three things I believe your mother would have wanted to be a part of. So, in a way, she is."

"Dad…" Reilly didn't know what to say. As terrible as it was, he barely thought of his mother. He barely remembered her. If it wasn't for the pictures on his shelf in his bedroom, he probably would have forgotten what she looked like. That's why they were there, so he didn't forget.

 "Your families in Texas have also provided for you when they pass; both sets of grandparents"

"Dad!" Riley was amazed. "They hardly know me."

"You're still their grandchild."

"But Dad, that doesn't seem right," Reilly frowned. "I only see them once a year."

"No sense arguing, Reilly," he chuckled.

Reilly glanced up at his dad…he wanted to ask about his mom, but didn't want to upset him. They never talked about her anymore.

"What?" His dad asked.

"Were you and Mom happy?"

"For the most part." He nodded thoughtfully.

"What do you mean?"

"We were young and working to get to know each other when you came along."

"I wasn't…planned?" Reilly teased.

"We were married, but you weren't exactly planned…but we never considered you a mistake either." His dad teased back.

"What did Mom do? For a job?"

"She worked in her dad's insurance office. That's why she had good life insurance when she passed away."

"The day she died?" Reilly asked hesitantly.

His dad glanced over at him with a slight concerned narrowing of the eyes. "We've never talked about that Reilly. Are you sure you want to know?"

"I think I should know." Reilly admitted.

"Ok, I understand that."

Reilly watched him trying to see if he was upset, it didn't look like it.

"The picture you have in your room, of you on the pony and your mother and I standing behind you?

"Yea."

"That was taken the day before she passed away."

Reilly thought about that. It could have been the last picture ever taken of her. He knew the picture well. She was a little shorter than his dad and her hair was dark but not black like his dad's. Her eyes were brown and even though Reilly had his dad's blue eyes, they were shaped like his mom's in the picture.

"Where at?"

"My parent's riding stables. We were headed there the next morning; I was training a couple horses for some clients. When she woke up she didn't feel well so she stayed home and we went to the stables."

He went quiet. Reilly turned to see him staring out into the darkness, his eyes seemed distant and sad so Reilly just waited.

He cleared his throat before speaking, "We spent the whole day with your grandparents so your mother could rest. When we got back home she was still in bed so I went in and checked on her." He stopped again, hesitated then continued. "They said she passed away right after we left." He looked at Reilly. "She passed away in her sleep; there was no pain or suffering…her heart just stopped."

There was sadness in his dad's eyes, Reilly turned away from it and stared into the darkness. Finding your wife dead…that must have been horrible. He'd never known…never guessed…never really thought about it. The truth was heartbreaking for his dad.

"You OK?"

Reilly nodded. "You?"

He nodded. "I don't think about it very often…less as time goes by. When I do, I think more about what would have been, not what happened."

Reilly nodded and looked over at his new truck.

"It's sure pretty." His dad smiled. "With that bright of blue, we'll spot you coming a couple miles away at the ranch."

"No sneaking up on anyone." Reilly smiled gloomily.

CHAPTER TWO

"Round two…" Dru said from behind him.

Reilly turned and grinned. "Wish we could go with round ten and eleven."

"That's a lot of horses," She laughed which made her blue eyes sparkle. Her long blonde hair was in a low pony tail down her back and the blue denim of her jacket made her eyes a deeper shade of blue.

Her laugh made him smile.

"Thirty three horses in one day?" His dad said from behind Dru. He shook his head. "I'm not sure I would be up for that."

They had driven to the ranch in the dark in time for a sunrise ride. Sunrises on the ranch were beautiful in May. The colors lit up the sky and reflected on the pond in pinks and blues. The different shades of green this time of year was spectacular. There were yellow, pink, and his favorite purple wild flowers covering hillsides and pastures. Pine trees, birch trees, pasture grass, flowers…all the vegetation was bright and gave the ranch a new spring life.

The air was crisp first thing in the morning, which felt good on the face while the body was warm in a light jacket. Cowboy hats helped keep the heat from escaping out of the top of the head and from ticks and bugs from getting in their hair and hitching a ride. The hats gave them portable shade for their eyes which wouldn't be hidden behind sunglasses until the sunlight became harsh in the afternoon.

They were riding the horses that would be ridden by the clients for the summer. Ten horses in all, three at a time for the first two rounds then Jessup was going to join them for the last.

"Did you check on Dusty?" Dru asked.

Reilly nodded. "She's fine, attached herself to the other orphaned calves Jessup's taking care of."

"I'm glad there's only five this year." Dru nodded.

Reilly stepped into the stirrup of his second horse of the day, and the little mare took three steps sideways. Not expecting it, his foot slipped out of the stirrup and he landed on the ground with a thud.

Both of his riding partners laughed. They knew he didn't fall far enough or hard enough to hurt himself…but just enough to damage his pride a little. He grinned looking up at them from the ground. They were mounted on the horses which made them appear even farther away.

"Nice!" He smiled up at them. "That is a caring reaction if I've ever seen one." He tried to make them feel guilty for laughing but knew it didn't work.

"Well you got the first dirt for the day," Dru laughed.

"Well, since I'm not as an experienced rider as you two PROFESSIONALS then let's hope it's the last." He joked and moved the mare next to the fence. He used the fence to keep her from stepping away from him sideways and used the reins to keep her from moving forward.

Once mounted, he turned with an "alright let's just get moving" look. The two adults moved out with a couple chuckles still escaping.

"Where to this time?" He asked as he trotted the mare in between them.

Dru smiled. "I've been on every inch of this ranch, a couple times over, so it's up to the two of you."

Reilly turned to his dad who shrugged.

"How about to the highest point on the ranch or the lowest point on the ranch?" Reilly suggested and turned back to Dru. She smiled thoughtfully.

"What?" He asked.

She turned and looked at him. "The highest point on the ranch is the original Eli's resting place. He was my father's horse for over twenty five years. We buried Eli at the place my father considered the most beautiful on the ranch, Rider's Point. That way, Eli could watch over the ranch. When Jet passed away, we did the same for her."

"That's cool," Reilly smiled.

"It is," She nodded.

"Dru?" He heard his dad say, so Reilly turned to him…he was looking at her with a concerned expression.

"What?" Reilly asked looking back.

She was nodding but looking forward. "Grayson, Scott, and I spread our parent's and grandparent's ashes on Rider's Point." She turned to Reilly with a warm smile. "So they could watch over us."

Reilly's heart plummeted. First the conversation with his dad the night before about his mom, and now this.

"It's OK, Reilly." She said and he turned back to her. Dru had an understanding smile. "It's my most favorite spot in the entire world."

Reilly shook his head; he didn't want to go there today.

"I have an idea!" She grinned at him. "But you have to promise not to show Wade."

Reilly sat up taller in the saddle. "OK, but don't tell him I have a secret from him or he wouldn't ever forgive me for not telling him."

"Deal." She turned her horse to head down the mountain. It was steep, so they instantly had to lean back to balance on the horses.

"When I was your age, my dad showed me where there was a cave down by the river." She grinned at Reilly's excited expression. "Matt and Nikki know but the others don't."

"Why?" Reilly asked.

"Because Wade would want to live there," she laughed.

It took them a half hour to make it down to the bottom. The horses were sweating and Reilly's back was just starting to ache from the angle of the descent.

They came to a stop about forty feet from the river, high on a rock bluff.

"You can see it from the river but not from land." She said as she dismounted from the horse.

They tied the horses to a small tree and the horses instantly dropped their heads to rest. Dru reached in her saddle bag for something, but Reilly couldn't see what it was.

She walked past him with a devilish grin and Reilly excitedly followed her up to the edge of the bluff. He didn't see a path and it looked like she was lost when she placed her back to the rock bluff, stepped sideways down the hill about five steps, then took a step forward and over a small bush.

"Dru!" Reilly's dad called out to her.

She looked up with a mischievous smile and kept moving. Reilly was right behind her, even though it looked like she was stepping off the bluff and going to land in the water below.

He was surprised to find a ledge on the other side of the small bush. He copied her stance and placed his back to the rocky bluff wall. Taking small side steps, she moved away from him.

"Come on." She laughed. "You won't fall."

"Dru, I'm not going to forgive you if we all go for a swim when we fall off." His dad told her.

Dru stopped, looked around Reilly to his dad, who had just stepped onto the ledge. She grinned. "Yes, you would."

He laughed. "You're right…I would."

Reilly chuckled. He was on an adventure with Dru and his dad…it couldn't get any better than this… and then…it did.

She seemed to disappear. Reilly had to look down to make sure she hadn't fallen off the ledge and down into the water.

"Keep moving," He heard Dru say so he took a couple more steps and then one large one to his left.

"Reilly?" He heard his dad's worried voice.

"It's OK Dad…keep moving." He told him and watched his dad appear from the ledge.

They were standing on a wide rock path, all three together. If they took one step forward they would plummet thirty feet to the river. Dru was giggling softly.

She reached out and grabbed his hand. Reilly's heart raced as she pulled him behind her. She took another left, he followed and then he was being pulled to the opening of a large cave. His dad quickly came up from behind.

"There is no way you're showing that trail to the kids!" His dad said firmly.

Eyes wide and excited, Reilly agreed. "Not in a million years."

Then he turned back to the cave opening that Dru was walking into.

"Dru…" His dad said exasperatedly.

She stepped back out and looked over at him. "What?" She said while trying to make her blue eyes look innocent…but the grin was devilish.

"How do you know there isn't a bear or mountain lion in there?" His dad asked in concern.

"I've been here hundreds of times over the last 39 years." She smiled.

"39?" His dad asked with an amused raise of an eyebrow and a tilt of the head.

"OK, fine…40." She admitted with a playful pout. "There has never been a bear in there. That is the only trail that leads in here and I don't think they could find it."

"And a mountain lion?" His dad asked.

"I watched for tracks." She smiled and turned. "Worry wart." She called over her shoulder.

Reilly eagerly followed her. His dad…not so eagerly.

They stood about ten feet in the mouth of the cave. Reilly watched Dru break something then a green emergency lite stick lit the interior of the cave. That's what she had pulled from the saddle bags.

"Wow…" Came from both him and his dad.

The cave was about twelve feet wide and went even farther into the mountainside than what the lite stick could reach. She started walking into the cave.

"Dru…" His dad said again.

"Seriously, Jack," She laughed, her blue eyes shining. "You would never make a good Indiana Jones."

"I'll stick with a John Wayne or Clint Eastwood." He joked back. "I didn't realize you were such a Tomb Raider."

"Scott, Grayson, and I have been here over and over." She told him. "We even spent the night in here a couple times."

"Seriously?" Reilly turned to her in surprise.

Dru nodded, then walked even farther back into the cave. It stopped about thirty feet in.

Lifting the light Dru highlighted the walls. There were drawings all over.

"Don't touch the walls," She instructed as they looked around the cave. "We think they are from the Indian tribes that lived in the area hundreds of years ago. We don't want anything to happen to them. I want my great-grandchildren to be able to come here and see them."

"And you want them to crawl along that ledge?" His dad teased.

"When they get Reilly's age." She smiled.

"Hieroglyphics?" Reilly asked. "Is that the word?"

His dad nodded proudly.

"You guys stay here," Dru smiled. "I'll be right back." She turned and left before either of them could say anything.

"Well, at least she left us the light." His dad laughed.

"Oh, I would have killed her if she had left us in the dark in here." Reilly joked as he walked around the cave. "This is really cool, Dad."

"I have to agree."

They looked over each of the drawings again as they waited for her to return.

When she reappeared at the cave opening, she was carrying a saddle bag and knelt at the opening of the cave to spread out their breakfast. Father and son happily joined her.

Reilly sat and leaned on the rock wall of the opening and watched the river flow by. The mountain on the other side of the river was all cliff. There was no way someone would be able to be on that side and see this cave. Like Dru said, it would only be visible by boat.

He looked over at Dru and his dad as they talked about her many trips to the caves. His dad looked over at him and smiled. Reilly grinned back. They both knew this was one of the best days ever.

"Has anyone fallen in?" Reilly asked.

"Scott, of course," Dru laughed. "He was trying to run across that ledge. Half way we heard him yell and we turned just in time to see him fall."

"Were you worried about him drowning?" Reilly asked.

She shook her head. "Not in this eddy. Living this close to the river, my parents made sure we were good swimmers." Then she tilted a head and frowned. "But don't ever do it on purpose because you never truly know with this river." She ordered. "It may look calm on the top, but it's raging underneath and will sweep you away. It's unforgiving…many people have gone under and have never been seen again."

"I promise." He said earnestly. "I never will."

They packed up their supplies and Reilly followed her across the ledge again.

"We're supposed to be warming up these horses for clients." Reilly pointed out. "I think they've stood more than they've ridden this morning."

"Well, we know they can go downhill…we'll test their uphill next." His dad laughed.

"So, where to now?" Reilly looked at Dru after they were mounted.

"I know where there's a ghost town." She announced with a grin.

"Seriously?" Reilly turned to her in excitement.

She nodded, "It's sort of a ghost town. The buildings are down but you can see where it was."

"Can we go?" His dad asked.

Both Reilly and Dru turned and looked at him in surprise.

"What?" He smiled, his dimples deepening. "Ghost towns are more John Wayne and Clint Eastwood than Indiana Jones. His are ancient ruins and caves…there is a difference."

They all laughed and Dru led them up the hill. She angled this time so the walk up to the top of the mountain wasn't as steep as when they came down.

"Let's switch to round three." His dad suggested. "I think this was a good enough warm up for these three."

"Jessup can go with us." Reilly pointed out.

It was Dru's turn to have a horse misbehave. When she stepped into the stirrup of her third horse of the day, a pretty brown and white paint mare, the horse tried to bolt forward. She had enough momentum to get in the saddle and had a tight rein, so she pulled the horse into a circle to keep the horse from taking off on her. To everyone's relief, she didn't hit the ground.

Once the horse was in control, she glanced up at Reilly and grinned.

"Yeah, yeah…" He shook his head in admiration. "You're the best ever." And he truly meant it.

She took the horse into the corral, a more controlled environment, and got on and off the horse about twenty times. The first couple times the horse still tried to run off, by the tenth time the horse was standing still, by the twentieth time, the horse was bored and nearly asleep.

Reilly wasn't surprised when she didn't have any more problems with the horse the rest of the day.

Jessup led the way to the ghost town. Reilly rode next to him with his dad and Dru following.

Jessup was just an inch or so taller than Reilly, maybe 5' 10" and was of average build. His light brown hair was always cut short and he had the perpetual five-o'clock shadow…even in the mornings.

Perched on his head was always a grey 'Gus' cowboy hat with the sloped crease toward the front of the hat in the cooler months; always a straw hat in the warmer months.

He'd never seen the older cowboy in anything other than cowboy boots and jeans; although he had heard once that Jessup used to be quite a swimmer in his younger days.

Reilly recognized all the roads they had ridden on, until Jessup turned down an elk trail that eventually met up with a long forgotten road. Grass, weeds, and small brush had grown over the road.

"Is this Tagger land?" Reilly asked Jessup.

"Nah, this land is owned by the State of Idaho. It's protected, but open to the public as long as they aren't on motor vehicles."

"So the ghost town is on state land?" Reilly asked.

Jessup nodded.

"Do Matt and Nikki know about it?" Reilly asked, secretly wishing they didn't.

"They know about every inch of this ranch and these spots that were found over the years." Jessup smiled. "You'll know them too, by the time Dru's done with you."

Reilly laughed and looked back at the woman in question. She was pointing to something on the hillside while she talked to his dad.

Reilly followed the direction they were looking and saw a couple of elk staring down at them. He started to look away when he saw something odd on the ground. He pulled the horse into a stop and backed her up, almost running into Dru.

"What are you doing?" Dru asked in amusement.

"I saw something in the brush." Reilly said as he stepped off the horse and handed her the reins.

When he made it back to the bush, where he saw the object, he had to search around the area to find it. Standing on the ground you couldn't see it, but up high on the horse it was visible.

Reilly got down on his knees and reached around the bush, grasped it in his hand and pulled out one of the largest elk horns he had ever seen. His eyes widened in surprise; he turned proudly to show the other riders.

"Dang, Reilly!" Dru grinned at him.

"I've never seen one so big." His dad smiled.

"That looks like a shed from last year." Jessup nodded excitedly. "People pay big money for a shed like that."

"I'm not selling it." Reilly informed them as he walked back to the horse. "I think I'm going to hang it in my room."

"That's nice enough, I'd let you put it in the living room." His dad said.

"Really? Cool." Reilly said handing the antler to Jessup so he could get on the horse.

"Don't crash with that in your hands." Dru warned. "You'd stab yourself."

They started walking again after Reilly placed the antler across his lap, with the tines pointing away from him.

"Don't tell any hunters where you found that," Jessup smiled. "We'd have hundreds of hunters up here looking for the big boy that carried a set like that around."

They made it to the ghost town and walked around the remains of each building. A couple were so weather worn-that Reilly wouldn't have recognized them as old buildings but it was still cool to see them.

"This seems like an odd place to set up a town." Reilly looked over at his dad.

"That's how many towns started." He explained. "They would just stop and start building."

"So why didn't they grow?" Reilly asked.

"Because there was nothing here to sustain a town; the river isn't close enough and the railroad didn't come up here so the people probably just gave up and left." He said as they walked back to the horses.

"It's cool and sad at the same time." Reilly stepped into the saddle wondering what it would have been like a hundred years before when the fallen logs had actually been buildings. He glanced around the beautiful green meadow that was decorated with bright yellow flowers. It was just a little taste of heaven…no wonder why they stopped.

The riders turned back toward the ranch, this time Jessup and Reilly followed Dru and his dad.

They were nearing the spot where Reilly found the elk antler when Dru stopped, stood up in the saddle and peered into the brush. She turned and grinned at Reilly as she stepped off the horse and made her way behind a cluster of trees and brush.

She reappeared with another elk antler in her hand. The same size as the one he found!

"It looks like a matching set." She grinned and handed the antler to his dad while she remounted.

Reilly walked up closer so they could hold them next to each other.

They lifted the heavy antlers side by side.

"That's from the same elk!" Jessup shook his head. "Can you imagine the elk's neck after losing a load off his head like that? Talk about a load off your shoulders!"

They all laughed and started back up the trail.

"So what are you going to do with yours?" Reilly yelled up to Dru.

"I like your idea. I think there's room on the wall at The Homestead to hang it in the living room." She was talking to him while twisted in the saddle. "It'll bring back good memories." She smiled happily at him.

She warmed his heart, Reilly thought as he returned her smile.

CHAPTER THREE

"Nikki hired someone," Dru said.

"Really? I thought Dad was in charge of hiring."

Dru nodded as she handed him the lead rope to one of the horses they were loading into the horse trailer. They were headed back down to The Stables with all the lease and rental horses.

"He does. She called and asked him first." Dru walked back to the barn to get one of the other horses. When she returned, she continued. "Evidently she wants to trade work for renting one of the horses this summer."

"Part of the job is riding the company horses." Reilly commented.

"She didn't know that. Nikki figured if she would rather ride horses than get paid, she was worth giving a chance to, so Nikki called Jack and discussed it with him."

"She?"

Dru handed him the rope and smiled. "She." Dru confirmed.

Reilly tied the last horse and stepped out of the trailer. Dru pushed the back gate closed and lowered the latch.

"That's ten horses, right?" Dru asked him.

"Five in each trailer." Reilly confirmed.

"You good with driving?" She asked him as they made their way to the bunkhouse to get their weekend bags.

Reilly nodded excitedly. "I'll be careful. Dad will be with me."

A half hour later, Reilly was behind the wheel of his dad's truck, his dad in the passenger seat and his enthusiasm for driving the horse trailer to town…diminished. Dru was driving in front of him, which gave him a little confidence.

"Dru said Nikki hired someone for the stalls." Reilly glanced at his dad.

"Keep your eyes on the road. Remember you have five horses and one dad in the truck that you're responsible for." He was leaning back as if relaxed, but Reilly knew he wasn't.

"OK." Reilly tried to calm himself, but his comment increased the stress making him grip the steering wheel tighter. The tension was growing in his back as he made his way around a large turn.

"The steepest part of the road, Parson's Grade starts around the next corner. If you're not comfortable with the speed Dru is going, then slow down."

"OK." Reilly didn't think he could grip the wheel any tighter; his knuckles were white.

"Her name is Kelly."

"Who?" Reilly was concentrating on his speed and the back end of Dru's trailer.

His dad chuckled. "The girl Nikki hired."

"Oh," Reilly had forgotten what they were talking about as they approached the steep grade. He could feel the trailer trying to push the truck so his dad showed him how to adjust the trailer brakes which made the truck and trailer brakes work together.

Neither spoke until they made it to the bottom of the long steep winding grade and the road leveled out. Reilly sighed loudly.

"Good job."

"Thanks," Reilly felt his stomach relax. "Dru isn't even in sight anymore."

"She's been driving it for over 25 years, it's better to go the speed you're comfortable with. You'll get used to it."

Reilly nodded. He had been excited when his dad suggested he drive, but now he just wanted it over with and was relieved when they finally pulled into The Stables parking lot.

Dru was already there; her trailer unloaded. She and Nikki were leaning against her silver truck when he stopped next to her.

"Great job." Dru smiled up at him as she headed to the back of the trailer.

Reilly could see the look of pride in her eyes. It made the whole stressful ride worth it.

"Thanks," He opened the door and followed. His dad was already there opening the trailer door.

Reilly stepped up into the trailer and untied the first horse. He backed the horse out of the trailer and held out the rope to the hand reaching for it. He didn't recognize the hand so he glanced up.

She had red hair, was the first thing Reilly thought. It was just long enough to tuck behind her ears. Then he saw her eyes, they were green, almost emerald and they were smiling at him.

His hand touched hers as he placed the rope in her hand. He pulled it back quickly, as if she burned him.

"Hi," She smiled…her eyes seemed to sparkle. "I'm Kelly."

Reilly didn't say anything, he just stared.

"And this is Reilly," He heard his dad say. "And I'm Jack."

Reilly realized he was staring, and turned quickly to get another horse and forgot to step up. He fell forward as the end of the trailer smashed into his shins. He quickly stood and stepped up into the trailer. He glanced back and saw she had already turned and was walking away with the horse. He was relieved she didn't see him tumble.

As he backed the next horse out of the trailer, he looked up to see his dad looking at him with a grin.

"What?" Reilly asked, his face warm. It wasn't like she was the first girl he'd seen, just the first one he had stumbled for.

His dad just shook his head and took the horse.

Reilly looked up and saw her walking back to the trailer. He turned quickly, told himself to step up, and headed to the third horse. Carefully backing the horse out of the trailer, he felt his heart start to race in anticipation of handing the rope to her again.

As he gave her the rope, he glanced at her and smiled. She returned the smile and his stomach tumbled as she turned and led the horse away. Reilly was still looking at her when she turned and looked back at him. She quickly turned around and kept walking...he was sure he heard a little giggle.

"Reilly."

Reilly turned to see who said his name. It was Dru. She was grinning as widely as his dad had been. He felt his face warm again, so he quickly stepped back into the trailer and grabbed the fourth horse. "Don't embarrass yourself again." He mumbled quietly.

He handed Dru the rope for the fourth horse. One more, Reilly thought and untied the horse. He turned the horse in the trailer and stepped out with the horse and kept walking, nodding at Nikki as she smiled and said she would close the trailer door.

Forcing himself to walk at a normal pace, he realized he had only seen Kelly briefly, twice, and he was already looking forward to seeing her again.

Reilly didn't see her when he entered the barn and eyes quickly darted from stall to stall searching for her then his pulse raced again when she stepped out of the stall he was headed for.

"I've made sure she had water and some hay." Kelly smiled and stepped to the side so he could walk into the stall. She was wearing jeans, and a dark green shirt that highlighted her red hair.

His hands were shaking, so he reached up quickly and unhooked the halter. A hand ran down the horse's side as he walked back out of the stall.

"She's pretty," Kelly commented and shut the door behind him.

Reilly turned and looked at the brown horse. "She's a sweetheart."

"I asked Miss Tagger if I could trade work for riding."

Who? Miss Tagger? He chuckled to himself.

"What?" She asked, turning her curious eyes to him.

"Sorry," He smiled. "I don't hear her called that very often. Most people just call her Nikki."

"Are you related?"

"No, but she is like a sister to me."

"You're not a Tagger?"

"No," He smiled, a lot of people thought that. "I'm Reilly Morgan, my dad is the manager of The Stables."

Neither of them had moved from the stall door.

"I'm Kelly Harris." She stretched out a hand.

He took it lightly and shook it politely…it was so warm…his stomach tumbled again. He let her hand go quickly so she didn't feel his hand tremble.

"I just moved to Clarkston with my grandparents." She told him.

"For the summer?"

Her shoulders went up slightly. "Don't know yet, either the summer or forever."

Reilly didn't know what to say to that, so he remained quiet.

"Do you know all the horses?"

Internally, he sighed in relief that she had changed the subject.

"I've ridden all of them. Last year and we've spent the last couple days riding them at the ranch."

"Can you recommend one for me?" She smiled at him again and Reilly felt his stomach tumble again.

He shrugged. "They're all good or the Taggers wouldn't own them, let alone let a customer ride one." He looked around the stalls, no horse heads were hanging over the low stall doors…they were too busy eating. "What type of riding do you like?"

"When I was little I rode gymkhana; poles, some barrels, key-hole…those kinds of games."

Reilly nodded. "They do a lot of that here. Is that what you want to do this summer?"

She shrugged. "I don't know."

"How long has it been since you've ridden?" Reilly didn't want this conversation to end.

"Five or six years…my mom was married to a guy with horses. When they divorced, we moved to the city and away from them."

"Which city?"

"Bellingham, up by Seattle."

They still hadn't moved away from the stall. He began to wonder how long his dad was going to let him stay.

"Do you work here too?" She asked.

Reilly nodded. "I help get horses ready for the clients and take them on trail rides. I help dad maintain the arenas, too."

Kelly's eyes lit up. "So we'll be working together?"

Reilly smiled at her pleased expression. "Yeah."

"Reilly come to the office please." Nikki's voice echoed from the intercom.

"Maybe we can ride together too?" She asked as they turned and headed for the door.

Reilly nodded eagerly. "I'll show you all the trails." He opened the outside door and stepped to the side so she could go through first.

"I'd really like that." Her green eyes twinkled at him as she stepped through the door.

His stomached flipped again.

"I better go finish in the other stable," She said as they walked. They stopped in the aisle between the two buildings. "It was really nice meeting you, Reilly Morgan."

He grinned at her. "It was really nice meeting you, Kelly Harris."

They parted, both looking back at each other and smiling.

The smile was still on his face as he opened the door to the office. He was thinking of her red hair.

"Reilly!" Nikki said loudly to pull him out of his trance. They were the only two in the room.

"What?" He smiled, trying to put on an innocent face.

They both laughed at his attempt.

"So are you going to thank me?" She grinned, her brown eyes twinkling in delight.

"Yes," He admitted. "Yes, I thank you." He felt…happy.

She was sitting behind the desk and leaned back in the chair. Her long dark hair held back by a wide black headband. He sat opposite of her. "Well, just remember, she's here to work, don't become a distraction for her."

"I won't, I promise."

"You'll be working here too in a couple weeks. Don't let her become a distraction to you either," She warned. "I don't want Jack to have to fire you or her or be mad at me for hiring her."

Reilly sat back in the chair and looked at her. "Nikki, I promise I won't…but…" He didn't know how to express what he wanted to say…he'd had crushes on girls at school but he'd never seen a girl like Kelly before.

"I will tell you if I see a problem." Nikki promised him. "The first attraction is kind of scary and exciting all at the same time."

Reilly was relieved that she knew what he was feeling. "She took me by surprise." He admitted sheepishly.

She giggled. "We could tell."

Reilly looked around. "Where are Dad and Dru?"

"They went to The Homestead to meet up with Grayson and Scott."

Reilly nodded and looked towards the door.

Nikki laughed out loud. "She'll still be here tomorrow."

Reilly rolled his eyes. "Am I that see through?"

"Yes!"

CHAPTER FOUR

"I thought you should ask out Marla." Grace said.

It was Tuesday; his first day of driving to school and his truck was a hit with his and Grace's friends. They had spent their lunch sitting in the bed of the pretty blue truck and now they were headed home after school.

"Why Marla?" Reilly looked confused at her, then quickly looked back at the road. He had just told her about Kelly. He had waited until after school, so they would have more time to talk about the newcomer.

"She's a horse person," Grace explained. "She likes riding and roping and is involved in rodeo. Plus, she's cute."

Reilly laughed. He had to agree with her, he had actually thought about asking Marla out, but his Dad said he couldn't date until he was sixteen. It was the same rule that Grace had from her parents. Until the day before, when he saw Kelly, he hadn't been too concerned about the rule. He had lain in bed all night thinking of her red hair and green eyes; the way they sparkled when she smiled.

"She would be a good choice." He agreed trying to get his mind back in the conversation with Grace.

"Who would you suggest for me…if I could date?" Grace asked.

Reilly thought about it for a minute then smirked. "Marla," He answered. "Same reasons."

Grace burst out in laughter. "Almost a good choice. Maybe she has a brother." Then she turned in her seat and looked at him. "That's what we need!"

"What?" He chuckled at her exuberance…she always made his heart lighten.

"A brother and sister that get along great together!" She laughed again. "That way you can date the sister, I'll date the brother, so WE can still hang out together."

Reilly laughed with her. "Why hadn't we thought of that before?"

"Does Kelly have a brother?"

"I have no clue. We didn't talk about that. Just that she's living with her grandparents for the summer….or forever."

"Forever?"

He shrugged. "I don't know."

"Are you going over there tonight?"

Reilly smiled. "Yeah."

"Can I go?"

Reilly hesitated, he wanted them to meet, but he wanted to know Kelly more first. He wanted to just be with Kelly.

"OK," Grace glanced over at him.

"OK, what?" Reilly said in surprise. "I didn't say anything."

"Yes, you did," She stared out the front window at the road. "Not saying anything…said it all."

"Gracie," He felt uneasy. "This doesn't have anything to do with us."

"I know," She said, but Reilly could tell she was upset.

"I only talked to her for about 15 minutes," He tried to explain. "I don't really know what's going on."

Grace nodded but remained quiet.

He hadn't really thought this was going to be a problem. They had talked about dating and hanging out with other people, but this was the first time they were faced with the reality of it.

They drove the rest of the way to The Homestead in silence.

"Just drop me off at the end of the driveway," She said as they neared her home.

"No," Reilly glanced at her, turned, and drove all the way to the house.

Grace opened the door and quickly walked to the back door. Reilly got out of his truck and followed her.

She turned and tilted her head at him. "What are you doing?"

"Following my best friend into the house to see what Cora has for us to eat." He smiled at her and pushed her through the door.

Grace smiled, "Go to The Stables you idiot."

"Nope," He walked through the door behind her.

"What's going on with you two?" Cora handed them both a bowl full of their favorite afternoon snack; peanut butter and bananas.

"Battle of wills again," Reilly accepted the bowl happily.

"You two amaze me." Cora smiled at them and sat with them at the small kitchen table.

"Why?" Grace asked as she stuffed another peanut butter smeared banana chunk in her mouth.

"You act like an old married couple." She leaned back in the chair and relaxed.

Reilly and Grace looked at each other and laughed.

"What's that supposed to mean?" Reilly asked, shoveling more food in his mouth.

"You know every mood the other person has, you accept it, and you play off it, without being mean." She smiled. "It reminds me of how Wes and I used to be."

"We're not a couple," Grace reminded her.

"No, Honey, you're not." Cora smiled at her. "You're something better."

"What?" Reilly asked. He adored Cora; she was always wise and fun. There were times they would get her talking about her past and she would keep them laughing all afternoon.

"You two are soul-mates and are very fortunate to find each other at such a young age." She told them.

Reilly and Grace looked at each other. "Soul mates?" They asked in unison.

"Aren't soul mates supposed to be couples?" Grace asked.

"Like you're looking for your soul mate to marry." Reilly added.

Cora shook her head, "Not always, Wes and I were, but they can be your best friend too; man or woman."

"We finish each other's sentences a lot." Grace nodded.

"And I always know her moods." Reilly nodded. "Sometimes before I even see or talk to her. Dad calls it the twin syndrome."

Cora took their empty bowls and headed for the kitchen sink, "Many people never find their soul-mates or spend their whole life looking. You'll be friends for life and will always be there for each other."

"So we trust each other and want what's best for each other." Grace said seriously.

"Of course." Cora smiled, a little confused.

Reilly looked over at Grace, wondering why she made the comment.

"And even though we might not see each other for a while, when we do, it'll be like we were never apart." Grace continued, looking at Cora.

"Exactly…" The older woman nodded.

Reilly and Grace's eyes met. Without saying anything they knew Cora was right.

"Go," Grace told him. "I'll be here."

Reilly stood, kissed the confused Cora on the cheek, put his hand on Grace's head and messed up her hair, then walked out the back door.

Anxious to see Kelly, he had to constantly watch his speed as he drove to The Stables.

Trying not to look like he was too anxious to see her, he went to the office first to check in.

His dad and Dru were finishing a conference call but waved him in and he sat quietly waiting for them. Some lady was talking about a wedding.

When his dad hung up the phone he looked at Dru and shook his head.

"What?" Reilly asked.

"She wanted a wedding in the West Stable, with the horses." Dru answered.

"You've done that before." Reilly remember helping clean up the building before and after.

"She has a guest list of 400." His dad told him.

"Where would they park?" Reilly asked in surprise, "Where would they sit?"

"Exactly…" Dru smiled at him.

"Are there any weddings booked this summer?" Reilly remembered how much work they were but they were also fun.

"Four or five," His dad answered. "In the arena and in the pasture overlooking the canyons, and behind the big arena."

Reilly nodded. His mind kept thinking of Kelly…wondering where she was… Did she really like him? He was sure she did.

"In preparation for all those wonderful wedding photographs, we need to get the storage building painted." He said.

Reilly nodded. "Ok. Do you have the supplies? I can start it tonight."

He rose, so Reilly did too. "Go home and change out of your school clothes. The paint and brushes are in my truck, I'll get them. Kelly brought painting clothes too, so she can help."

Reilly felt his pulse race…she was there. He tried to keep from smiling, but it didn't work well. He glanced at Dru as he followed his dad out the door. She smiled and winked at him; his heart warmed.

He couldn't have moved any faster in getting to the house, changing clothes, and returning. His heart was racing as he walked down the aisle and walked to the storage barn. It was beige, but had started to fade and discolor from the sun.

When he saw her, it was just like the first time again. He was surprised at how pretty her red hair was and how her emerald green eyes sparkled when she saw him. His heart raced, she was glad to see him!

His dad's voice finally penetrated his daze.

"Dru wants something bolder than beige, so we're going with a pine green." He looked down at the can and popped open the lid, then groaned. "I hope it blends in and not sticks out." He glanced up at the two painters. "Don't tell her I said so, but this could be a big mistake."

Reilly heard Kelly giggle and thought how it sounded like music.

"Well, Jack, it's a pretty color." Kelly said.

"Well, let's hope it's not too much." He shook his head then poured part of the paint in a paint tray for Kelly and part in a tray for Reilly.

"Fingers crossed." Kelly laughed nervously as she dipped the roller brush into the pan and turned to do the first swipe of green across the faded beige.

They all three stepped back and looked at the results.

"I hope it dries darker." Reilly commented; glancing at his dad's worried face.

"If it doesn't…" He looked at the two painters. "When Dru goes to the ranch next, we'll repaint it." He grinned mischievously.

The teenagers laughed and bent to fill their brushes with paint. His dad left shaking his head.

Reilly felt nervous and waited for Kelly to talk.

After a few minutes she stopped and stepped back to look at the color.

"I don't know, Reilly." She turned to him. "I kind of like it."

Reilly looked at the paint color then to her. He nodded. "It's drying darker….it looks like a pine tree."

"Might save us from having to repaint," She giggled.

She was just a little shorter than him so he glanced down into her green eyes.

"How old are you?" He asked.

"I turned sixteen last month." She answered. "How old are you?"

"I turn sixteen in January. You're a year ahead of me in school." He calculated.

She shook her head. "I didn't finish school when I was eight. So we're in the same grade."

He hesitated then finally asked. "Why didn't you finish school when you were eight?"

"My dad had…issues." She said quietly.

He didn't respond and just kept painting.

"Reilly?"

"Yeah?"

"Where's your mom?"

"She died when I was five."

She was silent long enough he looked over at her. She was staring at him with narrowed eyes.

"What?" He asked.

"I've never told anyone this before…" She frowned. "My dad died of a drug overdose when I was eight, that's why I didn't finish school that year."

She had trusted him with a secret. That meant something to him. "I won't tell anyone." He promised and wanted to ask about her mother but decided to wait until she offered the information.

"Tell me about school before you came here." He said and they painted and talked for the rest of the afternoon.

They laughed at each other's stories and finished the building faster than they expected. When just the trim was left, they walked back to the side they had started with to see what the color looked like when it dried.

They were both surprised. It was exactly the color of a pine tree and blended into the trees behind it.

His dad and Dru walked up behind them.

"Good job you two!" Dru smiled. "That was fast, you make a great team." She stepped back, looked at the color of the building, turned and looked at Reilly's dad. "It works."

He sighed. "I'm relieved to say…it does."

Dru gave him the "I told you so" look and then smiled at the two teenagers. "Let's get you cleaned up and call it a night."

The sun had started to go down as Reilly walked Kelly to her little white car. They watched a pink and yellow sunset light the sky.

"It's beautiful," She said looking up at the sky.

"We get some good ones out here." He agreed.

She opened the car door and turned to him. He stood frozen as she leaned in and gave him a kiss on the cheek.

"Thank you, Reilly Morgan."

He managed a smile, "Thank you, Kelly Harris."

He watched as she drove out of the parking lot.

"Wow." He finally whispered, as his trembling hand touched the spot where her lips had touched his cheek.

CHAPTER FIVE

Reilly lay flat on his stomach in the middle of the living room floor. The carpet burned at his cheek. He tried to move his left arm but it was stuck, he tried the right arm; it just barely moved. If he could brace himself with his right leg and lift, he could free the arm. Wiggling his leg, he found the wall. Stretching as far as he could, he braced on the wall and lifted his right side. His arm loosened and he freed it enough to grab his dad's arm. He heard a chuckle.

With as much strength as he could, he threw his legs over to the side and felt his father's grip on his arm loosen more.

"Good move," His dad admitted then slowly rolled to Reilly's right, which totally pinned Reilly under him.

"Dang, Dad!" Reilly started laughing. They had been wrestling for the last half hour and Reilly finally had to admit he lost.

"Alright," He spoke into the carpet. "I surrender."

He laughed and rolled off of him.

They both stretched out on the floor to catch their breath.

"You're getting stronger." His dad looked over at him; sweat droplets on his brow.

"Someday…" Reilly grinned at him.

They heard Reilly's phone alert him of a text message. Reilly didn't move.

"Grace?"

"Probably." He grinned at his dad.

"Gonna get it?"

"After one more round." Reilly jumped and landed on top of his unsuspecting dad who used Reilly's momentum and rolled…and quickly had his son pinned under him again.

Reilly felt him laughing. "Ten second pin."

"Surrender!" Reilly yelled into the carpet again.

His dad rolled off of him as they both laughed up at the ceiling.

Reilly sat up, breathing hard from the exertion. He glanced over at his dad who was bracing for Reilly to pounce again. Reilly stood, shaking his head.

"I'm done." He laughed and walked to the kitchen and filled a couple glasses with ice water. He retrieved his phone while his dad moved the two large recliners back into their normal position and then followed him out the front door and out to the deck. They sat comfortably in the chairs looking out at the star-lit night sky and enjoying the cool breeze. He loved it here.

Reilly checked his messages and stared at his phone.

"Grace?"

Reilly shook his head slowly. "Kelly." He glanced at his dad.

"You two have hit it off fast."

"I like her." Reilly admitted.

"It's mutual."

Reilly smiled.

TEXT FROM KELLY: I had a good time today

TEXT FROM REILLY: Me too, work tomorrow?

TEXT FROM KELLY: Yes, Th Fr off, work SA SU

TEXT FROM REILLY: I work weekend too.

TEXT FROM KELLY: Date if we work together?

Reilly didn't answer…how was he supposed to tell her his dad didn't think he was old enough to date…that sounded bad…like he was a little kid.

He looked over at his dad.

"What?" He asked without looking at him.

How did he do that?

"She wants to know about dating."

"You're six months out."

Reilly nodded but didn't know how to respond to her. If he didn't say yes, she would think he didn't like her.

"Tell her between school, work, the ranch and rodeo practice, you don't have time to date but look forward to spending time with her this summer."

Reilly's eyebrows went up in surprise, his dad was GOOD! And he could read minds…

TEXT FROM REILLY: School, Work, Practice can't, but spend every minute I can with you at stables

They waited patiently for her to respond.

Ten minutes later they glanced at each other, both deciding that she didn't like his answer.

"Sorry, Son."

Reilly nodded, he thought for sure she liked him enough to agree.

"What time is it?" His dad asked, suggesting she might have gone to bed.

Reilly looked at his phone. "Ten."

They both stood and walked into the kitchen. While his dad starting turning off the lights, Reilly headed up the stairs; half way, his phone received a message. Reilly quickly read it.

TEXT FROM KELLY: Every minute we can

Reilly grinned at his dad, who smiled back.

******

"So I get you before school, at school, and on the ride home. She gets you in the afternoon." Grace said on the way home the next day.

Reilly smiled at her plan. "She doesn't work Thursday or Friday so you and I can practice after school."

Grace nodded. "I sat and watched Wade, Sadie, and Nora taking turns on Rooster last night. I swear that horse has more patience than any human or any other animal…EVER."

Just the mention of Wade's name sent a twinge of guilt into his stomach. He hadn't seen Wade in a week.

He dropped Grace off at The Homestead and drove to The Stables. As usual, he headed for the office but stopped as he rounded the corner. His dad and Dru were standing in front of the office door.

Dru's arms were crossed in front of her and she looked really upset. His dad's hands were on his hips and he looked like he was glaring at her. Reilly stood in amazement. He'd never seen them argue.

He couldn't hear what they were saying because they were whispering, but it couldn't be good. Dru suddenly turned, stepped into the office and shut the door before his dad could follow her. An uneasy feeling went through Reilly as he watched him turn and walk to the back of the property.

Reilly stood frozen in place. What was he supposed to do? Go to his dad, Dru, or Kelly?

He slowly walked to the office and opened the door. Dru was sitting behind the desk, she looked like she was about to cry.

"Hey," She smiled at him. The smile didn't reach her eyes.

"Hey," He said back. "Do you know where Dad is?" He couldn't think of anything else to say.

"I think he's out back."

Reilly hesitated…she was always there for him; he should be there for her.

He stepped into the office and shut the door behind him.

"Are you OK?" Reilly asked taking a seat in front of the desk.

She nodded but her eyes glistened from the unshed tears.

"Dru?"

She looked over at him and smiled. "It's just been a tough day." She answered softly.

"Can I do anything to help?"

His question seemed to make her even more upset.

She shook her head. "I just don't like change."

"What's changing?" He asked nervously…his hands became moist and stomach was gurgling. He didn't like change either.

Her smile was more of a grimace as she looked from him to her computer.

"It's nothing for you to worry about," She smiled, trying to make him feel better.

"I'd like to help if I can." He offered.

Again, his offer seemed to upset her more.

"Reilly," Her gaze moved from the computer to look directly at him. He could tell she was trying to find the right words to say and not to cry. "You're one of my favorite people, and I really appreciate the offer, but I need to work this one out on my own."

Reilly nodded sadly. He hated to see her like this. He slowly stood and walked to the door then glanced back and saw a tear finally escape and roll down her cheek. He left quickly so he didn't embarrass her.

He walked to the back of the property to find his dad and ask why Dru was so upset and found him working the arena…that he had worked the day before.

It was the one thing he did when he didn't want to talk to anyone; he got on the tractor and drove.

Reilly silently watched him, wondering what to do.

"What's up Reilly Morgan?" Kelly said from behind him.

She had startled him. He turned and tried to smile.

"What's on the work agenda today?" He asked her, and tried to stop thinking of his dad and Dru.

"Jack said we should exercise the rental horses," She answered with a smile. "I'm so excited!"

Reilly heaved a sigh of relief. Something fun…

They saddled two of the horses and walked past the arena. His dad looked up long enough for Reilly to wave; he barely lifted his hand to return the wave.

Reilly and Kelly rode in silence until they were a safe distance from the buildings. Then he turned.

"Did you notice Dad and Dru fighting after you got here?"

Kelly shook her head. "They were in the office when I arrived so I just went back and started cleaning stalls. Jack came out to tell me about riding then he disappeared."

"They never fight," Reilly told her. "But I saw them arguing when I got here."

They rode in silence.

"Tell me about the first horse you can remember." He said to Kelly. He couldn't change things between his dad and Dru, but he could try and make the first ride with Kelly better.

The whole ride they talked about the different horses in their lives. Reilly told her about the Tagger Herd and especially Rufio and Cooper.

She was fascinated and swore to look them up on Facebook when she got home.

When they arrived back at the property, Dru was gone and his dad was in the office.

"Let's just put the horses away," Reilly told Kelly. "I'll see what Dad wants us to do next."

TEXT TO DAD: What should we do next?

TEXT TO REILLY: Have Kelly head home. You too, see you there.

"He says to head home." Reilly told her and walked her to her car again. His mind was so caught up with his dad and Dru's argument that he didn't think about the kiss she gave him the night before until they were standing next to her car.

"Thanks for the great ride, Reilly Morgan."

"I enjoyed it, Kelly Harris." He enjoyed their name game.

Again, he stood frozen as she leaned in and kissed him…on the LIPS this time! It was a fast kiss…but it was a kiss!

She smiled shyly, crawled into her car, and drove out of the parking lot.

Reilly was a statue as he watched her drive away. A smile crossed his face as he thought of the second that their lips had touched. Hers were so soft and warm.

He was still in the trance from her kiss when he opened the door of his truck. He glanced up just in time to see the lights of the office turn on. His dad wouldn't be home anytime soon.

Reilly's emotions were battling each other. His first kiss…at the same time as the first argument between his dad and Dru.

He was glad he had time alone at home before his dad got there.

TEXT TO DAD: I will fix dinner

TEXT FROM DAD: Thanks, be there in an hour

CHAPTER SIX

"Watch the tip of the rope, Wade." Grayson instructed.

"What?" Wade turned and looked at him.

"When you throw, aim the tip of the rope, not the whole rope…follow through with your hand." Grayson told him and demonstrated with his own rope.

Wade turned to his uncle.

"I was." Wade argued.

"No you weren't. You're just throwing the rope." Grayson smiled at him.

"How do I catch the calf if I don't throw the rope?" Wade looked confused.

"Pay attention to the tip when you're swinging, aim with the tip."

Wade swung the rope over and over around his head and watched the rope. He threw it when the tip was aimed at the dummy.

"Better," Grayson told him. "Try it without watching it."

Reilly, patiently waiting for his turn, watched Wade swinging the rope. Wade stared at the calf but Reilly could tell he was thinking of the rope. The rope sailed under the back legs of their mechanical steer. Wade pulled back hard and the noose tightened around the legs. He turned a proud smile at his uncle then at Reilly.

Reilly turned to see a smiling Grayson.

"Now, don't argue with me." Grayson's blue eyes crinkled on the sides when he smiled.

"Ok, I won't…this time." Wade grinned and loosened the rope so Reilly could throw.

Grayson left the arena and walked to the house. It was just the two of them at the arena now. Guy time…

"Let's get the horses." Reilly suggested and Wade quickly agreed.

With Rufio and Rooster saddled and standing patiently for them, they threw their lariats over and over again.

"My arms getting tired," Wade finally admitted.

Reilly nodded and coiled his rope and tied it to his saddle. Wade did the same then they began walking the horses around the arena with no destination in mind.

"It still seems weird to ride them." Reilly said, someday it would be natural but not yet.

Wade nodded. "Tomorrow night we ride Dollar and Cooper."

"It's a plan." He said and looked up to see the girls walking their horses into the arena. Grace stepped easily into the stirrup and swung herself up onto the cream colored Buttercup. They looked good together…but not as good as Sadie and Scarecrow. Sadie climbed onto the mounting block and then slid onto the big palomino. Sadie's hair was down, flowing down her back and around her shoulders. When she leaned towards the horse's neck, her hair fell forward and blended perfectly with Scarecrow's mane. They were perfect for each other.

Nora stepped up onto the mounting block and Arcturus sidestepped away from it… knowing she was going to slide into the saddle.

"Dang horse," Nora mumbled. Grace quickly moved Buttercup into Arcturus making the big dark horse step back into the mounting block.

"Thanks," Nora smiled up at Grace as she slid onto the saddle. "We're going to have to work on that. He can't be doing that in competition."

Reilly and Wade walked up to the girls and the five of them started walking their horses around the perimeter of the arena.

"Follow-the-leader?" Reilly asked. They all agreed.

"I have to switch horses." Wade reminded them. They trotted the horses when playing follow-the-leader and Rooster wasn't allowed to trot in the deep dirt of the arena with Wade on him.

They all nodded and walked back down to the gate. Wade dismounted and left to switch horses.

Reilly leaned forward, resting his arms on the saddle horn. He looked towards the big house. Dru's silver truck was in the driveway; it was there when he arrived after school.

"Cora said she didn't go to The Stables today." Grace whispered to him. Reilly had told her about the argument the night before.

"I have a bad feeling about this." Reilly whispered back. His stomach turned and not in the good way, like when he thought of Kelly.

"It'll be OK." She reassured him. "We argue sometimes and things get back to normal."

Reilly turned and looked at his best friend, "Have you ever cried when we fought?"

Grace stared at him a second, thinking, then shook her head slowly.

His shoulders slumped.

Wade returned with Dollar and they all started trotting around the arena. Grace took the first lead and led them around in figure eights and around barrels. They each practiced their reining as they weaved around the arena then made their way out the gate and along the farmer's fields behind the hay barn.

An hour later they were all lined up along the side of the arena, facing the fence panels.

Reilly turned and made sure everyone was even. "Ready?"

They all nodded. "Go!" He yelled.

Each rider started backing their horse up. Buttercup and Dollar took a couple steps then stopped. Grace and Wade frowned, then turned to watch the others. Sadie and Reilly moved Cooper and Scarecrow back a few more steps then the other two, then their horses stopped.

They grinned at each other and turned to watch Nora work Arcturus backwards across the arena. The horse moved slowly…but kept moving…even though it didn't look like Nora was asking him to move. When they reached the other side, Nora leaned down and stroked the horse's neck and grinned up at her fellow competitors.

"We win!" She hollered.

Reilly was impressed. Nora had Arcturus working well…once he let her on him.

"Does Isaiah do that too?" He asked her as she trotted back towards them.

"He's actually better at it." Nora said proudly.

The loud clanging of Cora's dinner bell echoed up to them. They had twenty minutes to get their horses back to the barn, brush them, feed them, then make it to the kitchen…or no dessert and everyone wanted Cora's dessert.

As they headed for the barn, Reilly sent a text to his dad.

TEXT TO DAD: Dinner?

His dad returned his message…too quickly…

TEXT TO REILLY: You can eat there, see you home later

Reilly frowned at his phone, the uneasy feeling coming back.

"What?" Grace said as they stepped off the horses.

He looked at her with a frown. "Something's not right."

He turned and looked at Dru's truck still sitting in the driveway.

"Talk to Dru." Grace whispered as she lifted her saddle off the horse.

Reilly grimaced and nodded. He knew his dad wouldn't talk; maybe he could try Dru again.

Ten minutes later he was following Grace into the kitchen.

"Staying for dinner?" Cora called out to him across the large kitchen. He grinned and nodded. "You must have heard what was for dinner." She teased.

He walked over to her and leaned over her shoulder to see what she had on the counter.

"Nice!" He hugged her from the back. "Lasagna!" She made the best lasagna…she made the best everything.

"Reilly, come check this out." Wade said excitedly from the living room.

Reilly followed the sound of his voice and found him facing the wall that led to the library.

"This is cool." Wade grinned at him.

On the wall was the elk horn that Dru had found at the ranch; the one that matched his. It was mounted on a leather covered board and sat angled, as if still on the elks head. He smiled when he remembered the look on her face when she came out of the brush. "It'll bring back good memories." Dru had said. She was right. The whole wonderful day flashed through Reilly's mind. The ride, caves, ghost town, the elk horns…the whole day had been perfect.

He stared at the horn wondering what had changed. They went from being really happy to really sad in just a couple days. He wanted to know why.

Cora called everyone to the dining room.

As he walked to the table, Reilly searched for Dru. She was talking to Scott towards the end of the table. His normal chair was one away from her…Grace usually sat between them. Reilly looked at Grace, just as she looked at him. He could tell that she was reading his mind and Grace sat in Reilly's chair, letting him sit next to Dru. He smiled…their minds just worked that way.

As he slid into the chair, Dru turned and looked at him in surprise, then a strained smile. Reilly's stomach turned again, as good as Cora's lasagna was…he didn't think he was going to be able to eat.

"How did the ride go?" She asked as she scooped a large portion of lasagna for him.

"It was fun," He tried to answer calmly. "Nobody's gonna beat Nora and Arcturus backing up though….she's killin' it."

"I've seen her practicing on that pretty hard." Dru nodded.

They ate quietly a moment before he saw her glance at him, she had a sad expression.

"Dru, what?" He whispered to her in a worried tone…she looked back at him in surprise.

Sitting down, they were nearly the same height; her legs were longer than his so, when they were standing she stood at least two inches taller than him. When she looked back at him they were eye to eye.

"I know something is wrong," He whispered; her eyes started to glisten from tears. He shook his head and turned back to his plate. "Never mind," He said gruffly. There was no way he could stand to make her cry and if she was that close to crying, then there really was something wrong. She only cried when it came to the horses!

He stared at his plate, not really seeing the food and he didn't really hear the people talking around him.

Reilly couldn't take the silence from her. He stood and pushed away from the table. Placing a hand on Gracie's head, he messed up her hair then quickly walked out of the dining room. A male voice called out to him but he didn't stop. He was out the door and almost to his truck when Dru caught up with him.

"Reilly!" She called out and he stopped but didn't turn or look at her.

"I can't see the tears in your eyes." Reilly's voice was low and shook when he spoke.

"OK," She said from right behind him. "I promise I won't look at you then." She tried to tease.

He waited for her to speak again as she walked up to him…her hand slid into his. She squeezed tightly so he wrapped his fingers around hers. She didn't speak so he did.

"Why do you guys do that?" Reilly finally asked looking down at their hands.

"What?" Her voice was low.

"Hold hands," He answered. "Ever since I was little, I saw you hold hands when times were tough or someone was sad."

"It's so natural for us that I never thought other people didn't do it." She said quietly. "Sometimes, a hug is too much…but we still need the touch of someone that cares. The warmth from the touch helps with the heart. So we hold hands to let the other person know that we love them, understand they are hurting or scared, and will always be there for them."

Reilly felt his heart hurt. "Will you always be there?" He asked hesitantly, he didn't know what he would do if she said no.

"Yes, Reilly, whenever you need me, I will always be here for you." Her voice shook when she said it, he knew she was crying.

Tears suddenly rushed to his eyes and he fought hard to contain them. There was something wrong…he knew it…but he also knew she wasn't going to talk to him about it. He squeezed her hand.

"I'll always be there for you, too." He whispered then released her hand and walked to his truck.

Without looking back, he drove home knowing his dad wouldn't talk about it either and there was nothing that Reilly could do to help.

CHAPTER SEVEN

Reilly opened his eyes and stared out the bedroom window. The sun was just starting to light the sky so he knew it was still early and he had time to lay in bed before he got ready for school.

His dad barely spoke to him after he arrived home from the Taggers. He asked what they had for dinner and if he had a good day in school. That was it. They had sat quietly and watched something on television before Reilly excused himself and went to his room. His dad had just nodded. Reilly had never seen him like this before; distant and depressed.

He rolled over onto his side and looked around. The light coming in the room was just enough he could see the pictures of his mother on the shelf. He stared for a while…wondering what it would have been like if she was still there. As his dad said; 'what would have been'. Reilly figured they would still be in Texas and would never have met the Taggers. He rolled onto his back.

A life without the Taggers? What would it have been like if his dad didn't answer the ad in the paper for the stable manager position? If he had never met Gracie, Wade, Sadie, Dru and the rest of the family? What would his dad be like, if he didn't work somewhere that he loved as much as The Stables?

Kelly had said her mom had moved her to a city where she didn't have horses for years. Cooper and Rufio had brought so much purpose into his life…what would his life have been like if he hadn't been there when they found the starving herd?

He sighed out loud. Then…out of nowhere…and for no apparent reason…he swore at the ceiling…said words his dad would have slapped him on the back of the head for saying. He said words that Gracie would have slapped him on the back of the head for saying. He repeated the words over and over and over…

When he stopped, he sighed again…that didn't help. He needed a more intelligent way to express his feelings…as his dad would say.

Reilly rolled over onto his stomach and thought of Kelly. He wouldn't see her again until tomorrow. He reached out and grabbed his phone to see if she had texted him. No messages from her, but there were ten from Grace. He sighed again as he read the messages.

Dru had gone to her room after he had left. Grace had tried to get any of the adults to talk to her but they wouldn't. Leah and Jordan seemed just as confused as they were. Her dad and Scott just wouldn't talk about it.

She would try again in the morning, no promises. They would talk when he picked her up for school. He placed the phone back on the table and rolled back over onto his back to stare at the ceiling.

No Gracie in his life…never meeting his soul mate. Cora was right, if his mother was alive, would they have ever met? The thought of her not being there, to balance his life…to anchor him, to liven his heart when he would drift…

He would never have known though…never had known the Taggers, he'd have other friends. What would his life had been like? Until yesterday it was perfect.

Reilly turned and looked at the alarm clock on the table. 6:44…it would go off at 6:45…he waited and stared at it until the beeps started. He flung his arm over and slapped it quiet.

Friday…it was Friday…tomorrow he would see Kelly he told himself and forced himself out of bed and into the shower.

As he stepped out of the bathroom he heard a truck outside and quickly ran to the window. He was looking for Dru…hoping it was Dru. It wasn't, it was Matt. He sighed again then thought maybe Matt would know what was going on and would talk to him about it. Reilly quickly dressed and headed down the stairs. Halfway down, he heard his dad talking.

Reilly did the one thing that he had never done before…he purposely eaves dropped on their conversation. If that was the only way to find out what was happening between his dad and Dru, then he was going to do it.

Reilly slowly took one more step down…

His dad said Texas…then he heard family… moving…he quit speaking.

Matt's voice reached him and Reilly's lungs stopped working when he heard what he said.

"We talked about Nikki and I moving in here after you move."

Their voices drifted away as they moved out of the house and Reilly heard the door close.

They were moving? To Texas? With family? His head began to spin and he had to sit down on the steps before he fell down them.

His whole body started to tingle…he realized he wasn't breathing and took in a deep breath and let it out.

"No." He said out loud. "No."

In a daze, he stood and walked to the front window to look out at Matt and his dad. Maybe… something… would tell him that Matt hadn't said what Reilly heard. "We talked about Nikki and I moving in here after you move." No…

They were standing next to Matt's truck, the door was open and Matt crawled in. He was looking sad as he talked. Matt knew what was happening…and Matt said he was moving into their house when they moved out.

The window of Matt's truck was rolled down and his arm rested in its place. Reilly's dad reached out and gripped Matt's arm just below the elbow as if to comfort him. Matt was staring out the front window; he nodded then turned tear filled eyes at Reilly's dad.

Reilly turned away from the window. His heart was racing; his breathing had nearly stopped again. Matt knew…it was bad enough that Matt had tears in his eyes. Reilly reached for his chest as the pain stabbed him in the chest. It was a gesture he'd seen Wade make after he broke his arm.

Wade…he was moving away from Wade…Gracie… Sadie…Dru…Cora…all of them…

Dru had said she was upset because she didn't like change…this was the change…

Reilly felt like his whole body was going to explode. He had to get out…before his dad got there…he couldn't talk to him right now…he didn't want him to confirm it…to tell him they were moving to Texas.

He ran for the back door and slid on his boots. The front door was opening so he quickly left by the back door. He was in his truck and down the driveway when his phone started ringing…it was his dad. Reilly just kept driving.

Half way to the main road he stopped and texted Grace to meet him at the end of the driveway. He knew when he didn't answer his dad would call The Homestead next.

The phone rang again. He glanced down…Dad again.

Reilly had to concentrate on driving to keep from speeding. As he neared The Homestead, he could see Grace running down the driveway…her mom running behind her.

His heart was racing…he had gotten Grace in trouble…he swerved in, leaned over and opened the door for Grace to jump in. She barely had the door closed when Reilly hit the gas pedal.

"Holy heck!" Grace yelled. "What the heck happened?" She was quickly buckling her seatbelt.

Reilly didn't say anything…he couldn't….his heart was still racing…his lungs hurt from not breathing. He just looked over at her with wide eyes.

"Breathe!" She yelled at him. So he did as he took the long turn towards Lewiston.

"I told Mom I was headed down the driveway and the phone rang." She started explaining. "She yelled at me to stop and for some reason I ran instead." She looked over at him. "I didn't understand why I did it then, but now…looking at you…I did the right thing."

Reilly just nodded, he needed to stop. He pulled into the rodeo grounds and pulled the truck in behind the horse stalls…they couldn't be seen from the road there.

As soon as he turned the truck off, he slid out of the truck, it was too confining…he needed open space around him.

"Breathe!" She yelled at him again as she ran around the side of the truck to him.

Reilly did, then he started bouncing…he couldn't stop moving…he was panicking…his heart was going to explode.

There was ringing…and singing…. Grace looked into the truck…her phone was singing and his phone was ringing.

"They're going to kill us." Grace said as she watched him bounce. "You found out what was wrong between Dru and Jack?"

"Yeah…" Reilly nearly shouted it.

"Reilly…you have to calm down." She yelled at him.

He stopped bouncing but started pacing back and forth instead.

"Well, that's not much better." She sounded frustrated.

He stopped, closed his eyes, and concentrated on breathing. After a minute he spoke, without opening his eyes.

"Dad is moving us to Texas."

She gasped. He opened his eyes and she was staring in disbelief.

He opened his arms and she stepped in. They held each other tightly.

As close as they were, they had very rarely hugged or held hands but right now, she was the one person he knew would understand his feelings, his fear, his pain because she would feel them too.

They were quiet until they both stopped shaking and the shock wore off. She stepped back.

"Now what?" She asked.

He shook his head. "I don't know."

"Well…" She started with half a smile. "We can't quite run away because that would just be stupid."

"The problem IS my leaving…" He smiled ironically, "Running away is leaving…Maybe if I don't let them know that I know…it will all just go away." He shook his head. "I don't know what to do Gracie." His heart was breaking.

"What was the Bonnie and Clyde thing for this morning?"

"Bonnie and Clyde?" He looked at her in confusion.

"Seriously…" She laughed nervously. "I felt like Bonnie running away from her mother and into the gangster Clyde's car."

They both laughed at the thought…then both stopped abruptly.

"Leah's gonna be really pissed." He told her.

Grace nodded with a deep sigh.

"Yeah, well your dad's gonna be just as pissed." She rolled her eyes. "So what do we do?"

He bit his lip and half smiled, "What if we told them we were playing at being Bonnie and Clyde…and see what they say?"

Grace started laughing. "Do you seriously thing they would buy that?"

He shrugged his shoulders. "I got nothing else and what do we have to lose?"

"We're fifteen…maybe they will. They think we're nuts anyway."

She handed him his phone. He hesitantly took it then sent his dad the most ridiculous text ever.

TEXT TO DAD: Sorry, playing Bonnie and Clyde with Grace

He waited…

His phone rang instead of a text message back.

"Dang." He looked at Grace…her phone rang too.

"Dang." She agreed.

They both answered and stood quietly while their parents yelled at them.

Reilly's ears were burning by the time he hit the end button on the phone. Grace was standing waiting for him.

"How bad?" He asked.

"Grounded for the weekend," She sighed. "If I ever do it again, she'll have my hide…whatever that means. You?"

"Taking the bus until school's out," He answered walking back to his truck.

"Dang," She said as she crawled in. "I was just getting used to this."

They rode quietly until they got to the school then agreed to meet at lunch to discuss again.

At lunch, neither of them had a resolution, but decided to keep quiet about their knowledge of the move.

"We make it difficult for them to break the news." Reilly decided.

"We'll kill them with kindness and you'll have to figure out a way to keep Jack from telling you when you're alone."

"Tonight we ride…I'll see if I can spend the night with Wade."

"After what we did this morning? Seriously?" Grace laughed.

"I'll have Wade ask…" Reilly grinned mischievously.

"That might just work."

CHAPTER EIGHT

He moved the reins to the left and Rufio tilted his head and moved to the left. Reilly smiled, the horse was getting better. They repeated to the left and right, and again.

Then he stopped and looked over at Nora. She was working with Isaiah on backing up. He watched her movements with the horse and wondered how a twelve year old could be so good at training.

"Cheater," He heard the giggle behind him. It was Sadie on Little Ghost.

The blonde grinned at him then her eyes moved to Nora. "I've been watching her, too." She admitted with another giggle.

"How can she be so good?" He turned his eyes back to Nora.

"Because of the type of riding she wants to be good in. We don't have to worry if people see us direct our horses…she does. Every movement is watched."

Reilly chuckled looking at her. "And how can you be so smart?"

Sadie turned her blue eyes to him, eyes that looked like Dru's.

"She tells me every day…a couple times a day." She giggled rolling her eyes.

They both laughed and then mimicked Nora's movements and were surprised when Rufio and Little Ghost responded and backed up.

They both looked at each other and laughed. The laughter increased when Nora trotted by and spoke; "Rock the movement, left foot, right foot, then repeat." She grinned and kept moving.

Reilly and Sadie did what she said and were amazed at the difference, both horses backed up evenly instead of moving too much to the right or to the left.

"Crikey." Reilly looked as Sadie.

"We'll never live it down…" Sadie shook her head and trotted off.

Reilly nodded and followed her.

"Where's Wade?" Reilly asked Sadie when he caught back up to her.

She shrugged. "I think he's staying overnight with one of his school friends. Mike I think."

"Dang," Reilly muttered.

"Why?" Sadie turned to him.

"Got in trouble with Dad this morning…"

"And Grace with Mom. Mom was REALLY mad when she got back to the house…that was weird." She frowned at him.

"You have no idea…" Reilly sighed, disappointed he was going to have to go home…then he sighed again when he realized he was sad about going home. That had never happened before.

"So you wanted Wade to see if you could stay here?" She asked.

Reilly nodded.

"Don't blame you. I imagine after this morning, it won't be fun at home." Sadie said wisely. "You need to give him time to look at it and laugh at how stupid it was."

Reilly nodded again; sometimes he forgot she was only ten.

"Are you good with math?" She asked.

"I get B's."

"OK, Grace isn't that good in math and Nora and I aren't getting along well enough for her to help me."

"You aren't?" Reilly was surprised. "I thought you guys were doing great today."

Sadie shook her head. "OK, so we won't be WHEN, I tell her we aren't."

It finally dawned on him what she was saying and he nodded, wondering if his head would ever get on track again.

"Us kids gotta stick together." She smiled and trotted towards Nora.

******

"Reilly, you did that wrong." Sadie shook her head and erased his answer. "It's like this…" She corrected the problem.

Reilly was sitting at the Tagger dining room table helping Sadie with her homework. He was spending the night in Wade's room.

"Dang Sadie," Reilly chuckled in amazement, the girl was a math wizard. "You don't need my help…you're a wizard at this."

"Duh," She whispered with a smirk. "But they didn't know that."

Reilly hid his face in his hands in case one of the adults was looking, and started laughing quietly.

He finally looked up at her. "You're awesome, Sadie."

"Thanks." She said with an appreciative smile.

They pretended to do math but instead played tic-tac-toe for an hour. She won most of the time.

"Alright you two, enough." Leah walked in and Sadie quickly closed the book over their games. "Come in and watch the movie with us."

They were headed for the living room when Leah grabbed Reilly's arm as he started to walk past her.

"Clyde," She spoke in a low tone which sent a shiver down his back. He looked into her narrowed eyes, his stomach churning. "Don't EVER have my daughter run from me again." She said firmly, her eyes boring into his.

"I didn't mean to." He stuttered. This was worse than facing his dad.

She nodded and let go of his arm.

He started to follow Sadie when he turned back to her. "Leah?"

She had walked into the kitchen, she turned to him. "Yes?"

"Both your daughters mean the world to me." He looked her straight in the eye and told her the truth. "I have no idea what I would do without them in my life. I would never do anything that would hurt them."

"I know, Reilly." She made the hand motion for him to go into the living room and followed him to the couch. They sat together watching the movie, with the two blonde girls sitting on the floor in front of them.

When the movie was reaching its critical point, and everyone was staring at the screen, Reilly looked around at the Taggers that surrounded him. The only one missing was Dru. Sadie said she was up in her room. He looked up at the ceiling, knowing her room was just above them and wondered how she was. Even if he could figure out how to keep his dad from moving them to Texas, he didn't think he could mend the issue between the two of them.

Nora, Sadie and Grace's laughter brought his attention back to the movie.

*****

Dru had already left when he skipped down the steps and entered the kitchen for breakfast. Cora smiled at him which always made him happy.

As he drove to The Stables, he was determined to find a way to keep the Taggers in his life. When he pulled into the parking lot he saw Kelly's car. He had completely forgotten she was going to be there. That's how screwed up his dad was making him right now!

Avoiding his dad, he went directly out to the barns to help with cleaning the stalls. He opened the door expecting to see Kelly and found his dad. Dang…

"Clyde." He frowned.

"Dad." Reilly headed for a straw fork then angled towards a stall.

"Not so fast." He said and stopped Reilly in his tracks.

Reilly turned slowly and looked at the upset expression on his dad's face.

"The Bonnie and Clyde crap was just that…crap." He stated. "What was going on?"

Reilly froze. He had no idea what to say. He stood there staring and wondering what to do.

"Hi, Reilly!" The voice of the angel Kelly sang from behind him. Reilly had never heard anything better in his life…at least at that moment.

Reilly slowly moved his eyes from his dad and turned to Kelly. His smile was pure relief. "Hi Kelly. How were your days off?" He turned back to his dad but only saw the door closing.

He stared at the door long after it closed. How do they get past this? He couldn't keep avoiding him forever. How does he convince him to stay in Idaho?

"What's going on?" Kelly stepped between him and the door.

Reilly smiled at her sparkling green eyes. His stomach tumbled.

What a roller coaster week! He turned all his attention on the pretty little red head that was smiling at him.

They decided to go on a horseback ride for lunch and made it half way down the main trail to the river when they stopped for lunch. The two of them had been laughing all day as they worked. He really needed a morning like that before his confrontation with his dad, which he knew was coming.

"How many horses do you think you've ridden in your lifetime?" Kelly asked as she helped him stuff their sandwich wrappings and empty water bottles into the saddle bags.

"Geez, between Texas, here at The Stables, the ranch and the Tagger Herd, I'd say dozens."

He turned and she was standing right next to him, close enough he could feel the warmth of her. She was standing on the rise of a sloped trail so she was level in height to him. His blue eyes went to her green eyes then down to her lips. He thought of the moment she had kissed him a couple nights before. They were soft and warm.

Reilly watched as she leaned in, he hesitated then leaned in too. For the next fifteen minutes they leaned in together.

When they finally parted, his heart was racing, his stomach turning, in the good way, and his face was flushed. He even noticed his lips were sore too.

She reached up and touched her lips, then looked up at him.

He smiled, she giggled; he was in heaven!

His dad was waiting for them when they arrived back at The Stables. His bubble was burst.

"Kelly, Nikki's in the office, she wants to show you the appointment calendar." He said politely. Kelly quickly headed to the office.

Reilly stood frozen, knowing the confrontation was coming.

His dad turned to him tiredly. "Dr. Mark's assistant dropped off some supplies for the ranch and Jessup needs them this afternoon."

Reilly looked at him in anticipation.

"You OK to drive up to the ranch yourself?"

"Absolutely," Reilly kept himself from smiling, another day of avoiding the confrontation.

"You'll come back tonight." He said sternly, bursting Reilly's bubble again.

They loaded the supplies into Reilly's truck. Other than getting away from the confrontation, he was really excited about driving his truck to the ranch for the first time.

He showed Reilly how to check the oil in the truck before he went on long trips. Then Reilly walked around the truck and made sure his tires were good before driving on the gravel roads at the ranch. He climbed into the front seat, checked his mirrors and turned the key to the engine so he could make sure he had enough gas.

"Jessup will fill it up at the ranch before you head back down. Don't forget."

"I won't." Reilly was anxious to leave before his dad said anything about the Bonnie and Clyde fiasco. Then he realized what he was thinking…he was in a hurry to get away from his dad. He felt awful. Why did this have to be happening? He loved his dad.

"Dad?" He said as he turned away.

He turned back and looked at Reilly, his eyes shadowed. Reilly realized how depressed and sad his dad looked, that made him feel even worse. He hadn't thought of how bad this week must be on him, too.

"What is it, Son?"

Reilly smiled weakly. "I'm sorry about yesterday."

He nodded and started to turn.

"Dad?"

He turned again.

"I love you."

"Reilly…" His dad shook his head tiredly. "I love you too, Son. Please drive careful, call me when you get there and when you head back. When you get to the bottom of Parson's Grade, stop at the pink house, there's service there and text me."

"I will." Reilly backed out and stopped to watch his dad walk back to the office. His shoulders were slumped and his head was down. Reilly sighed and turned to the road. He had a two hour drive ahead of him and should have been looking forward to it.

CHAPTER NINE

Reilly stopped at the pink house on the way to the ranch and sent his dad a text to let him know his location. He immediately texted him back, thanked him, and told him to drive safe.

Reilly chuckled. He just knew he was carrying the phone everywhere. It was probably in his shirt pocket so he could make sure he heard it.

The drive to the bottom of the grade was uneventful. When he made it to the steep grade, with all the winding corners, he slowed down to half the speed. It seemed like it took him forever to get to the top and his heart was racing nearly all the way. The first time a truck came down and they passed each other, Reilly had nearly driven off the road. It took him a minute to recover.

"Whew, I hope this gets better." He laughed nervously.

He tried to make up some time by going faster on the straight stretches. He still wasn't going as fast as all the Tagger Trio did on the road.

When he arrived at the ranch house, Jessup didn't walk out to greet him.

Reilly climbed out of the truck and unloaded the supplies. When he was done, he walked back out to the truck and looked around.

"This is the first time I have ever been here by myself." He said it out loud.

He looked around and wondered if he should wait for Jessup or if he should go ahead and head home. Then he noticed Jessup's truck was parked by the house. Maybe he was riding. He walked to the barn but didn't know what horse Jessup would be riding. There were half a dozen available for him to ride but he wouldn't know which ones they were.

Well, Sadie and Nora would know...

He walked into the barn but there were no horses there. He walked through the barn and into the corral, still no horses. He walked over to the edge and looked down the mountainside towards the river. It was the summer pasture for the horses. That's where he saw Jessup; sitting in the middle of the field with the horses grazing around him. His head was leaning forward.

Reilly's heart started pounding as he climbed the fence and headed to the man.

"Jessup?" He yelled out as he got closer. What were the odds that his first trip here by himself and he found Jessup... Reilly wasn't going to let himself think that.

"Jessup?" He yelled a little louder.

The foreman's head popped up and turned to look at him.

"Oh, hey, Reilly." He waved him over.

Reilly breathed a sigh of relief. "What are you doing?"

Jessup leaned back and lifted his arm. A leather horse headstall appeared. In his other hand was leather working tools.

"You're out here leather working?" Reilly asked in disbelief.

Jessup looked up and around the mountain side. "You know a better place to leather work?" He laughed.

When Reilly got closer he saw the small table sitting in front of the older man.

"No, I guess not." Reilly sat on a rock to watch him work.

"I didn't hear you drive up. What are you driving?"

Reilly grinned, "My new truck."

"You talked so much about it last weekend; I've been looking forward to seeing it."

Then Jessup told Reilly about his first truck.

"How long have you worked here?" Reilly asked.

"Fifteen years," He leaned back and stretched. "Came on board when they finished The Stables so Dru could spend time down there."

"Did you know them before you came here?"

Jessup shook his head. "No, met them in Billings, Montana a year after I broke my hip."

"Did you live there?"

Jessup chuckled. "No, I lived in Wyoming. It was a complete fluke that we met in Billings." He leaned forward and rested his elbows on his knees, forgetting the headstall. "I was recovering from my accident and had to sell a couple of my horses to pay the bills. I was selling at the horse auction and they were buying; plus looking for a foreman."

"How did you get hurt?" It was a question he had always wanted to ask.

Jessup looked over at him with a smirk. "The ranch owner decided to take everyone at the ranch skiing for Christmas; wasn't the best of ideas for a bunch of cowboys."

"You broke your hip snow skiing?" Reilly's jaw dropped.

Jessup laughed with him. "Never would have guessed it would you?"

Reilly shook his head. He tried to picture Jessup on skis in the snow; it was such a bizarre vision.

"Took a while for it to heal and then the ranch owner decided he didn't want me back, in case I did it again. I was only 42 at the time, so it wasn't like I was old and feeble…I'm still not." He started packing up his leather tools. "I took my horses to the auction in

Billings. Next thing I knew these three kids had bought all my horses then approached me to work for them."

"Kids…" Reilly smiled.

"Dru was only 25…kids." Jessup nodded.

"How did they know to hire you?"

Jessup shrugged. "Guess there were some mutual friends there that suggested me to them."

"I'm glad they did." Reilly said honestly.

"Me, too." Jessup nodded with a smile. "I have nothing but respect for the Trio. Hardest workers I've ever been around. They were open to learning as long as it benefited the company."

"Did they always get along as well as they do now?" Reilly was enjoying learning more about Dru and her brothers.

"Oh, hell no!" The man laughed. "They had some huge arguments to start with. Had one over a stupid boat that I thought was going to break them up."

"A boat? They don't have a boat."

Jessup laughed again. "Exactly! If they did, they probably wouldn't be together… Scott wanted it, Grayson wanted it, and Dru said it was wasting their money because they didn't have time for a boat. I think if she hadn't been able to sway Scott to see reason, they would have had a major issue."

"Scott swayed? I would think it would have been Grayson."

Jessup nodded. "Me too, but luckily enough they took a vote and the boat idea was put to rest."

"When did they start voting?"

"That was the first time. Grayson had just graduated from college and was taking more of a roll here at the ranch, as Dru moved on to The Stables. To make sure egos didn't get in the way they went to the voting system." He nodded at Reilly. "It's worked for them."

Jessup stood and tucked the leather tool box under an arm. Reilly grabbed the table for him.

"Thanks." Jessup smiled and started up the hill.

Reilly noticed the limp was more noticeable going uphill.

"Does it hurt?" He finally got up enough courage to ask.

"Not at all, thankfully," He walked to the gate instead of crawling over the fence. "I'm sure it will sooner or later, but I can do anything I want now. I just get a good massage every once in a while and visit the chiropractor a couple times a year. "

They reached the front of the house and Grayson's truck was there.

"I didn't know Grayson was coming up," Reilly was surprised. "Why did he need me to bring supplies up?"

"Came up early this morning. He's been riding down in the valley and found a few cows that needed some medical help. That's the supplies you brought up."

Reilly nodded as they made their way into the house. Grayson was just throwing steaks on the barbeque. "You staying up tonight?" He asked Reilly.

"Nah, Dad said I was supposed to come home tonight."

"You OK driving in the dark? You can stay for steak, then head down."

Reilly thought of the grade in the dark, he could barely do it in the daylight. He wasn't going to admit that to these two men though.

"I can stay. Dad said to call when I left."

"Good," Grayson said then turned to him with a glare. "Maybe you can explain to me why you had my wife running down my driveway chasing my daughter."

Reilly's heart sunk and he suddenly felt ill. He just stared up at Grayson and had no idea what to say. He didn't know what was worse; the look from Leah or from Grayson.

"What?" Jessup asked looking between the two of them.

Grayson stared at him, waiting for an answer.

Reilly started to tremble. He didn't want to lie to him but he also didn't want to tell him the truth. So they just stared at each other.

"Grayson," Jessup said.

Both Reilly and Grayson turned their heads to Jessup.

"If he hasn't said it by now…he isn't going to."

Grayson turned back to Reilly and Reilly turned back to Grayson.

"Someday," Grayson started. "You're going to tell me why and it better be good."

Reilly nodded; he would the day his dad told him they were moving to Texas. Hopefully Grayson would understand.

"Don't EVER do it again." Grayson said and turned back to the steaks.

The rest of the afternoon flew by as the men told Reilly stories of their first days together while they ate dinner.

Just as it was getting dark he got in his truck to leave. Reilly decided it had been a great afternoon, except the few minutes with Grayson. He liked the new independence.

Before he drove out of the driveway, Reilly sent a text to his dad letting him know he was headed home but would be going slow down the steep grade.

Reilly stopped the truck at the top of the grade, took a deep breath, then started down it slowly.

The stress started to get to him about half way down but he wasn't going to stop. He drove down the scary road at a turtle's pace. To keep his mind busy he thought of Kelly, then Dru, then Grace, then Wade, then his nerve wracking moment with Grayson.

With a sigh of relief, he saw the pink house appear in his headlights and knew he had finally made it all the way down. He pulled over to the side and sent his dad the text that said he made it, then tossed the phone onto the seat. As his muscles relaxed from the tense ride, he started to get tired, and the road was starting to blur in front of him. He hesitated pulling back out onto the road.

"What to do?" He asked out loud.

He got out of the truck and walked around it a couple times to let the brisk air help clear his mind. Feeling better, he got back in the truck, rolled down the windows so the cold air would smack in him the face, turned the radio on as loud as possible to assault his ears and mind. He started down the road.

There were lights headed his way, so he slowed down and waited for them to pass. They didn't get closer so he inched the truck forward. He laughed nervously at himself when he realized the headlights he was seeing was actually a porch light of a house. The stress was really getting to him.

He made it about another ten minutes down the road and pulled over again. His eyes had blurred again.

Reilly checked his phone for the time. It was 10:30. There was no cell phone reception where he was.

He sat quietly trying to decide what to do. He couldn't keep going.

"Thirty minutes…that's all I need." He said out loud then reached for the phone again. He set the alarm for 11:00 and set it on the dash. Thirty minutes, that's all he needed, he'd call his dad when he got closer and let him know he had taken a 30 minute nap.

That's the adult thing to do. He locked his doors, unbuckled his seat belt, leaned his seat back and closed his eyes.

CHAPTER TEN

There was pounding in his head…then someone yelling his name…then the pounding again. Reilly sat straight up and looked out into the darkness, where was he? What happened? The pounding came right next to his head. He turned and could see something hitting the window next to his head. Why was there a window by his head?

He shook his head to try and figure out what was happening. He looked around and saw he was in a truck…his truck…that made sense, but what was the pounding and the weird light coming from behind him. He turned…it was a pair of headlights. There was the pounding again. He turned to the window and could see someone on the other side…looking closer he realized it was Grayson. What the heck?

He opened the door to the truck.

"Reilly, what the hell are you doing?" Grayson grabbed his arm and roughly pulled him out of his truck.

He turned and saw Jessup limping up to them, a worried look on his face. "You OK?"

"Yeah…what's going on?" Reilly asked shaking, his mind a confused jumble.

"Reilly, why did you stop?" Grayson asked, he was still holding onto Reilly's arm, his fingers digging in, his voice gruff and his expression…angry.

"I got tired." Reilly explained, his head was still foggy. "I just stopped for 30 minutes."

"Reilly, it's 1:00 in the morning." Grayson finally let go of him with an angry push which made Reilly bounce off the side of the truck.

"What?" Reilly asked surprised. "I set the alarm clock for 11:00."

Grayson reached past him and picked up the phone. Reilly heard a few beeps go off then Grayson sighed. "It's set for a.m. instead of p.m."

Reilly groaned, "Grayson, I'm sorry."

Grayson nodded and checked his own phone. "I don't have service here."

"Me either." Jessup added.

"I was going to call Dad as soon as I got service." Reilly told them then he realized the whole situation. "Dad..." He looked up at Grayson.

"He called when you didn't arrive."

"I gotta call him." Reilly reached for his phone, panicking...his hands were shaking.

"You don't have service here either." Grayson told him and turned to Jessup. "Head up the hill until you get service and see if you can get through, let them know he's OK."

"Them?" Reilly turned nervous eyes to Grayson.

"Jack, Scott, and Jordan started from the bottom and we started from the top...looking for you."

The headlights from Jessup's truck flashed them, then disappeared as he turned around.

Reilly and Grayson stood in the black night with just the glow of the light from the truck's interior. There was no other light around them.

Reilly looked up at him nervously, heart racing. "I swear, Grayson, I thought I was doing the right thing."

"You did." His voice was calmer but still cold.

"Then why has this turned out to be so bad?"

"A little detail like a.m. and p.m."

Reilly started bouncing from his nerves. "It's really 1:00?"

Grayson nodded as he leaned his back against the truck.

"I thought it was the right thing."

"Reilly." Grayson said gruffly, which made Reilly jump away from him.

"I'm sorry." Reilly whispered and noticed, that even with the little light available, Grayson seemed pale. "I was just so tired."

Grayson sighed and leaned his head back against the truck.

"Grayson…"

"Reilly, stop talking…stop pacing…stop bouncing…just let me get back in control." Grayson exhaled loudly, his eyes were closed.

Reilly had never seen Grayson like this before. If Grayson was this bad…how bad was his dad?

For five minutes, Reilly forced himself not to bounce. He looked out into the darkness then back to the man he had scared. His mind kept racing back to his dad.

Finally, Grayson's head came down and he looked over at him. Reilly's heart raced.

"Our parents and grandparents were killed by a driver that fell asleep at the wheel." Grayson reminded him. "Pulling over to sleep…you did the right thing."

Reilly's heart nearly stopped as he stared at him. The fear that must have gone through him when Reilly didn't show up…when his dad called him…

"Grayson…" Reilly was near tears. There were no words to express how he felt bringing the horrors of Grayson's past back to him. "I…"

The older man raised an arm and Reilly stepped in for a rare embrace from him. As much as Reilly's body was shaking…Grayson's was hard as rock from the tension.

"Dad's gonna kill me." Reilly said when he finally stepped back.

"I doubt that." Grayson half chuckled; the tension and stress finally relaxing.

"I'd kill me." Reilly half joked; then asked seriously. "What should I have done differently?"

"Check your a.m. and p.m."

Reilly started bouncing again from the nerves this time, not the excitement. "Is that all?"

"Where you tired when you left?"

"No…just nervous about driving the grade in the dark."

"Then you did everything else right." Grayson assured him.

Lights appeared behind them, it was Jessup returning.

"They're about ten minutes out," Jessup told them as he stepped out of the truck. "You sure you're OK?" He asked Reilly.

Reilly nodded in rhythm with his nervous bouncing.

"Stop bouncing," Grayson told him. "You're making me nervous."

Reilly's feet hit the ground and stayed.

"Was he mad?" Reilly asked Jessup nervously.

"No, just relieved." Jessup assured him.

"Jessup, I'm really sorry." Reilly looked anxiously at the ranch foreman.

"I know, Reilly." Jessup chuckled. "I think we can see that."

They stood quietly waiting for his dad to arrive. Reilly felt ill, the steak dinner Grayson had cooked was threatening to come back up.

When they first saw the truck lights, Reilly started bouncing again. He forgot all about Grayson's request and could only think of his dad. He had to keep from running towards Scotts' truck when it pulled in behind his own. Jordan was sitting in between Scott, who was driving, and his dad opened the door before the truck was completely stopped.

Reilly tried to read his dad's expression…it was a mixture of relief and fear.

"Dad, I am so sorry." Reilly said as soon as he closed the truck door. It was all he could do to keep from running to him. The bouncing was more extreme.

Reilly pulled his eyes from his dad and looked at Jordan then to Scott. "I am so sorry." He told them but looked directly into Scott's eyes. He nodded to Reilly but didn't speak.

"I…" Reilly tried to tell him again that he was sorry but the words just jumbled in his mouth as he started to shake again. He could see the stress in Scott's eyes, and knew he had scared him like he did Grayson.

Scott did the same as Grayson of lifting an arm to embrace him. Reilly jumped at him and felt the same tension in Scott; that he had with Grayson.

When he stepped away from Scott he turned to Jordan and hugged her, she squeezed him harder than both men had.

He turned back to his dad, who had been upset with him when he left…the whole 24 hours before he had driven to the ranch…Reilly had been avoiding him and now the guilt and anxiety was running through him like wildfire.

"Dad…"

He opened his arms and Reilly ran to him wrapping his arms around him. His dad's arms embraced him and squeezed hard…then harder and tighter. He felt a shudder and wasn't sure if it was from him or his dad…or both.

"I'm sorry, I was just going to sleep for 30 minutes." He mumbled into his dad's shoulder.

"I know…" His voice shook when he spoke which made Reilly's have to fight the tears again.

The mixture of guilt from the last couple days of avoiding him and the guilt of causing them such stress and fear forced his eyes closed tight to keep the tears in.

Reilly stepped away from him and took a couple deep breaths to get in control. He didn't move from his dad's side but turned to the group.

Reilly opened his mouth to apologize again when Grayson held his hand up to him. "Reilly, we know." Grayson smiled to try to put him at ease.

Reilly chuckled nervously.

"Are you OK to drive?" Grayson asked him.

"No." Reilly said quickly. His nerves were shot.

"Good answer." Grayson smiled his approval, then turned to Scott.

"I'll drive him back down." Scott nodded.

Reilly's heart dropped and he glanced to his dad. He wanted to be with him; then he realized he probably shouldn't be driving either. Reilly turned to his dad as everyone started heading to their vehicles.

They stood quietly together.

"I don't know what else to say, Dad."

"I know."

"The last couple days have been terrible." Reilly sighed. "I know you and Dru are having problems."

"It's between Dru and me."

Reilly debated mentioning Texas, but knew it wasn't the time with everyone in the trucks waiting for them.

"But I added to your stress by being an idiot." Reilly admitted. "I tried to stay away just so we didn't talk about it."

"I could tell."

Reilly shook his head. "I'll never do it again, Dad, I promise."

"I know, Son." His dad reached out and brought him back into an embrace.

They weren't shaking as bad as they were the first time. His arms dropped and Reilly took a step back.

"Can I ride back with you and Jordan?" He glanced over at his truck with Scott in the driver's seat. "It's not Scott...I ..."

"I know." His dad smiled. "But right now, I don't think he should be alone either...it's late and he's tired and stressed."

Reilly glanced around at all the people and the vehicles. There wasn't any other possibility than to separate from his dad.

"OK," Reilly finally whispered regretfully and turned to his truck. "I'll see you at home."

His dad nodded and turned.

Reilly slid into the passenger side of his own truck and buckled his seat belt. They watched as Jordan pulled out onto the road and followed her.

They rode quietly for the first couple miles.

"How was the trip up the grade your first time alone?" Scott finally asked him.

Reilly smiled. "Scary....I don't think I could have driven slower."

"I remember the first time I drove it." Scott chuckled. "I was in a stick shift."

"No way." Reilly could feel the tension start to leave both of them.

"Every time I had to shift down I was wondering if I had any lower gears..." Scott laughed.

Reilly sighed, "How long will it take to get home?" He should have known the answer but his mind was so tired.

"It'll be another hour."

CHAPTER ELEVEN

Reilly turned to Scott. "Why can't I go home?"

"You have a house full of people wanting to see you." Scott explained in a low tone. "They were all pretty worried."

Reilly nodded. He hated the fact he scared everyone and felt he should go see them and apologize.

"Can I go home after?" He asked.

"It's pretty late." Scott reminded him. "Let's see what time it is after we get home."

Reilly frowned. He knew Scott was trying to be nice, but it was Scott's home, the Tagger home, Reilly wanted to go to his home…to his dad.

He turned and looked out into the darkness. The look on his dad's face when he stepped out of the truck would haunt him forever. The fear, relief, anger, and love…all rolled into that one look.

As he sighed, his breath shook. His eyes closed and tears fought to get out when he thought of what he put his dad through…thinking Reilly was wrecked and hurting or even worse… He had already found his wife dead and to think he was going to find his son that way…

"I WANT TO GO HOME." Reilly said louder than he expected.

"Reilly…" Scott started.

"You don't understand." Reilly turned to him. "I want to be with Dad." He didn't let Scott talk. "Did you know that Dad found my mom dead? Can you imagine how he felt thinking he might find me the same way?"

Scott turned to him with shock registering in his eyes.

"He must have thought …" A tear finally escaped. "I want to go home to Dad." He repeated.

Scott nodded but didn't say anything.

The rest of the ride was completed in silence.

Reilly nearly swore when Scott didn't take the turn to his house yet drove straight to The Homestead. He hated Scott at that moment.

When they pulled into the driveway, the swarm of Taggers spilled from the house. Reilly looked for his dad's truck, hoping that was why Scott didn't take him home. It wasn't there. He turned angry, hurt eyes to Scott, but the man was walking away from him towards the barn.

He forced a smile as Grace ran into his arms and hugged him tightly. He could feel her shaking. Wade was next, then Sadie, Nora, Cora…and it went on.

"It's three o'clock." Leah said as she hugged him. "Let's get everyone to bed." She wrapped her arm in his and pulled him to the house.

Reilly turned back to his truck, wanting to get inside and go home. His eyes went to the barn where Scott had disappeared. There was no sign of him.

******

Reilly lay quietly in Matt's bed. Grace and Nora were sleeping next to him; Sadie and Wade were sleeping in Wade's bed across the room. They couldn't get themselves to leave his side.

He slid off the side of the bed and looked back at Grace and Nora…they were still asleep.

He was still fully dressed and only needed to grab his boots before he walked out of the room. He was going home…no matter what they said.

He made his way out the room and down into the kitchen without a sound. The clock said it was 4 o'clock. He stepped out the back door and looked at his truck…he didn't know where the keys were. Scott probably still had them, so he turned to the key cabinet in the open coat closet. He was shocked when he opened the cabinet door and there wasn't a key to be found. It was empty…it normally had a dozen keys there for the vehicles, ATV's, tractor…

Maybe Scott left them in his truck. Sliding quietly out the door, he nearly ran to the truck. The keys weren't there. He turned and looked at the house then back to his truck. They had hidden all the keys from him? Anger and disappointment began to stir inside him.

He looked at the barn; he could saddle Rufio or Cooper but he had never ridden them on the road. Besides, they would make such a racket whinnying they would wake up the whole place.

So, he turned and headed down the driveway. He'd walk home. It might take an hour or two but he was still going home. He wanted to be with his dad and didn't understand why Scott hadn't taken him home. Dru would have…Reilly stopped.

Where was she? She wasn't there when they woke him up. She was never mentioned when they said they would let everyone know he was alright. She wasn't there when he arrived at The Homestead.

Reilly turned and looked back up the driveway. Her truck wasn't there. Where was she?

Dru had said she would be there whenever he needed her. "Yes, Reilly, whenever you need me, I will always be here for you." Those were her exact words. But where was she? He needed her now. He hadn't seen her since she had said them. How can she say something like that then not follow through?

He started walking again. This time he was mad at Scott and Dru which made his strides longer and faster. He turned when he hit the end of the driveway and started running. He wanted to be home.

Reilly was nearly out of breath from the running and from the hate he felt for Scott and Dru. How could they disappoint him like that…why?

He heard a vehicle behind him and moved over to the side of the road to make sure he was out of the way but the vehicle was slowing down. He turned quickly and saw Scott in one of the Tagger trucks. Reilly just kept walking.

"Get in." Scott yelled out to him.

Reilly didn't stop…he was going home. They would have to physically tie him down to keep him from his dad.

"I'm taking you home." Scott told him.

Reilly stopped and turned. He didn't know whether he should trust him or not.

"I promise….I'm taking you home." Scott said firmly. Reilly thought he sounded angry, too.

He opened the door hesitantly and looked over at him.

"I promise." Scott said again while looking him in the eye.

The way he said it made Reilly believe him, so he climbed into the truck.

They rode in silence again.

His dad was waiting for him by the backdoor when they arrived. He didn't say anything to Scott as he got out of the truck. He was still mad. The man should have brought him home in the first place.

He ran into his dad's arms and held him tightly. This was what he wanted…what he needed.

When they stepped into the house Reilly saw the one thing that could make him smile at that moment. The table between the recliners had been moved out of the way and the chairs pushed together, blankets and their pillows were in place. That's how they slept when Reilly was sick.

The lights were turned off and they crawled into the recliners. His dad pulled the blankets over them and tucked the blanket around him.

Reilly lay quietly staring out the window; his dad's breathing was the only thing he could hear. The sky was growing lighter as the sun came up.

"Where is she?" Reilly thought sadly. "Why isn't she here for him?" His heart was hurting from the disappointment and anger he felt towards her at that moment. He would never have dreamed that he would ever feel that way about her.

"Yes, Reilly, whenever you need me, I will always be here for you." Her words had begun to haunt him.

He looked over at his dad. The tears stung again at the thought of his face when he saw him on the side of the road.

Reilly reached out and placed his hand over his dad's. Their fingers grasped at each other's. Reilly looked over to see if he was awake. He wasn't…he was holding on in his sleep. The tears fell…for the love for his dad and the disappointment in the woman that taught him how important the human touch was.

******

His dad stepping out of the recliner made him open his eyes. Reilly watched as he walked into the kitchen and poured himself coffee. He turned and looked at Reilly, a smile spread across his face. Reilly smiled back and crawled out of the recliner.

Bringing him a glass of orange juice, they made their way to the big window that overlooked The Stables; their morning ritual. Other than checking on the property, there were beautiful sunrises from this view, but the sun was well up and the property quiet. It felt so good to get back to something so natural and honest for the two of them.

His dad put his arm around Reilly's shoulders and kissed him on the side of the head above the ear.

"I'm sorry, Dad." Reilly whispered.

"I know."

Reilly nodded, this was the time to tell him he knew about Texas. He started to turn and tell him, when he looked at the property below them. It took him a second to realize that Dru's truck was already there.

"Dru's there." Reilly said he surprise.

"She said she would feed this morning so we could sleep in." He answered and walked back into the kitchen.

Reilly stared in shock…wherever she had been the night before and early this morning…she knew…she knew what was going on. He had finally convinced himself that she was somewhere out of town and didn't know what had happened; that's how he finally convinced himself to fall asleep.

Staring at her truck now, the anger and disappointment welled up in him and made him ill.

"Yes, Reilly, whenever you need me, I will always be here for you."

Haunting words…he turned from the window.

CHAPTER TWELVE

"Come on. Your truck won't drive here by itself."

Reilly stood in the middle of the kitchen floor and stared at the back door. For the first time he could remember, he had no desire to go to The Homestead. He hesitantly walked out the door and crawled up into the truck. As they drove past The Stables, he noticed Dru's truck was gone but Kelly's car was there.

"Can I just hang out here and get the truck later?" Reilly asked with a calm voice but with an inner desperation.

His dad chuckled. "Truck first."

Reilly kept his mind busy thinking of Kelly and their lunch together the day before as they drove. The thought made Reilly grin. It seemed so long ago. His fingers went up to his lips as he remembered.

"You kissed her?"

Reilly turned in surprise and quickly lowered his hand as his face warmed.

"And you're blushing?" His dad gave him a knowing smile.

"Dad!"

He chuckled as they turned onto the driveway leading to The Homestead.

Reilly sighed. He didn't want to be here.

"Can I go back to The Stables?" Reilly asked when they stopped. Dru's truck was there. He didn't care if his dad thought he was in a hurry to get to Kelly, as long as he didn't realize he didn't want to be here. He didn't want to see her.

"In a bit," He answered as he walked towards the backdoor of the house.

Reilly took a step towards him then turned and walked quickly to the barn. He'd go see Rufio and Cooper first.

To his relief there were no adults in the barn; just Sadie, Wade, and the horses. The two ten-year olds smiled excitedly.

"Want to ride with us?" Sadie asked.

"Absolutely!" Reilly said too loudly and firmly.

They both looked at him in surprise then shrugged.

Within minutes they were saddled and walking towards the arena. Reilly peeked over at the house and saw Dru and his dad standing on the back porch watching him. It was the first time all week he had seen them together where they weren't arguing. They turned back into the house.

Maybe last night, when his dad saw how much the Taggers cared for him, he changed his mind about going to Texas…he hoped.

It really didn't matter anymore, as much as he loved the Tagger family, his dad was more important. He wasn't sure if it was because he was mad at Dru or not, but if his dad wanted to move to Texas then he would have to move.

"Come on, Reilly." Sadie yelled at him.

He looked up to see her on Little Ghost and Wade on Dollar trotting around the arena. It was time for follow the leader; he kicked Cooper into a trot.

By the time they were done riding, Reilly felt better. He had escaped the world by riding with these two cousins. Their energy and enthusiasm always brought him out of his funk…them and Grace. Gracie…he missed her…needed to talk to her…

"Hey!" The person of his thoughts appeared before him on top of Buttercup.

He nearly cried out but caught himself. He just grinned.

"You want to ride?" She smiled.

"Yes!" Again he nearly cried out…he was definitely delaying going to the house.

She looked at him in confusion. "Do you want to switch horses first?"

Reilly looked down at Cooper; sweat was beginning to dry on his sides.

"I'll wait." She smiled. "Thought we'd ride up behind the barn and in the fields this time."

"Great…be right back." Reilly headed down to the barn. When he walked through the doors, he stopped short and the little hairs on the back of his neck stood up.

Scott was there talking with Wade and Sadie.

Reilly forced himself to start moving and placed Cooper into his stall which was one of the first ones through the doors. He quickly brushed the horse, made sure he had water, grained him quickly then grabbed his gear and headed for his roan.

Rufio stood at attention at his stall door. The red roan horse loved to ride and Reilly knew he was excited to see the gear head his way.

As fast as he could, Reilly saddled the horse. His plan of ignoring Scott came to an abrupt end when he stepped out of the stall and right in front of him.

"Reilly…" Scott started.

Reilly could feel his back tense. "No." He said firmly and walked past him. Scott had to step back to keep from being stepped on by Rufio.

"I'm sorry." Scott yelled at him but Reilly just kept walking.

"What was that about?" Grace asked as he walked out of the barn.

Reilly stepped into the stirrup and swung onto the horse without talking or looking towards the barn.

"Reilly!" The voice came from the house. He didn't turn. He didn't want to talk to her.

Reilly looked at Grace, she understood, they kicked their horses into a trot and made their way behind the barn and up into the fields.

"Did Bonnie and Clyde ride horses?" Grace asked.

Reilly looked at her like she was crazy then smiled, remembering why she asked such a funny question.

"You know," Grace looked over at him. "This is going to get us into trouble again."

"I didn't hear anyone call my name." Reilly looked at her.

"Enough said." Grace nodded.

They rode quietly for a while.

"I knew you were OK." Grace said.

"What?"

"I knew you were OK." She repeated. "I'd know if something was wrong."

He looked at her. "I would know if you were hurt too."

She nodded and smiled.

They stopped on the hillside overlooking the Tagger property and looked out at the expanse of the property that was nestled in between farmer's fields. He promised himself that he would take a picture of this view before they left.

"If Dad wants to move, I go." He looked over at his soul-mate.

Tears glistened in her eyes as she nodded gloomily.

They rode the horses down to Angel's grave. It had nearly been a year since the horse had died. They dismounted.

"I would never have believed, a year ago, that Dad would have even thought of leaving." He looked back over the view of the property. "Or that I would agree."

"In three years we can do whatever we want." She reminded him.

He nodded and looked down at Angel's rock headstone remembering clearly the moment Sadie rest her head on his shoulder just before Angel died.

He looked over at The Homestead, to the pasture island in front of the house. He remembered the conversation with Wade…they would always be brothers.

Rufio rubbed his head on Reilly's arm which made him turn to the horse. His body felt like a shock wave ran through it. It wasn't just the Taggers! It was Cooper and Rufio too. They belonged to Tagger Enterprises. He would be leaving them! Reilly felt his throat constrict when he thought of the first time he saw Rufio; skeletal, weak, but still excited to see him. As he had touched the horse, the roan had leaned into him as if to thank him.

Reilly looked down at the barn…Cooper, he hadn't seen him in the stall at first. It had been so dark and Cooper so black, but when he did, Reilly had swore and called out to Dru. She was the first to take care of the horse.

The first night in the stalls he had stared at the two of them so hard his eyes had hurt, they were filling his heart in a place he didn't know existed; a place for unconditional love…and they gave it to him every day. When it was his time to feed, he had stepped into the stalls and fallen asleep between them. He had done it every night…that's why Dru had caught him in with them the night he named Rufio.

Reilly looked down at the house and thought of her. Why wasn't she there last night?

Rufio rubbed his arm again. Reilly touched the horse's nose and could feel Rufio's breath on the back of his hand. He turned his hand over and felt the warm air slide against his palm.

With the Taggers he could talk to them on the phone and Facebook Grace…but the horses? Pictures of them wouldn't be enough. His and Grace's dream of team roping together would be over…

He turned to Grace with a new determination. "What can we do to change his mind?"

She grinned. "That's better."

They remounted the horses and made their way back to the barn. "We have to find out what happened between Dru and your dad." Grace said.

Reilly thought of Dru again. He had to handle her disappearance the last 24 hours better. The only way he could keep the rest of the family was to let her go.

He let the anger towards her harden his heart. He wasn't letting Grace, Sadie, Wade, Nora, Matt, and Nikki along with Rufio and Cooper go because he was mad at Dru.

First thing he would have to do is apologize to Scott for being rude. They put the horses in the barn; brushed, watered, and fed.

Grace took his hand as they walked from the barn to the house. Reilly looked down at her hand grasping his.

"Yes, Reilly, whenever you need me, I will always be here for you."

He tightened his jaw and toughened his resolve. Then he turned the knob to the back door and with solid determination opened the door.

It took four steps into the hallway to see into the kitchen…and Dru was there. She turned to him. His fortitude vanished when he looked into her blue eyes. Hopeful…caring…loving…blue eyes… his heart melted. She was wearing a white shirt and her hair was down cascading around her shoulders. The woman looked…angelical.

He felt Grace's hands on his back, pushing him into the kitchen, she didn't realize that Dru was there.

"Reilly," Dru took a step towards him.

Reilly just shook his head, he couldn't do this. He walked down the hallway away from her, not knowing where he was going…Matt appeared in front of him.

Matt…who was moving into their house when they moved to Texas. He just couldn't imagine Matt moving his stuff into the house Reilly and his dad had lived in for nearly eight years.

"Hey, Reilly…" Matt smiled…it faded when he saw the look on Reilly face. "What's wrong?"

"I can't do this." Reilly looked him in the eye.

"Do what?" Matt asked with a tilt of the head.

"I can't pretend that everything is alright."

Matt shook his head. "What?" He was totally confused.

Wade and Nora walked into view as they were headed up the stairs. Reilly's eyes followed them until they disappeared.

"Reilly, what is it?" Matt asked, neither had moved.

Reilly looked back at him, Grace gripped his shirt behind him, she was realizing what was happening. He turned to her, Dru was standing directly behind Grace and her eyes registered surprise and confusion at his reaction.

Reilly looked down at Grace, "I can't." He told her then turned, walked past a stunned Matt, and through the living room, out the door, and just walked, straight out….he ended up in the pasture island. He sat on the bench and stared at the ground.

"Well, that didn't work." He said out loud.

His phone alerted him to a message.

Text from Grace: They are all confused, asking me questions

Text from Reilly: ??

Text from Grace: I told them nothing, they are headed to you

CHAPTER THIRTEEN

Reilly looked up and saw his dad and Dru walking out of the house and towards the pasture island.

"This is it," He felt himself start to bounce and forced himself to stop. "It's time to get this out into the open."

Shaking his head sadly, he stepped through the gate and into the pasture, but leaned his back against the fence to wait for them. It was time to act like an adult and face reality; and try to get his dad to change his mind.

Dru smiled nervously at him. Why would his dad bring her? Of all people? Why Dru to tell him they're leaving? She didn't even care enough to show up last night. Reilly couldn't look at them anymore and dropped his eyes to the ground.

"Reilly," His dad said as they got close.

"Dad." Reilly gritted his teeth.

"We need to talk to you." He said with a nervous tone.

Reilly took a deep breath and looked at the two of them. They both looked worried. Then why do this? He wanted to yell at them. Reilly felt his heart begin to hurt. How was he going to be able to change his dad's mind? Why was Dru there?

"I don't want this, Dad." Reilly pleaded. Dru's face register astonishment and then hurt. Almost like he'd slapped her…why?

"What?" His dad asked with eyes opened wide in surprise.

"I don't want to move." Reilly answered and saw them quickly glance at each other, neither of them spoke. He was sure it was because they didn't know he knew about Texas. "I heard you talking about moving to Texas and I don't want to leave. I know you two have had problems… and maybe can't work together anymore…but why Texas? I don't want to move. I love it here, please don't do this, Dad." He pleaded, desperation vibrating in his voice. Reilly had tried to remain calm but he could feel tears start to sting the back of his eyes and his hands began to shake.

"You heard me talking about Texas? When?" His dad frowned.

"You were talking to Matt about me needing to be with family." Reilly looked between the two. "The Taggers are family, Dad. Family is in your heart not in your blood." He argued. "I don't want to move to Texas." He looked down to the ground dejected. He'd finally said it…but it didn't make him feel any better.

"Is that why you were rude to Dru and Matt just now?" He asked.

Reilly nodded but didn't look up.

"You owe them an apology." He said firmly.

Reilly took a deep breath and let it out. "I'm sorry Dru. I really am. I would never want to do anything that would hurt Matt ….or you."

"It would be better if you looked at her when you said it." He said.

Reilly slowly raised his eyes to Dru. She was smiling at him, trying to put him at ease. His heart hurt again, why did she do that to him? How could his dad take him away from her? How could she not be there for him last night…this morning?

He quickly repeated his apology. She nodded and he dropped his confused and angry eyes again.

"That's sort of better." His dad said, "You only heard a portion of the conversation, Son. I have no intention of moving us back to Texas."

Reilly's head shot up and he looked at him to see if he was serious. Hope seared through him…then relief…he was serious.

He continued. "I consider the Taggers family also."

"I don't understand, Dad," Reilly said; his heart racing. "What was all the talk about moving?" He looked between the two of them. "And you two were so upset with each other."

His dad glanced over at Dru then back to him. "I was talking about us moving in here at The Homestead."

Reilly's mind was racing. Move here? With the Taggers? What? "I don't understand."

His dad stepped closer, his eye's registering concern…yet hope. "Dru and I started a relationship last October, when Rooster had his surgery."

"A relationship?" Reilly looked at them in surprise. "What?" His mind just couldn't comprehend what he was saying…a relationship?

"Dru and I have been seeing each other, as a couple, not just friends or for business."

Reilly shook his head in disbelief. He felt like all the blood was rushing into his head.

"Reilly, I asked Dru to marry me." He said with a nervous smile. "After our day of riding together Saturday, and the trip to the caves…the ghost town…I knew we were to be together forever…I knew it was time." He paused.

Reilly looked at his dad…stunned…the blood had stopped moving, his heart stopped beating…he wasn't even sure if he was breathing.

"Reilly…she said yes." His grin was full of joy.

Reilly had to reach behind him and grab the fence. His eyes went to Dru, she smiled with a hopeful expression…it was too much for his heart to bear…he had to drop his eyes away from her.

They weren't moving to Texas. They were moving to The Homestead. His dad was marrying Dru. Dru was going to be his step-mother; his MOM. He felt his throat constrict and the pressure of the tears again…now he was sure he was going to hyperventilate. He had dreamt of Dru being his mom for years. It was the only thing that he hadn't told Grace; how much he wanted Dru to be his mom. He wanted a mom.

He didn't know what it was like to have one of his own, just seeing the Tagger mothers fed his need. There were days he would have to leave the Homestead because watching Leah, Jordan, and Dru with the kids just seemed like torture. But it wasn't just a mom though; it was Dru.

Reilly glanced up and looked at her. Her blue eyes shimmered and looked hurt. He dropped his eyes again. Now he was hurting her, he knew it. He didn't know what to say. How could he tell her how happy he was? How much this meant to him? He took a deep breath again and let it out. He still couldn't believe this was happening. He felt numb.

"Are you alright with this, Son?" His dad asked in a low concerned voice.

Reilly squeezed his eyes shut to keep the tears from falling. His dad was asking him if he was alright with Dru being his mom…asking him if it was OK to move into the Tagger home. How unreal was that!?!

 Wade would be thrilled if he moved in permanently. Reilly shook his head to clear out all the thoughts running through it. He suddenly realized they might take that as a no.

Reilly opened his eyes and looked at her. Tears had started to fall from her anguished eyes.

How could he hurt her like this? Reilly knew he couldn't speak; his throat was constricted…if he said something he would breakdown and cry from years of wanting a mother. He didn't want that. How could he convey how much this meant to him without talking? How much she meant to him? Then, he remembered the one thing he knew she would understand.

Reilly slowly raised his hand out to her. He heard her gasp through the tears, and saw her quickly raise her hand to his. He dropped his gaze to watch her hand slide into his; the warmth of her fingers sliding around his own. *His mom…she was going to be his mom.* His heart was pounding so hard he was sure it would burst. Her hand tightened around his hand. It wasn't enough, just the hand, it wasn't enough…he quickly pulled her to him and threw his arms around her.

He could feel her arms come around him and hold him tightly; then…just a little tighter. That one simple move, made the tears fall from the years of needing a mom. The years of wishing SHE was his mom. He tucked his head into her neck and let the tears fall. She held him tighter which made him cry harder, sobs wracked through his body. This is what he was missing for all those years; a mother's arms holding him and comforting him. He needed her.

Reilly could feel her tears landing on his face as they held each other. He tried to stop crying but it just turned into shaking breaths.

"Take your time," She whispered to him. It was a loving, mothering voice, which made his head dizzy.

Reilly lifted his face from her neck and turned to rest it over her shoulder, but he didn't let her go and she didn't let him go.

"Can I get in on this?" He heard his dad.

"No," Reilly answered. He couldn't see his dad. "She's mine right now."

He felt her giggle and lean into him and rest her head against his. It was those little movements of true caring.

If this wasn't real…if it was another dream…he was going to explode. He had to make sure; "Dad?"

"Yes?"

"Is this a dream?"

"No. It's real."

"I've wanted this for years." Reilly admitted and felt her gasp. "I've dreamt of this so many times that it would hurt when I woke up. I would watch her with Matt and Nikki and I would just want to cry." His tears started falling again. "Dru?"

"Yes?" She whispered.

"Can I call you Mom?"

"Of course." Her arms tightened around him again and she buried her face in his shoulder.

He held her for a few more minutes, then told himself he couldn't do this forever, she would be there forever now, anytime he needed her; just like she promised. He smiled and released his grip on her. She hesitated then relaxed her arms. He stepped back and looked up at her.

His new 'soon to be mom' brought both her hands up to his face and gently wiped away the tear streaks. Her eyes seemed to glow with love.

"So," His dad chuckle. "You're good with this marriage thing then?"

Reilly smiled at the gleam in her eye. He never wanted to see that happiness leave her. He turned to his dad.

"Yeah, I think so." He answered with a chuckle. "I think I need to sit down."

Reilly opened the gate and they made their way to the two benches. He and Dru sat on one bench, her hand firmly gripped in his. His dad sat on the bench across from them.

"Whew," Reilly grinned. "I think it's going to take a bit for this to sink in." He leaned back and looked down at Dru's hand inside his own. He still couldn't believe this.

"I don't understand." Reilly looked at them. "You guys weren't even talking this week….you both were so upset."

She squeezed his hand which made him look up at her. "Jack asked me to marry him Wednesday morning…and I said no." She admitted with a grimace.

"No?" Riley stared up at her, stunned.

"I…I don't like change…wasn't ready….I was just so afraid that it would change our lives." She said nervously.

"What changed?" He asked. "Why did you change your mind?"

"Are you kidding me?" She looked at him seriously. "You disappeared and terrified me."

Reilly took in her concerned expression then looked at the ground. "I didn't think you cared."

"What?" She nearly yelled.

He glanced up at his dad then to her. "You weren't there…and I didn't see you after…you weren't here… You told me the other night that you would always be there for me….but you weren't…"

She turned him to her, tears threatening to fall again. "Reilly, I was nearly out of my mind. They had to hide all the keys to the trucks and Matt had to physically restrain me from leaving."

He looked at her in shock. "I thought they hid the keys from me, so I couldn't leave this morning."

She shook her head. "Jessup and Grayson were headed down from the ranch and Jack, Jordan and Scott had already left from here when I heard about it. They convinced themselves that I wouldn't be of any help. When they found you…" A tear slid down her cheek. "I was physically ill when they told me they found you and you were OK, the relief was just overwhelming. It was then that I realized that

I wasn't letting you…" Her eyes twinkled with humor when she looked at his dad. "….or Jack…out of my life."

"But you weren't here last night," He had been so hurt.

Dru squeezed his hand tightly.

"She was with me." His dad explained.

"I wanted to go home." Reilly told him. "But they said I had to stay here and you weren't here…I wanted to be home with you."

"My fault," Dru told him honestly. "I asked Scott to keep you here so I could go to Jack and beg his forgiveness and ask him to marry me." She squeezed his hand again. "I couldn't let another moment go by without knowing you were going to be with us forever." She paused and looked apologetic. "Scott called and told us you needed to be home, that you had left and were walking home. He was miserable for not taking you home and told us we didn't have a choice…even if he had to kick the door in, he was bringing you to Jack."

Reilly's head was spinning from all the information. "I thought you didn't care."

"She does." His dad said quickly.

"I absolutely do." She assured him.

They were all quiet for a moment. He knew they were letting him process all the information.

"Last year in the stall…?" Reilly looked up at her. He knew she would know what he was talking about.

"Yes?" She turned so she could see him better…her blue eyes soft and loving; his heart melted again.

"I told you that Rufio and Cooper gave me purpose." Reilly wanted her to understand how much this meant to him.

"When was this?" His dad asked.

Reilly looked over at him then up to Dru again. "You didn't tell him?"

"It was our moment," She smiled and squeezed his hand.

She was just killing him inside! He had to take another deep breath to stop the tears from coming again.

He looked up at his dad. "Right after we found the horses…the night I named Rufio."

He nodded.

Reilly turned to Dru, "I told you that they gave me purpose, and they absolutely do…they changed my life forever. But now, I realize what I needed and wanted." He took a deep breath, hoping she would understand. "I needed a mom; I wanted you to be my mom."

She wrapped her arms around him and pulled him close. "You have no idea what that means to me." She kissed him on top the head.

Reilly looked across at his dad who was watching the two of them with love shining in his eyes.

"Why didn't you tell us you were dating?" Reilly asked when she relaxed away from him.

"We needed to make sure, between us, before we had the pressure from the family." He explained. "I hope you understand…"

Reilly nodded, then chuckled. "Can you imagine, after my reaction the last ten minutes, what it would have been like if I'd known you were dating?"

They both nodded and laughed in agreement.

"I would never have forgiven you if you screwed it up." Reilly grinned at his dad.

"Oh, thanks," He looked at Dru and smiled. "We both wanted it for a long time…but were too scared to say anything to each other. The night before Rooster's surgery, we were all here, for Wade."

"When everyone went to bed, I was in the living room, crying of course," She lifted a shoulder in a slight shrug. "Jack put his arms around me to comfort me…and we just knew…how the other felt…"

Reilly looked between them as they smiled at each other. Their eyes shined…like when Grayson and Leah looked at each other. He could see it now…why didn't he see it before? Had anyone else seen what he didn't?

"Does everyone else know?" Reilly asked.

"Not everyone," His dad smiled. "Scott and Grayson, Matt figured it out on New Year's, and we think Nikki knows, that's it."

Reilly shook his head in disbelief. "I can't believe we're moving in…Wade is seriously going to freak!"

"Do you want to be the one to tell him?" His dad grinned.

"Oh, yes!" Excitement ran through him. "How? When?"

"Well, we hadn't really thought about it past telling you." Dru answered. "I'm thinking we see if Nikki and Matt would come out and tell them before anyone else."

Reilly looked at her in wonder then at his dad. "They're going to be my brother and sister!" He whispered in disbelief.

"I'm really glad you're good with this." She said and they laughed.

Reilly's phone started ringing. He quickly pulled it out of his pocket and saw it was Grace. He looked up at his dad. "She's probably looking out the window watching, she's been pretty upset too. Can I let her know everything is OK, that we're not moving to Texas?"

"Go ahead." He nodded.

Reilly pushed the accept button and answered the phone. "Gracie." He turned to the house and looked at the upstairs windows. It wasn't Grace, it was Wade.

"Are you OK?" Wade asked; his voice shook in concern. Reilly could see him at his bedroom window, leaning against the glass. "I couldn't help it, I stole Grace's phone and called." Wade explained.

Reilly jumped up off the bench and waved at him; grinning as wide as he could. "Dad and Dru are getting married! We're moving in!"

"WHAT?" Wade screamed on the phone and he could see him jumping in the window.

Reilly started bouncing too; he was so excited to tell Wade. Then he remembered what Dru had just said about telling Matt and Nikki first. He turned quickly to apologize but they were standing, with their arms around each other, looking up at Wade in the window and grinning at the 10 year old jumping up and down.

Reilly turned back and repeated himself. "They're getting married and Dad and I are moving in!"

Wade screamed again and disappeared from the window.

Reilly laughed and quickly pushed the speaker button and held out the phone so they could hear Wade yelling as he was running through the house; "Jack and Aunt Dru are getting married and Reilly is moving in with me!!"

They could tell he was running down the steps.

The front door flew open and Wade was running out the door. Reilly opened the gate into the pasture from the island as Wade opened the gate from the yard.

"I can't believe this!" Wade yelled as he ran across the pasture.

They could see everyone start walking out the front door.

"Well," Reilly turned to his dad and soon to be mom. "I think Wade let everyone know."

CHAPTER FOURTEEN

Wade stopped five feet in front of him, eyes wide in excitement. "You're going to be my cousin."

Reilly nodded as he watched Jordan and Leah pass him and head to Dru and his dad.

"Yeah, cool, huh?" Reilly asked him.

"So we're not going to be brothers anymore?" Wade's excitement started to fade.

"Wade," Reilly grinned. "No matter what, we'll always be brothers…we're going to be brother cousins."

Wade laughed but had to move quickly as Grace was racing into Reilly arms. They hugged in relief. He closed his eyes in happiness and released a long loud sigh, the anxiety and sadness released from his lungs. When he opened his eyes, he saw Scott.

He gently pushed Grace away from him and smiled at her. "Hold my place, I'll be right back."

"Alright." She laughed then ran to her aunt.

Reilly hesitantly walked up to Scott. They stared at each other a moment before Reilly spoke "I hated you." He said honestly.

"I hated me, and my sister, and your dad." Scott sighed. "It was one of the worst things I have ever done in my life."

"Thanks for finally taking me home." Reilly stretched his hand out. Scott gripped it firmly.

"I have one more explanation," Reilly said, thinking of Grayson, and started to turn.

"You think you do?" Scott glanced at him nervously. "I have to tell my wife I knew about this since last October and didn't tell her. She is NOT going to be happy."

Reilly's eyebrows shot up and he lifted his hands in the air. "I don't envy you there…that's a tough one."

Reilly turned and watched Scott walk up to his wife. Jordan turned with bright happy eyes, then, seeing the look on her husband's face, the smile faded. Scott spoke but Jordan just smiled again and threw her arms around her husband's neck.

Reilly looked for Grayson and Leah; they were standing next to Dru and his dad, both smiling happily. Grayson turned to look at him. Reilly took a deep breath and walked to them.

Grace met up with him half way over.

"Facing the music?"

He nodded then stopped. "Just me…" He told her…she nodded and walked back to her happy sister and cousins.

Reilly walked the short distance to her parents who were waiting.

"I said I would tell you when I could." Reilly stood confidently and hoped they would forgive him. He told them the story of Bonnie and Clyde.

When he finished, he waited for the consequences.

"You kids have seriously got to start talking to us instead of letting things get out of control." Leah told him. He nodded and watched her walk away, then turned back to Grace's dad.

"She didn't know why she ran?" Grayson asked him.

Reilly was surprised at his question. "She just said she knew something was wrong and ran, didn't know why she did it."

"That's curious," Grayson said and turned a worried expression to Reilly. "There has to be a reason, Reilly."

Reilly frowned, he didn't know why she ran; he hadn't given her a reason to.

They heard Grace's laugh and both turned to her, watched her for a minute then turned back to each other.

"She won't talk to us," Grayson told him, worry creasing his brow. "We tried. She completely shuts down when we ask about you."

Reilly nodded, he did the same thing to his dad when he asks about Grace. But this was different. "I'll find out, sir."

"I know what you two have is special, even if I don't fully understand it, but this time Reilly…"

"I'll let you know." Reilly finished for him, letting Grace's dad know he understood how important it was.

******

"We should have a party!" Jordan declared and everyone agreed except the bride-to-be.

"If we have a party, then it's an anniversary party for one year since Cora and the herd came to us." She said.

"They came into your life for a great reason." Wade grinned at her.

"That they did." Dru hugged him and then looked to Reilly.

Reilly grinned back, gave his future mom a kiss on the cheek and left to find Grace.

He found her in the kitchen with Cora. They were already making food plans for the party.

Reilly smiled politely to Cora and Jordan and took Grace's hand. As he pulled the confused girl away, he gave Leah a slight nod, she gave him a thankful smile in return.

As they stepped out the back door and headed for the barn, he saw Wade and Sadie were headed there, too. Reilly looked over to the men standing by the trucks and saw Grayson. Reilly nodded his head towards the barn. Grayson turned and called Sadie and Wade to him. The two kids changed their direction. Grace didn't see the exchange; he would never tell her either.

"Did you have this feeling Buttercup and Eli needed me?" Grace laughed as they made their way to the horse's stalls.

Reilly laughed and shook his head. "No, I haven't learned how to read horse minds."

"Yet…" She laughed her 'life is good' laugh.

He grabbed a bale of straw and walked it over to Buttercups stall, then went back for a second.

"What are you doing?" Grace asked confused.

Reilly smiled then threw some hay into Buttercup's feeder so she wouldn't try to eat their chairs. He opened the stall door and pulled the bales in and set them across from each other and out of Buttercups way.

He motioned for Grace to sit. She didn't, she stood at the door and looked at him in bewilderment.

"Why?" Grace asked cautiously.

Reilly sat on his bale and leaned back against the stall wall, stretching his legs out the length of the bale.

She took a hesitant step forward. "What are you doing?"

"We haven't talked about the last couple days…so here we are."

"This is weird, Reilly, even for us." She sat on the bale and mimicked his position. "You should be out with your dad and future mom."

He grinned at her. "Can you believe that?"

She instantly relaxed at his grin and sat cross legged on the bale. "We're cousins!"

He sighed. "Gracie, I have never been so shocked in all my life. And so freaking happy."

"You've always loved Dru." Grace tipped her head to the side.

"Adored her," Reilly admitted. "But after a couple years, I just gave up on the dream that they would get together."

"We never talked about her."

"No, I just didn't want to say it out loud."

"Is there anything else we've never talked about?"

"You tell me."

"I've got no secrets."

"Yes, you do." He laughed.

She looked at him in confusion.

Reilly sat up and crossed his legs in front of him and leaned towards her. "Bonnie and Clyde."

"What?"

"Why did you pull the Bonnie running to Clyde?"

Worry flickered in her eyes, he saw it and knew he hit a nerve.

"I was worried about you."

"Why?"

"Texas…"

"I hadn't told you about Texas yet…not until we stopped."

She didn't say anything.

"When I got home last night…this morning and you hugged me, you were shaking."

"Of course I was."

"Why?"

"Duh, I was worried about you."

"This morning, when we went riding, you said you weren't worried…you said you knew I was OK."

She didn't say anything; she just stood and walked to Buttercup. Leaning against the wall she ran a hand down the length of the horse.

"Mixed signals." She said as she fiddled with the horse's mane.

"Try again."

"What?"

"Try again, that doesn't work for me."

She frowned at him. "What is this about?"

"You telling me why you ran like Bonnie to Clyde's car."

She just glared at him.

"I gave you no reason to run from Leah. I went back and read the text, all it said was 'meet me at the end of the drive'. There is nothing there that said I was upset."

"You were early and wanted me to meet you at the end of the drive…so you were upset."

"Gracie, this is me…" He was desperate now, she wasn't giving him anything. "Why did you run from your mother? There wasn't anything in that text that said I was upset enough for you to run from Leah."

"I just knew, OK?" She nearly yelled at him. "It's just the way we are."

"Gracie," He said in a low reassuring voice. "Because we are, the way we are…I know there is something wrong…but I need you to tell me what it is." He stood and took a step to her.

Grace stepped closer to the horse.

He stopped and leaned against the stall wall a couple feet from her. He crossed his arms to show her he was relaxed and not interrogating her…even though he was trying to.

"We rode Friday night and I saw you yesterday morning before I went to work at The Stables." He said and she shrugged. "Then we didn't see, text, or speak until Scott brought me here this morning."

"I was surprised you didn't let me know you were headed to the ranch. Why didn't you take me with you?" She didn't look at him.

His eyes narrowed. "Dad said no."

She glanced up at him in surprise. "Jack did? Why?"

He chuckled, "He didn't want Bonnie with Clyde, I guess." She gave him a half smile. "You were grounded you know?"

She nodded. "Mom and Dad would have said yes so you didn't have to go by yourself."

He shook his head. "Not after Bonnie and Clyde. They may have said yes to Wade but he was at a friend's house."

She remained quiet.

"Before the Texas scare, nothing changed in our lives except for Dad and Dru not getting along."

The flicker of fear again.

"Did you know about Dad and Dru?" He hoped the answer was no, he couldn't forgive her if she did.

"Absolutely not," She shook her head. "I had no clue or I would have told you."

He sighed. His mind went back over the week…since he got back from the ranch after the weekend. Then, he got it, he knew what was wrong.

"Kelly."

Her head jerked up and she stared at him.

"You didn't like that I didn't want you to meet her yet."

"Yet…" She mumbled.

"Are you threatened by Kelly?"

Again, she didn't say anything.

He walked back to the bale and stretched out again. Then, he waited. Now that he figured out what was wrong he had to quit pushing. She needed to be the one to talk now. She had to work it out in her head and approach him, explain it to him.

Grace surprised him and walked out of the stall.

Dang…now what? He sat quietly trying to figure out what to do next. It wasn't just Grace he was worried about, but he was about to disappoint Grayson and Leah too.

He leaned his head back on the wall and looked up at the ceiling. "Oh, Gracie…I'm worried about you." He whispered.

"Why?" She stepped up to the stall door that only came up to her shoulders. She leaned her arms across the door top and looked in at him.

He tilted his head to the right and looked at her. "Because you've always talked to me when you've had a problem…now you won't…so this must be a big problem."

When she just looked at him and didn't speak…he asked again his voice earnest and pleading; "Is it Kelly?"

She made a face at him then sighed.

"I've only seen her four times Gracie…so why is it an issue?"

"It's not so much her…"

"OK, then what?"

She opened the stall door and made her way back to the straw bale, sitting on the end next to him.

"Your truck…Kelly…" She frowned.

"Our truck…and she will be our friend." Reilly corrected her.

Grace smiled hesitantly.

"What was the Bonnie and Clyde thing…why run from your mother?"

"When was the last time that the whole family didn't go to the ranch for Memorial Day weekend?"

He sat back in surprise. When he thought about her question, he had to admit the shocking truth. "They have always gone."

"Exactly," She leaned back. "That was surprising enough that it was just you, your dad, and Dru."

"But we know why now. I'm sure they just wanted to spend time together."

"With you."

"Yeah."

She shook her head, "Until thirty minutes ago, we didn't know that."

He nodded.

"Even before Memorial Day, Dru has never taken anyone with her to have dinner with her kids at college…it's their time together."

Reilly nodded, then, a smile crossed his face.

"What?" She asked confused.

"I thought it was a coincidence that she asked you to go with her, now I see it was Dad and her working together to give Dad and I time to look for my truck."

"So, I was right…they were keeping me away from you." She smirked.

Reilly felt a pang of guilt on that one. "It's a guy thing." He tried to smile through the guilt.

"It was a deliberate act to keep me away from you."

"OK," He nodded, "That is true, but buying the truck…it needed to be just me and Dad, Gracie."

"You were in on it?" She asked in surprise.

"Sort of," He sighed. "I was going to ask you if it could be just me and him."

"I would have understood that," Grace leaned back against the wall. "I wouldn't have liked it, but I would have understood it."

Reilly nodded.

"Then there was you, not wanting me to go with you to see Kelly."

He tilted his head. "You know why."

"Doesn't matter," She admitted. "Everything was piling up on top of each other; the truck, Memorial Day, Kelly…"

"So when your mother told you to get back to the house and not meet me at the end of the driveway?"

"It was just another attempt at keeping us apart," She nodded. "I just couldn't handle it. I didn't understand it then and I was scared."

"Scared?"

"We don't understand this…" She pointed between them. "So how can they understand it?"

"Cora said we're soul-mates…I agree with her. We just found each other early. I don't think they have an issue." Reilly frowned at her.

"I think they do." She argued. "Or did… I felt like I was being pulled away from you. That they were all keeping us apart."

Reilly didn't know what to say to make her feel better so he remained quiet and let her 'talk it out'.

"I didn't want anything to change. Your getting the truck made you more independent, I could see that. Your meeting Kelly…was OK…but I felt her pulling you away…the family doing the weird Memorial Day thing just really didn't make sense to me."

"Does it now?"

"Yeah…sort of…" She sighed. "It just got to be too much. I don't want things to change."

Reilly nodded his understanding.

"I can see it now that I wasn't running so much away from Mom, as I was away from everything changing."

"We're fifteen," He reminded her. "We're moving away from being kids."

"Exactly," She frowned. "Which means the changes are just beginning."

"But that doesn't mean the changes will be pulling us apart. Maybe they'll bring us together."

She sighed. "How?"

He stared at her as he thought quickly, then smiled. "We're going to be living in the same house now."

He saw her expression change, for the good.

"I didn't think of that." She smiled…a more relaxed and happy smile.

He moved up on the bale so he could be closer to her. "Everything will change for us Gracie," He warned. "But look at what just happened between Dru and Dad. Dru didn't want things to change so she told Dad no… can you imagine?" He shook his head and smiled at her. "And now, that she said yes…?"

"You'll have a mom." She grinned.

"You'll have a new cousin." He grinned back.

"And we're going to be living in the same house." Her grin grew wider.

"Just a sample of what it will be like when we go to college together." He said and could see the change in her since they first walked in, "Change isn't always bad."

"This could be awesome." She agreed excitedly.

He leaned back, "I don't think they understand what we have, but they understand how important it is."

She nodded.

"They won't ever…and we won't ever…try to break this up." He said pointing between the two of them.

They smiled, understanding and knowing.

"But we are going to have to find that brother and sister to date." She told him as they walked out of the stall.

He laughed. "I asked Kelly…she doesn't have a brother."

"Dang." Grace laughed.

CHAPTER FIFTEEN

Reilly made his way around his truck quickly. He told Kelly he wanted to impress his dad and 'mom to be', by opening the door for her, so she needed to wait for him. She was giggling when the door opened and stepped out. He was so nervous about her meeting Grace that he actually paid attention to what she was wearing. Boots, jeans, white tank top under a short sleeve western shirt. Almost exactly what Grace was wearing as she walked towards them. Kelly's western shirt was green that looked good with her red hair and green eyes; Grace's western shirt was blue that looked good with her blonde hair and blue eyes. Neither girl was wearing a hat today.

"Huh," Reilly muttered which made Kelly look up at him.

"What?" She asked. Her eyes looked worried.

He just shook his head and smiled. "Nothing."

Grace stopped in front of them and looked up at Reilly…expectantly. She tilted her head and raised an eyebrow…humor in her eyes.

It was a moment before he realized that she was waiting to be introduced…boy the nerves had really gotten to him.

"Grace this is Kelly Harris. Kelly this is Grace Tagger." He finally stammered.

"Hi Kelly." Grace stuck her hand out to the girl. Manners from the parents, he smiled.

"Hi Grace," Kelly smiled then shook Grace's hand. "I've heard so much about you…from Reilly and everyone at The Stables."

"Well, they're all pretty much family, so be careful what you believe." Grace laughed.

It was Grace's 'happy with life' laugh; Reilly smiled and could see Kelly's shoulders lower. She had been nervous, too. Grace's smile and laugh had a way of making everyone relax.

"Harris is your last name?" Grace asked Kelly.

Kelly nodded.

"I'm surprised is not O'Harris or O'Malley." Grace laughed and to Reilly's confused relief, Kelly laughed too.

"That's on my mom's side." Kelly explained. "But I get that a lot."

"What?" Reilly asked, looking confused at the two girls.

They both turned and looked at him in disbelief.

"What?" He asked again, this time feeling a little uneasy.

The girls turned back to each other and giggled.

Reilly stood next to the two, in relief that they seemed to hit it off, but confused as to why and how come he felt it was at his expense?

Grace just shook her head and turned back to Kelly. "I know you like to ride," She turned to walk towards the barn and Kelly followed. "What level are you? We'll see if we can round up a horse so we can ride out in the arena."

"You have an arena here?" Kelly asked excitedly and they left Reilly standing confused, relieved, and stunned next to his truck.

"Son?" His dad said from behind him.

Reilly turned and saw him and Dru walking across the driveway, they were holding hands. They always held hands now.

He loved seeing them together; knowing Dru was going to be his mom, and seeing the love between the two. How could they have hidden that so well for so long?

"Why are you standing here and they are headed to the barn?" Dru asked with a smile.

Reilly grinned and shook his head. "It took all of about 10 seconds for them to hit it off, but I think it was at my expense."

"Why?" They asked in unison.

He told them what Grace had said which caused the two of them to look at him in disbelief…just as the two teenagers had reacted.

"What?" He asked in exasperation, why did everyone have that reaction?

Much to his surprise, Dru turned to his dad and shook her head. "Really, Jack?" Then she grinned at Reilly and walked past him and headed to the barn.

"What?" Reilly turned to his dad, who was just staring at him and shaking his head.

"Reilly…Reilly…Reilly…" He muttered.

His dad schooled him on red hair, green eyes, and Irish names as they walked to the barn together.

When Reilly walked into the barn, Dru was walking out with a halter in hand.

She chuckled at him as she passed; "Run Reilly Run."

He was confused until the girls saw him…

"Welcome to the barn O'Reilly!" They both called out in an outlandish Irish brogue then burst out laughing. His dad joined them…and everyone else in the barn…until finally, he started laughing too.

******

Reilly bounced the lariat in his hand and watched Sadie make a throw. She nearly hit her target but it glanced off the back end and skidded to the left.

"Dang it!" She yelled.

"Relax, you'll get it." Grayson told her and patted Little Ghost on the rump as they walked by.

Both mechanical training calves were in the arena and Wade, Sadie, Grace, and Reilly were taking turns practicing from horse back. Nora and Kelly were sitting on the fence watching. Sadie and Reilly were roping the left calf, Grace and Wade the right calf.

Grayson turned to Grace and gave her instructions based on her previous throw. Grace nodded, lifted the rope, spun it around her head, and let it fly…and caught one of the back legs.

"Dang it!" She grinned down at her dad. He smiled and pushed Buttercup along.

Grayson turned to Reilly. "You ready?"

Reilly nodded, this was his first time throwing in front of Kelly and really wanted to impress her. She looked so happy, when he asked her to come over and watch them, and meet Grace and the Taggers. Now he wanted to show….something hit him in the leg and Rufio jumped off to the side.

Startled, Reilly looked over to see Grayson smiling at him, lariat in hand.

"Get out of your head," Grayson told him as he trotted Rufio back up to their starting position.

"What?" Reilly asked.

"When I ask if you're ready, BE ready." Grayson told him. "You were somewhere lost in your thoughts…probably little red head thoughts?" He grinned.

Reilly could feel his face warm but kept from looking at Kelly. "Yeah, I was." He admitted.

Grayson nodded. "When you're on the line you only think of the horse, your arm, the rope, the calf, the throw….got it?"

Reilly nodded and Grayson stepped back.

The horse, he repositioned Rufio. The arm, he lifted his arm paying attention to the bend in his shoulder and elbow. The rope, he twirled the rope over his head. The calf, he stared at the back legs…his target. The throw, just before the tip of the rope pointed at the calf he straightened his arm, twisted his wrist, flattened his palm and let go of the rope. The rope twisted in air and looped under the mechanical calf and Reilly yanked back on the lariat to capture the legs…and he did.

Cheers erupted from the fence and riders. Reilly looked over at Grayson to see him smiling proudly.

"Just remember not to let your head get in your way." Grayson said and patted Rufio on the hip to make him move out of the way for Sadie.

Reilly walked Rufio behind Sadie and smiled at Kelly. She grinned and waved back at him.

Wade and Rooster were next. Arm went up, lariat circled Wade's head and he let it fly. One back leg.

"Dang it!" He yelled with a grin.

They went around four more times before taking a break. Sadie missed on all but one where she caught one foot. Four 'dang its'! Grace missed completely on two and caught both feet on the last two. Only two 'dang its'! Reilly kept in mind what Grayson told him and caught all four times. Just grins, no 'dang its'! Wade caught one foot on each throw causing four 'dang its'.

Reilly walked up along the fence next to Kelly; Grace right beside him.

"That was great!" Kelly exclaimed excitedly.

"That was a first!" Grace told her then looked at Reilly. "What did Dad say to you?"

"He told me to think about the throwing and not about Kelly." Reilly admitted with a grin.

Kelly, Grace, and Nora started laughing.

Reilly felt the warmth on his cheeks again as he blushed…it was going to be a great summer.

******

The one year anniversary party for The Tagger herd and Cora coming to their lives was huge. And, whether Dru liked it or not, it became an engagement party for the bride and groom.

Jessup was down from the ranch, Nick up from Boise, Dr. Mark and all his clinic team were there, and Andy and his sons were there. Their neighbors at The Stables and The Homestead filled the front yard. All the horses were in the pasture just in front of the house.

Reilly stood on the top step of the porch looking down at the family and friends. He looked out at all the horses; the healthy horses. No one would believe that eleven of the horses in the pasture were near death last year. With Nikki's nutrition schedule, and now the exercise they received, their bodies had recovered.

Wade and Sadie were to his left, carrying their lariats. They were showing Andy's grandson how to throw the rope and catch the practice calf.

Kelly and Grace were in front of him. They were laughing at something…probably him again. Kelly was quickly becoming a great friend. He touched his lips again and smiled at her.

He heard Nora laughing. She was standing next to the fence and Arcturus was trying to eat the fake flower in her hair. She turned to the horse and stroked his nose then laid her hand on the star in the middle of the horse's forehead. He could see her close her eyes and smile contently. She seemed to do that a lot.

Jessup and Dr. Mark were working the barbeque, giving Cora a break from cooking. Nikki and Cora were sitting around the table with all the neighbors, laughing and having a good time.

Matt, Nick, Scott and Jordan were sitting with Andy and his family.

Grayson and Leah were standing next to the pasture fence playing with Eli, Rooster, Harvey, Little Ghost, and the rest of the herd were slowly walking up to them.

Reilly watched Grayson reach out and gently touch the side of Leah's cheek, just at the jawline. Her eyes glowed of love when she looked up at her husband. Their arms slid around each other's waists, their free arms still petting the multitude of horses in front of them. He wanted a love like that someday.

After his talk with Grace, he had met with them and told them about the conversation. He assured them that she was OK. They were thankful for his friendship with her and the fact that Reilly understood how important it was to tell them the information, although Grace would see it as breaking her trust. That was a fine line; one he would have to balance in the future.

Reilly looked over at the gate to his right. His dad and Dru were walking through, holding hands and laughing…he grinned at their contented smiles.

They had moved into the Tagger house the day before. Dru didn't see any reason to wait until after the wedding; she wanted both of them with her all the time. With all three of them working at The Stables and living at The Homestead, she was going to get her wish.

After eight years of living in the house above The Stables with his dad, just the two of them, it was hard to let go. Matt moved into his room and Nikki moved into his dad's. It was going to be really weird going back into the house with their stuff inside.

Packing up his mother's pictures brought tears to his eyes as he placed them in the box. Until Dru took them out of the box and put them on his shelf in his new bedroom. He was surprised.

"She is part of who you are." Dru had told him. "Never lose her in your heart, I've told Jack the same thing."

Reilly sighed and smiled at her across the lawn, his 'soon-to-be' mom smiled back.

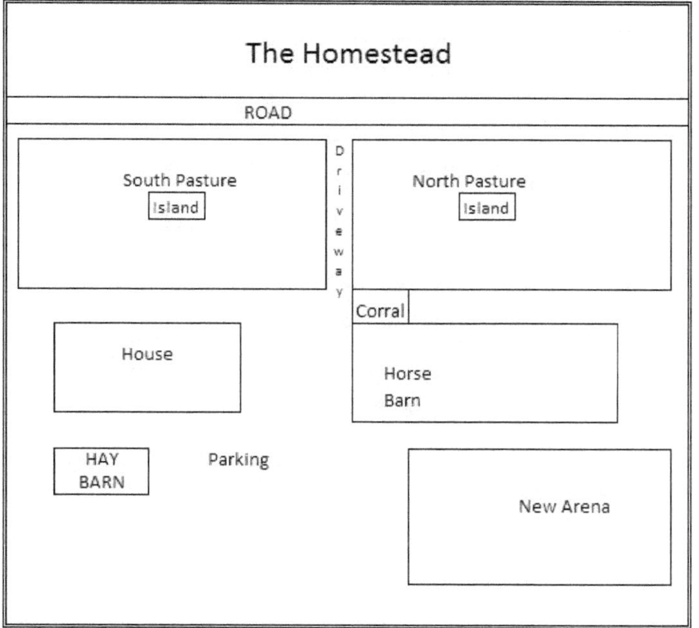

The Homestead
ROAD
Driveway
South Pasture
Island
North Pasture
Island
Corral
House
Horse
Barn
HAY
BARN
Parking
New Arena

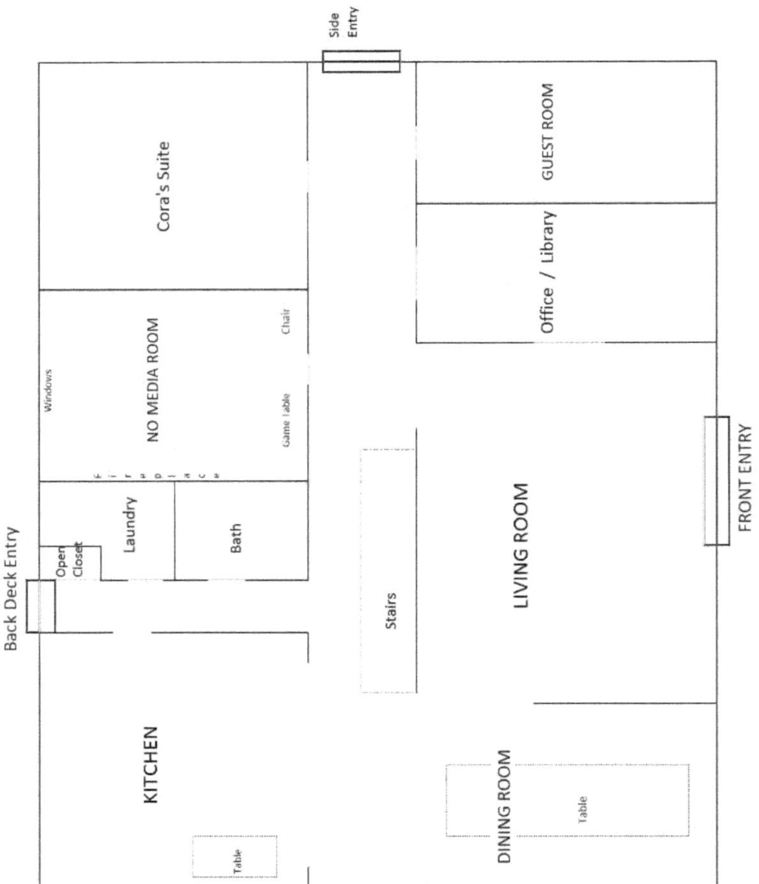

The Homestead Downstairs

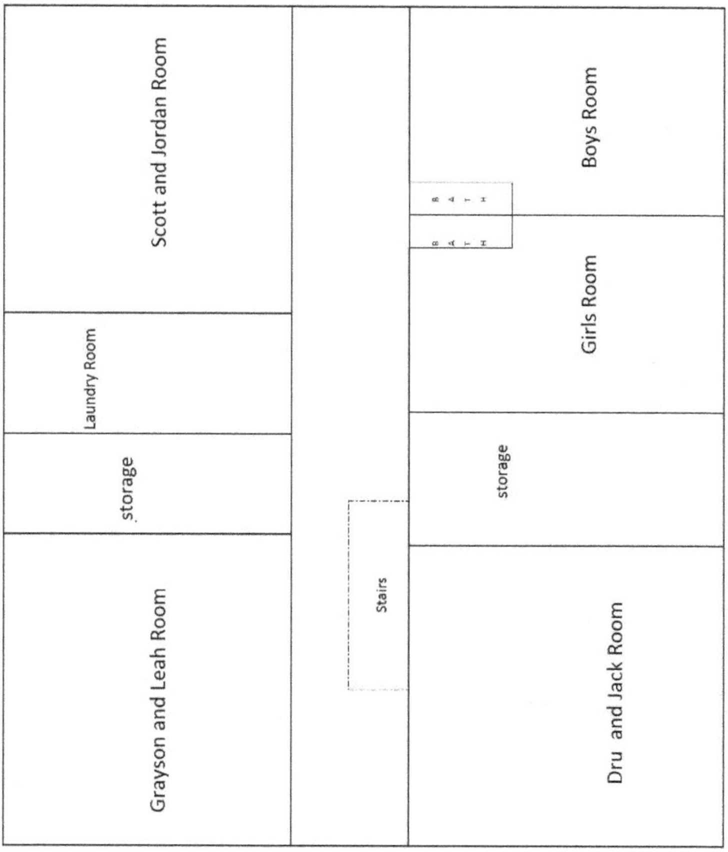

Scott and Jordan Room

Boys Room

BATH

BATH

Laundry Room

Girls Room

storage

storage

Stairs

Grayson and Leah Room

Dru and Jack Room

The Homestead Upstairs

The Tagger Family

Drucilla
Nikki
Matt —— Nick

Grayson
Leah
Grace
Sadie

Scott
Jordan
Nora
Wade

Jessup: Tagger Ranch

Jack Morgan: The Stables
Reilly

Cora Smith: The Homestead

Tagger Property History:
Mathew and Grace
Anderson and Nora
Mathew and Anne
Grayson Mathew, Scott Anderson, Drucilla Anne

ABOUT THE AUTHOR

I was raised with Shetlands and ponies and have loved horses since I watched a Shetland colt born when I was four.

Growing up, the TV show Bonanza was my favorite. I loved that western life and wanted to be Little Joe and Hoss' little sister. I wanted to live at the Ponderosa. Watching rodeos on television and attending when I could, was the closest I could get to the cowboy way of life.

That changed when I purchased my first 'big horse' when I was twenty-one and living in Alaska. I now have the great-granddaughter of that horse in my pasture.

I am also a photographer specializing in the equine industry; shows, races, jackpots, and rodeos. With my photography, I create my own covers.

The Tagger Herd Series was my first venture into fictional writing and I love the family and horses in the series.

My first 'stand-alone' novel was Hoofbeats in the Wind which ventured into rodeo.

My next book, Coffee With Cowboys delved deeper into the rodeo world and researching for the book was an adventure. I have met wonderful people from fans, stock contractors, and competitors. I thank every one of them that have helped make that book a possibility. It will always be special to me because of the people I met.

Bijou Bay was inspired by Idaho's Black Rock Ranch and the a true story I was fortunate enough to be told.

Writing, researching, photography, my two dogs, Morgan and Tagger, and Kit in the pasture, fill my world and keep me busy.

9 781733 952835